IRISH STORIES AND FOLKLORE

A COLLECTION OF THIRTY-SIX CLASSIC TALES

EDITED BY

STEPHEN BRENNAN

Skyhorse Publishing

First Edition

Skyhorse Publishing books may be purchased in bulk at special discounts for sales promotion, corporate gifts, fund-raising, or educational purposes. Special editions can also be created to specifications. For details, contact the Special Sales Department, Skyhorse Publishing, 307 West 36th Street, 11th Floor, New York, NY 10018 or info@skyhorsepublishing.com.

Visit our website at www.skyhorsepublishing.com.

10 9 8 7 6 5 4 3 2 1

Library of Congress Cataloging-in-Publication Data is available on file.

Cover design by Laura Klynstra

Print ISBN: 978-1-63450-106-4
Ebook ISBN: 978-1-63450-794-3

Printed in the United States of America

IRISH STORIES AND FOLKLORE

"The only land my family ever owned was in flowerpots."
—Sean O'Casey

CONTENTS

JAMIE FREEL AND THE YOUNG LADY

BY LETITIA MACLINTOCK

Down in Fannet, in times gone by, lived Jamie Freel and his mother. Jamie was the widow's sole support; his strong arm worked for her untiringly, and as each Saturday night came round he poured his wages into her lap, thanking her dutifully for the half-pence which she returned him for tobacco.

He was extolled by his neighbors as the best son ever known or heard of. But he had neighbors of whose opinions he was ignorant—neighbors who lived pretty close to him, whom he had never seen, who are, indeed, rarely seen by mortals, except on May Eves or Halloweens.

An old ruined castle, about a quarter of a mile from his cabin, was said to be the abode of the "wee folk." Every Halloween were the ancient windows lighted up, and passers by saw little figures flitting to and fro inside the building, while they heard the music of flutes and pipes.

It was well known that fairy revels took place; but nobody had the courage to intrude on them.

Jamie had often watched the little figures from a distance, and listened to the charming music, wondering what the inside of the castle was like; but one Halloween he got up, and took his cap, saying to his mother, "I'm awa to the castle to seek my fortune."

"What!" cried she. "Would you venture there—you that's the widow's only son? Dinna be sae venturesome and foolitch, Jamie! They'll kill you, an' then what'll come o' me?"

"Never fear, mother; nae harm'll happen me, but I maun gae."

He set out, and, as he crossed the potato field, came in sight of the castle, whose windows were ablaze with light that seemed to turn the russet leaves, still clinging to the crab-tree branches, into gold.

Halting in the grove at one side of the ruin, he listened to the elfin revelry, and the laughter and singing made him all the more determined to proceed.

Numbers of little people, the largest about the size of a child of five years old, were dancing to the music of flutes and fiddles, while others drank and feasted.

"Welcome, Jamie Freel! Welcome, welcome, Jamie!" cried the company, perceiving their visitor. The word "Welcome" was caught up and repeated by every voice in the castle.

Time flew, and Jamie was enjoying himself very much, when his hosts said, "We're going to ride to Dublin tonight to steal a young lady. Will you come, too, Jamie Freel?"

"Ay, that I will," cried the rash youth, thirsting for adventure.

A troop of horses stood at the door. Jamie mounted, and his steed rose with him into the air. He was presently flying over his mother's cottage, surrounded by the elfin troop, and on and on they went, over bold mountains, over little hills, over the deep Lough Swilley, over towns and cottages, where people were burning nuts and eating apples and keeping merry Halloween. It seemed to Jamie that they flew all round Ireland before they got to Dublin.

"This is Derry," said the fairies, flying over the cathedral spire; and what was said by one voice was repeated by all the rest, till fifty little voices were crying out, "Derry! Derry! Derry!"

In like manner was Jamie informed as they passed over each town on the route, and at length he heard the silvery voices cry, "Dublin! Dublin!"

It was no mean dwelling that was to be honored by the fairy visit, but one of the finest houses in Stephen's Green.

The troop dismounted near a window, and Jamie saw a beautiful face on a pillow in a splendid bed. He saw the young lady lifted and carried away, while the stick which was dropped in her place on the bed took her exact form.

The lady was placed before one rider and carried a short way, then given another, and the names of the towns were cried as before.

They were approaching home. Jamie heard "Rathmullan," "Milford," "Tamney," and then he knew they were near his own house.

"You've all had your turn at carrying the young lady," said he. "Why wouldn't I get her for a wee piece?"

"Ay, Jamie," replied they pleasantly, "you may take your turn at carrying her, to be sure."

Holding his prize very tightly he dropped down near his mother's door.

"Jamie Freel! Jamie Freel! is that the way you treat us?" cried they, and they, too, dropped down near the door.

Jamie held fast, though he knew not what he was holding, for the little folk turned the lady into all sorts of strange shapes. At one moment she was a black dog, barking and trying to bite; at another a glowing bar of iron, which yet had no heat; then again a sack of wool.

But still Jamie held her, and the baffled elves were turning away when a tiny woman, the smallest of the party, exclaimed, "Jamie Freel has her awa frae us, but he sall nae hae gude of her, for I'll mak' her deaf and dumb," and she threw something over the young girl.

While they rode off, disappointed, Jamie Freel lifted the latch and went in.

"Jamie man!" cried his mother, "you've been awa all night. What have they done on you?"

"Naething bad, mother; I hae the very best o' gude luck. Here's a beautiful young lady I hae brought you for company."

"Bless us and save us!" exclaimed his mother; and for some minutes she was so astonished she could not think of anything else to say.

Jamie told the story of the night's adventure, ending by saying, "Surely you wouldna have allowed me to let her gang with them to be lost for ever?"

"But a *lady*, Jamie! How can a lady eat we'er (our) poor diet and live in we'er poor way? I ax you that, you foolitch fellow!"

"Well, mother, sure it's better for her to be over here nor yonder," and he pointed in the direction of the castle.

Meanwhile the deaf and dumb girl shivered in her light clothing, stepping close to the humble turf fire.

"Poor crathur, she's quare and handsome! Nae wonder they set their hearts on her," said the old woman, gazing at their guest with pity and admiration. "We maun dress her first; but what in the name o' fortune hae I fit for the likes of her to wear?"

She went to her press in "the room" and took out her Sunday gown of brown drugget. She then opened a drawer and drew forth a pair of white stockings, a long snowy garment of fine linen, and a cap, her "dead dress," as she called it.

These articles of attire had long been ready for a certain triste ceremony, in which she would some day fill the chief part, and only saw the light occasionally when they were hung out to air; but she was willing to give even these to the fair trembling visitor, who was turning in dumb sorrow and wonder from her to Jamie, and from Jamie back to her.

The poor girl suffered herself to be dressed, and then sat down on a "creepie" in the chimney corner and buried her face in her hands.

"What'll we do to keep up a lady like thou?" cried the old woman.

"I'll work for you both, mother," replied the son.

"An' how could a lady live on we'er poor diet?" she repeated.

"I'll work for her," was all Jamie's answer.

He kept his word. The young lady was very sad for a long time, and tears stole down her cheeks many an evening, while the old woman span by the fire and Jamie made salmon nets, an accomplishment acquired by him in hopes of adding to the comfort of their guest.

But she was always gentle, and tried to smile when she perceived them looking at her; and by degrees she adapted herself to their ways and mode of life. It was not very long before she began to feed the pig, mash potatoes and meal for the fowls, and knit blue worsted socks.

So a year passed and Halloween came round again. "Mother," said Jamie, taking down his cap, "I'm off to the ould castle to seek my fortune."

"Are you mad, Jamie?" cried his mother in terror; "sure they'll kill you this time for what you done on them last year."

Jamie made light of her fears and went his way.

As he reached the crab-tree grove he saw bright lights in the castle windows as before, and heard loud talking. Creeping under the window he heard the wee folk say, "That was a poor trick Jamie Freel played us this night last year, when he stole the young lady from us."

"Ay," said the tiny woman, "an' I punished him for it, for there she sits a dumb image by the hearth, but he does na' know that three drops out o' this glass that I hold in my hand wad gie her her hearing and speech back again."

Jamie's heart beat fast as he entered the hall. Again he was greeted by a chorus of welcomes from the company—"Here comes Jamie Freel! Welcome, welcome, Jamie!"

As soon as the tumult subsided the little woman said, "You be to drink our health, Jamie, out o' this glass in my hand."

Jamie snatched the glass from her and darted to the door. He never knew how he reached his cabin, but he arrived there breathless and sank on a stove by the fire.

"You're kilt, surely, this time, my poor boy," said his mother.

"No, indeed, better luck than ever this time!" and he gave the lady three drops of the liquid that still remained at the bottom of the glass, notwithstanding his mad race over the potato field.

The lady began to speak, and her first words were words of thanks to Jamie.

The three inmates of the cabin had so much to say to one another that, long after cock-crow, when the fairy music had quite ceased, they were talking round the fire.

"Jamie," said the lady, "be pleased to get me paper and pen and ink that I may write to my father and tell him what has become of me."

She wrote, but weeks passed and she received no answer. Again and again she wrote, and still no answer.

At length she said, "You must come with me to Dublin, Jamie, to find my father."

"I hae no money to hire a car for you," he answered; "an' how can you travel to Dublin on your foot?"

But she implored him so much that he consented to set out with her and walk all the way from Fannet to Dublin. It was not as easy as the fairy journey; but at last they rang the bell at the door of the house in Stephen's Green.

"Tell my father that his daughter is here," said she to the servant who opened the door.

"The gentleman that lives here has no daughter, my girl. He had one, but she died better nor a year ago."

"Do you not know me, Sullivan?"

"No, poor girl, I do not."

"Let me see the gentleman. I only ask to see him."

"Well, that's not much to ax. We'll see what can be done."

In a few moments the lady's father came to the door.

"How dare you call me your father?" cried the old gentleman angrily. "You are an impostor. I have no daughter."

"Look in my face, father, and surely you'll remember me."

"My daughter is dead and buried. She died a long, long time ago." The old gentleman's voice changed from anger to sorrow. "You can go," he concluded.

"Stop, dear father, till you look at this ring on my finger. Look at your name and mine engraved on it."

"It certainly is my daughter's ring, but I do not know how you came by it. I fear in no honest way."

"Call my mother—*she* will be sure to know me," said the poor girl, who by this time was weeping bitterly.

"My poor wife is beginning to forget her sorrow. She seldom speaks of her daughter now. Why should I renew her grief by reminding her of her loss?"

But the young lady persevered till at last the mother was sent for.

"Mother," she began, when the old lady came to the door, "don't *you* know your daughter?"

"I have no daughter. My daughter died, and was buried a long, long time ago."

"Only look in my face and surely you'll know me."

The old lady shook her head.

"You have all forgotten me; but look at this mole on my neck. Surely, mother, you know me now?"

"Yes, yes," said her mother, "my Gracie had a mole on her neck like that; but then I saw her in the coffin, and saw the lid shut down upon her."

It became Jamie's turn to speak, and he gave the history of the fairy journey, of the theft of the young lady, of the figure he had seen laid in its place, of her life with his mother in Fannet, of last Halloween, and of the three drops that had released her from her enchantments.

She took up the story when he paused and told how kind the mother and son had been to her.

The parents could not make enough of Jamie. They treated him with every distinction, and when he expressed his wish to return to Fannet, said they did not know what to do to express their gratitude.

But an awkward complication arose. The daughter would not let him go without her. "If Jamie goes, I'll go, too," she said. "He saved me from the fairies, and has worked for me ever since. If it had not been for him, dear father and mother, you would never have seen me again. If he goes, I'll go, too."

This being her resolution, the old gentleman said that Jamie should become his son-in-law. The mother was brought from Fannet in a coach-and-four, and there was a splendid wedding.

They all lived together in the grand Dublin house, and Jamie was heir to untold wealth at his father-in-law's death.

THE NIGHTINGALE AND THE ROSE

BY OSCAR WILDE

"She said that she would dance with me if I brought her red roses," cried the young Student; "but in all my garden there is no red rose."

From her nest in the holm-oak tree the Nightingale heard him, and she looked out through the leaves, and wondered.

"No red rose in all my garden!" he cried, and his beautiful eyes filled with tears. "Ah, on what little things does happiness depend! I have read all that the wise men have written, and all the secrets of philosophy are mine, yet for want of a red rose is my life made wretched."

"Here at last is a true lover," said the Nightingale. "Night after night have I sung of him, though I knew him not: night after night have I told his story to the stars, and now I see him. His hair is dark as the hyacinth-blossom, and his lips are red as the rose of his desire; but passion has made his face like pale ivory, and sorrow has set her seal upon his brow."

"The Prince gives a ball tomorrow night," murmured the young Student, "and my love will be of the company. If I bring her a red rose she will dance with me till dawn. If I bring her a red rose, I shall hold her in my arms, and she will lean her head upon my shoulder, and her hand will be clasped in mine. But there is no red rose in my garden, so I shall sit lonely, and she will pass me by. She will have no heed of me, and my heart will break."

"Here indeed is the true lover," said the Nightingale. "What I sing of, he suffers–what is joy to me, to him is pain. Surely Love is a wonderful thing. It is more precious than emeralds, and dearer than fine opals. Pearls and pomegranates cannot buy it, nor is it set forth in the marketplace. It may not be purchased of the merchants, nor can it be weighed out in the balance for gold."

"The musicians will sit in their gallery," said the young Student, "and play upon their stringed instruments, and my love will dance to the sound of the harp and the violin. She will dance so lightly that her feet will not touch the floor, and the courtiers in their gay dresses will throng round her. But with me she will not dance, for I have no red rose to give her"; and he flung himself down on the grass, and buried his face in his hands, and wept.

"Why is he weeping?" asked a little Green Lizard, as he ran past him with his tail in the air.

"Why, indeed?" said a Butterfly, who was fluttering about after a sunbeam.

"Why, indeed?" whispered a Daisy to his neighbour, in a soft, low voice.

"He is weeping for a red rose," said the Nightingale.

"For a red rose?" they cried; "how very ridiculous!" and the little Lizard, who was something of a cynic, laughed outright.

But the Nightingale understood the secret of the Student's sorrow, and she sat silent in the oak-tree, and thought about the mystery of Love.

Suddenly she spread her brown wings for flight, and soared into the air. She passed through the grove like a shadow, and like a shadow she sailed across the garden.

In the centre of the grass-plot was standing a beautiful Rose-tree, and when she saw it she flew over to it, and lit upon a spray.

"Give me a red rose," she cried, "and I will sing you my sweetest song."

But the Tree shook its head.

"My roses are white," it answered; "as white as the foam of the sea, and whiter than the snow upon the mountain. But go to my brother who grows round the old sun-dial, and perhaps he will give you what you want."

So the Nightingale flew over to the Rose-tree that was growing round the old sun-dial.

"Give me a red rose," she cried, "and I will sing you my sweetest song."

But the Tree shook its head.

"My roses are yellow," it answered; "as yellow as the hair of the mermaiden who sits upon an amber throne, and yellower than the daffodil that blooms in the meadow before the mower comes with his scythe. But go to my brother who grows beneath the Student's window, and perhaps he will give you what you want."

So the Nightingale flew over to the Rose-tree that was growing beneath the Student's window.

"Give me a red rose," she cried, "and I will sing you my sweetest song."

But the Tree shook its head.

"My roses are red," it answered, "as red as the feet of the dove, and redder than the great fans of coral that wave and wave in the ocean-cavern. But the winter has chilled my veins, and the frost has nipped my buds, and the storm has broken my branches, and I shall have no roses at all this year."

"One red rose is all I want," cried the Nightingale, "only one red rose! Is there no way by which I can get it?"

"There is a way," answered the Tree; "but it is so terrible that I dare not tell it to you."

"Tell it to me," said the Nightingale, "I am not afraid."

"If you want a red rose," said the Tree, "you must build it out of music by moonlight, and stain it with your own heart's-blood. You must sing to me with your breast against a thorn. All night long you must sing to me, and the thorn must pierce your heart, and your life-blood must flow into my veins, and become mine."

"Death is a great price to pay for a red rose," cried the Nightingale, "and Life is very dear to all. It is pleasant to sit in the green wood, and to watch the Sun in his chariot of gold, and the Moon in her chariot of pearl. Sweet is the scent of the hawthorn, and sweet are the bluebells that hide in the valley, and the heather that blows on the hill. Yet Love is better than Life, and what is the heart of a bird compared to the heart of a man?"

So she spread her brown wings for flight, and soared into the air. She swept over the garden like a shadow, and like a shadow she sailed through the grove.

The young Student was still lying on the grass, where she had left him, and the tears were not yet dry in his beautiful eyes.

"Be happy," cried the Nightingale, "be happy; you shall have your red rose. I will build it out of music by moonlight, and stain it with my own heart's-blood. All that I ask of you in return is that you will be a true lover, for Love is wiser than Philosophy, though she is wise, and mightier than Power, though he is mighty. Flame-coloured are his wings, and coloured like flame is his body. His lips are sweet as honey, and his breath is like frankincense."

The Student looked up from the grass, and listened, but he could not understand what the Nightingale was saying to him, for he only knew the things that are written down in books.

But the Oak-tree understood, and felt sad, for he was very fond of the little Nightingale who had built her nest in his branches.

"Sing me one last song," he whispered; "I shall feel very lonely when you are gone."

So the Nightingale sang to the Oak-tree, and her voice was like water bubbling from a silver jar.

When she had finished her song the Student got up, and pulled a note-book and a lead-pencil out of his pocket.

"She has form," he said to himself, as he walked away through the grove–"that cannot be denied to her; but has she got feeling? I am afraid not. In fact, she is like most artists; she is all style, without any sincerity. She would not sacrifice herself for others. She thinks merely of music, and everybody knows that the arts are selfish. Still, it must be admitted that she has some beautiful notes in her voice. What a pity it is that they do not mean anything, or do any practical good." And he went into his room, and lay down on his little pallet-bed, and began to think of his love; and, after a time, he fell asleep.

And when the Moon shone in the heavens the Nightingale flew to the Rose-tree, and set her breast against the thorn. All night long she sang with her breast against the thorn, and the cold crystal Moon leaned down and listened. All night long she sang, and the thorn went deeper and deeper into her breast, and her life-blood ebbed away from her.

She sang first of the birth of love in the heart of a boy and a girl. And on the top-most spray of the Rose-tree there blossomed a marvellous rose, petal following petal, as song followed song. Pale was it, at first, as the mist that hangs over the river–pale as the feet of the morning, and silver as the wings of the dawn. As the shadow of a rose in a mirror of silver, as the shadow of a rose in a water-pool, so was the rose that blossomed on the topmost spray of the Tree.

But the Tree cried to the Nightingale to press closer against the thorn. "Press closer, little Nightingale," cried the Tree, "or the Day will come before the rose is finished."

So the Nightingale pressed closer against the thorn, and louder and louder grew her song, for she sang of the birth of passion in the soul of a man and a maid.

And a delicate flush of pink came into the leaves of the rose, like the flush in the face of the bridegroom when he kisses the lips of the bride. But the thorn had not yet reached her heart, so the rose's heart remained white, for only a Nightingale's heart's-blood can crimson the heart of a rose.

And the Tree cried to the Nightingale to press closer against the thorn. "Press closer, little Nightingale," cried the Tree, "or the Day will come before the rose is finished."

So the Nightingale pressed closer against the thorn, and the thorn touched her heart, and a fierce pang of pain shot through her. Bitter, bitter was the pain, and wilder and wilder grew her song, for she sang of the Love that is perfected by Death, of the Love that dies not in the tomb.

And the marvellous rose became crimson, like the rose of the eastern sky. Crimson was the girdle of petals, and crimson as a ruby was the heart.

But the Nightingale's voice grew fainter, and her little wings began to beat, and a film came over her eyes. Fainter and fainter grew her song, and she felt something choking her in her throat.

Then she gave one last burst of music. The white Moon heard it, and she forgot the dawn, and lingered on in the sky. The red rose heard it, and it trembled all over with ecstasy, and opened its petals to the cold morning air. Echo bore it to her purple cavern in the hills, and woke the sleeping shepherds from their dreams. It floated through the reeds of the river, and they carried its message to the sea.

"Look, look!" cried the Tree, "the rose is finished now"; but the Nightingale made no answer, for she was lying dead in the long grass, with the thorn in her heart.

And at noon the Student opened his window and looked out.

"Why, what a wonderful piece of luck!" he cried; "here is a red rose! I have never seen any rose like it in all my life. It is so beautiful that I am sure it has a long Latin name"; and he leaned down and plucked it.

Then he put on his hat, and ran up to the Professor's house with the rose in his hand.

The daughter of the Professor was sitting in the doorway winding blue silk on a reel, and her little dog was lying at her feet.

"You said that you would dance with me if I brought you a red rose," cried the Student. "Here is the reddest rose in all the world. You will wear it tonight next your heart, and as we dance together it will tell you how I love you."

But the girl frowned.

"I am afraid it will not go with my dress," she answered; "and, besides, the Chamberlain's nephew has sent me some real jewels, and everybody knows that jewels cost far more than flowers."

"Well, upon my word, you are very ungrateful," said the Student angrily; and he threw the rose into the street, where it fell into the gutter, and a cartwheel went over it.

"Ungrateful!" said the girl. "I tell you what, you are very rude; and, after all, who are you? Only a Student. Why, I don't believe you have even got silver buckles to your shoes as the Chamberlain's nephew has"; and she got up from her chair and went into the house.

"What a silly thing Love is," said the Student as he walked away. "It is not half as useful as Logic, for it does not prove anything, and it is always telling one of things that are not going to happen, and making one believe things that are not true. In fact, it is quite unpractical, and, as in this age to be practical is everything, I shall go back to Philosophy and study Metaphysics."

So he returned to his room and pulled out a great dusty book, and began to read.

A MODEST PROPOSAL

for preventing the children of poor people in Ireland, from being a burden on their parents or country, and for making them beneficial to the publick

BY JONATHAN SWIFT

It is a melancholy object to those, who walk through this great town, or travel in the country, when they see the streets, the roads and cabbin-doors crowded with beggars of the female sex, followed by three, four, or six children, all in rags, and importuning every passenger for an alms. These mothers instead of being able to work for their honest livelihood, are forced to employ all their time in strolling to beg sustenance for their helpless infants who, as they grow up, either turn thieves for want of work, or leave their dear native country, to fight for the Pretender in Spain, or sell themselves to the Barbadoes.

I think it is agreed by all parties, that this prodigious number of children in the arms, or on the backs, or at the heels of their mothers, and frequently of their fathers, is in the present deplorable state of the kingdom, a very great additional grievance; and therefore whoever could find out a fair, cheap and easy method of making these children sound and useful members of the common-wealth, would deserve so well of the publick, as to have his statue set up for a preserver of the nation.

But my intention is very far from being confined to provide only for the children of professed beggars: it is of a much greater extent, and shall take in the whole number of infants at a certain age, who are born of parents in effect as little able to support them, as those who demand our charity in the streets.

As to my own part, having turned my thoughts for many years, upon this important subject, and maturely weighed the several schemes of our projectors, I have always found them grossly mistaken in their computation. It is true, a child just dropt from its dam, may be supported by her milk, for a solar year, with little other nourishment: at most not above the value of two shillings, which the mother may certainly get, or the value in scraps, by her lawful occupation of begging; and it is exactly at one year old that I propose to provide for them in such a manner, as, instead of being a charge upon their parents, or the parish, or wanting food and raiment for the rest of their lives, they shall, on the contrary, contribute to the feeding, and partly to the clothing of many thousands.

There is likewise another great advantage in my scheme, that it will prevent those voluntary abortions, and that horrid practice of women murdering their bastard children, alas! too frequent among us, sacrificing the poor innocent babes, I doubt, more to avoid the expense than the shame, which would move tears and pity in the most savage and inhuman breast.

The number of souls in this kingdom being usually reckoned one million and a half, of these I calculate there may be about two hundred thousand couple whose wives are breeders; from which number I subtract thirty thousand couple, who are able to maintain their own children, (although I apprehend there cannot be so many, under the present distresses of the kingdom) but this being granted, there will remain an hundred and seventy thousand breeders. I again subtract fifty thousand, for those women who miscarry, or whose children die by accident or disease within the year. There only remain an hundred and twenty thousand children of poor parents annually born. The question therefore is, How this number shall be reared, and provided for? Which, as I have already said, under the present situation of affairs, is utterly impossible by all the methods hitherto proposed. For we can neither employ them in handicraft or agriculture; we neither build houses, (I mean in the country) nor cultivate land: they can very seldom pick up a livelihood by stealing till they arrive at six years old; except where they are of towardly parts, although I confess they learn the rudiments much earlier; during which time they can however be properly looked upon only as probationers: As I have been informed by a principal gentleman in the county of Cavan, who protested to me, that he never knew above one or two instances under the age of six, even in a part of the kingdom so renowned for the quickest proficiency in that art.

I am assured by our merchants, that a boy or a girl before twelve years old, is no saleable commodity, and even when they come to this age, they will not yield above three pounds, or three pounds and half a crown at most, on the exchange; which cannot turn to account either to the parents or kingdom, the charge of nutriments and rags having been at least four times that value.

I shall now therefore humbly propose my own thoughts, which I hope will not be liable to the least objection.

I have been assured by a very knowing American of my acquaintance in London, that a young healthy child well nursed, is, at a year old, a most delicious nourishing and wholesome food, whether stewed, roasted, baked, or boiled; and I make no doubt that it will equally serve in a fricasie, or a ragoust.

I do therefore humbly offer it to publick consideration, that of the hundred and twenty thousand children, already computed, twenty thousand may be reserved for breed, whereof only one fourth part to be males; which is more than we allow to sheep, black cattle, or swine, and my reason is, that these children are seldom the fruits of marriage, a circumstance not much regarded by our savages, therefore, one male will be sufficient to serve four females. That the remaining hundred thousand may, at a year old, be offered in sale to the persons of quality and fortune, through the kingdom, always advising the mother to let them suck plentifully in the last month, so as to render them plump, and fat for a good table. A child will make two dishes at an entertainment for friends, and when the family dines alone, the fore or hind quarter will make a reasonable dish, and seasoned with a little pepper or salt, will be very good boiled on the fourth day, especially in winter.

I have reckoned upon a medium, that a child just born will weigh 12 pounds, and in a solar year, if tolerably nursed, encreaseth to 28 pounds.

I grant this food will be somewhat dear, and therefore very proper for landlords, who, as they have already devoured most of the parents, seem to have the best title to the children.

Infant's flesh will be in season throughout the year, but more plentiful in March, and a little before and after; for we are told by a grave author, an eminent French physician, that fish being a prolifick dyet, there are more children born in Roman Catholick countries about nine months after Lent, the markets will be more glutted than usual, because the number of Popish infants, is at least three to one in this kingdom, and therefore it will have one other collateral advantage, by lessening the number of Papists among us.

I have already computed the charge of nursing a beggar's child (in which list I reckon all cottagers, laborers, and four-fifths of the farmers) to be about two shillings per annum, rags included; and I believe no gentleman would repine to give ten shillings for the carcass of a good fat child, which, as I have said, will make four dishes of excellent nutritive meat, when he hath only some particular friend, or his own family to dine with him. Thus the squire will learn to be a good landlord, and grow popular among his tenants, the mother will have eight shillings neat profit, and be fit for work till she produces another child.

Those who are more thrifty (as I must confess the times require) may flay the carcass; the skin of which, artificially dressed, will make admirable gloves for ladies, and summer boots for fine gentlemen.

As to our City of Dublin, shambles may be appointed for this purpose, in the most convenient parts of it, and butchers we may be assured will not be wanting; although I rather recommend buying the children alive, and dressing them hot from the knife, as we do roasting pigs.

A very worthy person, a true lover of his country, and whose virtues I highly esteem, was lately pleased, in discoursing on this matter, to offer a refinement upon my scheme. He said, that many gentlemen of this kingdom, having of late destroyed their deer, he conceived that the want of venison might be well supply'd by the bodies of young lads and maidens, not exceeding fourteen years of age, nor under twelve; so great a number of both sexes in every country being now ready to starve for want of work and service: And these to be disposed of by their parents if alive, or otherwise by their nearest relations. But with due deference to so excellent a friend, and so deserving a patriot, I cannot be altogether in his sentiments; for as to the males, my American acquaintance assured me from frequent experience, that their flesh was generally tough and lean, like that of our school-boys, by continual exercise, and their taste disagreeable, and to fatten them would not answer the charge. Then as to the females, it would, I think, with humble submission, be a loss to the publick, because they soon would become breeders themselves: And besides, it is not improbable that some scrupulous people might be apt to censure such a practice, (although indeed very unjustly) as a little bordering upon cruelty, which, I confess, hath always been with me the strongest objection against any project, how well soever intended.

But in order to justify my friend, he confessed, that this expedient was put into his head by the famous Salmanaazor, a native of the island Formosa, who came from thence to London, above twenty years ago, and in conversation told my friend, that in his country, when any young person happened to be put to death, the executioner sold the carcass to persons of quality, as a prime dainty; and that, in his time, the body of a plump girl of fifteen, who was crucified for an attempt to poison the Emperor, was sold to his imperial majesty's prime minister of state, and other great mandarins of the court in joints from the gibbet, at four hundred crowns. Neither indeed can I deny, that if the same use were made of several plump young girls in this town, who without one single groat to their fortunes, cannot stir abroad without a chair, and appear at a play-house and assemblies in foreign fineries which they never will pay for; the kingdom would not be the worse.

Some persons of a desponding spirit are in great concern about that vast number of poor people, who are aged, diseased, or maimed; and I have been desired to employ my thoughts what course may be taken, to ease the nation of so grievous an incumbrance. But I am not in the least pain upon that matter, because it is very well known, that they are every day dying, and rotting, by cold and famine, and filth, and vermin, as fast as can be reasonably expected. And as to the young laborers, they are now in almost as hopeful a condition. They cannot get work, and consequently pine away from want of nourishment, to a degree, that if at any time they are accidentally hired to common labor, they have not strength to perform it, and thus the country and themselves are happily delivered from the evils to come.

I have too long digressed, and therefore shall return to my subject. I think the advantages by the proposal which I have made are obvious and many, as well as of the highest importance.

For first, as I have already observed, it would greatly lessen the number of Papists, with whom we are yearly over-run, being the principal breeders of the nation, as well as our most dangerous enemies, and who stay at home on purpose with a design to deliver the kingdom to the Pretender, hoping to take their advantage by the absence of so many good Protestants, who have chosen rather to leave their country, than stay at home and pay tithes against their conscience to an Episcopal curate.

Secondly, The poorer tenants will have something valuable of their own, which by law may be made liable to a distress, and help to pay their landlord's rent, their corn and cattle being already seized, and money a thing unknown.

Thirdly, Whereas the maintenance of an hundred thousand children, from two years old, and upwards, cannot be computed at less than ten shillings a piece per annum, the nation's stock will be thereby increased fifty thousand pounds per annum, besides the profit of a new dish, introduced to the tables of all gentlemen of fortune in the kingdom, who have any refinement in taste. And the money will circulate among our selves, the goods being entirely of our own growth and manufacture.

Fourthly, The constant breeders, besides the gain of eight shillings sterling per annum by the sale of their children, will be rid of the charge of maintaining them after the first year.

Fifthly, This food would likewise bring great custom to taverns, where the vintners will certainly be so prudent as to procure the best receipts for dressing it to perfection; and consequently have their houses frequented by all the fine gentlemen, who justly value themselves upon their knowledge in good eating; and a skilful cook, who understands how to oblige his guests, will contrive to make it as expensive as they please.

Sixthly, This would be a great inducement to marriage, which all wise nations have either encouraged by rewards, or enforced by laws and penalties. It would increase the care and tenderness of mothers towards their children, when they were sure of a settlement for life to the poor babes, provided in some sort by the publick, to their annual profit instead of expense. We should soon see an honest emulation among the married women, which of them could bring the fattest child to the market. Men would become as fond of their wives, during the time of their pregnancy, as they are now of their mares in foal, their cows in calf, or sow when they are ready to farrow; nor offer to beat or kick them (as is too frequent a practice) for fear of a miscarriage.

Many other advantages might be enumerated. For instance, the addition of some thousand carcasses in our exportation of barrel'd beef: the propagation of swine's flesh, and improvement in the art of making good bacon, so much wanted among us by the great destruction of pigs, too frequent at our tables; which are no way comparable in taste or magnificence to a well grown, fat yearly child, which roasted whole will make a considerable figure at a Lord Mayor's feast, or any other publick entertainment. But this, and many others, I omit, being studious of brevity.

Supposing that one thousand families in this city, would be constant customers for infants flesh, besides others who might have it at merry meetings, particularly at weddings and christenings, I compute that Dublin would take off annually about twenty thousand carcasses; and the rest of the kingdom (where probably they will be sold somewhat cheaper) the remaining eighty thousand.

I can think of no one objection, that will possibly be raised against this proposal, unless it should be urged, that the number of people will be thereby much lessened in the kingdom. This I freely own, and 'twas indeed one principal design in offering it to the world. I desire the reader will observe, that I calculate my remedy for this one individual Kingdom of Ireland, and for no other that ever was, is, or, I think, ever can be upon Earth. Therefore let no man talk to me of other expedients: Of taxing our absentees at five shillings a pound: Of using neither cloths, nor household furniture, except what is of our own growth and manufacture: Of utterly rejecting the materials and instruments that promote foreign luxury: Of curing the expensiveness of pride, vanity, idleness, and gaming in our women: Of introducing a vein of parsimony, prudence and temperance: Of learning to love our country, wherein we differ even from Laplanders, and the inhabitants of Topinamboo: Of quitting our animosities and factions, nor acting any longer like the Jews, who were murdering one another at the very moment their city was taken: Of being a little cautious not to sell our country and consciences for nothing: Of teaching landlords to have at least one degree of mercy towards their tenants. Lastly, of putting a spirit of honesty, industry, and skill into our shop-keepers, who, if a resolution could now be taken to buy only our native goods, would immediately unite to cheat and exact upon us in the price, the measure, and the goodness, nor could ever yet be brought to make one fair proposal of just dealing, though often and earnestly invited to it.

Therefore I repeat, let no man talk to me of these and the like expedients, till he hath at least some glimpse of hope, that there will ever be some hearty and sincere attempt to put them into practice.

But, as to my self, having been wearied out for many years with offering vain, idle, visionary thoughts, and at length utterly despairing of success, I fortunately fell upon this proposal, which, as it is wholly new, so it hath something solid and real, of no expense and little trouble, full in our own power, and whereby we can incur no danger in disobliging England. For this kind of commodity will not bear exportation, and flesh being of too tender a consistence, to admit a long continuance in salt, although perhaps I could name a country, which would be glad to eat up our whole nation without it.

After all, I am not so violently bent upon my own opinion, as to reject any offer, proposed by wise men, which shall be found equally innocent, cheap, easy, and effectual. But before something of that kind shall be advanced in contradiction to my scheme, and offering a better, I desire the author or authors will be pleased maturely to consider two points. First, As things now stand, how they will be able to find food and raiment for a hundred thousand useless mouths and backs. And secondly, There being a round million of creatures in humane figure throughout this kingdom, whose whole subsistence put into a common stock, would leave them in debt two million of pounds sterling, adding those who are beggars by profession, to the bulk of farmers, cottagers and laborers, with their wives and children, who are beggars in effect; I desire those politicians who dislike my overture, and may perhaps be so bold to attempt an answer, that they will first ask the parents of these mortals, whether they would not at this day think it a great happiness to have been sold for food at a year old, in the manner I prescribe, and thereby have avoided such a perpetual scene of misfortunes, as they have since gone through, by the oppression of landlords, the impossibility of paying rent without money or trade, the want of common sustenance, with neither house nor cloths to cover them from the inclemencies of the weather, and the most inevitable prospect of entailing the like, or greater miseries, upon their breed for ever.

I profess, in the sincerity of my heart, that I have not the least personal interest in endeavoring to promote this necessary work, having no other motive than the publick good of my country, by advancing our trade, providing for infants, relieving the poor, and giving some pleasure to the rich. I have no children, by which I can propose to get a single penny; the youngest being nine years old, and my wife past child-bearing.

THE PURSUIT OF THE GILLA DAKER

BY PATRICK WESTON JOYCE

Now, it chanced at one time during the chase, while they were hunting over the plain of Cliach, that Finn went to rest on the hill of Collkilla, which is now called Knockainy and he had his hunting-tents pitched on a level spot near the summit, and some of his chief heroes tarried with him.

When the King and his companions had taken their places on the hill, the Feni unleashed their gracefully shaped, sweet-voiced hounds through the woods and sloping glens. And it was sweet music to Finn's ear, the cry of the long-snouted dogs, as they routed the deer from their covers and the badgers from their dens; the pleasant, emulating shouts of the youths; the whistling and signalling of the huntsmen; and the encouraging cheers of the mighty heroes, as they spread themselves through the glens and woods, and over the broad green plain of Cliach.

Then did Finn ask who of all his companions would go to the highest point of the hill directly over them to keep watch and ward and to report how the chase went on. For, he said, the Dedannans were ever on the watch to work the Feni mischief by their druidical spells, and more so during the chase than at other times.

Finn Ban Mac Bresal stood forward and offered to go; and, grasping his broad spears, he went to the top, and sat viewing the plain to the four points of the sky. And the King and his companions brought forth the chess-board and chess-men and sat them down to a game.

Finn Ban Mac Bresal had been watching only a little time when he saw on a plain to the east a Fomor of vast size coming towards the hill, leading a horse. As he came nearer Finn Ban observed that he was the ugliest-looking giant his eyes ever lighted on. He had a large, thick body, bloated and swollen out to a great size; clumsy, crooked legs; and broad, flat feet turned inwards. His hands and arms and shoulders were bony and thick and very strong-looking; his neck was long and thin; and while his head was poked forward, his face was turned up, as he stared straight at Finn Mac Bresal. He had thick lips, and long, crooked teeth; and his face was covered all over with bushy hair.

He was fully armed; but all his weapons were rusty and soiled and slovenly looking. A broad shield of a dirty, sooty color, rough and battered, hung over his back; he had a long, heavy, straight sword at his left hip; and he held in his left hand two thick-handled, broad-headed spears, old and rusty, and seeming as if they had not been handled for years. In his right hand he held an iron club, which he dragged after him with its end on the ground; and, as it trailed along, it tore up a track as deep as the furrow a farmer ploughs with a team of oxen.

The horse he led was even larger in proportion than the giant himself, and quite as ugly. His great carcass was covered all over with tangled scraggy hair, of a sooty black; you could count his ribs and all the points of his big bones through his hide; his legs were crooked and knotty; his neck was twisted; and as for his jaws, they were so long and heavy that they made his head look twice too large for his body.

The giant held him by a thick halter, and seemed to be dragging him forward by main force, the animal was so lazy and so hard to move. Every now and then, when the beast tried to stand still, the giant would give him a blow on the ribs with his big iron club, which sounded as loud as the thundering of a great billow against the rough-headed rocks of the coast. When he gave him a pull forward by the halter, the wonder was that he did not drag the animal's head away from his body; and, on the other hand, the horse often gave the halter such a tremendous tug backwards that it was equally wonderful how the arm of the giant was not torn away from his shoulder.

When at last he had come up he bowed his head and bended his knee, and saluted the King with great respect.

Finn addressed him; and after having given him leave to speak he asked him who he was, and what was his name, and whether he belonged to one of the noble or ignoble races; also what was his profession or craft, and why he had no servant to attend to his horse.

The big man made answer and said, "King of the Feni, whether I come of a noble or of an ignoble race, that, indeed, I cannot tell, for I know not who my father and mother were. As to where I came from, I am a Fomor of Lochlann in the north; but I have no particular dwelling-place, for I am continually travelling about from one country to another, serving the great lords and nobles of the world, and receiving wages for my service.

"In the course of my wanderings I have often heard of you, O King, and of your greatness and splendor and royal bounty; and I have come now to ask you to take me into your service for one year; and at the end of that time I shall fix my own wages, according to my custom.

"You ask me also why I have no servant for this great horse of mine. The reason of that is this: at every meal I eat my master must give me as much food and drink as would be enough for a hundred men; and whosoever the lord or chief may be that takes me into his service, it is quite enough for him to have to provide for me, without having also to feed my servant.

"Moreover, I am so very heavy and lazy that I should never be able to keep up with a company on march if I had to walk; and this is my reason for keeping a horse at all.

"My name is the Gilla Dacker, and it is not without good reason that I am so called. For there never was a lazier or worse servant than I am, or one that grumbles more at doing a day's work for his master. And I am the hardest person in the world to deal with; for, no matter how good or noble I may think my master, or how kindly he may treat me, it is hard words and foul reproaches I am likely to give him for thanks in the end.

"This, O Finn, is the account I have to give of myself, and these are my answers to your questions."

"Well," answered Finn, "according to your own account you are not a very pleasant fellow to have anything to do with; and of a truth there is not much to praise in your appearance. But things may not be so bad as you say; and, anyhow, as I have never yet refused any man service and wages, I will not now refuse you."

Whereupon Finn and the Gilla Dacker made covenants, and the Gilla Dacker was taken into service for a year.

"And now," said the Gilla Dacker, "as to this same horse of mine, I find I must attend to him myself, as I see no one here worthy of putting a hand near him. So I will lead him to the nearest stud, as I am wont to do, and let him graze among your horses. I value him greatly, however, and it would grieve me very much if any harm were to befall him; so," continued he, turning to the King, "I put him under your protection, O King, and under the protection of all the Feni that are here present."

At this speech the Feni all burst out laughing to see the Gilla Dacker showing such concern for his miserable, worthless old skeleton of a horse.

Howbeit, the big man, giving not the least heed to their merriment, took the halter off the horse's head and turned him loose among the horses of the Feni.

But now, this same wretched-looking old animal, instead of beginning to graze, as everyone thought he would, ran in among the horses of the Feni, and began straightway to work all sorts of mischief. He cocked his long, hard, switchy tail straight out like a rod, and, throwing up his hind legs, he kicked about on this side and on that, maiming and disabling several of the horses. Sometimes he went tearing through the thickest of the herd, butting at them with his hard, bony forehead; and he opened out his lips with a vicious grin and tore all he could lay hold on with his sharp, crooked teeth, so that none were safe that came in his way either before or behind.

At last he left them, and was making straight across to a small field where Conan Mail's horses were grazing by themselves, intending to play the same tricks among them. But Conan, seeing this, shouted in great alarm to the Gilla Dacker to bring away his horse, and not let him work any more mischief; and threatening, if he did not do so at once, to go himself and knock the brains out of the vicious old brute on the spot.

But the Gilla Dacker told Conan that he saw no way of preventing his horse from joining the others, except someone put the halter on him. "And," said he to Conan, "there is the halter; and if you are in any fear for your own animals, you may go yourself and bring him away from the field."

Conan was in a mighty rage when he heard this; and as he saw the big horse just about to cross the fence, he snatched up the halter, and, running forward with long strides, he threw it over the animal's head and thought to lead him back. But in a moment the horse stood stock still, and his body and legs became as stiff as if they were made of wood; and though Conan pulled and tugged with might and main, he was not able to stir him an inch from his place.

At last Fergus Finnvel, the poet, spoke to Conan and said,

"I never would have believed, Conan Mail, that you could be brought to do horse-service for any knight or noble in the whole world; but now, indeed, I see that you have made yourself a horse-boy to an ugly foreign giant, so hateful-looking and low-born that not a man of the Feni would have anything to say to him. As you have, however, to mind this old horse in order to save your own, would it not be better for you to mount him and revenge yourself for all the trouble he is giving you, by riding him across the country, over the hill-tops, and down into the deep glens and valleys, and through stones and bogs and all sorts of rough places, till you have broken the heart in his big ugly body?"

Conan, stung by the cutting words of the poet and by the jeers of his companions, jumped upon the horse's back, and began to beat him mightily with his heels and with his two big heavy fists to make him go; but the horse seemed not to take the least notice, and never stirred.

"I know the reason he does not go," said Fergus Finnvel; "he has been accustomed to carry a horseman far heavier than you—that is to say, the Gilla Dacker; and he will not move till he has the same weight on his back."

At this Conan Mail called out to his companions, and asked which of them would mount with him and help to avenge the damage done to their horses.

"I will go," said Coil Croda the Battle Victor, son of Criffan; and up he went. But the horse never moved.

Dara Donn Mac Morna next offered to go, and mounted behind the others; and after him Angus Mac Art Mac Morna. And the end of it was that fourteen men of the Clann Baskin and Clann Morna got up along with Conan; and all began to thrash the horse together with might and main. But they were none the better for it, for he remained standing stiff and immovable as before. They found, moreover, that their seat was not at all an easy one—the animal's back was so sharp and bony.

When the Gilla Dacker saw the Feni beating his horse at such a rate he seemed very angry, and addressed the King in these words:

King of the Feni, I now see plainly that all the fine accounts I heard about you and the Feni are false, and I will not stay in your service—no, not another hour. You can see for yourself the ill usage these men are giving my horse without cause; and I leave you to judge whether anyone could put up with it—anyone who had the least regard for his horse. The time is, indeed, short since I entered your service, but I now think it a great deal too long; so pay me my wages and let me go my ways."

But Finn said, "I do not wish you to go; stay on till the end of your year, and then I will pay you all I promised you."

"I swear," answered the Gilla Dacker, "that if this were the very last day of my year, I would not wait till morning for my wages after this insult. So, wages or no wages, I will now seek another master; but from this time forth I shall know what to think of Finn Mac Cumal and his Feni!"

With that the Gilla Dacker stood up as straight as a pillar, and, turning his face towards the south-west, he walked slowly away.

When the horse saw his master leaving the hill he stirred himself at once and walked quietly after him, bringing the fifteen men away on his back. And when the Feni saw this they raised a loud shout of laughter, mocking them.

The Gilla Dacker, after he had walked some little way, looked back, and, seeing that his horse was following, he stood for a moment to tuck up his skirts. Then, all at once changing his pace, he set out with long, active strides; and if you know what the speed of a swallow is flying across a mountain-side, or the dry fairy wind of a March day sweeping over the plains, then you can understand the swiftness of the Gilla Dacker as he ran down the hill-side towards the south-west.

Neither was the horse behindhand in the race; for though he carried a heavy load, he galloped like the wind after his master, plunging and bounding forward with as much freedom as if he had nothing at all on his back.

The men now tried to throw themselves off; but this, indeed, they were not able to do, for the good reason that they found themselves fastened firmly, hands and feet and all, to the horse's back.

And now Conan, looking round, raised his big voice and shouted to Finn and the Feni, asking them were they content to let their friends be carried off in that manner by such a horrible, foul-looking old spectre of a horse.

Finn and the others, hearing this, seized their arms and started off in pursuit. Now, the way the Gilla Daker and his horse took was first through Fermore, which is at the present day called Hy Conall Gavra; next over the wide, healthy summit of Slieve Lougher; from that to Corca Divna; and they ran along by Slieve Mish till they reached Cloghan Kincat, near the deep green sea.

And so the great horse continued his course without stop or stay, bringing the sixteen Feni with him through the sea. Now, this is how they fared in the sea while the horse was farther and farther to the west: they had always a dry, firm strand under them, for the waters retired before the horse; while behind them was a wild, raging sea, which followed close after and seemed ready every moment to topple over their heads. But, though the billows were tumbling and roaring all round, neither horse nor riders were wetted by as much as a drop of brine or a dash of spray.

Then Finn spoke and asked the chiefs what they thought best to be done; and they told him they would follow whatsoever counsel he and Fergus Finnvel, the poet, gave them. Then Finn told Fergus to speak his mind; and Fergus said:

"My counsel is that we go straightway to Ben Edar, where we shall find a ship ready to sail. For our forefathers, when they wrested the land from the gifted, bright-complexioned Dedannans, bound them by covenant to maintain this ship for ever, fitted with all things needful for a voyage, even to the smallest article, as one of the privileges of Ben Edar; so that if at any time one of the noble sons of Gael Glas wished to sail to distant lands from Erin, he should have a ship lying at hand in the harbor ready to begin his voyage."

They agreed to this counsel, and turned their steps without delay northwards towards Ben Edar. They had not gone far when they met two noble-looking youths, fully armed, and wearing over their armor beautiful mantles of scarlet silk, fastened by brooches of gold. The strangers saluted the King with much respect; and the King saluted them in return. Then, having given them leave to converse, he asked them who they were, whither they had come, and who the prince or chief was that they served. And the elder answered:

"My name is Feradach, and my brother's name is Foltlebar; and we are the two sons of the King of Innia. Each of us professes an art; and it has long been a point of dispute between us which art is the better, my brother's or mine.

"Hearing that there is not in the world a wiser or more far-seeing man than thou art, O King, we have come to ask thee to take us into thy service among thy household troops for a year, and at the end of that time to give judgment between us in this matter."

Finn asked them what were the two arts they professed.

"My art," answered Feradach, "is this. If at any time a company of warriors need a ship, give me only my joiner's axe and my crann-tavall, and I am able to provide a ship for them without delay. The only think I ask them to do is this—to cover their heads close, and keep them covered, while I give the crann-tavall three blows of my axe. Then I tell them to uncover their heads; and lo, there lies the ship in harbor ready to sail!"

Then Foltlebar spoke and said, "This, O King, is the art I profess. On land I can track the wild duck over nine ridges and nine glens, and follow her without being once thrown out till I drop upon her in her nest. And I can follow up a track on sea quite as well as on land if I have a good ship and crew."

Finn replied, "You are the very men I want; and I now take you both into my service. At this moment I need a good ship and a skilful pilot more than any two things in the whole world."

Whereupon Finn told them the whole story of the Gilla Dacker's doings from beginning to end. "And we are now," said he, "on our way to Ben Edar to seek a ship that we may follow this giant and his horse and rescue our companions."

Then Feradach said, "I will get you a ship—a ship that will sail as swiftly as a swallow can fly!"

And Foltlebar said, "I will guide your ship in the track of the Gilla Dacker till ye lay hands on him, in whatsoever quarter of the world he may have hidden himself!"

And so they turned back to Cloghan Kincat. And when they had come to the beach Feradach told them to cover their heads, and they did so. Then he struck three blows of his axe on the crann-tavall; after which he made them look. And lo, they saw a ship fully fitted out with oars and sails and with all things needed for a long voyage riding before them in the harbor!

Then they went on board and launched their ship on the cold, bright sea; and Foltlebar was their pilot and steersman. And they set their sail and plied their slender oars, and the ship moved swiftly westward till they lost sight of the shores of Erin; and they saw nothing all round them but a wide girdle of sea. After some days' sailing a great storm came from the west, and the black waves rose up against them so that they had much ado to keep their vessel from sinking. But through all the roaring of the tempest, through the rain and blinding spray, Foltlebar never stirred from the helm or changed his course, but still kept close on the track of the Gilla Dacker.

At length the storm abated and the sea grew calm. And when the darkness had cleared away they saw to the west, a little way off, a vast rocky cliff towering over their heads to such a height that its head seemed hidden among the clouds. It rose up sheer from the very water, and looked at that distance as smooth as glass, so that at first sight there seemed no way to reach the top.

Foltlebar, after examining to the four points of the sky, found the track of the Gilla Dacker as far as the cliff, but no farther. And he accordingly told the heroes that he thought it was on the top of that rock the giant lived; and that, anyhow, the horse must have made his way up the face of the cliff with their companions.

When the heroes heard this they were greatly cast down and puzzled what to do; for they saw no way of reaching the top of the rock; and they feared they should have to give up the quest and return without their companions. And they sat down and looked up at the cliff with sorrow and vexation in their hearts.

Fergus Finnvel, the poet, then challenged the hero Dermat O'Dyna to climb the rock in pursuit of the Gilla Dacker, and he did so, and on reaching the summit found himself in a beautiful fairy plain. He fared across it and came to a great tree laden with fruit beside a well as clear as crystal. Hard by, on the brink of the well, stood a tall pillar stone, and on its top lay a golden-chased drinking horn. He filled the horn from the well and drank, but had scarcely taken it from his lips when he saw a fully armed wizard champion advancing to meet him with looks and gestures of angry menace. The wizard upbraided him for entering his territory without leave and for drinking out of his well from his drinking horn, and thereupon challenged him to fight. For four days long they fought, the wizard escaping from Dermat every even-fall by leaping into the well and disappearing down through it. But on the fourth evening Dermat closed with the wizard when about to spring into the water, and fell with him into the well.

On reaching the bottom the wizard wrested himself away and started running, and Dermat found himself in a strangely beautiful country with a royal palace hard by, in front of which armed knights were engaged in warlike exercises. Through them the wizard ran, but, when Dermat attempted to follow, his way was barred by their threatening weapons. Nothing daunted, he fell upon them in all his battle fury, and routed them so entirely that they fled and shut themselves up in the castle or took refuge in distant woods.

Overcome with his battle toil (and smarting all over with wounds) Dermat fell into a dead sleep, from which he was wakened by a friendly blow from the flat of a sword held by a young, golden-haired hero, who proved to be the brother of the Knight of Valor, King of that country of Tir-fa-tonn, whom in the guise of the Knight of the Fountain, Dermat had fought and chased away.

A part of the kingdom belonging to him had been seized by his wizard brother, and he now seeks and obtains Dermat's aid to win it back for him.

When Dermat at last meets Finn and the other Feni who had gone in pursuit of him into the Kingdom of Sorca, at the summit of the great rock, he is able to relate how he headed the men of the Knight of Valor against the Wizard King, and slew him and defeated his army.

"And now," continued he, bringing forth the Knight of Valor from among the strange host, "this is he who was formerly called the Knight of Valor, but who is now the King of Tir-fa-tonn. Moreover, this King has told me, having himself found it out by his druidical art, that it was Avarta the Dedannan (the son of Illahan of the Many-colored Raiment) who took the form of the Gilla Dacker, and who brought the sixteen Feni away to the Land of Promise, where he now holds them in bondage."

Then Foltlebar at once found the tracks of the Gilla Dacker and his horse. He traced them from the very edge of the rock across the plain to the sea at the other side; and they brought round their ship and began their voyage. But this time Foltlebar found it very hard to keep on the track; for the Gilla Dacker, knowing that there were not in the world men more skilled in following up a quest than the Feni, took great pains to hide all traces of the flight of himself and his horse; so that Foltlebar was often thrown out; but he always recovered the track after a little time.

And so they sailed from island to island and from bay to bay, over many seas and by many shores, ever following the track, till at length they arrived at the Land of Promise. And when they had made the land, and knew for a certainty that this was indeed the Land of Promise, they rejoiced greatly; for in this land Dermat O'Dyna had been nurtured by Mannanan Mac Lir of the Yellow Hair.

Then they held council as to what was best to be done; and Finn's advice was that they should burn and spoil the country in revenge of the outrage that had been done to his people. Dermat, however, would not hear of this. And he said:

"Not so, O King. The people of this land are of all men the most skilled in druidic art; and it is not well that they should be at feud with us. Let us rather send to Avarta a trusty herald to demand that he should set our companions at liberty. If he does so, then we shall be at peace; if he refuse, then shall we proclaim war against him and his people, and waste this land with fire and sword till he be forced, even by his own people, to give us back our friends."

This advice was approved by all. And then Finn said:

"But how shall heralds reach the dwelling of this enchanter; for the ways are not open and straight, as in other lands, but crooked and made for concealment, and the valleys and plains are dim and shadowy and hard to be traversed?"

But Foltlebar, nothing daunted by the dangers and the obscurity of the way, offered to go with a single trusty companion; and they took up the track and followed it without being once thrown out, till they reached the mansion of Avarta. There they found their friends amusing themselves on the green outside the palace walls; for, though kept captive in the island, yet were they in no wise restrained, but were treated by Avarta with much kindness. When they saw the heralds coming towards them their joy knew no bounds; they crowded round to embrace them, and asked them many questions regarding their home and their friends.

At last Avarta himself came forth and asked who these strangers were; and Foltlebar replied:

"We are of the people of Finn Mac Cumal, who has sent us as heralds to thee. He and his heroes have landed on this island guided hither by me; and he bade us tell thee that he has come to wage war and to waste this land with fire and sword as a punishment for that thou hast brought away his people by foul spells, and even now keepest them in bondage."

When Avarta heard this he made no reply, but called a council of his chief men to consider whether they should send back to Finn an answer of war or of peace. And they, having much fear of the Feni, were minded to restore Finn's people and to give him his own award in satisfaction for the injury done to him; and to invite Finn himself and those who had come with him to a feast of joy and friendship in the house of Avarta.

Avarta himself went with Foltlebar to give this message. And after he and Finn had exchanged friendly greetings, he told them what the council had resolved; and Finn and Dermat and the others were glad at heart. And Finn and Avarta put hand in hand and made a league of friendship.

So they went with Avarta to his house, where they found their lost friends; and, being full of gladness, they saluted and embraced each other. Then a feast was prepared; and they were feasted for three days, and they ate and drank and made merry.

On the fourth day a meeting was called on the green to hear the award. Now, it was resolved to make amends on the one hand to Finn, as King of the Feni, and on the other to those who had been brought away by the Gilla Dacker. And when all were gathered together Finn was first asked to name his award; and this is what he said:

"I shall not name an award, O Avarta; neither shall I accept an eric from thee. But the wages I promised thee when we made our covenant at Knockainy, that I will give thee. For I am thankful for the welcome thou hast given us here; and I wish that there should be peace and friendship between us for ever."

But Conan, on his part, was not so easily satisfied; and he said to Finn:

"Little hast thou endured, O Finn, in this matter; and thou mayst well waive thy award. But hadst thou, like us, suffered from the sharp bones and the rough carcass of the Gilla Dacker's monstrous horse in a long journey from Erin to the Land of Promise, across wide seas, through tangled woods, and over rough-headed rocks, thou wouldst then, methinks, name an award."

At this, Avarta and the others who had seen Conan and his companions carried off on the back of the big horse could scarce keep from laughing; and Avarta said to Conan:

"Name thy award, and I will fulfill it every jot; for I have heard of thee, Conan, and I dread to bring the gibes and taunts of thy foul tongue on myself and my people."

"Well, then," said Conan, "my award is this: that you choose fifteen of the best and noblest men in the Land of Promise, among whom are to be your own best beloved friends; and that you cause them to mount on the back of the big horse, and that you yourself take hold of his tail. In this manner you shall fare to Erin, back again by the self-same track the horse took when he brought us hither—through the same surging seas, through the same thick thorny woods, and over the same islands and rough rocks and dark glens. And this, Avarta, is my award," said Conan.

Now, Finn and his people were rejoiced exceedingly when they heard Conan's award—that he asked from Avarta nothing more than like for like. For they feared much that he might claim treasure of gold and silver, and thus bring reproach on the Feni.

Avarta promised that everything required by Conan should be done, binding himself in solemn pledges. Then the heroes took their leave; and having launched their ship on the broad, green sea, they sailed back by the same course to Erin. And they marched to their camping-place at Knockainy, where they rested in their tents.

Avarta then chose his men. And he placed them on the horse's back, and he himself caught hold of the tail; and it is not told how they fared till they made harbor and landing-place at Cloghan Kincat. They delayed not, but straightway journeyed over the self-same track as before till they reached Knockainy.

Finn and his people saw them afar off coming towards the hill with great speed; the Gilla Dacker, quite as large and as ugly as ever, running before the horse; for he had let go the tail at Cloghan Kincat. And the Feni could not help laughing heartily when they saw the plight of the fifteen chiefs on the great horse's back; and they said with one voice that Conan had made a good award that time.

When the horse reached the spot from which he had at first set out the men began to dismount. Then the Gilla Dacker, suddenly stepping forward, held up his arm and pointed earnestly over the heads of the Feni towards the field where the horses were standing; so that the heroes were startled, and turned round every man to look. But nothing was to be seen except the horses grazing quietly inside the fence.

Finn and the others now turned round again with intent to speak to the Gilla Dacker and bring him and his people into the tents; but much did they marvel to find them all gone. The Gilla Dacker and his great horse and fifteen nobles of the Land of Promise had disappeared in an instant; and neither Finn himself nor any of his chiefs ever saw them afterwards.

THE KEENING WOMAN

BY PATRICK PEARSE

'Coilin,' says my father to me one morning after the breakfast, and I putting my books together to be stirring to school— 'Coilin,' says he, 'I have a task for you to-day. Sean will tell the master it was myself kept you at home to-day, or it's the way he'll be thinking you're miching, like you were last week. Let you not forget now, Sean.'

'I will not, father,' says Sean, and a lip on him. He wasn't too thankful it to be said that it's not for him my father had the task. This son was well satisfied, for my lessons were always a trouble to me, and the master promised me a beating the day before unless I'd have them at the tip of my mouth the next day.

'What you'll do, Coilin,' says my father when Sean was gone off, 'is to bring the ass and the little car with you to Screeb, and draw home a load of sedge. Michileen Maire is cutting it for me. We'll be starting, with God's help, to put the new roof on the house after to-morrow, if the weather stands.'

'Michileen took the ass and car with him this morning,' says I.

'You'll have to leg it, then, *a mhic O*,' says my father. 'As soon as Michileen has an ass-load cut, fetch it home with you on the car, and let Michileen tear till he's black. We might draw the other share to-morrow.'

It wasn't long till I was knocking steps out of the road. I gave my back to Kilbrickan and my face to Turlagh. I left Turlagh behind me, and I made for Gortmore. I stood a spell looking at an oared boat that was on Loch Ellery, and another spell playing with some Inver boys that were late going to Gortmore school. I left them at the school gate, and I reached Glencana. I stood, for the third time watching a big eagle that was sunning himself on Carrigacapple. East with me, then, till I was in Derrybanniv, and the hour and a half wasn't spent when I cleared Glashaduff bridge.

There was a house that time a couple of hundred yards east from the bridge, near the road, on your right-hand side and you drawing towards Screeb. It was often before that I saw an old woman standing in the door of that house, but I had no acquaintance on her, nor did she ever put talk or topic on me. A tall, thin woman she was, her head as white as the snow, and two dark eyes, as they would be two burning sods, flaming in her head. She was a woman that would scare me if I met her in a lonely place in the night. Times she would be knitting or carding, and she crooning low to herself; but the thing she would be mostly doing when I travelled, would be standing in the door, and looking from her up and down the road, exactly as she'd be waiting for someone that would be away from her, and she expecting him home.

She was standing there that morning as usual, her hand to her eyes, and she staring up the road. When she saw me going past, she nodded her head to me. I went over to her.

'Do you see a person at all coming up the road?' says she.

'I don't,' says I.

'I thought I saw someone. It can't be that I'm astray. See, isn't that a young man making up on us?' says she.

'Devil a one do I see,' says I. 'There's not a person at all between the spot we're on and the turning of the road.'

'I was astray, then,' says she. 'My sight isn't as good as it was. I thought I saw him coming. I don't know what's keeping him.'

'Who's away from you?' says myself.

'My son that's away from me,' says she.

'Is he long away?'

'This morning he went to Uachtar Ard.'

'But, sure, he couldn't be here for a while,' says I. 'You'd think he'd barely be in Uachtar Ard by now, and he doing his best, unless it was by the morning train he went from the Burnt House.'

'What's this I'm saying?' says she. 'It's not to-day he went, but yesterday,—or the day ere yesterday, maybe. . . I'm losing my wits.'

'If it's on the train he's coming,' says I, 'he'll not be here for a couple of hours yet.'

'On the train?' says she. 'What train?'

'The train that does be at the Burnt House at noon.'

'He didn't say a word about a train,' says she. 'There was no train coming as far as the Burnt House yesterday.'

'Isn't there a train coming to the Burnt House these years?' says I, wondering greatly. She didn't give me any answer, however. She was staring up the road again. There came a sort of dread on me of her, and I was about gathering off.

'If you see him on the road,' says she 'tell him to make hurry.'

'I've no acquaintance on him,' says I.

'You'd know him easy. He's the playboy of the people. A young, active lad, and he well set-up. He has a white head on him, like is on yourself, and grey eyes . . . like his father had. Bawneens he's wearing.'

'If I see him,' says I, 'I'll tell him you're waiting for him.'

'Do, son,' says she.

With that I stirred on with me east, and left her standing in the door.

She was there still, and I coming home a couple of hours after that, and the load of sedge on the car.

'He didn't come yet?' says I to her.

'No, *a mhuirnín*. You didn't see him?'

'No.'

'No? What can have happened him?'

There were signs of rain on the day.

'Come in till the shower's over,' says she. 'It's seldom I do have company.'

I left the ass and the little car on the road, and I went into the house.

'Sit and drink a cup of milk,' says she.

I sat on the bench in the corner, and she gave me a drink of milk and a morsel of bread. I was looking all round the house, and I eating and drinking. There was a chair beside the fire, and a white shirt and a suit of clothes laid on it.

'I have these ready against he will come,' says she. 'I washed the bawneens yesterday after his departing,—no, the day ere yesterday—I don't know right which day I washed them; but, anyhow, they'll be clean and dry before him when he does come. . . What's your own name?' says she, suddenly, after a spell of silence.

I told her.

'*Muise,* my love you are!' says she. 'The very name that was—that is—on my own son. Whose are you?'

I told her.

'And do you say you're a son of Sean Feichin's?' says she. 'Your father was in the public-house in Uachtar Ard that night. . . .' She stopped suddenly with that, and there came some change on her. She put her hand to her head. You'd think that it's madness was struck on her. She sat before the fire then, and she stayed for a while dreaming into the heart of the fire. It was short till she began moving herself to and fro over the fire, and crooning or keening in a low voice. I didn't understand the words right, or it would be better for me to say that it's not on the words I was thinking but on the music. It seemed to me that there was the loneliness of the hills in the dead time of night, or the loneliness of the grave when nothing stirs in it but worms, in that music. Here are the words as I heard them from my father after that—

Sorrow on death, it is it that blackened my heart,
That carried off my love and that left me ruined,
Without friend, without companion under the roof of my house
But this sorrow in my middle, and I lamenting.
Going the mountain one evening,
The birds spoke to me sorrowfully,
The melodious snipe and the voiceful curlew,
Telling me that my treasure was dead.
I called on you, and your voice I did not hear,
I called again, and an answer I did not get.
I kissed your mouth, and O God, wasn't it cold!
Och, it's cold your bed is in the lonely graveyard.
And O sod-green grave, where my child is,
O narrow, little grave, since you are his bed,
My blessing on you, and the thousand blessings
On the green sods that are over my pet.
Sorrow on death, its blessing is not possible—
It lays fresh and withered together;
And, O pleasant little son, it is it is my affliction,
Your sweet body to be making clay!

When she had that finished, she kept on moving herself to and fro, and lamenting in a low voice. It was a lonesome place to be, in that backward house, and you to have no company but yon solitary old woman, mourning to herself by the fireside. There came a dread and a creeping on me, and I rose to my feet.

'It's time for me to be going home,' says I. 'The evening's clearing.'

'Come here,' says she to me.

I went hither to her. She laid her two hands softly on my head, and she kissed my forehead.

'The protection of God to you, little son,' says she. 'May He let the harm of the year over you, and may He increase the good fortune and happiness of the year to you and to your family.'

With that she freed me from her. I left the house, and pushed on home with me.

'Where were you, Coilin, when the shower caught you?' says my mother to me that night. 'It didn't do you any hurt.'

'I waited in the house of yon old woman on the east side of Glashaduff bridge,' says I. 'She was talking to me about her son. He's in Uachtar Ard these two days, and she doesn't know why he hasn't come home ere this.'

My father looked over at my mother.

'The Keening Woman,' says he.

'Who is she ?' says I.

'The Keening Woman,' says my father. 'Muirne of the Keens.'

'Why was that name given to her?' says I.

'For the keens she does be making,' answered my father. 'She's the most famous keening-woman in Connemara or in the Joyce Country. She's always sent for when anyone dies. She keened my father, and there's a chance but she'll keen myself. But, may God comfort her, it's her own dead she does be keening always, it's all the same what corpse is in the house.'

'And what's her son doing in Uachtar Ard?' says I.

'Her son died twenty years since, Coilin,' says my mother.

'He didn't die at all,' says my father, and a very black look on him. 'He *was murdered.*'

'Who murdered him?'

It's seldom I saw my father angry, but it's awful his anger was when it would rise up in him. He took a start out of me when he spoke again, he was that angry.

'Who murdered your own grandfather? Who drew the red blood out of my grandmother's shoulders with a lash? Who would do it but the English? My curse on—'

My mother rose, and she put her hand on his mouth.

'Don't give your curse to anyone, Sean,' says she. My mother was that kindhearted, she wouldn't like to throw the bad word at the devil himself. I believe she'd have pity in her heart for Cain and for Judas, and for Diarmaid of the Galls.

'It's time for us to be saying the Rosary,' says she. 'Your father will tell you about Coilin Muirne some other night.'

'Father,' says I, and we going on our knees, 'we should say a prayer for Coilin's soul this night.'

'We'll do that, son,' says my father kindly.

Sitting up one night, in the winter that was on us, my father told us the story of Muirne from start to finish. It's well I mind him in the firelight, a broad-shouldered man, a little stooped, his share of hair going grey, lines in his forehead, a sad look in his eyes. He was mending an old sail that night, and I was on my knees beside him in the name of helping him. My mother and my sisters were spinning frieze. Seaneen was stretched on his face on the floor, and he in grips of a book. 'Twas small the heed he gave to the same book, for it's the pastime he had, to be tickling the soles of my feet and taking an odd pinch out of my calves; but as my father stirred out in the story Sean gave over his trickery, and it is short till he was listening as interested as anyone. It would be hard not to listen to my father when he'd tell a story like that by the hearthside. He was a sweet storyteller. It's often I'd think there was music in his voice; a low, deep music like that in the bass of the organ in Tuam Cathedral.

Twenty years are gone, Coilin (says my father), since the night myself and Coilin Muirne (may God give him grace) and three or four others of the neighbours were in Neachtan's public-house in Uachtar Ard. There was a fair in the town the same day, and we were drinking a glass before taking the road home on ourselves. There were four or five men in it from Carrowroe and from the Joyce Country, and six or seven of the people of the town. There came a stranger in, a thin, black man that nobody knew. He called for a glass.

'Did ye hear, people,' says he to us, and he drinking with us, 'that the lord is to come home to-night?'

'What business has the devil here?' says someone.

'Bad work he's up to, as usual,' says the black man. 'He has settled to put seven families out of their holdings.'

'Who's to be put out?' says one of us.

'Old Thomas O'Drinan from the Glen,—I'm told the poor fellow's dying, but it's on the roadside he'll die, if God hasn't him already; a man of the O'Conaire's that lives in a cabin on this side of Loch Shindilla; Manning from Snamh Bo; two in Annaghmaan; a woman at the head of the Island; and Anthony O'Greelis from Lower Camus.'

'Anthony's wife is heavy in child,' says Cuimin O'Niadh.

'That won't save her, the creature,' says the black man. 'She's not the first woman out of this country that bore her child in a ditch-side of the road.'

There wasn't a word out of anyone of us.

'What sort of men are ye?' says the black man,—'ye are not men, at all. I was born and raised in a countryside, and, my word to you, the men of that place wouldn't let the whole English army together throw out seven families on the road without them knowing the reason why. Are ye afraid of the man that's coming here tonight?'

'It's easy to talk,' said Cuimin, 'but what way can we stop the bodach?'

'Murder him this night,' says a voice behind me. Everybody started. I myself turned round. It was Coilin Muirne that spoke. His two eyes were blazing in his head, a flame in his cheeks, and his head thrown high.

'A man that spoke that, whatever his name and surname,' says the stranger. He went hither and gripped Coilin's hand.

'Drink a glass with me,' says he.

Coilin drank the glass. The others wouldn't speak.

'It's time for us to be shortening the road,' says Cuimin, after a little spell.

We got a move on us. We took the road home. The night was dark. There was no wish for talk on any of us, at all. When we came to the head of the street Cuimin stood in the middle of the road.

'Where's Coilin Muirne?' says he.

We didn't feel him from us till Cuimin spoke. He wasn't in the company.

Myself went back to the public-house. Coilin wasn't in it. I questioned the pot-boy. He said that Coilin and the black man left the shop together five minutes after our going. I searched the town. There wasn't tale or tidings of Coilin anywhere. I left the town and I followed the other men. I hoped it might be that he'd be to find before me. He wasn't, nor the track of him.

It was very far in the night when we reached Glashaduff bridge. There was a light in Muirne's house. Muirne herself was standing in the door.

'God save you, men,' says she, coming over to us.'Is Coilin with you?'

'He isn't, maise,' says I. 'He stayed behind us in Uachtar Ard.'

'Did he sell?' says she.

'He did, and well,' says I. 'There's every chance that he'll stay in the town till morning. The night's black and cold in itself. Wouldn't it be as well for you to go in and lie down?'

'It's not worth my while,' says she. 'I'll wait up till he comes. May God hasten you.'

We departed. There was, as it would be, a load on my heart. I was afraid that there was something after happening to Coilin. I had ill notions of that black man I lay down on my bed after coming home, but I didn't sleep.

The next morning myself and your mother were eating breakfast, when the latch was lifted from the door, and in comes Cuimin O'Niadh. He could hardly draw his breath.

'What's the news with you, man?,' says I.

'Bad news,' says he. 'The lord was murdered last night. He was got on the road a mile to the east of Uachtar Ard, and a bullet through his heart. The soldiers were in Muirne's house this morning on the track of Coilin, but he wasn't there. He hasn't come home yet. It's said it was he murdered the lord. You mind the words he said last night?'

I leaped up, and out the door with me. Down the road, and east to Muirne's house. There was no one before me but herself. The furniture of the house was this way and that way, where the soldiers were searching. Muirne got up when she saw me in the door.

'Sean O'Conaire,' says she, 'for God's pitiful sake, tell me where's my son? You were along with him. Why isn't he coming home to me?'

'Let you have patience, Muirne,' says I. 'I'm going to Uachtar Ard after him.'

I struck the road. Going in the street of Uachtar Ard, I saw a great ruck of people. The bridge and the street before the chapel were black with people. People were making on the spot from every art. But, a thing that put terror on my heart, there wasn't a sound out of that terrible gathering—only the eyes of every man stuck in a little knot that was in the right-middle of the crowd. Soldiers that were in that little knot, black coats and red coats on them, and guns and swords in their hands; and among the black coats and red coats I saw a country boy, and bawneens on him. Coilin Muirne that was in it, and he in holds of the soldiers. The poor boy's face was as white as my shirt, but he had the beautiful head of him lifted proudly, and it wasn't the head of a coward, that head.

He was brought to the barracks, and that crowd following him. He was taken to Galway that night. He was put on his trial the next month. It was sworn that he was in the public-house that night. It was sworn that the black man was discoursing on the landlords. It was sworn that he said the lord would be coming that night to throw the people out of their holdings the next day. It was sworn that Coilin Muirne was listening attentively to him. It was sworn that Coilin said those words, 'Murder him this night,' when Cuimin O'Niadh said, 'What way can we stop the bodach?' It was sworn that the black man praised him for saying those words, that he shook hands with him, that they drank a glass together. It was sworn that Coilin remained in the shop after the going of the Rossnageeragh people, and that himself and the black man left the shop together five minutes after that. There came a peeler then, and he swore he saw Coilin and the black man leaving the town, and that it wasn't the Rossnageeragh road they took on themselves, but the Galway road. At eight o'clock they left the town. At half after eight a shot was fired at the lord on the Galway road. Another peeler swore he heard the report of the shot. He swore he ran to the place, and, closing up to the place, he saw two men running away. A thin man one of them was, and he dressed like a gentleman would be.

A country boy the other man was.

'What kind of clothes was the country boy wearing?' says the lawyer.

'A suit of bawneens,' says the peeler.

'Is that the man you saw?' says the lawyer, stretching his finger towards Coilin.

'I would say it was.'

'Do you swear it?'

The peeler didn't speak for a spell.

'Do you swear it?' says the lawyer again.

'I do,' says the peeler. The peeler's face at that moment was whiter than the face of Coilin himself.

A share of us swore then that Coilin never fired a shot out of a gun; that he was a decent, kindly boy that wouldn't hurt a fly, if he had the power for it. The parish priest swore that he knew Coilin from the day he baptized him; that it was his opinion that he never committed a sin, and that he wouldn't believe from anyone at all that he would slay a man. It was no use for us. What good was our testimony against the testimony of the police? Judgment of death was given on Coilin.

His mother was present all that time. She didn't speak a word from start to finish, but her two eyes stuck in the two eyes of her son, and her two hands knitted under her shawl.

'He won't be hanged,' says Muirne that night. 'God promised me that he won't be hanged.'

A couple of days after that we heard that Coilin wouldn't be hanged, that it's how his soul would be spared him on account of him being so young as he was, but that he'd be kept in gaol for the term of his life.

'He won't be kept,' says Muirne. 'O Jesus,' she would say, 'don't let them keep my son from me.'

It's marvellous the patience that woman had, and the trust she had in the Son of God. It's marvellous the faith and the hope and the patience of women.

She went to the parish priest. She said to him that if he'd write to the people of Dublin, asking them to let Coilin out to her, it's certain he would be let out.

'They won't refuse you, Father,' says she.

The priest said that there would be no use at all in writing, that no heed would be paid to his letter, but that he himself would go to Dublin and that he would speak with the great people, and that, maybe, some good might come out of it. He went. Muirne was full-sure her son would be home to her by the end of a week or two. She readied the house before him. She put lime on it herself, inside and outside. She set two neighbours to put a new thatch on it. She spun the makings of a new suit of clothes for him; she dyed the wool with her own hands; she brought it to the weaver, and she made the suit when the frieze came home.

We thought it long while the priest was away. He wrote a couple of times to the master, but there was nothing new in the letters. He was doing his best, he said, but he wasn't succeeding too well. He was going from person to person, but it's not much satisfaction anybody was giving him. It was plain from the priest's letters that he hadn't much hope he'd be able to do anything. None of us had much hope, either. But Muirne didn't lose the wonderful trust she had in God.

'The priest will bring my son home with him,' she used say.

There was nothing making her anxious but fear that she wouldn't have the new suit ready before Coilin's coming. But it was finished at last; she had everything ready, repair on the house, the new suit laid on a chair before the fire,—and still no word of the priest.

'Isn't it Coilin will be glad when he sees the comfort I have in the house,' she would say. 'Isn't it he will look spruce going the road to Mass of a Sunday, and that suit on him!'

It's well I mind the evening the priest came home. Muirne was waiting for him since morning, the house cleaned up, and the table laid.

'Welcome home,' she said, when the priest came in. She was watching the door, as she would be expecting someone else to come in. But the priest closed the door after him.

'I thought that it's with yourself he'd come, Father,' says Muirne. 'But, sure it's the way he wouldn't like to come on the priest's car. He was shy like that always, the creature.'

'Oh, poor Muirne,' says the priest, holding her by the two hands, 'I can't conceal the truth from you. He's not coming, at all. I didn't succeed in doing anything. They wouldn't listen to me.'

Muirne didn't say a word. She went over and she sat down before the fire. The priest followed her and laid his hand on her shoulder.

'Muirne,' says he, like that.

'Let me be, Father, for a little while,' says she. 'May God and His Mother reward you for what you've done for me. But leave me to myself for a while. I thought you'd bring him home to me, and it's a great blow on me that he hasn't come.'

The priest left her to herself. He thought he'd be no help to her till the pain of that blow would be blunted.

The next day Muirne wasn't to be found. Tale or tidings no one had of her. Word nor wisdom we never heard of her till the end of a quarter. A share of us thought that it's maybe out of her mind the creature went, and a lonely death to come on her in the hollow of some mountain, or drowning in a boghole. The neighbours searched the hills round about, but her track wasn't to be seen.

One evening myself was digging potatoes in the garden, when I saw a solitary woman making on me up the road. A tall, thin woman. Her head well-set. A great walk under her. 'If Muirne ni Fhiannachta is living,' says I to myself, 'it's she that's in it.' 'Twas she, and none else. Down with me to-the road.

'Welcome home, Muirne,' says I to her. 'Have you any news?'

'I have, then,' says she, 'and good news. I went to Galway. I saw the Governor of the gaol. He said to me that he wouldn't be able to do a taste, that it's the Dublin people would be able to let him out of gaol, if his letting-out was to be got. I went off to Dublin. O, Lord, isn't it many a hard, stony road I walked, isn't it many a fine town I saw before I came to Dublin? 'Isn't it a great country, Ireland is?' I used say to myself every evening when I'd be told I'd have so many miles to walk before I'd see Dublin. But, great thanks to God and to the Glorious Virgin, I walked in on the street of Dublin at last, one cold, wet evening. I found a lodging. The morning of the next day I enquired for the Castle. I was put on the way. I went there. They wouldn't let me in at first, but I was at them till I got leave of talk with some man. He put me on to another man, a man that was higher than himself. He sent me to another man. I said to them all I wanted was to see the Lord Lieutenant of the Queen. I saw him at last. I told him my story. He said to me that he couldn't do anything. I gave my curse to the Castle of Dublin, and out the door with me. I had a pound in my pocket. I went aboard a ship, and the morning after I was in Liverpool of the English. I walked the long roads of England from Liverpool to London. When I came to London I asked knowledge of the Queen's Castle. I was told. I went there. They wouldn't let me in. I went there every day, hoping that I'd see the Queen coming out. After a week I saw her coming out. There were soldiers and great people about her. I went over to the Queen before she went in to her coach.

There was a paper, a man in Dublin wrote for me, in my hand. An officer seized me. The Queen spoke to him, and he freed me from him. I spoke to the Queen. She didn't understand me. I stretched the paper to her. She gave the paper to the officer, and he read it. He wrote certain words on the paper, and he gave it back to me. The Queen spoke to another woman that was along with her. The woman drew out a crown piece and gave it to me. I gave her back the crown piece, and I said that it's not silver I wanted, but my son. They laughed. It's my opinion they didn't understand me. I showed them the paper again. The officer laid his finger on the words he was after writing. I curtseyed to the Queen and went off with me. A man read for me the words the officer wrote. It's what was in it, that they would write to me about Coilin without delay. I struck the road home then, hoping that, maybe, there would be a letter before me. 'Do you think, Sean,' says Muirne, finishing her story, 'has the priest any letter?' There wasn't a letter at all in the house before me coming out the road; but I'm thinking it's to the priest they'd send the letter, for it's a chance the great people might know him.'

'I don't know did any letter come,' says I. 'I would say there didn't, for if there did the priest would be telling us.'

'It will be here some day yet,' says Muirne. 'I'll go in to the priest, anyhow, and I'll tell him my story.'

In the road with her, and up the hill to the priest's house. I saw her going home again that night, and the darkness falling. It's wonderful how she was giving it to her footsoles, considering what she suffered of distress and hardship for a quarter.

A week went by. There didn't come any letter. Another week passed. No letter came. The third week, and still no letter. It would take tears out of the grey stones to be looking at Muirne, and the anxiety that was on her. It would break your heart to see her going in the road to the priest every morning. We were afraid to speak to her about Coilin. We had evil notions. The priest had evil notions. He said to us one day that he heard from another priest in Galway that it's not more than well Coilin was, that it's greatly the prison was preying on his health, that he was going back daily. That story wasn't told to Muirne.

One day myself had business with the priest, and I went in to him. We were conversing in the parlour when we heard a person's footstep on the street outside. Never a knock on the house-door, or on the parlour-door, but in into the room with Muirne ni Fhiannachta, and a letter in her hand. It's with trouble she could talk.

'A letter from the Queen, a letter from the Queen!' says she.

The priest took the letter. He opened it. I noticed that his hand was shaking, and he opening it. There came the colour of death in his face after reading it. Muirne was standing out opposite him, her two eyes blazing in her head, her mouth half open.

'What does she say, Father?' says she. 'Is she sending him home to me?'

'It's not from the Queen this letter came, Muirne,' says the priest, speaking slowly, like as there would be some impediment on him, 'but from the Governor of the gaol in Dublin.'

'And what does he say? Is he sending him home to me?'

The priest didn't speak for a minute. It seemed to me that he was trying to mind certain words, and the words, as you would say, going from him.

'Muirne,' says he at last, 'he says that poor Coilin died yesterday.'

At the hearing of those words, Muirne burst a-laughing. The like of such laughter I never heard. That laughter was ringing in my ears for a month after that. She made a couple of terrible screeches of laughter, and then she fell in a faint on the floor.

She was fetched home, and she was on her bed for a half year. She was out of her mind all that time. She came to herself at long last, and no person at all would think there was a thing the matter with her,—only the delusion that her son isn't returned home yet from the fair of Uachtar Ard. She does be expecting him always, standing or sitting in the door half the day, and everything ready for his home-coming. She doesn't understand that there's any change on the world since that night. 'That's the reason, Coilin,' says my father to me, 'that she didn't know the railway was coming as far as Burnt House. Times she remembers herself, and she starts keening like you saw her. 'Twas herself that made yon keen you heard from her. May God comfort her, says my father,' putting an end to his story.

'And daddy,' says I, 'did any letter come from the Queen after that?'

'There didn't, nor the colour of one.'

'Do you think, daddy, was it Coilin that killed the lord?'

'I know it wasn't,' says my father. 'If it was he'd acknowledge it. I'm as certain as I'm living this night that it's the black man killed the lord. I don't say that poor Coilin wasn't present.'

'Was the black man ever caught?' says my sister.

'He wasn't, maise,' says my father. 'Little danger on him.'

'Where did he belong, the black man, do you think, daddy?' says I.

'I believe, before God,' says my father, 'that it's a peeler from Dublin Castle was in it. Cuimin O'Niadh saw a man very like him giving evidence against another boy in Tuam a year after that.'

'Daddy,' says Seaneen suddenly, 'when I'm a man I'll kill that black man.'

'God save us,' says my mother.

My father laid his hand on Seaneen's head.

'Maybe, little son,' says he, 'we'll all be taking tally-ho out of the black soldiers before the clay will come on us.'

'It's time for the Rosary,' says my mother.

GRACE

BY JAMES JOYCE

Two gentlemen who were in the lavatory at the time tried to lift him up: but he was quite helpless. He lay curled up at the foot of the stairs down which he had fallen. They succeeded in turning him over. His hat had rolled a few yards away and his clothes were smeared with the filth and ooze of the floor on which he had lain, face downwards. His eyes were closed and he breathed with a grunting noise. A thin stream of blood trickled from the corner of his mouth.

These two gentlemen and one of the curates carried him up the stairs and laid him down again on the floor of the bar. In two minutes he was surrounded by a ring of men. The manager of the bar asked everyone who he was and who was with him. No one knew who he was but one of the curates said he had served the gentleman with a small rum.

"Was he by himself?" asked the manager.

"No, sir. There was two gentlemen with him."

"And where are they?"

No one knew; a voice said:

"Give him air. He's fainted."

The ring of onlookers distended and closed again elastically. A dark medal of blood had formed itself near the man's head on the tessellated floor. The manager, alarmed by the grey pallor of the man's face, sent for a policeman.

His collar was unfastened and his necktie undone. He opened eyes for an instant, sighed and closed them again. One of gentlemen who had carried him upstairs held a dinged silk hat in his hand. The manager asked repeatedly did no one know who the injured man was or where had his friends gone. The door of the bar opened and an immense constable entered. A crowd which had followed him down the laneway collected outside the door, struggling to look in through the glass panels.

The manager at once began to narrate what he knew. The constable, a young man with thick immobile features, listened. He moved his head slowly to right and left and from the manager to the person on the floor, as if he feared to be the victim of some delusion. Then he drew off his glove, produced a small book from his waist, licked the lead of his pencil and made ready to indite. He asked in a suspicious provincial accent:

"Who is the man? What's his name and address?"

A young man in a cycling-suit cleared his way through the ring of bystanders. He knelt down promptly beside the injured man and called for water. The constable knelt down also to help. The young man washed the blood from the injured man's mouth and then called for some brandy. The constable repeated the order in an authoritative voice until a curate came running with the glass. The brandy was forced down the man's throat. In a few seconds he opened his eyes and looked about him. He looked at the circle of faces and then, understanding, strove to rise to his feet.

"You're all right now?" asked the young man in the cycling-suit.

"Sha,'s nothing," said the injured man, trying to stand up.

He was helped to his feet. The manager said something about a hospital and some of the bystanders gave advice. The battered silk hat was placed on the man's head. The constable asked:

"Where do you live?"

The man, without answering, began to twirl the ends of his moustache. He made light of his accident. It was nothing, he said: only a little accident. He spoke very thickly.

"Where do you live?" repeated the constable.

The man said they were to get a cab for him. While the point was being debated a tall agile gentleman of fair complexion, wearing a long yellow ulster, came from the far end of the bar. Seeing the spectacle, he called out:

"Hallo, Tom, old man! What's the trouble?"

"Sha,'s nothing," said the man.

The new-comer surveyed the deplorable figure before him and then turned to the constable, saying:

"It's all right, constable. I'll see him home."

The constable touched his helmet and answered:

"All right, Mr. Power!"

"Come now, Tom," said Mr. Power, taking his friend by the arm. "No bones broken. What? Can you walk?"

The young man in the cycling-suit took the man by the other arm and the crowd divided.

"How did you get yourself into this mess?" asked Mr. Power.

"The gentleman fell down the stairs," said the young man.

"I''ery 'uch o'liged to you, sir," said the injured man.

"Not at all."

"'ant we have a little. . .?"

"Not now. Not now."

The three men left the bar and the crowd sifted through the doors in to the laneway. The manager brought the constable to the stairs to inspect the scene of the accident. They agreed that the gentleman must have missed his footing. The customers returned to the counter and a curate set about removing the traces of blood from the floor.

When they came out into Grafton Street, Mr. Power whistled for an outsider. The injured man said again as well as he could.

"I''ery 'uch o'liged to you, sir. I hope we'll 'eet again. 'y na'e is Kernan."

The shock and the incipient pain had partly sobered him.

"Don't mention it," said the young man.

They shook hands. Mr. Kernan was hoisted on to the car and, while Mr. Power was giving directions to the carman, he expressed his gratitude to the young man and regretted that they could not have a little drink together.

"Another time," said the young man.

The car drove off towards Westmoreland Street. As it passed Ballast Office the clock showed half-past nine. A keen east wind hit them, blowing from the mouth of the river. Mr. Kernan was huddled together with cold. His friend asked him to tell how the accident had happened.

"I'an't 'an," he answered, "'y 'ongue is hurt."

"Show."

The other leaned over the well of the car and peered into Mr. Kernan's mouth but he could not see. He struck a match and, sheltering it in the shell of his hands, peered again into the mouth which Mr. Kernan opened obediently. The swaying movement of the car brought the match to and from the opened mouth. The lower teeth and gums were covered with clotted blood and a minute piece of the tongue seemed to have been bitten off. The match was blown out.

"That's ugly," said Mr. Power.

"Sha, 's nothing," said Mr. Kernan, closing his mouth and pulling the collar of his filthy coat across his neck.

Mr. Kernan was a commercial traveller of the old school which believed in the dignity of its calling. He had never been seen in the city without a silk hat of some decency and a pair of gaiters. By grace of these two articles of clothing, he said, a man could always pass muster. He carried on the tradition of his Napoleon, the great Blackwhite, whose memory he evoked at times by legend and mimicry. Modern business methods had spared him only so far as to allow him a little office in Crowe Street, on the window blind of which was written the name of his firm with the address—London, E. C. On the mantelpiece of this little office a little leaden battalion of canisters was drawn up and on the table before the window stood four or five china bowls which were usually half full of a black liquid. From these bowls Mr. Kernan tasted tea. He took a mouthful, drew it up, saturated his palate with it and then spat it forth into the grate. Then he paused to judge.

Mr. Power, a much younger man, was employed in the Royal Irish Constabulary Office in Dublin Castle. The arc of his social rise intersected the arc of his friend's decline, but Mr. Kernan's decline was mitigated by the fact that certain of those friends who had known him at his highest point of success still esteemed him as a character. Mr. Power was one of these friends. His inexplicable debts were a byword in his circle; he was a debonair young man.

The car halted before a small house on the Glasnevin road and Mr. Kernan was helped into the house. His wife put him to bed while Mr. Power sat downstairs in the kitchen asking the children where they went to school and what book they were in. The children—two girls and a boy, conscious of their father's helplessness and of their mother's absence, began some horseplay with him. He was surprised at their manners and at their accents, and his brow grew thoughtful. After a while Mrs. Kernan entered the kitchen, exclaiming:

"Such a sight! O, he'll do for himself one day and that's the holy alls of it. He's been drinking since Friday."

Mr. Power was careful to explain to her that he was not responsible, that he had come on the scene by the merest accident. Mrs. Kernan, remembering Mr. Power's good offices during domestic quarrels, as well as many small, but opportune loans, said:

"O, you needn't tell me that, Mr. Power. I know you're a friend of his, not like some of the others he does be with. They're all right so long as he has money in his pocket to keep him out from his wife and family. Nice friends! Who was he with tonight, I'd like to know?"

Mr. Power shook his head but said nothing.

"I'm so sorry," she continued, "that I've nothing in the house to offer you. But if you wait a minute I'll send round to Fogarty's at the corner."

Mr. Power stood up.

"We were waiting for him to come home with the money. He never seems to think he has a home at all."

"O, now, Mrs. Kernan," said Mr. Power, "we'll make him turn over a new leaf. I'll talk to Martin. He's the man. We'll come here one of these nights and talk it over."

She saw him to the door. The carman was stamping up and down the footpath, and swinging his arms to warm himself.

"It's very kind of you to bring him home," she said.

"Not at all," said Mr. Power.

He got up on the car. As it drove off he raised his hat to her gaily.

"We'll make a new man of him," he said. "Good-night, Mrs. Kernan."

Mrs. Kernan's puzzled eyes watched the car till it was out of sight. Then she withdrew them, went into the house and emptied her husband's pockets.

She was an active, practical woman of middle age. Not long before she had celebrated her silver wedding and renewed her intimacy with her husband by waltzing with him to Mr. Power's accompaniment. In her days of courtship, Mr. Kernan had seemed to her a not ungallant figure: and she still hurried to the chapel door whenever a wedding was reported and, seeing the bridal pair, recalled with vivid pleasure how she had passed out of the Star of the Sea Church in Sandymount, leaning on the arm of a jovial well-fed man, who was dressed smartly in a frock-coat and lavender trousers and carried a silk hat gracefully balanced upon his other arm. After three weeks she had found a wife's life irksome and, later on, when she was beginning to find it unbearable, she had become a mother. The part of mother presented to her no insuperable difficulties and for twenty-five years she had kept house shrewdly for her husband. Her two eldest sons were launched. One was in a draper's shop in Glasgow and the other was clerk to a tea-merchant in Belfast. They were good sons, wrote regularly and sometimes sent home money. The other children were still at school.

Mr. Kernan sent a letter to his office next day and remained in bed. She made beef-tea for him and scolded him roundly. She accepted his frequent intemperance as part of the climate, healed him dutifully whenever he was sick and always tried to make him eat a breakfast. There were worse husbands. He had never been violent since the boys had grown up, and she knew that he would walk to the end of Thomas Street and back again to book even a small order.

Two nights after, his friends came to see him. She brought them up to his bedroom, the air of which was impregnated with a personal odour, and gave them chairs at the fire. Mr. Kernan's tongue, the occasional stinging pain of which had made him somewhat irritable during the day, became more polite. He sat propped up in the bed by pillows and the little colour in his puffy cheeks made them resemble warm cinders. He apologised to his guests for the disorder of the room, but at the same time looked at them a little proudly, with a veteran's pride.

He was quite unconscious that he was the victim of a plot which his friends, Mr. Cunningham, Mr. M'Coy and Mr. Power had disclosed to Mrs. Kernan in the parlour. The idea had been Mr. Power's, but its development was entrusted to Mr. Cunningham. Mr. Kernan came of Protestant stock and, though he had been converted to the Catholic faith at the time of his marriage, he had not been in the pale of the Church for twenty years. He was fond, moreover, of giving side-thrusts at Catholicism.

Mr. Cunningham was the very man for such a case. He was an elder colleague of Mr. Power. His own domestic life was not very happy. People had great sympathy with him, for it was known that he had married an unpresentable woman who was an incurable drunkard. He had set up house for her six times; and each time she had pawned the furniture on him.

Everyone had respect for poor Martin Cunningham. He was a thoroughly sensible man, influential and intelligent. His blade of human knowledge, natural astuteness particularised by long association with cases in the police courts, had been tempered by brief immersions in the waters of general philosophy. He was well informed. His friends bowed to his opinions and considered that his face was like Shakespeare's.

When the plot had been disclosed to her, Mrs. Kernan had said:

"I leave it all in your hands, Mr. Cunningham."

After a quarter of a century of married life, she had very few illusions left. Religion for her was a habit, and she suspected that a man of her husband's age would not change greatly before death. She was tempted to see a curious appropriateness in his accident and, but that she did not wish to seem bloody-minded, would have told the gentlemen that Mr. Kernan's tongue would not suffer by being shortened. However, Mr. Cunningham was a capable man; and religion was religion. The scheme might do good and, at least, it could do no harm. Her beliefs were not extravagant. She believed steadily in the Sacred Heart as the most generally useful of all Catholic devotions and approved of the sacraments. Her faith was bounded by her kitchen, but, if she was put to it, she could believe also in the banshee and in the Holy Ghost.

The gentlemen began to talk of the accident. Mr. Cunningham said that he had once known a similar case. A man of seventy had bitten off a piece of his tongue during an epileptic fit and the tongue had filled in again, so that no one could see a trace of the bite.

"Well, I'm not seventy," said the invalid.

"God forbid," said Mr. Cunningham.

"It doesn't pain you now?" asked Mr. M'Coy.

Mr. M'Coy had been at one time a tenor of some reputation. His wife, who had been a soprano, still taught young children to play the piano at low terms. His line of life had not been the shortest distance between two points and for short periods he had been driven to live by his wits. He had been a clerk in the Midland Railway, a canvasser for advertisements for *The Irish Times* and for *The Freeman's Journal,* a town traveller for a coal firm on commission, a private inquiry agent, a clerk in the office of the Sub-Sheriff, and he had recently become secretary to the City Coroner. His new office made him professionally interested in Mr. Kernan's case.

"Pain? Not much," answered Mr. Kernan. "But it's so sickening. I feel as if I wanted to retch off."

"That's the boose," said Mr. Cunningham firmly.

"No," said Mr. Kernan. "I think I caught a cold on the car. There's something keeps coming into my throat, phlegm or——"

"Mucus." said Mr. M'Coy.

"It keeps coming like from down in my throat; sickening."

"Yes, yes," said Mr. M'Coy, "that's the thorax."

He looked at Mr. Cunningham and Mr. Power at the same time with an air of challenge. Mr. Cunningham nodded his head rapidly and Mr. Power said:

"Ah, well, all's well that ends well."

"I'm very much obliged to you, old man," said the invalid.

Mr. Power waved his hand.

"Those other two fellows I was with——"

"Who were you with?" asked Mr. Cunningham.

"A chap. I don't know his name. Damn it now, what's his name? Little chap with sandy hair. . . ."

"And who else?"

"Harford."

"Hm," said Mr. Cunningham.

When Mr. Cunningham made that remark, people were silent. It was known that the speaker had secret sources of information. In this case the monosyllable had a moral intention. Mr. Harford sometimes formed one of a little detachment which left the city shortly after noon on Sunday with the purpose of arriving as soon as possible at some public-house on the outskirts of the city where its members duly qualified themselves as bona fide travellers. But his fellow-travellers had never consented to overlook his origin. He had begun life as an obscure financier by lending small sums of money to workmen at usurious interest. Later on he had become the partner of a very fat, short gentleman, Mr. Goldberg, in the Liffey Loan Bank. Though he had never embraced more than the Jewish ethical code, his fellow-Catholics, whenever they had smarted in person or by proxy under his exactions, spoke of him bitterly as an Irish Jew and an illiterate, and saw divine disapproval of usury made manifest through the person of his idiot son. At other times they remembered his good points.

"I wonder where did he go to," said Mr. Kernan.

He wished the details of the incident to remain vague. He wished his friends to think there had been some mistake, that Mr. Harford and he had missed each other. His friends, who knew quite well Mr. Harford's manners in drinking were silent. Mr. Power said again:

"All's well that ends well."

Mr. Kernan changed the subject at once.

"That was a decent young chap, that medical fellow," he said. "Only for him——"

"O, only for him," said Mr. Power, "it might have been a case of seven days, without the option of a fine."

"Yes, yes," said Mr. Kernan, trying to remember. "I remember now there was a policeman. Decent young fellow, he seemed. How did it happen at all?"

"It happened that you were peloothered, Tom," said Mr. Cunningham gravely.

"True bill," said Mr. Kernan, equally gravely.

"I suppose you squared the constable, Jack," said Mr. M'Coy.

Mr. Power did not relish the use of his Christian name. He was not straight-laced, but he could not forget that Mr. M'Coy had recently made a crusade in search of valises and portmanteaus to enable Mrs. M'Coy to fulfil imaginary engagements in the country. More than he resented the fact that he had been victimised he resented such low playing of the game. He answered the question, therefore, as if Mr. Kernan had asked it.

The narrative made Mr. Kernan indignant. He was keenly conscious of his citizenship, wished to live with his city on terms mutually honourable and resented any affront put upon him by those whom he called country bumpkins.

"Is this what we pay rates for?" he asked. "To feed and clothe these ignorant bostooms . . . and they're nothing else."

Mr. Cunningham laughed. He was a Castle official only during office hours.

"How could they be anything else, Tom?" he said.

He assumed a thick, provincial accent and said in a tone of command:

"65, catch your cabbage!"

Everyone laughed. Mr. M'Coy, who wanted to enter the conversation by any door, pretended that he had never heard the story. Mr. Cunningham said:

"It is supposed—they say, you know—to take place in the depot where they get these thundering big country fellows, omadhauns, you know, to drill. The sergeant makes them stand in a row against the wall and hold up their plates."

He illustrated the story by grotesque gestures.

"At dinner, you know. Then he has a bloody big bowl of cabbage before him on the table and a bloody big spoon like a shovel. He takes up a wad of cabbage on the spoon and pegs it across the room and the poor devils have to try and catch it on their plates: *65, catch your cabbage*."

Everyone laughed again: but Mr. Kernan was somewhat indignant still. He talked of writing a letter to the papers.

"These yahoos coming up here," he said, "think they can boss the people. I needn't tell you, Martin, what kind of men they are."

Mr. Cunningham gave a qualified assent.

"It's like everything else in this world," he said. "You get some bad ones and you get some good ones."

"O yes, you get some good ones, I admit," said Mr. Kernan, satisfied.

"It's better to have nothing to say to them," said Mr. M'Coy. "That's my opinion!"

Mrs. Kernan entered the room and, placing a tray on the table, said:

"Help yourselves, gentlemen."

Mr. Power stood up to officiate, offering her his chair. She declined it, saying she was ironing downstairs, and, after having exchanged a nod with Mr. Cunningham behind Mr. Power's back, prepared to leave the room. Her husband called out to her:

"And have you nothing for me, duckie?"

"O, you! The back of my hand to you!" said Mrs. Kernan tartly.

Her husband called after her:

"Nothing for poor little hubby!"

He assumed such a comical face and voice that the distribution of the bottles of stout took place amid general merriment.

The gentlemen drank from their glasses, set the glasses again on the table and paused. Then Mr. Cunningham turned towards Mr. Power and said casually:

"On Thursday night, you said, Jack."

"Thursday, yes," said Mr. Power.

"Righto!" said Mr. Cunningham promptly.

"We can meet in M'Auley's," said Mr. M'Coy. "That'll be the most convenient place."

"But we mustn't be late," said Mr. Power earnestly, "because it is sure to be crammed to the doors."

"We can meet at half-seven," said Mr. M'Coy.

"Righto!" said Mr. Cunningham.

"Half-seven at M'Auley's be it!"

There was a short silence. Mr. Kernan waited to see whether he would be taken into his friends' confidence. Then he asked:

"What's in the wind?"

"O, it's nothing," said Mr. Cunningham. "It's only a little matter that we're arranging about for Thursday."

"The opera, is it?" said Mr. Kernan.

"No, no," said Mr. Cunningham in an evasive tone, "it's just a little. . . spiritual matter."

"O," said Mr. Kernan.

There was silence again. Then Mr. Power said, point blank:

"To tell you the truth, Tom, we're going to make a retreat."

"Yes, that's it," said Mr. Cunningham, "Jack and I and M'Coy here—we're all going to wash the pot."

He uttered the metaphor with a certain homely energy and, encouraged by his own voice, proceeded:

"You see, we may as well all admit we're a nice collection of scoundrels, one and all. I say, one and all," he added with gruff charity and turning to Mr. Power. "Own up now!"

"I own up," said Mr. Power.

"And I own up," said Mr. M'Coy.

"So we're going to wash the pot together," said Mr. Cunningham.

A thought seemed to strike him. He turned suddenly to the invalid and said:

"D'ye know what, Tom, has just occurred to me? You might join in and we'd have a four-handed reel."

"Good idea," said Mr. Power. "The four of us together."

Mr. Kernan was silent. The proposal conveyed very little meaning to his mind, but, understanding that some spiritual agencies were about to concern themselves on his behalf, he thought he owed it to his dignity to show a stiff neck. He took no part in the conversation for a long while, but listened, with an air of calm enmity, while his friends discussed the Jesuits.

"I haven't such a bad opinion of the Jesuits," he said, intervening at length. "They're an educated order. I believe they mean well, too."

"They're the grandest order in the Church, Tom," said Mr. Cunningham, with enthusiasm. "The General of the Jesuits stands next to the Pope."

"There's no mistake about it," said Mr. M'Coy, "if you want a thing well done and no flies about, you go to a Jesuit. They're the boyos have influence. I'll tell you a case in point. . . ."

"The Jesuits are a fine body of men," said Mr. Power.

"It's a curious thing," said Mr. Cunningham, "about the Jesuit Order. Every other order of the Church had to be reformed at some time or other but the Jesuit Order was never once reformed. It never fell away."

"Is that so?" asked Mr. M'Coy.

"That's a fact," said Mr. Cunningham. "That's history."

"Look at their church, too," said Mr. Power. "Look at the congregation they have."

"The Jesuits cater for the upper classes," said Mr. M'Coy.

"Of course," said Mr. Power.

"Yes," said Mr. Kernan. "That's why I have a feeling for them. It's some of those secular priests, ignorant, bumptious——"

"They're all good men," said Mr. Cunningham, "each in his own way. The Irish priesthood is honoured all the world over."

"O yes," said Mr. Power.

"Not like some of the other priesthoods on the continent," said Mr. M'Coy, "unworthy of the name."

"Perhaps you're right," said Mr. Kernan, relenting.

"Of course I'm right," said Mr. Cunningham. "I haven't been in the world all this time and seen most sides of it without being a judge of character."

The gentlemen drank again, one following another's example. Mr. Kernan seemed to be weighing something in his mind. He was impressed. He had a high opinion of Mr. Cunningham as a judge of character and as a reader of faces. He asked for particulars.

"O, it's just a retreat, you know," said Mr. Cunningham. "Father Purdon is giving it. It's for business men, you know."

"He won't be too hard on us, Tom," said Mr. Power persuasively.

"Father Purdon? Father Purdon?" said the invalid.

"O, you must know him, Tom," said Mr. Cunningham stoutly. "Fine, jolly fellow! He's a man of the world like ourselves."

"Ah, . . . yes. I think I know him. Rather red face; tall."

"That's the man."

"And tell me, Martin. . . . Is he a good preacher?"

"Munno. . . . It's not exactly a sermon, you know. It's just kind of a friendly talk, you know, in a common-sense way."

Mr. Kernan deliberated. Mr. M'Coy said:

"Father Tom Burke, that was the boy!"

"O, Father Tom Burke," said Mr. Cunningham, "that was a born orator. Did you ever hear him, Tom?"

"Did I ever hear him!" said the invalid, nettled. "Rather! I heard him. . . ."

"And yet they say he wasn't much of a theologian," said Mr Cunningham.

"Is that so?" said Mr. M'Coy.

"O, of course, nothing wrong, you know. Only sometimes, they say, he didn't preach what was quite orthodox."

"Ah! . . . he was a splendid man," said Mr. M'Coy.

"I heard him once," Mr. Kernan continued. "I forget the subject of his discourse now. Crofton and I were in the back of the . . . pit, you know . . . the——"

"The body," said Mr. Cunningham.

"Yes, in the back near the door. I forget now what. . . . O yes, it was on the Pope, the late Pope. I remember it well. Upon my word it was magnificent, the style of the oratory. And his voice! God! hadn't he a voice! *The Prisoner of the Vatican*, he called him. I remember Crofton saying to me when we came out——"

"But he's an Orangeman, Crofton, isn't he?" said Mr. Power.

"'Course he is," said Mr. Kernan, "and a damned decent Orangeman too. We went into Butler's in Moore Street—faith, I was genuinely moved, tell you the God's truth—and I remember well his very words. 'Kernan,' he said, 'we worship at different altars, he said, but our belief is the same.' Struck me as very well put."

"There's a good deal in that," said Mr. Power. "There used always to be crowds of Protestants in the chapel where Father Tom was preaching."

"There's not much difference between us," said Mr. M'Coy.

"We both believe in——"

He hesitated for a moment.

". . . in the Redeemer. Only they don't believe in the Pope and in the mother of God."

"But, of course," said Mr. Cunningham quietly and effectively, "our religion is the religion, the old, original faith."

"Not a doubt of it," said Mr. Kernan warmly.

Mrs. Kernan came to the door of the bedroom and announced:

"Here's a visitor for you!"

"Who is it?"

"Mr. Fogarty."

"O, come in! come in!"

A pale, oval face came forward into the light. The arch of its fair trailing moustache was repeated in the fair eyebrows looped above pleasantly astonished eyes. Mr. Fogarty was a modest grocer. He had failed in business in a licensed house in the city because his financial condition had constrained him to tie himself to second-class distillers and brewers. He had opened a small shop on Glasnevin Road where, he flattered himself, his manners would ingratiate him with the housewives of the district. He bore himself with a certain grace, complimented little children and spoke with a neat enunciation. He was not without culture.

Mr. Fogarty brought a gift with him, a half-pint of special whisky. He inquired politely for Mr. Kernan, placed his gift on the table and sat down with the company on equal terms. Mr. Kernan appreciated the gift all the more since he was aware that there was a small account for groceries unsettled between him and Mr. Fogarty. He said:

"I wouldn't doubt you, old man. Open that, Jack, will you?"

Mr. Power again officiated. Glasses were rinsed and five small measures of whisky were poured out. This new influence enlivened the conversation. Mr. Fogarty, sitting on a small area of the chair, was specially interested.

"Pope Leo XIII," said Mr. Cunningham, "was one of the lights of the age. His great idea, you know, was the union of the Latin and Greek Churches. That was the aim of his life."

"I often heard he was one of the most intellectual men in Europe," said Mr. Power. "I mean, apart from his being Pope."

"So he was," said Mr. Cunningham, "if not the most so. His motto, you know, as Pope, was Lux upon Lux—Light upon Light."

"No, no," said Mr. Fogarty eagerly. "I think you're wrong there. It was Lux in Tenebris, I think—Light in Darkness."

"O yes," said Mr. M'Coy, "Tenebrae."

"Allow me," said Mr. Cunningham positively, "it was Lux upon Lux. And Pius IX his predecessor's motto was Crux upon Crux—that is, Cross upon Cross—to show the difference between their two pontificates."

The inference was allowed. Mr. Cunningham continued.

"Pope Leo, you know, was a great scholar and a poet."

"He had a strong face," said Mr. Kernan.

"Yes," said Mr. Cunningham. "He wrote Latin poetry."

"Is that so?" said Mr. Fogarty.

Mr. M'Coy tasted his whisky contentedly and shook his head with a double intention, saying:

"That's no joke, I can tell you."

"We didn't learn that, Tom," said Mr. Power, following Mr. M'Coy's example, "when we went to the penny-a-week school."

"There was many a good man went to the penny-a-week school with a sod of turf under his oxter," said Mr. Kernan sententiously. "The old system was the best: plain honest education. None of your modern trumpery. . . ."

"Quite right," said Mr. Power.

"No superfluities," said Mr. Fogarty.

He enunciated the word and then drank gravely.

"I remember reading," said Mr. Cunningham, "that one of Pope Leo's poems was on the invention of the photograph—in Latin, of course."

"On the photograph!" exclaimed Mr. Kernan.

"Yes," said Mr. Cunningham.

He also drank from his glass.

"Well, you know," said Mr. M'Coy, "isn't the photograph wonderful when you come to think of it?"

"O, of course," said Mr. Power, "great minds can see things."

"As the poet says: *Great minds are very near to madness,*" said Mr. Fogarty.

Mr. Kernan seemed to be troubled in mind. He made an effort to recall the Protestant theology on some thorny points and in the end addressed Mr. Cunningham.

"Tell me, Martin," he said. "Weren't some of the popes—of course, not our present man, or his predecessor, but some of the old popes—not exactly . . . you know . . . up to the knocker?"

There was a silence. Mr. Cunningham said:

"O, of course, there were some bad lots . . . But the astonishing thing is this. Not one of them, not the biggest drunkard, not the most . . . out-and-out ruffian, not one of them ever preached *ex cathedra* a word of false doctrine. Now isn't that an astonishing thing?"

"That is," said Mr. Kernan.

"Yes, because when the Pope speaks *ex cathedra,*" Mr. Fogarty explained, "he is infallible."

"Yes," said Mr. Cunningham.

"O, I know about the infallibility of the Pope. I remember I was younger then. . . . Or was it that——?"

Mr. Fogarty interrupted. He took up the bottle and helped the others to a little more. Mr. M'Coy, seeing that there was not enough to go round, pleaded that he had not finished his first measure. The others accepted under protest. The light music of whisky falling into glasses made an agreeable interlude.

"What's that you were saying, Tom?" asked Mr. M'Coy.

"Papal infallibility," said Mr. Cunningham, "that was the greatest scene in the whole history of the Church."

"How was that, Martin?" asked Mr. Power.

Mr. Cunningham held up two thick fingers.

"In the sacred college, you know, of cardinals and archbishops and bishops there were two men who held out against it while the others were all for it. The whole conclave except these two was unanimous. No! They wouldn't have it!"

"Ha!" said Mr. M'Coy.

"And they were a German cardinal by the name of Dolling. . . or Dowling. . . or——"

"Dowling was no German, and that's a sure five," said Mr. Power, laughing.

"Well, this great German cardinal, whatever his name was, was one; and the other was John MacHale."

"What?" cried Mr. Kernan. "Is it John of Tuam?"

"Are you sure of that now?" asked Mr. Fogarty dubiously. "I thought it was some Italian or American."

"John of Tuam," repeated Mr. Cunningham, "was the man."

He drank and the other gentlemen followed his lead. Then he resumed:

"There they were at it, all the cardinals and bishops and archbishops from all the ends of the earth and these two fighting dog and devil until at last the Pope himself stood up and declared infallibility a dogma of the Church *ex cathedra*. On the very moment John MacHale, who had been arguing and arguing against it, stood up and shouted out with the voice of a lion: '*Credo*!'"

"I believe!" said Mr. Fogarty.

"Credo!" said Mr. Cunningham. "That showed the faith he had. He submitted the moment the Pope spoke."

"And what about Dowling?" asked Mr. M'Coy.

"The German cardinal wouldn't submit. He left the church."

Mr. Cunningham's words had built up the vast image of the church in the minds of his hearers. His deep, raucous voice had thrilled them as it uttered the word of belief and submission. When Mrs. Kernan came into the room, drying her hands she came into a solemn company. She did not disturb the silence, but leaned over the rail at the foot of the bed.

"I once saw John MacHale," said Mr. Kernan, "and I'll never forget it as long as I live."

He turned towards his wife to be confirmed.

"I often told you that?"

Mrs. Kernan nodded.

"It was at the unveiling of Sir John Gray's statue. Edmund Dwyer Gray was speaking, blathering away, and here was this old fellow, crabbed-looking old chap, looking at him from under his bushy eyebrows."

Mr. Kernan knitted his brows and, lowering his head like an angry bull, glared at his wife.

"God!" he exclaimed, resuming his natural face, "I never saw such an eye in a man's head. It was as much as to say: *I have you properly taped, my lad*. He had an eye like a hawk."

"None of the Grays was any good," said Mr. Power.

There was a pause again. Mr. Power turned to Mrs. Kernan and said with abrupt joviality:

"Well, Mrs. Kernan, we're going to make your man here a good holy pious and God-fearing Roman Catholic."

He swept his arm round the company inclusively.

"We're all going to make a retreat together and confess our sins—and God knows we want it badly."

"I don't mind," said Mr. Kernan, smiling a little nervously.

Mrs. Kernan thought it would be wiser to conceal her satisfaction. So she said:

"I pity the poor priest that has to listen to your tale."

Mr. Kernan's expression changed.

"If he doesn't like it," he said bluntly, "he can. . . do the other thing. I'll just tell him my little tale of woe. I'm not such a bad fellow——"

Mr. Cunningham intervened promptly.

"We'll all renounce the devil," he said, "together, not forgetting his works and pomps."

"Get behind me, Satan!" said Mr. Fogarty, laughing and looking at the others.

Mr. Power said nothing. He felt completely out-generalled. But a pleased expression flickered across his face.

"All we have to do," said Mr. Cunningham, "is to stand up with lighted candles in our hands and renew our baptismal vows."

"O, don't forget the candle, Tom," said Mr. M'Coy, "whatever you do."

"What?" said Mr. Kernan. "Must I have a candle?"

"O yes," said Mr. Cunningham.

"No, damn it all," said Mr. Kernan sensibly, "I draw the line there. I'll do the job right enough. I'll do the retreat business and confession, and . . . all that business. But. . . no candles! No, damn it all, I bar the candles!"

He shook his head with farcical gravity.

"Listen to that!" said his wife.

"I bar the candles," said Mr. Kernan, conscious of having created an effect on his audience and continuing to shake his head to and fro. "I bar the magic-lantern business."

Everyone laughed heartily.

"There's a nice Catholic for you!" said his wife.

"No candles!" repeated Mr. Kernan obdurately. "That's off!"

The transept of the Jesuit Church in Gardiner Street was almost full; and still at every moment gentlemen entered from the side door and, directed by the lay-brother, walked on tiptoe along the aisles until they found seating accommodation. The gentlemen were all well dressed and orderly. The light of the lamps of the church fell upon an assembly of black clothes and white collars, relieved here and there by tweeds, on dark mottled pillars of green marble and on lugubrious canvases. The gentlemen sat in the benches, having hitched their trousers slightly above their knees and laid their hats in security. They sat well back and gazed formally at the distant speck of red light which was suspended before the high altar.

In one of the benches near the pulpit sat Mr. Cunningham and Mr. Kernan. In the bench behind sat Mr. M'Coy alone: and in the bench behind him sat Mr. Power and Mr. Fogarty. Mr. M'Coy had tried unsuccessfully to find a place in the bench with the others, and, when the party had settled down in the form of a quincunx, he had tried unsuccessfully to make comic remarks. As these had not been well received, he had desisted. Even he was sensible of the decorous atmosphere and even he began to respond to the religious stimulus. In a whisper, Mr. Cunningham drew Mr. Kernan's attention to Mr. Harford, the moneylender, who sat some distance off, and to Mr. Fanning, the registration agent and mayor maker of the city, who was sitting immediately under the pulpit beside one of the newly elected councillors of the ward. To the right sat old Michael Grimes, the owner of three pawnbroker's shops, and Dan Hogan's nephew, who was up for the job in the Town Clerk's office. Farther in front sat Mr. Hendrick, the chief reporter of *The Freeman's Journal,* and poor O'Carroll, an old friend of Mr. Kernan's, who had been at one time a considerable commercial figure. Gradually, as he recognised familiar faces, Mr. Kernan began to feel more at home. His hat, which had been rehabilitated by his wife, rested upon his knees. Once or twice he pulled down his cuffs with one hand while he held the brim of his hat lightly, but firmly, with the other hand.

A powerful-looking figure, the upper part of which was draped with a white surplice, was observed to be struggling into the pulpit. Simultaneously the congregation unsettled, produced handkerchiefs and knelt upon them with care. Mr. Kernan followed the general example. The priest's figure now stood upright in the pulpit, two-thirds of its bulk, crowned by a massive red face, appearing above the balustrade.

Father Purdon knelt down, turned towards the red speck of light and, covering his face with his hands, prayed. After an interval, he uncovered his face and rose. The congregation rose also and settled again on its benches. Mr. Kernan restored his hat to its original position on his knee and presented an attentive face to the preacher. The preacher turned back each wide sleeve of his surplice with an elaborate large gesture and slowly surveyed the array of faces. Then he said:

"For the children of this world are wiser in their generation than the children of light. Wherefore make unto yourselves friends out of the mammon of iniquity so that when you die they may receive you into everlasting dwellings."

Father Purdon developed the text with resonant assurance. It was one of the most difficult texts in all the Scriptures, he said, to interpret properly. It was a text which might seem to the casual observer at variance with the lofty morality elsewhere preached by Jesus Christ. But, he told his hearers, the text had seemed to him specially adapted for the guidance of those whose lot it was to lead the life of the world and who yet wished to lead that life not in the manner of worldlings. It was a text for business men and professional men. Jesus Christ, with His divine understanding of every cranny of our human nature, understood that all men were not called to the religious life, that by far the vast majority were forced to live in the world, and, to a certain extent, for the world: and in this sentence He designed to give them a word of counsel, setting before them as exemplars in the religious life those very worshippers of Mammon who were of all men the least solicitous in matters religious.

He told his hearers that he was there that evening for no terrifying, no extravagant purpose; but as a man of the world speaking to his fellow-men. He came to speak to business men and he would speak to them in a businesslike way. If he might use the metaphor, he said, he was their spiritual accountant; and he wished each and every one of his hearers to open his books, the books of his spiritual life, and see if they tallied accurately with conscience.

Jesus Christ was not a hard taskmaster. He understood our little failings, understood the weakness of our poor fallen nature, understood the temptations of this life. We might have had, we all had from time to time, our temptations: we might have, we all had, our failings. But one thing only, he said, he would ask of his hearers. And that was: to be straight and manly with God. If their accounts tallied in every point to say:

"Well, I have verified my accounts. I find all well."

But if, as might happen, there were some discrepancies, to admit the truth, to be frank and say like a man:

"Well, I have looked into my accounts. I find this wrong and this wrong. But, with God's grace, I will rectify this and this. I will set right my accounts."

KING O'TOOLE AND HIS GOOSE

BY S. LOVER

"By Gor, I thought all the world, far and near, heerd o' King O'Toole—well, well, but the darkness of mankind is ontellible! Well, sir, you must know, as you didn't hear it afore, that there was a king, called King O'Toole, who was a fine ould king in the ould ancient times, long ago; and it was him that owned the churches in the early days. The king, you see, was the right sort; he was the rale boy, and loved sport as he loved his life, and huntin' in partic'lar; and from the risin' o' the sun, up he got, and away he wint over the mountains beyant afther the deer; and the fine times them wor.

"Well, it was all mighty good, as long as the king had his health; but, you see, in coorse of time the king grew ould, by raison he was stiff in his limbs, and when he got sthriken in years, his heart failed him, and he was lost intirely for want o' divarshin, bekase he couldn't go a huntin' no longer; and, by dad, the poor king was obleeged at last for to get a goose to divart him. Oh, you may laugh, if you like, but it's truth I'm tellin' you; and the way the goose divarted him was this-a-way: You see, the goose used for to swim acrass the lake, and go divin' for throut, and cotch fish on a Friday for the king, and flew every other day round about the lake, divartin' the poor king. All went on mighty well, antil, by dad, the goose got sthriken in years like her master, and couldn't divart him no longer, and then it was that the poor king was lost complate. The king was walkin' one mornin' by the edge of the lake, lamentin' his cruel fate, and thinkin' o' drownin' himself, that could get no divarshun in life, when all of a suddint, turnin' round the corner beyant, who should he meet but a mighty dacent young man comin' up to him.

"'God save you,' says the king to the young man.

"'God save you kindly, King O'Toole,' says the young man. 'Thrue for you,' says the king. 'I am King O'Toole,' says he, 'prince and plennypennytinchery o' these parts,' says he; 'but how kem ye to know that?' says he. 'Oh, never mind,' says St. Kavin.

"You see it was Saint Kavin, sure enough—the saint himself in disguise, and nobody else. 'Oh, never mind,' says he, 'I know more than that. May I make bowld to ax how is your goose, King O'Toole?' says he. 'Blur-an-agers, how kem ye to know about my goose?' says the king. 'Oh, no matther; I was given to understand it,' says Saint Kavin. After some more talk the king says, 'What are you?' 'I'm an honest man,' says Saint Kavin. 'Well, honest man,' says the king, 'and how is it you make your money so aisy?' 'By makin' ould things as good as new,' says Saint Kavin. 'Is it a tinker you are?' says the king. 'No,' says the saint; 'I'm no tinker by thrade, King O'Toole; I've a betther thrade than a tinker,' says he—'what would you say,' says he, 'if I made your ould goose as good as new?'

"My dear, at the word o' making his goose as good as new, you'd think the poor ould king's eyes was ready to jump out iv his head. With that the king whistled, and down kem the poor goose, all as one as a hound, waddlin' up to the poor cripple, her masther, and as like him as two pays. The minute the saint clapt his eyes on the goose, 'I'll do the job for you,' says he, 'King O'Toole.' 'By *Jaminee*!' says King O'Toole, 'if you do, bud I'll say you're the cleverest fellow in the sivin parishes.' 'Oh, by dad,' says St. Kavin, 'you must say more nor that—my horn's not so soft all out,' says he, 'as to repair your ould goose for nothin'; what'll you gi' me if I do the job for you?—that's the chat,' says St. Kavin. 'I'll give you whatever you ax,' says the king; 'isn't that fair?' 'Divil a fairer,' says the saint; 'that's the way to do business. Now,' says he, 'this is the bargain I'll make with you, King O'Toole: will you gi' me all the ground the goose flies over, the first offer, afther I make her as good as new?' 'I will,' says the king. 'You won't go back o' your word?' says St. Kavin. 'Honor bright!' says King O'Toole, howldin' out his fist. 'Honor bright!' says St. Kavin, back agin, 'it's a bargain. Come here!' says he to the poor ould goose—'come here, you unfort'nate ould cripple, and it's I that'll make you the sportin' bird.' With that, my dear, he took up the goose by the two wings—'Criss o' my crass an you,' says he, markin' her to grace with the blessed sign at the same minute—and throwin' her up in the air, 'whew,' says he, jist givin' her a blast to help her; and with that, my jewel, she tuk to her heels, flyin' like one o' the aigles themselves, and cuttin' as many capers as a swallow before a shower of rain.

"Well, my dear, it was a beautiful sight to see the king standin' with his mouth open, lookin' at his poor ould goose flyin' as light as a lark, and betther nor ever she was: and when she lit at his fut, patted her an the head, and, '*Ma vourneen*,' says he, 'but you are the *darlint* o' the world.' 'And what do you say to me,' says Saint Kavin, 'for makin' her the like?' 'By gor,' says the king, 'I say nothin' bates the art o' man, barrin' the bees.' 'And do you say no more nor that?' says Saint Kavin. 'And that I'm behoulden to you,' says the king. 'But will you gi'e me all the ground the goose flew over?' says Saint Kavin. 'I will,' says King O'Toole, 'and you're welkim to it,' says he, 'though it's the last acre I have to give.' 'But you'll keep your word thrue?' says the saint. 'As thrue as the sun,' says the king. 'It's well for you, King O'Toole, that you said that word,' says he; 'for if you didn't say that word, *the devil receave the bit o' your goose id ever fly agin.*' Whin the king was as good as his word, Saint Kavin was *plazed* with him, and thin it was that he made himself known to the king. 'And,' says he, 'King O'Toole, you're a decent man, for I only kem here to *thry you.* You don't know me,' says he, 'bekase I'm disguised.' 'Musha! thin,' says the king, 'who are you?' 'I'm Saint Kavin,' said the saint, blessin' himself. 'Oh, queen iv heaven!' says the king, makin' the sign o' the crass betune his eyes, and fallin' down on his knees before the saint; 'is it the great Saint Kavin,' says he, 'that I've been discoorsin' all this time without knowin' it,' says he, 'all as one as if he was a lump iv a *gossoon*?—and so you're a saint?' says the king. 'I am,' says Saint Kavin. 'By gor, I thought I was only talking to a dacent boy,' says the king. 'Well, you know the differ now,' says the saint. 'I'm Saint Kavin,' says he, 'the greatest of all the saints.' And so the king had his goose as good as new, to divart him as long as he lived: and the saint supported him afther he kem into his property, as I tould you, until the day iv his death—and that was soon afther; for the poor goose thought he was ketchin' a throut one Friday; but, my jewel, it was a mistake he made—and instead of a throut, it was a thievin' horse-eel; and by gor, instead iv the goose killin' a throut for the king's supper,—by dad, the eel killed the king's goose—and small blame to him; but he didn't ate her, bekase he darn't ate what Saint Kavin laid his blessed hands on."

THE HOST OF THE AIR

BY WILLIAM BUTLER YEATS

O'Driscoll drove with a song,
The wild duck and the drake,
From the tall and the tufted reeds
Of the drear Hart Lake.

And he saw how the reeds grew dark
At the coming of night tide,
And dreamed of the long dim hair
Of Bridget his bride.

He heard while he sang and dreamed
A piper piping away,
And never was piping so sad,
And never was piping so gay.

And he saw young men and young girls
Who danced on a level place
And Bridget his bride among them,
With a sad and a gay face.

The dancers crowded about him,
And many a sweet thing said,
And a young man brought him red wine

And a young girl white bread.

But Bridget drew him by the sleeve,
Away from the merry bands,
To old men playing at cards
With a twinkling of ancient hands.

The bread and the wine had a doom,
For these were the host of the air;
He sat and played in a dream
Of her long dim hair.

He played with the merry old men
And thought not of evil chance,
Until one bore Bridget his bride
Away from the merry dance.

He bore her away in his arms,
The handsomest young man there,
And his neck and his breast and his arms
Were drowned in her long dim hair.

O'Driscoll scattered the cards
And out of his dream awoke:
Old men and young men and young girls
Were gone like a drifting smoke;

But he heard high up in the air
A piper piping away,
And never was piping so sad,
And never was piping so gay.

CHRONICLE OF THE VOYAGES OF SAINT BRENDAN

BY STEPHEN VINCENT BRENNAN

Remember Brendan, not as a graven saint, he was a man and suffered so; in no ways proud, he sought the will of the Lord God full meekly and contrite of heart. And I have seen his eyes start from his head at some marvel, and I have seen the cold gray oceans break over him for days, and I have seen him spit salt seas and tremble with the cold. But no thing overmanned him, because in every tempest he saw the hand of God, and in every trial he sought the will of God, and trusted so, and was not afraid, and thereby gave us heart and courage. And we brethren took example from him, and thereby saved our souls.

Remember Brendan, later called *Saint,* born in the land of Munster, hard by the loch Lein. A holy man of fierce abstinence, known for his great works and the father of almost three thousand monks, he lived at Clonfert then, where we knew him at the first and last.

Recall the night, just past compline it was, when the holy abbot Barrind, later called *Saint*, came out of the darkness into our circle to visit Brendan.

And each of them was joyful of the other. And when Brendan began to tell Barrind of the many wonders he had seen voyaging in the sea and visiting in diverse lands, Barrind at once began to sigh and anon he threw himself prostrate upon the ground and prayed hard and then began to weep. Now Brendan comforted him the best he could, and lifting him up said: *"Brother Abbot, have you not come to be joyful with us, to speak the word of God and to give us heart? Therefore for God's love, do not be afraid, but tell us what marvels you have seen in the great ocean, that encompasses all the world."*

So Barrind began to tell Brendan and all the gathered monks of a great wonder. These were his words:

"I have a son, his name is Meroc, who had a great desire to seek about by ship in diverse countries to find a solitary place wherein he might dwell secretly out of the business of the world, in order to better serve God quietly in devotion. I counseled him to sail to an island in the sea, nearby the mountain of stones, which everybody knows. So he made ready and sailed there with his monks. And when he came there, he liked the place full well, and there settled where he and his monks served our Lord devoutly. And then I saw in a vision that this monk Meroc was sailed right far westward into the sea more than three days sailing, and suddenly to those voyagers there came a dark cloud of fog that overcovered them, so that for a great part of the day they saw no light; then as our Lord willed, the fog passed away, and they saw a fair island, and thereward they drew. In that island was joy and mirth enough and all the earth of that island shone as brightly as the sun, and there were the fairest trees and herbs that ever any man saw, and here were many precious stones shining bright, and every herb was ripe, and every tree full of fruit; so that it was a glorious sight and a heavenly joy to abide there. Then there came to them a fair young man, and courteously he welcomed them all, and called every monk by his name, and said they were much bound to praise the name of our Lord Jesu, who would out of his grace show them that glorious place, where it is always day and never night, and that this place is called the garden of paradise. But by this island is another island whereon no man may come. And the fair young man said to them, 'You have been here half a year without meat or drink or sleep.' They supposed they had been there only half a day, so merry and joyful they were. The young man told them that this was the place where Adam and Eve lived first, and ever would have lived, if they had not broken the commandment of God. Then the fair young man brought them to their ship again and said they might no longer abide there, and when they were all shipped, suddenly the young man vanished away out of their sight. And then within a short time after, by the purveyance of the Lord Jesu, Meroc and the brothers returned to their own island where I and the other brothers received them goodly, and demanded where they had been so long. And they said that they had been in the Land of the Blest, before the Gates of Paradise. And they asked of us, 'Cannot you tell from the sweetness of our clothes that we have been in Paradise?' And I and the other brothers said, 'We do believe you have been in God's Paradise, but we don't know where this Paradise is.'"

At hearing this we all lay prostrate and said, *"The Lord God is just in all his works and merciful and loving to his servants, once again he has nourished our wonder with his holy spirit."*

On the day following Barrind's visit, Brendan gathered twelve of the brothers and closed us up in the oratory saying, *"If it is God's will, I will seek that holy land of which the brother Abbott spoke. Does this appeal to you? What do you say?"*

We answered Brendan thus, *"Not our will, but God's. To know God's will, we leave our families, give away what we possess, put away the lives we led and follow you, if it is the will of God."*

To better know the will of God we fasted forty days, tho not oftener than for three days running as is the rule. And during this time we sought the blessing of the holy father Edna, later called *Saint*, in his western island. We stayed there three days and three nights only.

Old Edna's blessing got, we took ourselves to a lonely inlet place we called Brendan's Butt, for he had known this spot as a boy and there sat many hours, looking away out over the ocean to the west, his seat upon a butt of stone. Here we built a vessel sufficient for a voyage of seven years. With iron tools we ribbed and framed it of ash and oak, the stepping for the mast was oak, and covered it in ox hides, well tanned, stitched together and greased with lard. Therein we put provisions for a forty days journey and many spares of ox hide, and then we got ourselves aboard and here lived devoutly twelve days, afloat but well in sight of land.

On the day set for our departure we received the sacrament and got ourselves aboard, when just as Brendan blessed us all, there came another two of his monks who prayed him that they might come with us. And he said, *"You may sail with us, but one of you shall die and go to hell ere we return."* Even so, they would go with us.

And then Brendan bade the brethren raise the sail, and forth we voyaged in God's name, so that on the morrow we were out of sight of any land. For eleven days and nights we sailed plain, and then we saw an island afar from us. We sailed thitherward as fast as we could, and soon a great reach of stone appeared afar off above the waves, and for three days we worked our way around the island before we found an inlet fit for a landing. At last we found a little haven and there we beached our leather boat.

Suddenly, bounding up to us, there came a fair hound who laid down at Brendan's feet cheering him. So Brendan said to us, *"Be of good heart, for the Lord has sent his messenger to lead us into some good place."* And the hound brought us to a fair hall, where we found tables spread with good meat and drink. Then Brendan spoke the grace and then we brethren sat down and ate and drank. And there were beds made ready for us that we might sleep after our long labor. But Brendan did not sleep, but prayed the night away upon his knees.

On the morrow we returned again to our skin boat, pushed off and sailed a long time in the sea before we found any land. At last, by the purveyance of God, we saw a full fair island of green pasture, whereon were the whitest sheep that we had ever seen. And every sheep was as big as any ox. Just after dragging our ship ashore, we were welcomed by a goodly old man who said, *"This is the Isle of Sheep. Here it is never cold but ever summer. This is why the sheep are so huge, they feed all year on the best grasses and herbs anywhere."* When the old man took his leave he told us, *"Voyage on, and by God's grace, you soon will come upon a place like paradise, whereon you ought to spend your Eastertide."*

We sailed forth and soon came upon another island, but because of shallows and broken stone and the fury of the seas, we bore off and beached our skin ship instead upon a rock, where nothing grew, a small desolate island. Or so we thought, for when we lit the fire so that we might bake our grain and dress our meat, the island began to move under us. And all a panic then, amazed and full of fear, we threw ourselves into the boat, and pulled and twisted at the oars, swatting and thumping one another in our haste to be away. And lo, the island seemed to dip and we floated free and soon were well away. And all that night we spied the beacon of our fire leaping and dancing in the cold, dark ocean. Brendan must have smelled the terror on us, for he said, *"Do not be afraid. It is only a great fish, the biggest in the sea. He labors night and day to swallow his own tail, but he cannot because of his great size. He is called Jasconius."*

And then anon we oared three days and nights before we sighted any land and the weariness was heavy on us. But soon after, as God would, we saw a fair island, full of flowers, herbs, and trees, whereof we thanked God of his good grace, and then anon we found a little stream and followed it, walking our hide boat well in land. And then anon we found a full fair well, and thereby grew a mighty tree, full of boughs, and on every bough sat a white bird, and they so thick upon the tree, their number being so great, and their song being so merry that it was a heavenly noise to hear. Then Brendan fell to his knees and wept for joy, and made his prayers devoutly unto our Lord God that he might understand the meaning of the bird song. And then at once a white bird flew from the tree to Brendan. She flapped and fluttered, she hooked and danced and called, and made a merry noise full like a flute. It seemed to us, no holy hymn ever was so joyful. And Brendan said, *"If you are the messengers of God, tell me why you sit so thick upon the tree and why you sing so merrily?"*

And the bird said, "*Once upon a time, we were angels in heaven, but when our master Lucifer fell down into hell for his high pride, we fell with him for our offenses, some higher, some lower, depending on the quality of their trespass; and because our trespass was but little, our Lord has sent us here, out of all pain to live in great joy and mirth, here to serve him on this tree in the best manner that we can. Today is Sunday, can you not guess why we are all white as snow?*"

And when we all remembered, we fell upon our knees and hymned praise to our good Lord Jesu Christ. And the white bird sang to Brendan, "*It is twelve month past that you departed from your abbey. In the seventh year you shall come unto the place of your desire. For each of those years you shall spend the Eastertide here with us, as you do today.*"

Then all the birds began to sing evensong so merrily that it was truly a heavenly noise to hear. And after supper Brendan and all of us went to bed, and slept well, and on the morrow we rose early, to hear the birds sing matins, and later prime and all such services of the holy rule.

We all abided there with Brendan eight full weeks, til after Trinity Sunday when we again sailed for the Isle of Sheep, and there we victualed well and were blessed again by the goodly old man, and returned again to our leather boat, and waited for the wind to blow fair. And ere we put out, the bird of the tree came again to us, and danced upon our prow and flapped and fluttered and sang, "*I am come to tell you that you shall sail from here to an island whereon there is an abbey of twenty-four monks, and there you shall hold your Christmas, but Eastertide, do not forget, you spend with us.*"

And then the bird flew off.

The wind with us now, we sailed forth into the ocean, but soon fell a great tempest on us, which we were greatly troubled by for a long time and sorely belabored. And we saw, by the purveyance of God, a little island afar off, and full meekly we prayed to our Lord to send us thither in safety. It took eleven days, and in this time we monks were so weary of the long pull and the mountain gray oceans that we set little price upon our lives, and cried continually to our Lord to show us mercy and bring us to that little island in safety. And by the purveyance of God we came at last into a little haven, but so narrow that only one ship might come in. And after we had come to anchor, the brethren went ashore, and when we had long walked about, at last we found two fair wells; one was of fair clear water, and the other was somewhat troubley and thick. At this we thanked our Lord full humbly that had brought us here, and made to drink the water, but Brendan charged us thus, "Take no water without license. If we abstain us a while longer, our Lord will purvey for us in the best wise."

And soon after came to us a good old hoar-haired man, who welcomed us full meekly and kissed Brendan, but did not speak, and by this we understood that he observed a rule of silence. And he led us past many a fair well til we came to an abbey, where we were received with much honor and solemn procession. And then the Abbott welcomed Brendan and all our fellowship, and kissed him full meekly, but did not speak. And he drew Brendan by the hand, and led us into a fair hall, and sat us down in a row on benches; and the Abbott of that place, in observance of the new commandment, washed all our feet with fair clear water. And afterward, in silence still, led us into the refractory, there to seat ourselves among the brothers of the abbey. And anon came one who served us well of meat and drink. For every monk had set before him a fair white loaf and white roots and herbs, which we found right delicious, tho none of us could name; and we drank of the water of the fair clear well that we had seen before when first we came ashore, that Brendan had forbade us. And then the Abbott came, and breaking silence, prayed us eat and drink, *"For every day the Lord sends a good old man that covers this table with meat and drink for us. But we know not how it comes, for we do nothing to procure it, and yet our Lord feeds us. And we are twenty-four monks in number, yet every day of the week he sends us twelve loaves, and every Sunday and feast day, twenty-four loaves, and the bread we leave at dinner we eat at supper. And now at your coming our Lord has sent us forty-eight loaves, that all of us may be merry together as brethren. And we have lived twenty-nine years here in this abbey: tho we did first come out of the abbey of Saint Patrick in Ireland eighty years ago. And here in this land it is ever fair weather, and none of us is ever sick since we came here."*

And then Brendan and the Abbott and all the company went into the church, and we said evensong together, and devoutly. And when we looked upward at the crucifix, we saw our Lord hanging on a cross made of fine crystal and curiously wrought; and in the choir were twenty-four seats for twenty-four monks, and seven unlit tapers, and the Abbott's seat was made close upon the altar in the middle of the choir. And then Brendan asked the Abbott, *"How long have you kept silence one with another?"*

And the Abbott answered Brendan, *"For this twenty-nine years, no one has spoken to another."*

And Brendan wept for joy at this, and desired of the Abbott, *"That we might all dwell here with you."*

And the Abbott answered Brendan, *"That will not do, for our Lord has showed to you in what manner you will be guided til the seventh year is done, and after that term you will return with your monks to Ireland in safety; except that one of the two monks that came last to you will dwell in the island of anchorites, and the other will burn in hell."*

And as we knelt with Brendan in the church, we saw a bright shining angel fly in at the window that lighted all the tapers in the church and flew out again and then to heaven. And Brendan marveled greatly how fair the light burned but wasted not. And the Abbott said to us that it is written how Moses saw a bush afire, yet it burned not, *"and therefore marvel not, for the might of our Lord is now as great as ever it was."*

And when we had dwelled there even til Christmas was gone twelve days and eight days more, we took leave of this holy Abbott and his convent, and returned again to our skinned-ship. And then we sailed from thence toward the island of the abbey of Saint Hillary, but aching cold and furious tempests troubled us til just before the start of Lent, when we bespied an island, not far off; and then we pulled for it but weakly, our strength all spent, our stomachs empty, our bodies raw with thirst. And when at last we gained the island, and dragged our battered boat upon the beach, we found a well of clear water, and diverse roots that grew about it, and multitudes of sweet fleshed fish that swarmed in the river that flowed to the sea. And Brendan said, *"Let us gather up this bounty which the Lord makes a gift to us, and then let us renew our bodies with meat and drink, and our spirits in hymns devoutly sung."*

And we obeyed Brendan, and we dug many roots and put them in the fire to bake, likewise we netted many fish and cleaned and baked them also. But when we made to drink, our holy father Brendan said, *"Of this clear water drink only what is meet for your good health, lest this gift of God do you some harm."*

And after grace was said, we fell to meat and drink, and then when we had eaten and drunk, we began to sing the holy office and promptly, one by one, each man fell to sleep. Tho Brendan did not sleep, but prayed three days and nights upon his knees, and full devoutly for our awakening. And so at length we did awaken, and those of us who had drank three cups of that clear water slept three days and nights, and those who drank two cups slept two, and one cup only one day and night. And Brendan gathered us about the fire and said, *"Brothers, we see here how a gift of God may do us harm. As Lent is neigh, let us now get ourselves to sea; take only meat and drink for one meal every three days, as is the rule, enough to last this holy season out."*

And then again we pulled our hide boat upon God's ocean, and for three full days the wind blew foul, and then a sudden all grew still. The wind blew not and the sea calmed and flattened and seemed to set into a thing solid. And

Brendan said, *"Brothers, lay off your oars, let us drift; and in this show true submission to the will of God."*

And then we drifted twenty days. And this was a time of meditation and prayer, and of perfect observance of the rule, and of good fellowship among the brethren. Then at last by the purveyance of the Lord, the wind arose and blew fresh til Palm Sunday.

And then at last we came again unto the Isle of Sheep, and were received again by the goodly old man, who brought us again into the fair hall, and served us. And after soup on Holy Thursday, he washed our feet, and gave us each the kiss of peace, alike our Lord had done with his disciples. And on the Friday of the passion of our Lord we sacrificed the lamb of innocence, and on the Saturday we did all holy rite and prayed together full devoutly, that we might find ourselves prepared for the miracle of the resurrection of our Lord Jesu. And at eventide we toiled our skin vessel into the sea, and as Brendan bid us, pulled our ashen oars against the seas that blow shorewards at eventide. And Brendan made his seat upon the oaken tiller and captained us unto a place in the sea that he did chose. And on that Easter vigil, just at the hour of lauds, when all the world is blue with first light, he bid us lay upon our oars, and Brendan asked unto us, *"Do you not know where it is you are?"*

And we did not know, but Brendan did know; and lo, we seemed to rise up heavenward, and the seas fell away from our frail craft, and we beheld ourselves again upon Jasconius' back. And we beheld the smear of char where twelve months past we laid a fire to bake our meat, and we were amazed, and Brendan seeing this said, *"Do not be afraid."*

And one by one we stepped out upon this living isle. And Brendan said,

"How splendid is the will of our good Lord, that even savage monsters do his bidding and make this place upon a fish's back to keep the holy service of the resurrection."

And after Mass was said, and Brendan sacrificed the spotless lamb of innocence, we got ourselves again aboard our skin vessel, and lo Jasconius dove beneath the sea, and we sailed free. And on that same morning we gained the island where the tree of the birds was, and that same bird welcomed Brendan and sang full merrily.

And there we dwelled from Easter til Trinity Sunday, as we had done the year before, in full great joy and mirth; and daily we heard the merry service of the birds sitting in the tree. And then the one bird told Brendan that he should return again at Christmas to the abbey of the monks, *"and Easterday, do not forget, you spend with us. But every other day of your journey, you labor in the full great peril of the ocean, from year to year til the seventh year has been accomplished when you shall find the Land of the Blest, before the gates of Paradise, and dwell there forty days in full great joy and mirth; and after you shall return home in safety to your own abbey and there end your life and be admitted to blessed heaven, which our Lord bought for you with his most precious blood."*

And then an angel of our Lord ordained all things needful to our voyage, in vitals and all other things necessary. And then we thanked our Lord for the great goodness that he had often shown us in our great need. And then we sailed forth in the great sea ocean, abiding in the mercy of our Lord through great troubles and tempests.

THE CANTERVILLE GHOST

BY OSCAR WILDE

When Mr. Hiram B. Otis, the American Minister, bought Canterville Chase, every one told him he was doing a very foolish thing, as there was no doubt at all that the place was haunted. Indeed, Lord Canterville himself, who was a man of the most punctilious honor, had felt it his duty to mention the fact to Mr. Otis when they came to discuss terms.

'We have not cared to live in the place ourselves,' said Lord Canterville, 'since my grandaunt, the Dowager Duchess of Bolton, was frightened into a fit, from which she never really recovered, by two skeleton hands being placed on her shoulders as she was dressing for dinner, and I feel bound to tell you, Mr. Otis, that the ghost has been seen by several living members of my family, as well as by the rector of the parish, the Rev. Augustus Dampier, who is a Fellow of King's College, Cambridge. After the unfortunate accident to the Duchess, none of our younger servants would stay with us, and Lady Canterville often got very little sleep at night, in consequence of the mysterious noises that came from the corridor and the library.'

'My Lord,' answered the Minister, 'I will take the furniture and the ghost at a valuation. I come from a modern country, where we have everything that money can buy; and with all our spry young fellows painting the Old World red, and carrying off your best actresses and prima-donnas, I reckon that if there were such a thing as a ghost in Europe, we'd have it at home in a very short time in one of our public museums, or on the road as a show.'

'I fear that the ghost exists,' said Lord Canterville, smiling, 'though it may have resisted the overtures of your enterprising impresarios. It has been well known for three centuries, since 1584 in fact, and always makes its appearance before the death of any member of our family.'

'Well, so does the family doctor for that matter, Lord Canterville. But there is no such thing, sir, as a ghost, and I guess the laws of Nature are not going to be suspended for the British aristocracy.'

'You are certainly very natural in America,' answered Lord Canterville, who did not quite understand Mr. Otis's last observation, 'and if you don't mind a ghost in the house, it is all right. Only you must remember I warned you.'

A few weeks after this, the purchase was completed, and at the close of the season the Minister and his family went down to Canterville Chase. Mrs. Otis, who, as Miss Lucretia R. Tappan, of West 53rd Street, had been a celebrated New York belle, was now a very handsome, middle-aged woman, with fine eyes, and a superb profile. Many American ladies on leaving their native land adopt an appearance of chronic ill-health, under the impression that it is a form of European refinement, but Mrs. Otis had never fallen into this error. She had a magnificent constitution, and a really wonderful amount of animal spirits. Indeed, in many respects, she was quite English, and was an excellent example of the fact that we have really everything in common with America nowadays, except, of course, language. Her eldest son, christened Washington by his parents in a moment of patriotism, which he never ceased to regret, was a fair-haired, rather good-looking young man, who had qualified himself for American diplomacy by leading the German at the Newport Casino for three successive seasons, and even in London was well known as an excellent dancer. Gardenias and the peerage were his only weaknesses. Otherwise he was extremely sensible. Miss Virginia E. Otis was a little girl of fifteen, lithe and lovely as a fawn, and with a fine freedom in her large blue eyes. She was a wonderful amazon, and had once raced old Lord Bilton on her pony twice round the park, winning by a length and a half, just in front of the Achilles statue, to the huge delight of the young Duke of Cheshire, who proposed for her on the spot, and was sent back to Eton that very night by his guardians, in floods of tears. After Virginia came the twins, who were usually called 'The Stars and Stripes,' as they were always getting swished. They were delightful boys, and with the exception of the worthy Minister the only true republicans of the family.

As Canterville Chase is seven miles from Ascot, the nearest railway station, Mr. Otis had telegraphed for a waggonette to meet them, and they started on their drive in high spirits. It was a lovely July evening, and the air was delicate with the scent of the pine-woods. Now and then they heard a wood pigeon brooding over its own sweet voice, or saw, deep in the rustling fern, the burnished breast of the pheasant. Little squirrels peered at them from the beech-trees as they went by, and the rabbits scudded away through the brushwood and over the mossy knolls, with their white tails in the air. As they entered the avenue of Canterville Chase, however, the sky became suddenly overcast with clouds, a curious stillness seemed to hold the atmosphere, a great flight of rooks passed silently over their heads, and, before they reached the house, some big drops of rain had fallen.

Standing on the steps to receive them was an old woman, neatly dressed in black silk, with a white cap and apron. This was Mrs. Umney, the housekeeper, whom Mrs. Otis, at Lady Canterville's earnest request, had consented to keep on in her former position. She made them each a low curtsey as they alighted, and said in a quaint, old-fashioned manner, 'I bid you welcome to Canterville Chase.' Following her, they passed through the fine Tudor hall into the library, a long, low room, paneled in black oak, at the end of which was a large stained-glass window. Here they found tea laid out for them, and, after taking off their wraps, they sat down and began to look round, while Mrs. Umney waited on them.

Suddenly Mrs. Otis caught sight of a dull red stain on the floor just by the fireplace and, quite unconscious of what it really signified, said to Mrs. Umney, 'I am afraid something has been spilt there.'

'Yes, madam,' replied the old housekeeper in a low voice, 'blood has been spilt on that spot.'

'How horrid,' cried Mrs. Otis; 'I don't at all care for blood-stains in a sitting-room. It must be removed at once.'

The old woman smiled, and answered in the same low, mysterious voice, 'It is the blood of Lady Eleanore de Canterville, who was murdered on that very spot by her own husband, Sir Simon de Canterville, in 1575. Sir Simon survived her nine years, and disappeared suddenly under very mysterious circumstances. His body has never been discovered, but his guilty spirit still haunts the Chase. The blood-stain has been much admired by tourists and others, and cannot be removed.'

'That is all nonsense,' cried Washington Otis; 'Pinkerton's Champion Stain Remover and Paragon Detergent will clean it up in no time,' and before the terrified housekeeper could interfere he had fallen upon his knees, and was rapidly scouring the floor with a small stick of what looked like a black cosmetic. In a few moments no trace of the blood-stain could be seen.

'I knew Pinkerton would do it,' he exclaimed triumphantly, as he looked round at his admiring family; but no sooner had he said these words than a terrible flash of lightning lit up the sombre room, a fearful peal of thunder made them all start to their feet, and Mrs. Umney fainted.

'What a monstrous climate!' said the American Minister calmly, as he lit a long cheroot. 'I guess the old country is so overpopulated that they have not enough decent weather for everybody. I have always been of opinion that emigration is the only thing for England.'

'My dear Hiram,' cried Mrs. Otis, 'what can we do with a woman who faints?'

'Charge it to her like breakages,' answered the Minister; 'she won't faint after that'; and in a few moments Mrs. Umney certainly came to. There was no doubt, however, that she was extremely upset, and she sternly warned Mr. Otis to beware of some trouble coming to the house.

'I have seen things with my own eyes, sir,' she said, 'that would make any Christian's hair stand on end, and many and many a night I have not closed my eyes in sleep for the awful things that are done here.' Mr. Otis, however, and his wife warmly assured the honest soul that they were not afraid of ghosts, and, after invoking the blessings of Providence on her new master and mistress, and making arrangements for an increase of salary, the old housekeeper tottered off to her own room.

* * * * *

The storm raged fiercely all that night, but nothing of particular note occurred. The next morning, however, when they came down to breakfast, they found the terrible stain of blood once again on the floor. 'I don't think it can be the fault of the Paragon Detergent,' said Washington, 'for I have tried it with everything. It must be the ghost.' He accordingly rubbed out the stain a second time, but the second morning it appeared again. The third morning also it was there, though the library had been locked up at night by Mr. Otis himself, and the key carried upstairs. The whole family were now quite interested; Mr. Otis began to suspect that he had been too dogmatic in his denial of the existence of ghosts, Mrs. Otis expressed her intention of joining the Psychical Society, and Washington prepared a long letter to Messrs. Myers and Podmore on the subject of the Permanence of Sanguineous Stains when connected with Crime. That night all doubts about the objective existence of phantasmata were removed for ever.

The day had been warm and sunny; and, in the cool of the evening, the whole family went out for a drive. They did not return home till nine o'clock, when they had a light supper. The conversation in no way turned upon ghosts, so there were not even those primary conditions of receptive expectation which so often precede the presentation of psychical phenomena. The subjects discussed, as I have since learned from Mr. Otis, were merely such as form the ordinary conversation of cultured Americans of the better class, such as the immense superiority of Miss Fanny Davenport over Sarah Bernhardt as an actress; the difficulty of obtaining green corn, buckwheat cakes, and hominy, even in the best English houses; the importance of Boston in the development of the world-soul; the advantages of the baggage check system in railway travelling; and the sweetness of the New York accent as compared to the London drawl. No mention at all was made of the supernatural, nor was Sir Simon de Canterville alluded to in any way. At eleven o'clock the family retired, and by half-past all the lights were out. Some time after, Mr. Otis was awakened by a curious noise in the corridor, outside his room. It sounded like the clank of metal, and seemed to be coming nearer every moment. He got up at once, struck a match, and looked at the time. It was exactly one o'clock. He was quite calm, and felt his pulse, which was not at all feverish. The strange noise still continued, and with it he heard distinctly the sound of footsteps. He put on his slippers, took a small oblong phial out of his dressing-case, and opened the door. Right in front of him he saw, in the wan moonlight, an old man of terrible aspect. His eyes were as red burning coals; long grey hair fell over his shoulders in matted coils; his garments, which were of antique cut, were soiled and ragged, and from his wrists and ankles hung heavy manacles and rusty gyves.

'My dear sir,' said Mr. Otis, 'I really must insist on your oiling those chains, and have brought you for that purpose a small bottle of the Tammany Rising Sun Lubricator. It is said to be completely efficacious upon one application, and there are several testimonials to that effect on the wrapper from some of our most eminent native divines. I shall leave it here for you by the bedroom candles, and will be happy to supply you with more should you require it.' With these words the United States Minister laid the bottle down on a marble table, and, closing his door, retired to rest.

For a moment the Canterville ghost stood quite motionless in natural indignation; then, dashing the bottle violently upon the polished floor, he fled down the corridor, uttering hollow groans, and emitting a ghastly green light. Just, however, as he reached the top of the great oak staircase, a door was flung open, two little white-robed figures appeared, and a large pillow whizzed past his head! There was evidently no time to be lost, so, hastily adopting the Fourth Dimension of Space as a means of escape, he vanished through the wainscoting, and the house became quite quiet.

On reaching a small secret chamber in the left wing, he leaned up against a moonbeam to recover his breath, and began to try and realize his position. Never, in a brilliant and uninterrupted career of three hundred years, had he been so grossly insulted. He thought of the Dowager Duchess, whom he had frightened into a fit as she stood before the glass in her lace and diamonds; of the four housemaids, who had gone off into hysterics when he merely grinned at them through the curtains of one of the spare bedrooms; of the rector of the parish, whose candle he had blown out as he was coming late one night from the library, and who had been under the care of Sir William Gull ever since, a perfect martyr to nervous disorders; and of old Madame de Tremouillac, who, having wakened up one morning early and seen a skeleton seated in an armchair by the fire reading her diary, had been confined to her bed for six weeks with an attack of brain fever, and, on her recovery, had become reconciled to the Church, and broken off her connection with that notorious skeptic Monsieur de Voltaire. He remembered the terrible night when the wicked Lord Canterville was found choking in his dressing-room, with the knave of diamonds halfway down his throat, and confessed, just before he died, that he had cheated Charles James Fox out of £50,000 at Crockford's by means of that very card, and swore that the ghost had made him swallow it. All his great achievements came back to him again, from the butler who had shot himself in the pantry because he had seen a green hand tapping at the window pane, to the beautiful Lady Stutfield, who was always obliged to wear a black velvet band round her throat to hide the mark of five fingers burnt upon her white skin, and who drowned herself at last in the carp-pond at the end of the King's Walk. With the enthusiastic egotism of the true artist he went over his most celebrated performances, and smiled bitterly to himself as he recalled to mind his last appearance as 'Red Ruben, or the Strangled Babe,' his *début* as 'Gaunt Gibeon, the Blood-sucker of Bexley Moor,' and the *furore* he had excited one lovely June evening by merely playing ninepins with his own bones upon the lawn-tennis ground. And after all this, some wretched modern Americans were to come and offer him the Rising Sun Lubricator, and throw pillows at his head! It was quite unbearable. Besides, no ghosts in history had ever been treated in this manner. Accordingly, he determined to have vengeance, and remained till daylight in an attitude of deep thought.

* * * * *

The next morning when the Otis family met at breakfast, they discussed the ghost at some length. The United States Minister was naturally a little annoyed to find that his present had not been accepted. 'I have no wish,' he said, 'to do the ghost any personal injury, and I must say that, considering the length of time he has been in the house, I don't think it is at all polite to throw pillows at him'—a very just remark, at which, I am sorry to say, the twins burst into shouts of laughter. 'Upon the other hand,' he continued, 'if he really declines to use the Rising Sun Lubricator, we shall have to take his chains from him. It would be quite impossible to sleep, with such a noise going on outside the bedrooms.'

For the rest of the week, however, they were undisturbed, the only thing that excited any attention being the continual renewal of the blood-stain on the library floor. This certainly was very strange, as the door was always locked at night by Mr. Otis, and the windows kept closely barred. The chameleon-like color, also, of the stain excited a good deal of comment. Some mornings it was a dull (almost Indian) red, then it would be vermilion, then a rich purple, and once when they came down for family prayers, according to the simple rites of the Free American Reformed Episcopalian Church, they found it a bright emerald-green. These kaleidoscopic changes naturally amused the party very much, and bets on the subject were freely made every evening. The only person who did not enter into the joke was little Virginia, who, for some unexplained reason, was always a good deal distressed at the sight of the blood-stain, and very nearly cried the morning it was emerald-green.

The second appearance of the ghost was on Sunday night. Shortly after they had gone to bed they were suddenly alarmed by a fearful crash in the hall. Rushing downstairs, they found that a large suit of old armor had become detached from its stand, and had fallen on the stone floor, while, seated in a high-backed chair, was the Canterville ghost, rubbing his knees with an expression of acute agony on his face. The twins, having brought their pea-shooters with them, at once discharged two pellets on him, with that accuracy of aim which can only be attained by long and careful practice on a writing-master, while the United States Minister covered him with his revolver, and called upon him, in accordance with Californian etiquette, to hold up his hands! The ghost started up with a wild shriek of rage, and swept through them like a mist, extinguishing Washington Otis's candle as he passed, and so leaving them all in total darkness. On reaching the top of the staircase he recovered himself, and determined to give his celebrated peal of demoniac laughter. This he had on more than one occasion found extremely useful. It was said to have turned Lord Raker's wig grey in a single night, and had certainly made three of Lady Canterville's French governesses give warning before their month was up. He accordingly laughed his most horrible laugh, till the old vaulted roof rang and rang again, but hardly had the fearful echo died away when a door opened, and Mrs. Otis came out in a light blue dressing-gown. 'I am afraid you are far from well,' she said, 'and have brought you a bottle of Dr. Dobell's tincture. If it is indigestion, you will find it a most excellent remedy.' The ghost glared at her in fury, and began at once to make preparations for turning himself into a large black dog, an accomplishment for which he was justly renowned, and to which the family doctor always attributed the permanent idiocy of Lord Canterville's uncle, the Hon. Thomas Horton. The sound of approaching footsteps, however, made him hesitate in his fell purpose, so he contented himself with becoming faintly phosphorescent, and vanished with a deep churchyard groan, just as the twins had come up to him.

On reaching his room he entirely broke down, and became a prey to the most violent agitation. The vulgarity of the twins, and the gross materialism of Mrs. Otis, were naturally extremely annoying, but what really distressed him most was, that he had been unable to wear the suit of mail. He had hoped that even modern Americans would be thrilled by the sight of a Spectre In Armor, if for no more sensible reason, at least out of respect for their national poet Longfellow, over whose graceful and attractive poetry he himself had whiled away many a weary hour when the Cantervilles were up in town. Besides, it was his own suit. He had worn it with great success at the Kenilworth tournament, and had been highly complimented on it by no less a person than the Virgin Queen herself. Yet when he had put it on, he had been completely overpowered by the weight of the huge breastplate and steel casque, and had fallen heavily on the stone pavement, barking both his knees severely, and bruising the knuckles of his right hand.

For some days after this he was extremely ill, and hardly stirred out of his room at all, except to keep the blood-stain in proper repair. However, by taking great care of himself, he recovered, and resolved to make a third attempt to frighten the United States Minister and his family. He selected Friday, the 17th of August, for his appearance, and spent most of that day in looking over his wardrobe, ultimately deciding in favor of a large slouched hat with a red feather, a winding-sheet frilled at the wrists and neck, and a rusty dagger. Towards evening a violent storm of rain came on, and the wind was so high that all the windows and doors in the old house shook and rattled. In fact, it was just such weather as he loved. His plan of action was this. He was to make his way quietly to Washington Otis's room, gibber at him from the foot of the bed, and stab himself three times in the throat to the sound of slow music. He bore Washington a special grudge, being quite aware that it was he who was in the habit of removing the famous Canterville blood-stain, by means of Pinkerton's Paragon Detergent. Having reduced the reckless and foolhardy youth to a condition of abject terror, he was then to proceed to the room occupied by the United States Minister and his wife, and there to place a clammy hand on Mrs. Otis's forehead, while he hissed into her trembling husband's ear the awful secrets of the charnel-house. With regard to little Virginia, he had not quite made up his mind. She had never insulted him in any way, and was pretty and gentle. A few hollow groans from the wardrobe, he thought, would be more than sufficient, or, if that failed to wake her, he might grabble at the counterpane with palsy-twitching fingers. As for the twins, he was quite determined to teach them a lesson. The first thing to be done was, of course, to sit upon their chests, so as to produce the stifling sensation of nightmare. Then, as their beds were quite close to each other, to stand between them in the form of a green, icy-cold corpse, till they became paralyzed with fear, and finally, to throw off the winding-sheet, and crawl round the room, with white bleached bones and one rolling eye-ball, in the character of 'Dumb Daniel, or the Suicide's Skeleton,' a *rôle* in which he had on more than one occasion produced a great effect, and which he considered quite equal to his famous part of 'Martin the Maniac, or the Masked Mystery.'

At half-past ten he heard the family going to bed. For some time he was disturbed by wild shrieks of laughter from the twins, who, with the light-hearted gaiety of schoolboys, were evidently amusing themselves before they retired to rest, but at a quarter past eleven all was still, and, as midnight sounded, he sallied forth. The owl beat against the window panes, the raven croaked from the old yew-tree, and the wind wandered moaning round the house like a lost soul; but the Otis family slept unconscious of their doom, and high above the rain and storm he could hear the steady snoring of the Minister for the United States. He stepped stealthily out of the wainscoting, with an evil smile on his cruel, wrinkled mouth, and the moon hid her face in a cloud as he stole past the great oriel window, where his own arms and those of his murdered wife were blazoned in azure and gold. On and on he glided, like an evil shadow, the very darkness seeming to loathe him as he passed. Once he thought he heard something call, and stopped; but it was only the baying of a dog from the Red

Farm, and he went on, muttering strange sixteenth-century curses, and ever and anon brandishing the rusty dagger in the midnight air. Finally he reached the corner of the passage that led to luckless Washington's room. For a moment he paused there, the wind blowing his long grey locks about his head, and twisting into grotesque and fantastic folds the nameless horror of the dead man's shroud. Then the clock struck the quarter, and he felt the time was come. He chuckled to himself, and turned the corner; but no sooner had he done so, than, with a piteous wail of terror, he fell back, and hid his blanched face in his long, bony hands. Right in front of him was standing a horrible spectre, motionless as a carven image, and monstrous as a madman's dream! Its head was bald and burnished; its face round, and fat, and white; and hideous laughter seemed to have writhed its features into an eternal grin. From the eyes streamed rays of scarlet light, the mouth was a wide well of fire, and a hideous garment, like to his own, swathed with its silent snows the Titan form. On its breast was a placard with strange writing in antique characters, some scroll of shame it seemed, some record of wild sins, some awful calendar of crime, and, with its right hand, it bore aloft a falchion of gleaming steel.

Never having seen a ghost before, he naturally was terribly frightened, and, after a second hasty glance at the awful phantom, he fled back to his room, tripping up in his long winding-sheet as he sped down the corridor, and finally dropping the rusty dagger into the Minister's jack-boots, where it was found in the morning by the butler. Once in the privacy of his own apartment, he flung himself down on a small pallet-bed, and hid his face under the clothes. After a time, however, the brave old Canterville spirit asserted itself, and he determined to go and speak to the other ghost as soon as it was daylight. Accordingly, just as the dawn was touching the hills with silver, he returned towards the spot where he had first laid eyes on the grisly phantom, feeling that, after all, two ghosts were better than one, and that, by the aid of his new friend, he might safely grapple with the twins. On reaching the spot, however, a terrible sight met his gaze. Something had evidently happened to the spectre, for the light had entirely faded from its hollow eyes, the gleaming falchion had fallen from its hand, and it was leaning up against the wall in a strained and uncomfortable attitude. He rushed forward and seized it in his arms, when, to his horror, the head slipped off and rolled on the floor, the body assumed a recumbent posture, and he found himself clasping a white dimity bed-curtain, with a sweeping-brush, a kitchen cleaver, and a hollow turnip lying at his feet! Unable to understand this curious transformation, he clutched the placard with feverish haste, and there, in the grey morning light, he read these fearful words:—

YE OLDE GHOSTE

Ye Onlie True and Originale Spook. Beware of Ye Imitationes. All others are Counterfeite.

The whole thing flashed across him. He had been tricked, foiled, and outwitted! The old Canterville look came into his eyes; he ground his toothless gums together; and, raising his withered hands high above his head, swore, according to the picturesque phraseology of the antique school, that when Chanticleer had sounded twice his merry horn, deeds of blood would be wrought, and Murder walk abroad with silent feet.

Hardly had he finished this awful oath when, from the red-tiled roof of a distant homestead, a cock crew. He laughed a long, low, bitter laugh, and waited. Hour after hour he waited, but the cock, for some strange reason, did not crow again. Finally, at half-past seven, the arrival of the housemaids made him give up his fearful vigil, and he stalked back to his room, thinking of his vain hope and baffled purpose. There he consulted several books of ancient chivalry, of which he was exceedingly fond, and found that, on every occasion on which his oath had been used, Chanticleer had always crowed a second time. 'Perdition seize the naughty fowl,' he muttered, 'I have seen the day when, with my stout spear, I would have run him through the gorge, and made him crow for me an 'twere in death!' He then retired to a comfortable lead coffin, and stayed there till evening.

* * * * *

The next day the ghost was very weak and tired. The terrible excitement of the last four weeks was beginning to have its effect. His nerves were completely shattered, and he started at the slightest noise. For five days he kept his room, and at last made up his mind to give up the point of the blood-stain on the library floor. If the Otis family did not want it, they clearly did not deserve it. They were evidently people on a low, material plane of existence, and quite incapable of appreciating the symbolic value of sensuous phenomena. The question of phantasmic apparitions, and the development of astral bodies, was of course quite a different matter, and really not under his control. It was his solemn duty to appear in the corridor once a week, and to gibber from the large oriel window on the first and third Wednesday in every month, and he did not see how he could honorably escape from his obligations. It is quite true that his life had been very evil, but, upon the other hand, he was most conscientious in all things connected with the supernatural. For the next three Saturdays, accordingly, he traversed the corridor as usual between midnight and three o'clock, taking every possible precaution against being either heard or seen. He removed his boots, trod as lightly as possible on the old worm-eaten boards, wore a large black velvet cloak, and was careful to use the Rising Sun Lubricator for oiling his chains. I am bound to acknowledge that it was with a good deal of difficulty that he brought himself to adopt this last mode of protection. However, one night, while the family were at dinner, he slipped into Mr. Otis's bedroom and carried off the bottle. He felt a little humiliated at first, but afterwards was sensible enough to see that there was a great deal to be said for the invention, and, to a certain degree, it served his purpose. Still, in spite of everything, he was not left unmolested. Strings were continually being stretched across the corridor, over which he tripped in the dark, and on one occasion, while dressed for the part of 'Black Isaac, or the Huntsman of Hogley Woods,' he met with a severe fall, through treading on a butter-slide, which the twins had constructed from the entrance of the Tapestry Chamber to the top of the oak staircase. This last insult so enraged him, that he resolved to make one final effort to assert his dignity and social position, and determined to visit the insolent young Etonians the next night in his celebrated character of 'Reckless Rupert, or the Headless Earl.'

He had not appeared in this disguise for more than seventy years; in fact, not since he had so frightened pretty Lady Barbara Modish by means of it, that she suddenly broke off her engagement with the present Lord Canterville's grandfather, and ran away to Gretna Green with handsome Jack Castleton, declaring that nothing in the world would induce her to marry into a family that allowed such a horrible phantom to walk up and down the terrace at twilight. Poor Jack was afterwards shot in a duel by Lord Canterville on Wandsworth Common, and Lady Barbara died of a broken heart at Tunbridge Wells before the year was out, so, in every way, it had been a great success. It was, however, an extremely difficult 'make-up,' if I may use such a theatrical expression in connection with one of the greatest mysteries of the supernatural, or, to employ a more scientific term, the higher-natural world, and it took him fully three hours to make his preparations. At last everything was ready, and he was very pleased with his appearance. The big leather riding-boots that went with the dress were just a little too large for him, and he could only find one of the two horse-pistols, but, on the whole, he was quite satisfied, and at a quarter past one he glided out of the wainscoting and crept down the corridor. On reaching the room occupied by the twins, which I should mention was called the Blue Bed Chamber, on account of the color of its hangings, he found the door just ajar. Wishing to make an effective entrance, he flung it wide open, when a heavy jug of water fell right down on him, wetting him to the skin, and just missing his left shoulder by a couple of inches. At the same moment he heard stifled shrieks of laughter proceeding from the four-post bed. The shock to his nervous system was so great that he fled back to his room as hard as he could go, and the next day he was laid up with a severe cold. The only thing that at all consoled him in the whole affair was the fact that he had not brought his head with him, for, had he done so, the consequences might have been very serious.

He now gave up all hope of ever frightening this rude American family, and contented himself, as a rule, with creeping about the passages in list slippers, with a thick red muffler round his throat for fear of draughts, and a small arquebuse, in case he should be attacked by the twins. The final blow he received occurred on the 19th of September. He had gone downstairs to the great entrance-hall, feeling sure that there, at any rate, he would be quite unmolested, and was amusing himself by making satirical remarks on the large Saroni photographs of the United States Minister and his wife, which had now taken the place of the Canterville family pictures. He was simply but neatly clad in a long shroud, spotted with churchyard mould, had tied up his jaw with a strip of yellow linen, and carried a small lantern and a sexton's spade. In fact, he was dressed for the character of 'Jonas the Graveless, or the Corpse-Snatcher of Chertsey Barn,' one of his most remarkable impersonations, and one which the Cantervilles had every reason to remember, as it was the real origin of their quarrel with their neighbor, Lord Rufford. It was about a quarter past two o'clock in the morning, and, as far as he could ascertain, no one was stirring. As he was strolling towards the library, however, to see if there were any traces left of the blood-stain, suddenly there leaped out on him from a dark corner two figures, who waved their arms wildly above their heads, and shrieked out 'BOO!' in his ear.

Seized with a panic, which, under the circumstances, was only natural, he rushed for the staircase, but found Washington Otis waiting for him there with the big garden-syringe; and being thus hemmed in by his enemies on every side, and driven almost to bay, he vanished into the great iron stove, which, fortunately for him, was not lit, and had to make his way home through the flues and chimneys, arriving at his own room in a terrible state of dirt, disorder, and despair.

After this he was not seen again on any nocturnal expedition. The twins lay in wait for him on several occasions, and strewed the passages with nutshells every night to the great annoyance of their parents and the servants, but it was of no avail. It was quite evident that his feelings were so wounded that he would not appear. Mr. Otis consequently resumed his great work on the history of the Democratic Party, on which he had been engaged for some years; Mrs. Otis organized a wonderful clam-bake, which amazed the whole county; the boys took to lacrosse, euchre, poker, and other American national games; and Virginia rode about the lanes on her pony, accompanied by the young Duke of Cheshire, who had come to spend the last week of his holidays at Canterville Chase. It was generally assumed that the ghost had gone away, and, in fact, Mr. Otis wrote a letter to that effect to Lord Canterville, who, in reply, expressed his great pleasure at the news, and sent his best congratulations to the Minister's worthy wife.

The Otises, however, were deceived, for the ghost was still in the house, and though now almost an invalid, was by no means ready to let matters rest, particularly as he heard that among the guests was the young Duke of Cheshire, whose grand-uncle, Lord Francis Stilton, had once bet a hundred guineas with Colonel Carbury that he would play dice with the Canterville ghost, and was found the next morning lying on the floor of the card-room in such a helpless paralytic state, that though he lived on to a great age, he was never able to say anything again but 'Double Sixes.' The story was well known at the time, though, of course, out of respect to the feelings of the two noble families, every attempt was made to hush it up; and a full account of all the circumstances connected with it will be found in the third volume of Lord Tattle's *Recollections of the Prince Regent and his Friends*. The ghost, then, was naturally very anxious to show that he had not lost his influence over the Stiltons, with whom, indeed, he was distantly connected, his own first cousin having been married *en secondes noces* to the Sieur de Bulkeley, from whom, as every one knows, the Dukes of Cheshire are lineally descended. Accordingly, he made arrangements for appearing to Virginia's little lover in his celebrated impersonation of 'The Vampire Monk, or, the Bloodless Benedictine,' a performance so horrible that when old Lady Startup saw it, which she did on one fatal New Year's Eve, in the year 1764, she went off into the most piercing shrieks, which culminated in violent apoplexy, and died in three days, after disinheriting the Cantervilles, who were her nearest relations, and leaving all her money to her London apothecary. At the last moment, however, his terror of the twins prevented his leaving his room, and the little Duke slept in peace under the great feathered canopy in the Royal Bedchamber, and dreamed of Virginia.

* * * * *

A few days after this, Virginia and her curly-haired cavalier went out riding on Brockley meadows, where she tore her habit so badly in getting through a hedge, that, on her return home, she made up her mind to go up by the back staircase so as not to be seen. As she was running past the Tapestry Chamber, the door of which happened to be open, she fancied she saw some one inside, and thinking it was her mother's maid, who sometimes used to bring her work there, looked in to ask her to mend her habit. To her immense surprise, however, it was the Canterville Ghost himself! He was sitting by the window, watching the ruined gold of the yellowing trees fly through the air, and the red leaves dancing madly down the long avenue. His head was leaning on his hand, and his whole attitude was one of extreme depression. Indeed, so forlorn, and so much out of repair did he look, that little Virginia, whose first idea had been to run away and lock herself in her room, was filled with pity, and determined to try and comfort him. So light was her footfall, and so deep his melancholy, that he was not aware of her presence till she spoke to him.

'I am so sorry for you,' she said, 'but my brothers are going back to Eton to-morrow, and then, if you behave yourself, no one will annoy you.'

'It is absurd asking me to behave myself,' he answered, looking round in astonishment at the pretty little girl who had ventured to address him, 'quite absurd. I must rattle my chains, and groan through keyholes, and walk about at night, if that is what you mean. It is my only reason for existing.'

'It is no reason at all for existing, and you know you have been very wicked. Mrs. Umney told us, the first day we arrived here, that you had killed your wife.'

'Well, I quite admit it,' said the Ghost petulantly, 'but it was a purely family matter, and concerned no one else.'

'It is very wrong to kill any one,' said Virginia, who at times had a sweet Puritan gravity, caught from some old New England ancestor.

'Oh, I hate the cheap severity of abstract ethics! My wife was very plain, never had my ruffs properly starched, and knew nothing about cookery. Why, there was a buck I had shot in Hogley Woods, a magnificent pricket, and do you know how she had it sent up to table? However, it is no matter now, for it is all over, and I don't think it was very nice of her brothers to starve me to death, though I did kill her.'

'Starve you to death? Oh, Mr. Ghost, I mean Sir Simon, are you hungry? I have a sandwich in my case. Would you like it?'

'No, thank you, I never eat anything now; but it is very kind of you, all the same, and you are much nicer than the rest of your horrid, rude, vulgar, dishonest family.'

'Stop!' cried Virginia, stamping her foot, 'it is you who are rude, and horrid, and vulgar, and as for dishonesty, you know you stole the paints out of my box to try and furbish up that ridiculous blood-stain in the library. First you took all my reds, including the vermilion, and I couldn't do any more sunsets, then you took the emerald-green and the chrome-yellow, and finally I had nothing left but indigo and Chinese white, and could only do moonlight scenes, which are always depressing to look at, and not at all easy to paint. I never told on you, though I was very much annoyed, and it was most ridiculous, the whole thing; for who ever heard of emerald-green blood?'

'Well, really,' said the Ghost, rather meekly, 'what was I to do? It is a very difficult thing to get real blood nowadays, and, as your brother began it all with his Paragon Detergent, I certainly saw no reason why I should not have your paints. As for color, that is always a matter of taste: the Cantervilles have blue blood, for instance, the very bluest in England; but I know you Americans don't care for things of this kind.'

'You know nothing about it, and the best thing you can do is to emigrate and improve your mind. My father will be only too happy to give you a free passage, and though there is a heavy duty on spirits of every kind, there will be no difficulty about the Custom House, as the officers are all Democrats. Once in New York, you are sure to be a great success. I know lots of people there who would give a hundred thousand dollars to have a grandfather, and much more than that to have a family Ghost.'

'I don't think I should like America.'

'I suppose because we have no ruins and no curiosities,' said Virginia satirically.

'No ruins! no curiosities!' answered the Ghost; 'you have your navy and your manners.'

'Good evening; I will go and ask papa to get the twins an extra week's holiday.'

'Please don't go, Miss Virginia,' he cried; 'I am so lonely and so unhappy, and I really don't know what to do. I want to go to sleep and I cannot.'

'That's quite absurd! You have merely to go to bed and blow out the candle. It is very difficult sometimes to keep awake, especially at church, but there is no difficulty at all about sleeping. Why, even babies know how to do that, and they are not very clever.'

'I have not slept for three hundred years,' he said sadly, and Virginia's beautiful blue eyes opened in wonder; 'for three hundred years I have not slept, and I am so tired.'

Virginia grew quite grave, and her little lips trembled like rose-leaves. She came towards him, and kneeling down at his side, looked up into his old withered face.

'Poor, poor Ghost,' she murmured; 'have you no place where you can sleep?'

'Far away beyond the pine-woods,' he answered, in a low dreamy voice, 'there is a little garden. There the grass grows long and deep, there are the great white stars of the hemlock flower, there the nightingale sings all night long. All night long he sings, and the cold, crystal moon looks down, and the yew-tree spreads out its giant arms over the sleepers.'

Virginia's eyes grew dim with tears, and she hid her face in her hands.

'You mean the Garden of Death,' she whispered.

'Yes, Death. Death must be so beautiful. To lie in the soft brown earth, with the grasses waving above one's head, and listen to silence. To have no yesterday, and no to-morrow. To forget time, to forgive life, to be at peace. You can help me. You can open for me the portals of Death's house, for Love is always with you, and Love is stronger than Death is.'

Virginia trembled, a cold shudder ran through her, and for a few moments there was silence. She felt as if she was in a terrible dream.

Then the Ghost spoke again, and his voice sounded like the sighing of the wind.

'Have you ever read the old prophecy on the library window?'

'Oh, often,' cried the little girl, looking up; 'I know it quite well. It is painted in curious black letters, and it is difficult to read. There are only six lines:

When a golden girl can win
Prayer from out the lips of sin,
When the barren almond bears,
And a little child gives away its tears,
Then shall all the house be still
And peace come to Canterville.'
'But I don't know what they mean.'

'They mean,' he said sadly, 'that you must weep for me for my sins, because I have no tears, and pray with me for my soul, because I have no faith, and then, if you have always been sweet, and good, and gentle, the Angel of Death will have mercy on me. You will see fearful shapes in darkness, and wicked voices will whisper in your ear, but they will not harm you, for against the purity of a little child the powers of Hell cannot prevail.'

Virginia made no answer, and the Ghost wrung his hands in wild despair as he looked down at her bowed golden head. Suddenly she stood up, very pale, and with a strange light in her eyes. 'I am not afraid,' she said firmly, 'and I will ask the Angel to have mercy on you.'

He rose from his seat with a faint cry of joy, and taking her hand bent over it with old-fashioned grace and kissed it. His fingers were as cold as ice, and his lips burned like fire, but Virginia did not falter, as he led her across the dusky room. On the faded green tapestry were broidered little huntsmen. They blew their tasselled horns and with their tiny hands waved to her to go back. 'Go back! little Virginia,' they cried, 'go back!' but the Ghost clutched her hand more tightly, and she shut her eyes against them. Horrible animals with lizard tails, and goggle eyes, blinked at her from the carven chimney-piece, and murmured 'Beware! little Virginia, beware! we may never see you again,' but the Ghost glided on more swiftly, and Virginia did not listen. When they reached the end of the room he stopped, and muttered some words she could not understand. She opened her eyes, and saw the wall slowly fading away like a mist, and a great black cavern in front of her. A bitter cold wind swept round them, and she felt something pulling at her dress. 'Quick, quick,' cried the Ghost, 'or it will be too late,' and, in a moment, the wainscoting had closed behind them, and the Tapestry Chamber was empty.

* * * * *

About ten minutes later, the bell rang for tea, and, as Virginia did not come down, Mrs. Otis sent up one of the footmen to tell her. After a little time he returned and said that he could not find Miss Virginia anywhere. As she was in the habit of going out to the garden every evening to get flowers for the dinner-table, Mrs. Otis was not at all alarmed at first, but when six o'clock struck, and Virginia did not appear, she became really agitated, and sent the boys out to look for her, while she herself and Mr. Otis searched every room in the house. At half-past six the boys came back and said that they could find no trace of their sister anywhere. They were all now in the greatest state of excitement, and did not know what to do, when Mr. Otis suddenly remembered that, some few days before, he had given a band of gypsies permission to camp in the park. He accordingly at once set off for Blackfell Hollow, where he knew they were, accompanied by his eldest son and two of the farm-servants. The little Duke of Cheshire, who was perfectly frantic with anxiety, begged hard to be allowed to go too, but Mr. Otis would not allow him, as he was afraid there might be a scuffle. On arriving at the spot, however, he found that the gypsies had gone, and it was evident that their departure had been rather sudden, as the fire was still burning, and some plates were lying on the grass. Having sent off Washington and the two men to scour the district, he ran home, and despatched telegrams to all the police inspectors in the county, telling them to look out for a little girl who had been kidnapped by tramps or gypsies. He then ordered his horse to be brought round, and, after insisting on his wife and the three boys sitting down to dinner, rode off down the Ascot Road with a groom. He had hardly, however, gone a couple of miles when he heard somebody galloping after him, and, looking round, saw the little Duke coming up on his pony, with his face very flushed and no hat. 'I'm awfully sorry, Mr. Otis,' gasped out the boy, 'but I can't eat any dinner as long as Virginia is lost. Please, don't be angry with me; if you had let us be engaged last year, there would never have been all this trouble. You won't send me back, will you? I can't go! I won't go!'

The Minister could not help smiling at the handsome young scapegrace, and was a good deal touched at his devotion to Virginia, so leaning down from his horse, he patted him kindly on the shoulders, and said, 'Well, Cecil, if you won't go back I suppose you must come with me, but I must get you a hat at Ascot.'

'Oh, bother my hat! I want Virginia!' cried the little Duke, laughing, and they galloped on to the railway station. There Mr. Otis inquired of the station-master if any one answering the description of Virginia had been seen on the platform, but could get no news of her. The station-master, however, wired up and down the line, and assured him that a strict watch would be kept for her, and, after having bought a hat for the little Duke from a linen-draper, who was just putting up his shutters, Mr. Otis rode off to Bexley, a village about four miles away, which he was told was a well-known haunt of the gypsies, as there was a large common next to it. Here they roused up the rural policeman, but could get no information from him, and, after riding all over the common, they turned their horses' heads homewards, and reached the Chase about eleven o'clock, dead-tired and almost heart-broken. They found Washington and the twins waiting for them at the gate-house with lanterns, as the avenue was very dark. Not the slightest trace of Virginia had been discovered. The gypsies had been caught on Brockley meadows, but she was not with them, and they had explained their sudden departure by saying that they had mistaken the date of Chorton Fair, and had gone off in a hurry for fear they might be late. Indeed, they had been quite distressed at hearing of Virginia's disappearance, as they were very grateful to Mr. Otis for having allowed them to camp in his park, and four of their number had stayed behind to help in the search. The carp-pond had been dragged, and the whole Chase thoroughly gone over, but without any result. It was evident that, for that night at any rate, Virginia was lost to them; and it was in a state of the deepest depression that Mr. Otis and the boys walked up to the house, the groom following behind with the two horses and the pony. In the hall they found a group of frightened servants, and lying on a sofa in the library was poor Mrs. Otis, almost out of her mind with terror and anxiety, and having her forehead bathed with eau-de-cologne by the old housekeeper. Mr. Otis at once insisted on her having something to eat, and ordered up supper for the whole party. It was a melancholy meal, as hardly any one spoke, and even the twins were awestruck and subdued, as they were very fond of their sister. When they had finished, Mr. Otis, in spite of the entreaties of the little Duke, ordered them all to bed, saying that nothing more could be done that night, and that he would telegraph in the morning to Scotland Yard for some detectives to be sent down immediately. Just as they were passing out of the dining-room, midnight began to boom from the clock tower, and when the last stroke sounded they heard a crash and a sudden shrill cry; a dreadful peal of thunder shook the house, a strain of unearthly music floated through the air, a panel at the top of the staircase flew back with a loud noise, and out on the landing, looking very pale and white, with a little casket in her hand, stepped Virginia. In a moment they had all rushed up to her. Mrs. Otis clasped her passionately in her arms, the Duke smothered her with violent kisses, and the twins executed a wild war-dance round the group.

'Good heavens! child, where have you been?' said Mr. Otis, rather angrily, thinking that she had been playing some foolish trick on them. 'Cecil and I have been riding all over the country looking for you, and your mother has been frightened to death. You must never play these practical jokes any more.'

'Except on the Ghost! except on the Ghost!' shrieked the twins, as they capered about.

'My own darling, thank God you are found; you must never leave my side again,' murmured Mrs. Otis, as she kissed the trembling child, and smoothed the tangled gold of her hair.

'Papa,' said Virginia quietly, 'I have been with the Ghost. He is dead, and you must come and see him. He had been very wicked, but he was really sorry for all that he had done, and he gave me this box of beautiful jewels before he died.'

The whole family gazed at her in mute amazement, but she was quite grave and serious; and, turning round, she led them through the opening in the wainscoting down a narrow secret corridor, Washington following with a lighted candle, which he had caught up from the table. Finally, they came to a great oak door, studded with rusty nails. When Virginia touched it, it swung back on its heavy hinges, and they found themselves in a little low room, with a vaulted ceiling, and one tiny grated window. Imbedded in the wall was a huge iron ring, and chained to it was a gaunt skeleton, that was stretched out at full length on the stone floor, and seemed to be trying to grasp with its long fleshless fingers an old-fashioned trencher and ewer, that were placed just out of its reach. The jug had evidently been once filled with water, as it was covered inside with green mould. There was nothing on the trencher but a pile of dust. Virginia knelt down beside the skeleton, and, folding her little hands together, began to pray silently, while the rest of the party looked on in wonder at the terrible tragedy whose secret was now disclosed to them.

'Hallo!' suddenly exclaimed one of the twins, who had been looking out of the window to try and discover in what wing of the house the room was situated. 'Hallo! the old withered almond-tree has blossomed. I can see the flowers quite plainly in the moonlight.'

'God has forgiven him,' said Virginia gravely, as she rose to her feet, and a beautiful light seemed to illumine her face.

'What an angel you are!' cried the young Duke, and he put his arm round her neck and kissed her.

* * * * *

Four days after these curious incidents a funeral started from Canterville Chase at about eleven o'clock at night. The hearse was drawn by eight black horses, each of which carried on its head a great tuft of nodding ostrich-plumes, and the leaden coffin was covered by a rich purple pall, on which was embroidered in gold the Canterville coat-of-arms. By the side of the hearse and the coaches walked the servants with lighted torches, and the whole procession was wonderfully impressive. Lord Canterville was the chief mourner, having come up specially from Wales to attend the funeral, and sat in the first carriage along with little Virginia. Then came the United States Minister and his wife, then Washington and the three boys, and in the last carriage was Mrs. Umney. It was generally felt that, as she had been frightened by the ghost for more than fifty years of her life, she had a right to see the last of him. A deep grave had been dug in the corner of the churchyard, just under the old yew-tree, and the service was read in the most impressive manner by the Rev. Augustus Dampier. When the ceremony was over, the servants, according to an old custom observed in the

Canterville family, extinguished their torches, and, as the coffin was being lowered into the grave, Virginia stepped forward and laid on it a large cross made of white and pink almond-blossoms. As she did so, the moon came out from behind a cloud, and flooded with its silent silver the little churchyard, and from a distant copse a nightingale began to sing. She thought of the ghost's description of the Garden of Death, her eyes became dim with tears, and she hardly spoke a word during the drive home.

The next morning, before Lord Canterville went up to town, Mr. Otis had an interview with him on the subject of the jewels the ghost had given to Virginia. They were perfectly magnificent, especially a certain ruby necklace with old Venetian setting, which was really a superb specimen of sixteenth-century work, and their value was so great that Mr. Otis felt considerable scruples about allowing his daughter to accept them.

'My lord,' he said, 'I know that in this country mortmain is held to apply to trinkets as well as to land, and it is quite clear to me that these jewels are, or should be, heirlooms in your family. I must beg you, accordingly, to take them to London with you, and to regard them simply as a portion of your property which has been restored to you under certain strange conditions. As for my daughter, she is merely a child, and has as yet, I am glad to say, but little interest in such appurtenances of idle luxury. I am also informed by Mrs. Otis, who, I may say, is no mean authority upon Art—having had the privilege of spending several winters in Boston when she was a girl—that these gems are of great monetary worth, and if offered for sale would fetch a tall price. Under these circumstances, Lord Canterville, I feel sure that you will recognize how impossible it would be for me to allow them to remain in the possession of any member of my family; and, indeed, all such vain gauds and toys, however suitable or necessary to the dignity of the British aristocracy, would be completely out of place among those who have been brought up on the severe, and I believe immortal, principles of republican simplicity. Perhaps I should mention that Virginia is very anxious that you should allow her to retain the box as a memento of your unfortunate but misguided ancestor. As it is extremely old, and consequently a good deal out of repair, you may perhaps think fit to comply with her request. For my own part, I confess I am a good deal surprised to find a child of mine expressing sympathy with mediævalism in any form, and can only account for it by the fact that Virginia was born in one of your London suburbs shortly after Mrs. Otis had returned from a trip to Athens.'

Lord Canterville listened very gravely to the worthy Minister's speech, pulling his grey moustache now and then to hide an involuntary smile, and when Mr. Otis had ended, he shook him cordially by the hand, and said, 'My dear sir, your charming little daughter rendered my unlucky ancestor, Sir Simon, a very important service, and I and my family are much indebted to her for her marvelous courage and pluck. The jewels are clearly hers, and, egad, I believe that if I were heartless enough to take them from her, the wicked old fellow would be out of his grave in a fortnight, leading me the devil of a life. As for their being heirlooms, nothing is an heirloom that is not so mentioned in a will or legal document, and the existence of these jewels has been quite unknown. I assure you I have no more claim on them than your butler, and when Miss Virginia grows up I daresay she will be pleased to have pretty things to wear. Besides, you forget, Mr. Otis, that you took the furniture and the ghost at a valuation, and anything that belonged to the ghost passed at once into your possession, as, whatever activity Sir Simon may have shown in the corridor at night, in point of law he was really dead, and you acquired his property by purchase.'

Mr. Otis was a good deal distressed at Lord Canterville's refusal, and begged him to reconsider his decision, but the good-natured peer was quite firm, and finally induced the Minister to allow his daughter to retain the present the ghost had given her, and when, in the spring of 1890, the young Duchess of Cheshire was presented at the Queen's first drawing-room on the occasion of her marriage, her jewels were the universal theme of admiration. For Virginia received the coronet, which is the reward of all good little American girls, and was married to her boy-lover as soon as he came of age. They were both so charming, and they loved each other so much, that every one was delighted at the match, except the old Marchioness of Dumbleton, who had tried to catch the Duke for one of her seven unmarried daughters, and had given no less than three expensive dinner-parties for that purpose, and, strange to say, Mr. Otis himself. Mr. Otis was extremely fond of the young Duke personally, but, theoretically, he objected to titles, and, to use his own words, 'was not without apprehension lest, amid the enervating influences of a pleasure-loving aristocracy, the true principles of republican simplicity should be forgotten.' His objections, however, were completely overruled, and I believe that when he walked up the aisle of St. George's, Hanover Square, with his daughter leaning on his arm, there was not a prouder man in the whole length and breadth of England.

The Duke and Duchess, after the honeymoon was over, went down to Canterville Chase, and on the day after their arrival they walked over in the afternoon to the lonely churchyard by the pine-woods. There had been a great deal of difficulty at first about the inscription on Sir Simon's tombstone, but finally it had been decided to engrave on it simply the initials of the old gentleman's name, and the verse from the library window. The Duchess had brought with her some lovely roses, which she strewed upon the grave, and after they had stood by it for some time they strolled into the ruined chancel of the old abbey. There the Duchess sat down on a fallen pillar, while her husband lay at her feet smoking a cigarette and looking up at her beautiful eyes. Suddenly he threw his cigarette away, took hold of her hand, and said to her, 'Virginia, a wife should have no secrets from her husband.'

'Dear Cecil! I have no secrets from you.'

'Yes, you have,' he answered, smiling, 'you have never told me what happened to you when you were locked up with the ghost.'

'I have never told any one, Cecil,' said Virginia gravely.

'I know that, but you might tell me.'

'Please don't ask me, Cecil, I cannot tell you. Poor Sir Simon! I owe him a great deal. Yes, don't laugh, Cecil, I really do. He made me see what Life is, and what Death signifies, and why Love is stronger than both.'

The Duke rose and kissed his wife lovingly.

'You can have your secret as long as I have your heart,' he murmured.

'You have always had that, Cecil.'

'And you will tell our children some day, won't you?'

Virginia blushed.

THE ORANGE-MAN; OR, THE HONEST BOY AND THE THIEF

BY MARIA EDGEWORTH

Charles was the name of the honest boy; and Ned was the name of the thief. Charles never touched what was not his own: *this* is being an honest boy.

Ned often took what was not his own: this is being a thief.

Charles's father and mother, when he was a very little boy, had taught him to be honest, by always punishing him when he meddled with what was not his own: but when Ned took what was not his own, his father and mother did not punish him; so he grew up to be a thief.

Early one summer's morning, as Charles was going along the road to school, he met a man leading a horse, which was laden with panniers.

The man stopped at the door of a public-house which was by the road side; and he said to the landlord, who came to the door, "I won't have my horse unloaded; I shall only stop with you whilst I eat my breakfast.—Give my horse to some one to hold here on the road, and let the horse have a little hay to eat."

The landlord called; but there was no one in the way; so he beckoned to Charles, who was going by, and begged him to hold the horse.

"Oh," said the man, "but can you engage him to be an honest boy? for these are oranges in my baskets; and it is not every little boy one can leave with oranges."

"Yes," said the landlord, "I have known Charles from the cradle upwards, and I never caught him in a lie or a theft; all the parish knows him to be an honest boy; I'll engage your oranges will be as safe with him as if you were by yourself."

"Can you so?" said the orange man; "then I'll engage, my lad, to give you the finest orange in my basket, when I come from breakfast, if you'll watch the rest whilst I am away."—

"Yes," said Charles, "I *will* take care of your oranges."

So the man put the bridle into his hand, and he went into the house to eat his breakfast.

Charles had watched the horse and the oranges about five minutes, when he saw one of his school-fellows coming towards him. As he came nearer, Charles saw that it was Ned.

Ned stopped as he passed, and said, "Good-morrow to you, Charles; what are you doing there? whose horse is that? and what have you got in the baskets?"

"There are oranges in the baskets," said Charles; "and a man, who has just gone into the inn, here, to eat his breakfast, bid me take care of them, and so I did; because he said he would give me an orange when he came back again."

"An orange!" cried Ned; "are you to have a whole orange?—I wish I was to have one! However, let me look how large they are." Saying this, Ned went towards the pannier, and lifted up the cloth that covered it. "La! what fine oranges!" he exclaimed, the moment he saw them: "Let me touch them, to feel if they are ripe."

"No," said Charles, "you had better not; what signifies it to you whether they are ripe, you know, since you are not to eat them. You should not meddle with them; they are not yours—You must not touch them."

"Not touch them! surely," said Ned, "there's no harm in *touching* them. You don't think I mean to steal them, I suppose." So Ned put his hand into the orange-man's basket, and he took up an orange, and he felt it; and when he had felt it, he smelled it. "It smells very sweet," said he, "and it feels very ripe; I long to taste it; I will only just suck one drop of juice at the top." Saying these words, he put the orange to his mouth.

Little boys, who wish to be honest, beware of temptation; do not depend too much upon yourselves; and remember, that it is easier to resolve to do right at first, than at last. People are led on, by little and little, to do wrong.

The *sight* of the oranges tempted Ned to *touch* them; the touch tempted him to *smell* them; and the smell tempted him to *taste* them.

"What are you about, Ned?" cried Charles, taking hold of his arm. "You said, you only wanted to smell the orange; do, put it down, for shame!"

"Don't say *for shame* to me," cried Ned, in a surly tone; "the oranges are not yours, Charles!"

"No, they are not mine; but I promised to take care of them, and so I will:—so put down that orange!"

"Oh, if it comes to that, I won't," said Ned, "and let us see who can make me, if I don't choose it;—I'm stronger than you."

"I am not afraid of you for all that," replied Charles, "for I am in the right." Then he snatched the orange out of Ned's hand, and he pushed him with all his force from the basket.

Ned, immediately returning, hit him a violent blow, which almost stunned him.

Still, however, this good boy, without minding the pain, persevered in defending what was left in his care; he still held the bridle with one hand, and covered the basket with his other arm, as well as he could.

Ned struggled in vain, to get his hands into the pannier again; he could not; and, finding that he could not win by strength, he had recourse to cunning. So he pretended to be out of breath and to desist; but he meant, as soon as Charles looked away, to creep softly round to the basket, on the other side.

Cunning people, though they think themselves very wise, are almost always very silly.

Ned, intent upon one thing, the getting round to steal the oranges, forgot that if he went too close to the horse's heels, he should startle him. The horse indeed, disturbed by the bustle near him, had already left off eating his hay, and began to put down his ears; but when he felt something touch his hind legs, he gave a sudden kick, and Ned fell backwards, just as he had seized the orange.

Ned screamed with the pain; and at the scream all the people came out of the public house to see what was the matter; and amongst them came the orange-man.

Ned was now so much ashamed, that he almost forgot the pain, and wished to run away; but he was so much hurt, that he was obliged to sit down again.

The truth of the matter was soon told by Charles, and as soon believed by all the people present who knew him: for he had the character of being an honest boy; and Ned was known to be a thief and a liar.

So nobody pitied Ned for the pain he felt. "He deserves it," says one. "Why did he meddle with what was not his own?"—"Pugh! he is not much hurt, I'll answer for it," said another. "And if he was, it's a lucky kick for him, if it keeps him from the gallows," says a third. Charles was the only person who said nothing; he helped Ned away to a bank: for brave boys are always good-natured.

"Oh, come here," said the orange-man, calling him; "Come here, my honest lad! What! You got that black eye in keeping my oranges, did you?—That's a stout little fellow," said he, taking him by the hand, and leading him into the midst of the people.

Men, women, and children, had gathered around, and all the children fixed their eyes upon Charles, and wished to be in his place.

In the mean time, the orange-man took Charles's hat off his head, and filled it with fine China oranges. "There, my little friend," said he, "take them, and God bless you with them! If I could but afford it, you should have all that is in my basket."

Then the people, and especially the children, shouted for joy; but as soon as there was silence, Charles said to the orange-man, "Thank'e, master, with all my heart; but I can't take your oranges, only that one I earned; take the rest back again: as for a black eye, that's nothing! but I won't be paid for it; no more than for doing what's honest. So I can't take your oranges, master; but I thank you as much as if I had them." Saying these words, Charles offered to pour the oranges back into the basket; but the man would not let him.

"Then," said Charles, "if they are honestly mine, I may give them away;" so he emptied the hat amongst the children, his companions. "Divide them amongst you," said he; and without waiting for their thanks, he pressed through the crowd, and ran towards home. The children all followed him, clapping their hands, and thanking him.

The little thief came limping after. Nobody praised him, nobody thanked him; he had no oranges to eat, nor had he any to give away. *People must be honest, before they can be generous.* Ned sighed as he went towards home; "And all this," said he to himself, "was for one orange; it was not worth while."

No: it is never worth while to do wrong.

Little boys who read this story, consider which would you rather have been, *the honest boy*, or *the thief.*

THE PRIEST'S SOUL

BY LADY WILDE

In former days there were great schools in Ireland, where every sort of learning was taught to the people, and even the poorest had more knowledge at that time than many a gentleman has now. But as to the priests, their learning was above all, so that the fame of Ireland went over the whole world, and many kings from foreign lands used to send their sons all the way to Ireland to be brought up in the Irish schools.

Now, at this time there was a little boy learning at one of them who was a wonder to everyone for his cleverness. His parents were only labouring people, and of course poor; but young as he was, and as poor as he was, no king's or lord's son could come up to him in learning. Even the masters were put to shame; for when they were trying to teach him he would tell them something they never heard of before, and show them their ignorance. One of his great triumphs was in argument; and he would go on till he proved to you that black was white, and then when you gave in, for no one could beat him in talk, he would turn round and show you that white was black, or maybe that there was no colour at all in the world. When he grew up his poor father and mother were so proud of him that they resolved to make him a priest, which they did at last, though they nearly starved themselves to get the money. Well, such another learned man was not in Ireland, and he was as great in argument as ever, so that no one could stand before him. Even the bishops tried to talk to him, but he showed them at once they knew nothing at all.

Now, there were no schoolmasters in those times, but it was the priests taught the people; and as this man was the cleverest in Ireland, all the foreign kings sent their sons to him, as long as he had house-room to give them. So he grew very proud, and began to forget how low he had been, and worst of all, even to forget God, who had made him what he was. And the pride of arguing got hold of him, so that from one thing to another he went on to prove that there was no Purgatory, and then no Hell, and then no Heaven, and then no God; and at last that men had no souls, but were no more than a dog or a cow, and when they died there was an end of them. "Whoever saw a soul?" he would say. "If you can show me one, I will believe." No one could make any answer to this; and at last they all came to believe that as there was no other world, everyone might do what they liked in this; the priest setting the example, for he took a beautiful young girl to wife. But as no priest or bishop in the whole land could be got to marry them, he was obliged to read the service over for himself. It was a great scandal, yet no one dared to say a word, for all the king's sons were on his side, and would have slaughtered anyone who tried to prevent his wicked goings-on. Poor boys; they all believed in him, and thought every word he said was the truth. In this way his notions began to spread about, and the whole world was going to the bad, when one night an angel came down from Heaven, and told the priest he had but twenty-four hours to live.

He began to tremble, and asked for a little more time.

But the angel was stiff, and told him that could not be.

"What do you want time for, you sinner?" he asked.

"Oh, sir, have pity on my poor soul!" urged the priest.

"Oh, no! You have a soul, then," said the angel. "Pray, how did you find that out?"

"It has been fluttering in me ever since you appeared," answered the priest. "What a fool I was not to think of it before."

"A fool, indeed," said the angel. "What good was all your learning, when it could not tell you that you had a soul?"

"Ah, my lord," said the priest, "If I am to die, tell me how soon I may be in Heaven?"

"Never," replied the angel. "You denied there was a Heaven."

"Then, my lord, may I go to Purgatory?"

"You denied Purgatory also; you must go straight to Hell," said the angel.

"But, my lord, I denied Hell also," answered the priest, "so you can't send me there either."

The angel was a little puzzled.

"Well," said he, "I'll tell you what I can do for you. You may either live now on earth for a hundred years, enjoying every pleasure, and then be cast into Hell for ever; or you may die in twenty-four hours in the most horrible torments, and pass through Purgatory, there to remain till the Day of Judgment, if only you can find some one person that believes, and through his belief mercy will be vouchsafed to you, and your soul will be saved."

The priest did not take five minutes to make up his mind.

"I will have death in the twenty-four hours," he said, "so that my soul may be saved at last."

On this the angel gave him directions as to what he was to do, and left him.

Then immediately the priest entered the large room where all the scholars and the kings' sons were seated, and called out to them—

"Now, tell me the truth, and let none fear to contradict me; tell me what is your belief—have men souls?"

"Master," they answered, "once we believed that men had souls; but thanks to your teaching, we believe so no longer. There is no Hell, and no Heaven, and no God. This is our belief, for it is thus you taught us."

Then the priest grew pale with fear, and cried out—"Listen! I taught you a lie. There is a God, and man has an immortal soul. I believe now all I denied before."

But the shouts of laughter that rose up drowned the priest's voice, for they thought he was only trying them for argument.

"Prove it, master," they cried. "Prove it. Who has ever seen God? Who has ever seen the soul?"

And the room was stirred with their laughter.

The priest stood up to answer them, but no word could he utter. All his eloquence, all his powers of argument had gone from him; and he could do nothing but wring his hands and cry out, "There is a God! there is a God! Lord have mercy on my soul!"

And they all began to mock him! and repeat his own words that he had taught them—

"Show him to us; show us your God." And he fled from them, groaning with agony, for he saw that none believed; and how, then, could his soul be saved?

But he thought next of his wife. "She will believe," he said to himself; "women never give up God."

And he went to her; but she told him that she believed only what he taught her, and that a good wife should believe in her husband first and before and above all things in Heaven or earth.

Then despair came on him, and he rushed from the house, and began to ask every one he met if they believed. But the same answer came from one and all—"We believe only what you have taught us," for his doctrine had spread far and wide through the country.

Then he grew half mad with fear, for the hours were passing, and he flung himself down on the ground in a lonesome spot, and wept and groaned in terror, for the time was coming fast when he must die.

Just then a little child came by. "God save you kindly," said the child to him.

The priest started up.

"Do you believe in God?" he asked.

"I have come from a far country to learn about him," said the child. "Will your honor direct me to the best school they have in these parts?"

"The best school and the best teacher is close by," said the priest, and he named himself.

"Oh, not to that man," answered the child, "for I am told he denies God, and Heaven, and Hell, and even that man has a soul, because he cannot see it; but I would soon put him down."

The priest looked at him earnestly. "How?" he inquired.

"Why," said the child, "I would ask him if he believed he had life to show me his life."

"But he could not do that, my child," said the priest. "Life cannot be seen; we have it, but it is invisible."

"Then if we have life, though we cannot see it, we may also have a soul, though it is invisible," answered the child.

When the priest heard him speak these words, he fell down on his knees before him, weeping for joy, for now he knew his soul was safe; he had met one at last that believed. And he told the child his whole story—all his wickedness, and pride, and blasphemy against the great God; and how the angel had come to him, and told him of the only way in which he could be saved, through the faith and prayers of someone that believed.

"Now, then," he said to the child, "take this penknife and strike it into my breast, and go on stabbing the flesh until you see the paleness of death on my face. Then watch—for a living thing will soar up from my body as I die, and you will then know that my soul has ascended to the presence of God. And when you see this thing, make haste and run to my school, and call on all my scholars to come and see that the soul of their master has left the body, and that all he taught them was a lie, for that there is a God who punishes sin, and a Heaven, and a Hell, and that man has an immortal soul destined for eternal happiness or misery."

"I will pray," said the child, "to have courage to do this work."

And he kneeled down and prayed. Then when he rose up he took the penknife and struck it into the priest's heart, and struck and struck again till all the flesh was lacerated; but still the priest lived, though the agony was horrible, for he could not die until the twenty-four hours had expired.

At last the agony seemed to cease, and the stillness of death settled on his face.

Then the child, who was watching, saw a beautiful living creature, with four snow-white wings, mount from the dead man's body into the air and go fluttering round his head.

So he ran to bring the scholars; and when they saw it, they all knew it was the soul of their master; and they watched with wonder and awe until it passed from sight into the clouds.

And this was the first butterfly that was ever seen in Ireland; and now all men know that the butterflies are the souls of the dead, waiting for the moment when they may enter Purgatory, and so pass through torture to purification and peace.

But the schools of Ireland were quite deserted after that time, for people said, "What is the use of going so far to learn, when the wisest man in all Ireland did not know if he had a soul till he was near losing it, and was only saved at last through the simple belief of a little child."

THE RISING OF THE MOON

BY JOHN KEEGAN CASEY

"Oh! then tell me, Shawn O'Ferrall, Tell me why you hurry so?"
"Hush ma bouchal, hush and listen," And his cheeks were all a-glow.
"I bear orders from the captain, Get you ready quick and soon,
For the pikes must be together at the risin' of the moon."
At the risin' of the moon, at the risin' of the moon,
For the pikes must be together at the risin' of the moon.

"Oh! then tell me, Shawn O'Ferrall, Where the gatherin' is to be?"
"In the ould spot by the river, Right well known to you and me.
One word more—for signal token Whistle up the marchin' tune,
With your pike upon your shoulder, by the risin' of the moon."
By the risin' of the moon, by the risin' of the moon,
With your pike upon your shoulder, by the risin' of the moon.

Out from many a mudwall cabin Eyes were watching thro' that night,
Many a manly chest was throbbing For the blessed warning light.
Murmurs ran along the valleys Like the banshee's lonely croon,
And a thousand blades were flashing at the risin' of the moon.
At the risin' of the moon, at the risin' of the moon,
And a thousand blades were flashing at the risin' of the moon.

There beside the singing river That dark mass of men was seen,
Far above the shining weapons Hung their own beloved green.

"Death to ev'ry foe and traitor! Forward! strike the marchin' tune,
And hurrah, my boys, for freedom! 'Tis the risin' of the moon."
'Tis the risin' of the moon, 'Tis the risin' of the moon,
And hurrah my boys for freedom! 'Tis the risin' of the moon.

Well they fought for poor old Ireland, And full bitter was their fate
(Oh! what glorious pride and sorrow Fill the name of Ninety-Eight).
Yet, thank God, e'en still are beating Hearts in manhood's burning noon,
Who would follow in their footsteps, At the risin' of the moon!
At the rising of the moon, at the risin' of the moon,
Who would follow in their footsteps, at the risin' of the moon.

HIGH TEA AT MCKEOWN'S

BY EDITH SOMERVILLE AND MARTIN ROSS

"Papa!" said the youngest Miss Purcell, aged eleven, entering the drawing-room at Mount Purcell in a high state of indignation and a flannel dressing-gown that had descended to her in unbroken line of succession from her eldest sister, "isn't it my turn for the foxy mare to-morrow? Nora had her at Kilmacabee, and it's a rotten shame—"

The youngest Miss Purcell here showed signs of the imminence of tears, and rooted in the torn pocket of the dressing-gown for the hereditary pocket-handkerchief that went with it.

Sir Thomas paused in the act of cutting the end off a long cigar, and said briefly:

"Neither of you'll get her. She's going ploughing the Craughmore."

The youngest Miss Purcell knew as well as her sister Nora that the latter had already commandeered the foxy mare, and, with the connivance of the cowboy, had concealed her in the cow-house; but her sense of tribal honor, stimulated by her sister's threatening eye, withheld her from opening this branch of the subject.

"Well, but Johnny Mulcahy won't plough to-morrow because he's going to the Donovan child's funeral. Tommy Brien's just told me so, and he'll be drunk when he comes back, and tomorrow'll be the first day that Carnage and Trumpeter are going out—"

The youngest Miss Purcell paused, and uttered a loud sob.

"My darling baby," remonstrated Lady Purcell from behind a reading-lamp, "you really ought not to run about the stable-yard at this hour of the night, or, indeed, at any other time!"

"Baby's always bothering to come out hunting," remarked an elder sister, "and you know yourself, mamma, that the last time she came was when she stole the postman's pony, and he had to run all the way to Drinagh, and you said yourself she was to be kept in the next day for a punishment."

"How ready you are with your punishments! What is it to you if she goes out or no?" demanded Sir Thomas, whose temper was always within easy reach.

"She can have the cob, Tom," interposed stout and sympathetic Lady Purcell, on whom the tears of her youngest born were having their wonted effect, "I'll take the donkey chaise if I go out."

"The cob is it?" responded Sir Thomas, in the stalwart brogue in which he usually expressed himself. "The cob has a leg on him as big as your own since the last day one of them had him out!" The master of the house looked round with exceeding disfavor on his eight good-looking daughters. "However, I suppose it's as good to be hanged for a sheep as a lamb, and if you don't want him—"

The youngest Miss Purcell swiftly returned her handkerchief to her pocket, and left the room before any change of opinion was possible.

Mount Purcell was one of those households that deserve to be subsidized by any country neighborhood in consideration of their unfailing supply of topics of conversation. Sir Thomas was a man of old family, of good income and of sufficient education, who, while reserving the power of comporting himself like a gentleman, preferred as a rule to assimilate his demeanor to that of one of his own tenants (with whom, it may be mentioned, he was extremely popular). Many young men habitually dined out on Sir Thomas's brogue and his unwearying efforts to dispose of his eight daughters.

His wife was a handsome, amiable, and by no means unintelligent lady upon whose back the eight daughters had ploughed and had left long furrows. She was not infrequently spoken of as "that un*for*tunate Lady Purcell!" with a greater or less broadening of the accent on the second syllable according to the social standard of the speaker. Her tastes were comprehended and sympathized with by her gardener, and by the clerk at Mudie's who refilled her box. The view taken of her by her husband and family was mainly a negative one, and was tinged throughout by the facts that she was afraid to drive anything more ambitious than the donkey, and had been known to mistake the kennel terrier for a hound puppy. She had succeeded in transmitting to her daughters her very successful complexion and blue eyes, but her responsibility for them had apparently gone no further. The Misses Purcell faced the world and its somewhat excessive interest in them with the intrepid *esprit de corps* of a square of British infantry, but among themselves they fought, as the coachman was wont to say—and no one knew better than the coachman—"both bitther an regular, like man and wife!" They ranged in age from about five and twenty downwards, sportswomen, warriors, and buccaneers, all of them, and it would be difficult to determine whether resentment or a certain secret pride bulked the larger in their male parent's mind in connection with them.

"Are you going to draw Clashnacrona to-morrow?" asked Muriel, the second of the gang (Lady Purcell, it should have been mentioned, had also been responsible for her daughters' names), rising from her chair and pouring what was left of her after dinner coffee into her saucer, a proceeding which caused four pairs of lambent eyes to discover themselves in the coiled mat of red setters that occupied the drawing-room hearthrug.

"No, I am not," said Sir Thomas, "and, what's more, I'm coming in early. I'm a fool to go hunting at all at this time o' year, with half the potatoes not out of the ground." He rose, and using the toe of his boot as the coulter of a plough, made a way for himself among the dogs to the centre of the hearthrug. "Be hanged to these dogs! I declare I don't know am I more plagued with dogs or daughters! Lucy!"

Lady Purcell dutifully disinterred her attention from a catalogue of Dutch bulbs.

"When I get in to-morrow I'll go call on that Local Government Board Inspector who's staying in Drinagh. They tell me he's a very nice fellow and he's rolling in money. I daresay I'll ask him to dinner. He was in the army one time, I believe. They often give these jobs to soldiers. If any of you girls come across him," he continued, bending his fierce eyebrows upon his family, "I'll trouble you to be civil to him and show him none of your infernal airs because he happens to be an Englishman! I hear he's bicycling all over the country and he might come out to see the hounds."

Rosamund, the eldest, delivered herself of an almost imperceptible wink in the direction of Violet, the third of the party. Sir Thomas's diplomacies were thoroughly appreciated by his offspring. "It's time some of you were cleared out from under my feet!" he told them. Nevertheless when, some four or five years before, a subaltern of Engineers engaged on the Government survey of Ireland had laid his career, plus fifty pounds per annum and some impalpable expectations, at the feet of Muriel, the clearance effected by Sir Thomas had been that of Lieutenant Aubrey Hamilton. "Is it marry one of my daughters to that penniless pup!" he had said to Lady Purcell, whose sympathies had, as usual, been on the side of the detrimental. "Upon my honor, Lucy, you're a bigger fool than I thought you—and that's saying a good deal!"

It was near the beginning of September, and but a sleepy half dozen or so of riders had turned out to meet the hounds the following morning, at Liss Cranny Wood. There had been rain during the night and, though it had ceased, a wild wet wind was blowing hard from the north-west. The yellowing beech trees twisted and swung their grey arms in the gale. Hats flew down the wind like driven grouse; Sir Thomas's voice, in the middle of the covert, came to the riders assembled at the cross roads on the outskirts of the wood in gusts, fitful indeed, but not so fitful that Nora, on the distrained foxy mare, was not able to gauge to a nicety the state of his temper. From the fact of her unostentatious position in the rear it might safely be concluded that it, like the wind, was still rising. The riders huddled together in the lee of the trees, their various elements fused in the crucible of Sir Thomas's wrath into a compact and anxious mass. There had been an unusually large entry of puppies that season, and Sir Thomas's temper, never at its best on a morning of cubbing, was making exhaustive demands on his stock of expletives. Rabbits were flying about in every direction, each with a shrieking puppy or two in its wake. Jerry, the Whip, was galloping *ventre à terre* along the road in the vain endeavor to overtake a couple in headlong flight to the farm where they had spent their happier earlier days. At the other side of the wood the Master was blowing himself into apoplexy in the attempt to recall half a dozen who were away in full cry after a cur-dog, and a zealous member of the hunt looked as if he were playing polo with another puppy that doubled and dodged to evade the lash and the duty of getting to covert. Hither and thither among the beech trees went that selection from the Master's family circle, exclusive of the furtive Nora, that had on this occasion taken the field. It was a tradition in the country that there were never fewer than four Miss Purcells out, and that no individual Miss Purcell had more than three days' hunting in the season. Whatever may have been the truth of this, the companion legend that each Miss Purcell slept with two hound puppies in her bed was plausibly upheld by the devotion with which the latter clung to the heels of their nurses.

In the midst of these scenes of disorder an old fox rightly judging that this was no place for him, slid out of the covert, and crossed the road just in front of where Nora, in a blue serge skirt and a red Tam-o'-Shanter cap, lurked on the foxy mare. Close after him came four or five couple of old hounds, and, prominent among her elders, yelped the puppy that had been Nora's special charge. This was not cubbing, and no one knew it better than Nora; but the sight of Carnage among the prophets—Carnage, whose noblest quarry hitherto had been the Mount Purcell turkey-cock—overthrew her scruples. The foxy mare, a ponderous creature, with a mane like a Nubian lion and a mouth like steel, required nearly as much room to turn in as a man-of-war, and while Nora, by vigorous use of her heel and a reliable ash plant, was getting her head round, her sister Muriel, on a raw-boned well-bred colt—Sir Thomas, as he said, made the best of a bad job, and utilized his daughters as roughriders—shot past her down the leafy road, closely followed by a stranger on a weedy bay horse, which Nora instantly recognized as the solitary hireling of the neighborhood.

Through the belt of wood and out into the open country went the five couple, and after them went Muriel, Nora and the strange man. There had been an instant when the colt had thought that it seemed a pity to leave the road, but, none the less, he had the next instant found himself in the air, a considerable distance above a low stone wall, with a tingling streak across his ribs, and a bewildering sensation of having been hustled. The field in which he alighted was a sloping one and he ramped down it very enjoyably to himself, with all the weight of his sixteen hands and a half concentrated in his head, when suddenly a tall grassy bank confronted him, with, as he perceived with horror, a ditch in front of it. He tried to swerve, but there seemed something irrevocable about the way in which the bank faced him, and if his method of "changing feet" was not strictly conventional, he achieved the main point and found all four safely under him when he landed, which was as much—if not more than as much—as either he or Muriel expected. The Miss Purcells were a practical people, and were thankful for minor mercies.

It was at about this point that the stranger on the hireling drew level; he had not been at the meet, and Muriel turned her head to see who it was that was kicking old McConnell's screw along so well. He lifted his cap, but he was certainly a stranger. She saw a discreetly clipped and pointed brown beard, with a rather long and curling moustache.

"Fed on furze!" thought Muriel, with a remembrance of the foxy mare's upper lip when she came in "off the hill."

Then she met the strange man's eyes—was he quite a stranger? What was it about the greeny-grey gleam of them that made her heart give a curious lift, and then sent the color running from it to her face and back again to her heart?

"I thought you were going to cut me—Muriel!" said the strange man.

In the meantime the five couple and Carnage were screaming down the heathery side of Liss Cranny Hill, on a scent that was a real comfort to them after nearly five miserable months of kennels and road-work, and a glorious wind under their sterns. Jerry, the Whip, was riding like a madman to stop them; they knew that well, and went the faster for it. Sir Thomas was blowing his horn inside out. But Jerry was four fields behind, and Sir Thomas was on the wrong side of the wood, and Miss Muriel and the strange gentleman were coming on for all they were worth, and were as obviously bent on having a good time as they were. Carnage flung up her handsome head and squealed with pure joy, as she pitched herself over the big bounds fence at the foot of the hill, and flopped across the squashy ditch on the far side. There was grass under her now, beautiful firm dairy grass, and that entrancing perfume was lying on it as thick as butter—Oh! it was well to be hunting! thought Carnage, with another most childish shriek, legging it after her father and mother and several other blood relations in a way that did Muriel's heart good to see.

The fox, as good luck would have it, had chosen the very pick of Sir Thomas's country, and Muriel and the stranger had it all to themselves. She looked over her shoulder. Away back in a half-dug potato field Nora and a knot of laborers were engaged in bitter conflict with the foxy mare on the subject of a bank with a rivulet in front of it. To refuse to jump running water had been from girlhood the resolve of the foxy mare; it was plain that neither Nora's ash plant, nor the stalks of rag-wort, torn from the potato ridges, with which the countrymen flagellated her from behind, were likely to make her change her mind. Farther back still were a few specks, motionless apparently, but representing, as Muriel was well aware, the speeding indignant forms of those Miss Purcells who had got left. As for Sir Thomas—well, it was no good going to meet the devil half-way! was the filial reflection; of Sir Thomas's second daughter, as, with a clatter of stones, she and the colt dropped into a road, and charged on over the bank on the other side, the colt leaving a hind leg behind him in it, and sending thereby a clod of earth flying into the stranger's face. The stranger only laughed, and catching hold of the much enduring hireling he drove him level with the colt, and lifted him over the ensuing bank and gripe in a way subsequently described by Jerry as having "covered acres."

But the old fox's hitherto straight neck was getting a twist in it. Possibly he had summered himself rather too well, and found himself a little short of training for the point that he had first fixed on. At all events, he swung steadily round, and headed for the lower end of the long belt of Liss Cranny Wood; and, as he and his pursuers so headed, Retributive Justice, mounted on a large brown horse, very red in the face, and followed by a string of hounds and daughters, galloped steadily toward the returning sinners.

It is probably superfluous to reproduce for sporting readers the exact terms in which an infuriated master of hounds reproves an erring flock. Sir Thomas, even under ordinary circumstances, had a stirring gift of invective. It was currently reported that after each day's hunting Lady Purcell made a house-to-house visitation of conciliation to all subscribers of five pounds and upwards. On this occasion the Master, having ordered his two daughters home without an instant's delay, proceeded to a satiric appreciation of the situation at large and in detail, with general reflections as to the advantage to tailors of sticking to their own trade, and direct references of so pointed a character to the mental abilities of the third delinquent, that that gentleman's self-control became unequal to further strain, and he also retired abruptly from the scene.

Nora and Muriel meanwhile pursued their humbled, but unrepentant, way home. It was blowing as hard as ever. Muriel's hair had only been saved from complete overthrow by two hair-pins yielded, with pelican-like devotion, by a sister. Nora had lost the Tam-o'-Shanter, and had torn her blue serge skirt. The foxy mare had cast a shoe, and the colt was unaffectedly done.

"He's mad for a drink!" said Muriel, as he strained towards the side of the bog road, against which the waters of a small lake, swollen by the recent rains, were washing in little waves under the lash of the wind—"I think I'll let him just wet his mouth."

She slackened the reins, and the thirsty colt eagerly thrust his muzzle into the water. As he did so he took another forward step, and instantly, with a terrific splash, he and his rider were floundering in brown water up to his withers in the ditch below the submerged edge of the road. To Muriel's credit it must be said that she bore this unlooked-for immersion with the nerve of a Baptist convert. In a second she had pulled the colt round parallel with the bank, and in another she had hurled herself from the saddle and was dragging herself, like a wounded otter, up on to the level of the road.

"Well you've done it now, Muriel!" said Nora dispassionately. "How pleased Sir Thomas will be when the colt begins to cough to-morrow morning! He's bound to catch cold out of this. Look out! Here's that man that went the run with us. I'd try and wipe some of the mud off my face if I were you!"

A younger sister of fifteen is not apt to err on the side of over sympathy, but the deficiencies of Nora were more than made up for by the solicitude of the stranger with the pointed beard. He hauled the colt from his watery nest, he dried him down with handfuls of rushes, he wiped the saddle with his own beautiful silk pocket-handkerchief. For a stranger he displayed—so it struck Nora—a surprising knowledge of the locality. He pointed out that Mount Purcell was seven miles away, and that the village of Drinagh, where he was putting up—("Oho! so he's the inspector Sir Thomas was going to be so civil to!" thought the younger Miss Purcell with an inward grin)—was only two or three miles away.

"You know, Nora," said Muriel with an unusually conciliatory manner, "it isn't at all out of our way, and the colt *ought* to get a proper rub down and a hot drink."

"I should have thought he'd had about as much to drink as he wanted, hot or cold!" said Nora.

But Nora had not been a younger sister for fifteen years for nothing, and it was for Drinagh that the party steered their course.

Their arrival stirred McKeown's Hotel (so-called) to its depths. Destiny had decreed that Mrs. McKeown, being, as she expressed it, "an epicure about boots," should choose this day of all others to go to "town" to buy herself a pair, leaving the direction of the hotel in the hands of her husband, a person of minor importance, and of Mary Ann Whooly, a grey-haired kitchen-maid, who milked the cows and made the beds, and at a distance in the back-yard was scarcely distinguishable from the surrounding heaps of manure.

The Inspector's hospitality knew no limits, and failed to recognize that those of McKeown's Hotel were somewhat circumscribed. He ordered hot whisky and water, mutton chops, dry clothes for Miss Purcell, fires, tea, buttered toast, poached eggs and other delicacies simultaneously and immediately, and the voice of Mary Ann Whooly imploring Heaven's help for herself and its vengeance upon her inadequate assistants was heard far in the streets of Drinagh.

"Sure herself" (herself was Mrs. McKeown) "has her box locked agin me, and I've no clothes but what's on me!" she protested, producing after a long interval a large brown shawl and a sallow-complexioned blanket, "but the Captain's after sending these. Faith, they'll do ye grand! Arrah, why not, asthore! Sure he'll never look at ye!"

These consisted of a long covert coat, a still longer pair of yellow knitted stockings, and a pair of pumps.

"Sure they're the only best we have," continued Mary Ann Whooly, pooling, as it were, her wardrobe with that of the lodger. "God's will must be, Miss Muriel, my darlin' gerr'l!"

It says a good deal for the skill of Nora as a tire-woman that her sister's appearance ten minutes afterwards was open to no reproach, save possibly that of eccentricity, and the Inspector's gaze—which struck the tire-woman as being of a singularly enamored character for so brief an acquaintance—was so firmly fixed upon her sister's countenance that nothing else seemed to signify. It was by this time past two o'clock, and the repast, which arrived in successive relays, had, at all events, the merit of combining the leading features of breakfast, lunch and afternoon tea in one remarkable procession. Julia Connolly, having inaugurated the entertainment with tumblers of dark brown steaming whisky and water, was impelled from strength to strength by her growing sense of the greatness of the occasion, and it would be hard to say whether the younger Miss Purcell was more gratified by the mound of feather-light pancakes which followed on the tea and buttered toast, or by the almost cringing politeness of her elder sister.

"How civil she is!" thought Nora scornfully; "for all she's so civil she'll have to lend me her saddle next week, or I'll tell them the whole story!" (Them meant the sisterhood.) "I bet he was holding her hand just before the pancakes came in!"

At about this time Lady Purcell, pursuing her peaceful way home in her donkey chaise, was startled by the sound of neighing and by the rattle of galloping hoofs behind her, and her consternation may be imagined when the foxy mare and the colt, saddled but riderless, suddenly ranged up one on either side of her chaise. Having stopped themselves with one or two prodigious bounds that sent the mud flying in every direction, they proceeded to lively demonstrations of friendship towards the donkey, which that respectable animal received with every symptom of annoyance. Lady Purcell had never in her life succeeded in knowing one horse from another, and what horses these were she had not the faintest idea; but the side saddles were suggestive of her Amazon brood; she perceived that one of the horses had been under water, and by the time she had arrived at her own hall door, with the couple still in close attendance upon her, anxiety as to the fate of her daughters and exhaustion from much scourging of the donkey, upon whom the heavy coquetries of the foxy mare had had a most souring effect, rendered the poor lady but just capable of asking if Sir Thomas had returned.

"He is, my Lady, but he's just after going down to the farm, and he's going on to call on the English gentleman that's at Mrs. McKeown's."

"And the young ladies?" gasped Lady Purcell.

The answer suited with her fears. Lady Purcell was not wont to take the initiative, still less one of her husband's horses, without his approval; but the thought of the saturated side-saddle lent her decision, and as soon as a horse and trap could be got ready she set forth for Drinagh.

It need not for a moment be feared that such experienced campaigners as the Misses Muriel and Nora Purcell had forgotten that their father had settled to call upon their temporary host, what time the business of the morning should be ended, or that they had not arranged a sound scheme of retirement, but when the news was brought to them that during the absence of the stable-boy—"to borrow a half score of eggs and a lemon for pancakes," it was explained—their horses had broken forth from the cow-shed and disappeared, it may be admitted that even their stout hearts quailed.

"Oh, it will be all right!" the Inspector assured them, with the easy optimism of the looker-on in domestic tragedy; "your father will see there was nothing else for you to do."

"That's all jolly fine," returned Nora, "but *I'm* going out to borrow Casey's car" (Casey was the butcher), "and I'll just tell old Mary Ann to keep a sharp look out for Sir Thomas, and give us warning in time."

It is superfluous to this simple tale to narrate the conversation that befell on the departure of Nora. It was chiefly of a retrospective character, with disquisitions on such abstractions as the consolations that sometimes follow on the loss of a wealthy great-aunt, the difficulties of shaving with a "tennis elbow," the unchanging quality of certain emotions. This later topic was still under discussion when Nora burst into the room.

"Here's Sir Thomas!" she panted. "Muriel, fly! There's no time to get downstairs, but Mary Ann Whooly said we could go into the room off this sitting-room till he's gone."

Flight is hardly the term to be applied to the second Miss Purcell's retreat, and it says a good deal for the Inspector's mental collapse that he saw nothing ludicrous in her retreating back, clad as it was in his own covert coat, with a blanket like the garment of an Indian brave trailing beneath it. Nora tore open a door near the fireplace, and revealed a tiny room containing a table, a broken chair, and a heap of feathers near an old feather bed on the floor.

"Get in, Muriel!" she cried.

They got in, and as the door closed on them Sir Thomas entered the room.

During the morning the identity of the stranger on whom he had poured the vials of his wrath, with the Local Government Board Inspector whom he was prepared to be delighted to honor, had been brought home to Sir Thomas, and nothing could have been more handsome and complete than the apology that he now tendered. He generously admitted the temptation endured in seeing hounds get away with a good fox on a day devoted to cubbing, and even went so far as to suggest that possibly Captain Clarke—

"Hamilton-Clarke," said the Inspector.

"Had ridden so hard in order to stop them."

"Er—quite so," said the Inspector.

Something caused the dressing-room door to rattle, and Captain Hamilton-Clarke grew rather red.

"My wife and I hope," continued Sir Thomas, urbanely, "that you will come over to dine with us to-morrow evening, or possibly to-night."

He stopped. A trap drove rapidly up to the door, and Lady Purcell's voice was heard agitatedly inquiring "if Miss Muriel and Miss Nora were there? Casey had just told her—"

The rest of the sentence was lost.

"Why, that *is* my wife!" said Sir Thomas. "What the deuce does she want here?"

A strange sound came from behind the door of the dressing-room: something between a stifled cry and a laugh. The Inspector's ears became as red as blood. Then from within there was heard a sort of rush, and something fell against the door. There followed a wholly uncontrolled yell and a crash, and the door was burst open.

It has, I think, been mentioned that in the corner of the dressing-room in which the Misses Purcell had taken refuge there was on the floor the remains of a feather bed. The feathers had come out through a ragged hole in one corner of it; Nora, in the shock of hearing of Lady Purcell's arrival, trod on the corner of the bed and squeezed more of the feathers out of it. A gush of fluff was the result, followed by a curious and unaccountable movement in the bed, and then from the hole there came forth a corpulent and very mangy old rat. Its face was grey and scaly, and horrid pink patches adorned its fat person. It gave one beady glance at Nora, and proceeded with hideous composure to lope heavily across the floor towards the hole in the wall by which it had at some bygone time entered the room. But the hole had been nailed up, and as the rat turned to seek another way of escape the chair upon which Muriel had incontinently sprung broke down, depositing her and her voluminous draperies on top of the rat.

I cannot feel that Miss Purcell is to be blamed that at this moment all power of self-control, of reason almost, forsook her. Regardless of every other consideration, she snatched the blankets and the covert-coat skirts into one massive handful, and with, as has been indicated, a yell of housemaid stridency, flung herself against the door and dashed into the sitting-room, closely followed by Nora, and rather less closely by the rat. The latter alone retained its presence of mind, and without an instant's delay hurried across the room and retired by the half-open door. Immediately from the narrow staircase there arose a series of those acclaims that usually attend the progress of royalty, and, in even an intenser degree, of rats. There came a masculine shout, a shrill and ladylike scream, a howl from Mary Ann Whooly, accompanied by the clang and rattle of a falling coal box, and then Lady Purcell, pale and breathless, appeared at the doorway of the sitting-room.

"Sure the young lady isn't in the house at all, your ladyship!" cried the pursuing voice of Mary Ann Whooly, faithful, even at this supreme crisis, to a lost cause.

Lady Purcell heard her not. She was aware only of her daughter Muriel, attired like a scarecrow in a cold climate, and of the attendant fact that the arm of the Local Government Board Inspector was encircling Muriel's waist, as far as circumstances and a brown woolen shawl would permit. Nora, leaning halfway out of the window, was calling at the top of her voice for Sir Thomas's terrier; Sir Thomas was very loudly saying nothing in particular, much as an angry elderly dog barks into the night. Lady Purcell wildly concluded that the party was rehearsing a charade—the last scene of a very vulgar charade.

"Muriel!" she exclaimed, "*what* have you got on you? And who—" She paused and stared at the Inspector. "Good gracious!" she cried, "why, it's Aubrey Hamilton!"

TEIG O'KANE AND THE CORPSE

BY DOUGLAS HYDE

There was once a grown-up lad in the County Leitrim, and he was strong and lively, and the son of a rich farmer. His father had plenty of money, and he did not spare it on the son. Accordingly, when the boy grew up he liked sport better than work, and, as his father had no other children, he loved this one so much that he allowed him to do in everything just as it pleased himself. He was very extravagant, and he used to scatter the gold money as another person would scatter the white. He was seldom to be found at home, but if there was a fair, or a race, or a gathering within ten miles of him, you were dead certain to find him there. And he seldom spent a night in his father's house, but he used to be always out rambling, and, like Shawn Bwee long ago, there was "the love of every girl in the breast of his shirt," and it's many's the kiss he got and he gave, for he was very handsome, and there wasn't a girl in the country but would fall in love with him, only for him to fasten his two eyes on her, and it was for that someone made this *rann* on him—

> "Feuch an rógaire 'g iarraidh póige,
> Ni h-iongantas mór é a bheith mar atá
> Ag leanamhaint a gcómhnuidhe d'árnán na gráineóige
> Anuas 's anios 's nna chodladh 'sa' lá."

i.e.—"Look at the rogue, its for kisses he's rambling,
> It isn't much wonder, for that was his way;
> He's like an old hedgehog, at night he'll be scrambling
> From this place to that, but he'll sleep in the day."

At last he became very wild and unruly. He wasn't to be seen day nor night in his father's house, but always rambling or going on his *kailee* (night-visit) from place to place and from house to house, so that the old people used to shake their heads and say to one another, "it's easy seen what will happen to the land when the old man dies; his son will run through it in a year, and it won't stand him that long itself."

He used to be always gambling and card-playing and drinking, but his father never minded his bad habits, and never punished him. But it happened one day that the old man was told that the son had ruined the character of a girl in the neighborhood, and he was greatly angry, and he called the son to him, and said to him, quietly and sensibly—"Avic," says he, "you know I loved you greatly up to this, and I never stopped you from doing your choice thing whatever it was, and I kept plenty of money with you, and I always hoped to leave you the house and land, and all I had after myself would be gone; but I heard a story of you to-day that has disgusted me with you. I cannot tell you the grief that I felt when I heard such a thing of you, and I tell you now plainly that unless you marry that girl I'll leave house and land and everything to my brother's son. I never could leave it to anyone who would make so bad a use of it as you do yourself, deceiving women and coaxing girls. Settle with yourself now whether you'll marry that girl and get my land as a fortune with her, or refuse to marry her and give up all that was coming to you; and tell me in the morning which of the two things you have chosen."

"Och! *Domnoo Sheery*! father, you wouldn't say that to me, and I such a good son as I am. Who told you I wouldn't marry the girl?" says he.

But his father was gone, and the lad knew well enough that he would keep his word too; and he was greatly troubled in his mind, for as quiet and as kind as the father was, he never went back of a word that he had once said, and there wasn't another man in the country who was harder to bend than he was.

The boy did not know rightly what to do. He was in love with the girl indeed, and he hoped to marry her sometime or other, but he would much sooner have remained another while as he was, and follow on at his old tricks—drinking, sporting, and playing cards; and, along with that, he was angry that his father should order him to marry, and should threaten him if he did not do it.

"Isn't my father a great fool," says he to himself. "I was ready enough, and only too anxious, to marry Mary; and now since he threatened me, faith I've a great mind to let it go another while."

His mind was so much excited that he remained between two notions as to what he should do. He walked out into the night at last to cool his heated blood, and went on to the road. He lit a pipe, and as the night was fine he walked and walked on, until the quick pace made him begin to forget his trouble. The night was bright, and the moon half full. There was not a breath of wind blowing, and the air was calm and mild. He walked on for nearly three hours, when he suddenly remembered that it was late in the night, and time for him to turn. "Musha! I think I forgot myself," says he; "it must be near twelve o'clock now."

The word was hardly out of his mouth, when he heard the sound of many voices, and the trampling of feet on the road before him. "I don't know who can be out so late at night as this, and on such a lonely road," said he to himself.

He stood listening, and he heard the voices of many people talking through other, but he could not understand what they were saying. "Oh, wirra!" says he, "I'm afraid. It's not Irish or English they have; it can't be they're Frenchmen!" He went on a couple of yards further, and he saw well enough by the light of the moon a band of little people coming towards him, and they were carrying something big and heavy with them. "Oh, murder!" says he to himself, "sure it can't be that they're the good people that's in it!" Every *rib* of hair that was on his head stood up, and there fell a shaking on his bones, for he saw that they were coming to him fast.

He looked at them again, and perceived that there were about twenty little men in it, and there was not a man at all of them higher than about three feet or three feet and a half, and some of them were grey, and seemed very old. He looked again, but he could not make out what was the heavy thing they were carrying until they came up to him, and then they all stood round about him. They threw the heavy thing down on the road, and he saw on the spot that it was a dead body.

He became as cold as the Death, and there was not a drop of blood running in his veins when an old little grey *maneen* came up to him and said, "Isn't it lucky we met you, Teig O'Kane?"

Poor Teig could not bring out a word at all, nor open his lips, if he were to get the world for it, and so he gave no answer.

"Teig O'Kane," said the little grey man again, "isn't it timely you met us?"

Teig could not answer him.

"Teig O'Kane," says he, "the third time, isn't it lucky and timely that we met you?"

But Teig remained silent, for he was afraid to return an answer, and his tongue was as if it was tied to the roof of his mouth.

The little grey man turned to his companions, and there was joy in his bright little eye. "And now," says he, "Teig O'Kane hasn't a word, we can do with him what we please. Teig, Teig," says he, "you're living a bad life, and we can make a slave of you now, and you cannot withstand us, for there's no use in trying to go against us. Lift that corpse."

Teig was so frightened that he was only able to utter the two words, "I won't;" for as frightened as he was, he was obstinate and stiff, the same as ever.

"Teig O'Kane won't lift the corpse," said the little *maneen*, with a wicked little laugh, for all the world like the breaking of a *lock* of dry *kippeens*, and with a little harsh voice like the striking of a cracked bell. "Teig O'Kane won't lift the corpse—make him lift it;" and before the word was out of his mouth they had all gathered round poor Teig, and they all talking and laughing through other.

Teig tried to run from them, but they followed him, and a man of them stretched out his foot before him as he ran, so that Teig was thrown in a heap on the road. Then before he could rise up the fairies caught him, some by the hands and some by the feet, and they held him tight, in a way that he could not stir, with his face against the ground. Six or seven of them raised the body then, and pulled it over to him, and left it down on his back. The breast of the corpse was squeezed against Teig's back and shoulders, and the arms of the corpse were thrown around Teig's neck. Then they stood back from him a couple of yards, and let him get up. He rose, foaming at the mouth and cursing, and he shook himself, thinking to throw the corpse off his back. But his fear and his wonder were great when he found that the two arms had a tight hold round his own neck, and that the two legs were squeezing his hips firmly, and that, however strongly he tried, he could not throw it off, any more than a horse can throw off its saddle. He was terribly frightened then, and he thought he was lost. "Ochone! for ever," said he to himself, "it's the bad life I'm leading that has given the good people this power over me. I promise to God and Mary, Peter and Paul, Patrick and Bridget, that I'll mend my ways for as long as I have to live, if I come clear out of this danger—and I'll marry the girl."

The little grey man came up to him again, and said he to him, "Now, Tei-*geen*," says he, "you didn't lift the body when I told you to lift it, and see how you were made to lift it; perhaps when I tell you to bury it you won't bury it until you're made to bury it!"

"Anything at all that I can do for your honor," said Teig, "I'll do it," for he was getting sense already, and if it had not been for the great fear that was on him, he never would have let that civil word slip out of his mouth.

The little man laughed a sort of laugh again. "You're getting quiet now, Teig," says he. "I'll go bail but you'll be quiet enough before I'm done with you. Listen to me now, Teig O'Kane, and if you don't obey me in all I'm telling you to do, you'll repent it. You must carry with you this corpse that is on your back to Teampoll-Démus, and you must bring it into the church with you, and make a grave for it in the very middle of the church, and you must raise up the flags and put them down again the very same way, and you must carry the clay out of the church and leave the place as it was when you came, so that no one could know that there had been anything changed. But that's not all. Maybe that the body won't be allowed to be buried in that church; perhaps some other man has the bed, and, if so, it's likely he won't share it with this one. If you don't get leave to bury it in Teampoll-Démus, you must carry it to Carrick-fhad-vic-Orus, and bury it in the churchyard there; and if you don't get it into that place, take it with you to Teampoll-Ronan; and if that churchyard is closed on you, take it to Imlogue-Fada; and if you're not able to bury it there, you've no more to do than to take it to Kill-Breedya, and you can bury it there without hindrance. I cannot tell you what one of those churches is the one where you will have leave to bury that corpse under the clay, but I know that it will be allowed you to bury him at some church or other of them. If you do this work rightly, we will be thankful to you, and you will have no cause to grieve; but if you are slow or lazy, believe me we shall take satisfaction of you."

When the grey little man had done speaking, his comrades laughed and clapped their hands together. "Glic! Glic! Hwee! Hwee!" they all cried; "go on, go on, you have eight hours before you till daybreak, and if you haven't this man buried before the sun rises, you're lost." They struck a fist and a foot behind on him, and drove him on in the road. He was obliged to walk, and to walk fast, for they gave him no rest.

He thought himself that there was not a wet path, or a dirty *boreen*, or a crooked contrary road in the whole county, that he had not walked that night. The night was at times very dark, and whenever there would come a cloud across the moon he could see nothing, and then he used often to fall. Sometimes he was hurt, and sometimes he escaped, but he was obliged always to rise on the moment and to hurry on. Sometimes the moon would break out clearly, and then he would look behind him and see the little people following at his back. And he heard them speaking amongst themselves, talking and crying out, and screaming like a flock of sea-gulls; and if he was to save his soul he never understood as much as one word of what they were saying.

He did not know how far he had walked, when at last one of them cried out to him, "Stop here!" He stood, and they all gathered round him.

"Do you see those withered trees over there?" says the old boy to him again. "Teampoll-Démus is among those trees, and you must go in there by yourself, for we cannot follow you or go with you. We must remain here. Go on boldly."

Teig looked from him, and he saw a high wall that was in places half broken down, and an old grey church on the inside of the wall, and about a dozen withered old trees scattered here and there round it. There was neither leaf nor twig on any of them, but their bare crooked branches were stretched out like the arms of an angry man when he threatens. He had no help for it, but was obliged to go forward. He was a couple of hundred yards from the church, but he walked on, and never looked behind him until he came to the gate of the churchyard. The old gate was thrown down, and he had no difficulty in entering. He turned then to see if any of the little people were following him, but there came a cloud over the moon, and the night became so dark that he could see nothing. He went into the churchyard, and he walked up the old grassy pathway leading to the church. When he reached the door, he found it locked. The door was large and strong, and he did not know what to do. At last he drew out his knife with difficulty, and stuck it in the wood to try if it were not rotten, but it was not.

"Now," said he to himself, "I have no more to do; the door is shut, and I can't open it."

Before the words were rightly shaped in his own mind, a voice in his ear said to him, "Search for the key on the top of the door, or on the wall."

He started. "Who is that speaking to me?" he cried, turning round; but he saw no one. The voice said in his ear again, "Search for the key on the top of the door, or on the wall."

"What's that?" said he, and the sweat running from his forehead; "who spoke to me?"

"It's I, the corpse, that spoke to you!" said the voice.

"Can you talk?" said Teig.

"Now and again," said the corpse.

Teig searched for the key, and he found it on the top of the wall. He was too much frightened to say any more, but he opened the door wide, and as quickly as he could, and he went in, with the corpse on his back. It was as dark as pitch inside, and poor Teig began to shake and tremble.

"Light the candle," said the corpse.

Teig put his hand in his pocket, as well as he was able, and drew out a flint and steel. He struck a spark out of it, and lit a burnt rag he had in his pocket. He blew it until it made a flame, and he looked round him. The church was very ancient, and part of the wall was broken down. The windows were blown in or cracked, and the timber of the seats was rotten. There were six or seven old iron candlesticks left there still, and in one of these candlesticks Teig found the stump of an old candle, and he lit it. He was still looking round him on the strange and horrid place in which he found himself, when the cold corpse whispered in his ear, "Bury me now, bury me now; there is a spade and turn the ground." Teig looked from him, and he saw a spade lying beside the altar. He took it up, and he placed the blade under a flag that was in the middle of the aisle, and leaning all his weight on the handle of the spade, he raised it. When the first flag was raised it was not hard to raise the others near it, and he moved three or four of them out of their places. The clay that was under them was soft and easy to dig, but he had not thrown up more than three or four shovelfuls, when he felt the iron touch something soft like flesh. He threw up three or four more shovelfuls from around it, and then he saw that it was another body that was buried in the same place.

"I am afraid I'll never be allowed to bury the two bodies in the same hole," said Teig, in his own mind. "You corpse, there on my back," says he, "will you be satisfied if I bury you down here?" But the corpse never answered him a word.

"That's a good sign," said Teig to himself. "Maybe he's getting quiet," and he thrust the spade down in the earth again. Perhaps he hurt the flesh of the other body, for the dead man that was buried there stood up in the grave, and shouted an awful shout. "Hoo! hoo!! hoo!!! Go! go!! go!!! or you're a dead, dead, dead man!" And then he fell back in the grave again. Teig said afterwards, that of all the wonderful things he saw that night, that was the most awful to him. His hair stood upright on his head like the bristles of a pig, the cold sweat ran off his face, and then came a tremor over all his bones, until he thought that he must fall.

But after a while he became bolder, when he saw that the second corpse remained lying quietly there, and he threw in the clay on it again, and he smoothed it overhead and he laid down the flags carefully as they had been before. "It can't be that he'll rise up any more," said he.

He went down the aisle a little further, and drew near to the door, and began raising the flags again, looking for another bed for the corpse on his back. He took up three or four flags and put them aside, and then he dug the clay. He was not long digging until he laid bare an old woman without a thread upon her but her shirt. She was more lively than the first corpse, for he had scarcely taken any of the clay away from about her, when she sat up and began to cry, "Ho, you *bodach* (clown)! Ha, you *bodach*! Where has he been that he got no bed?"

Poor Teig drew back, and when she found that she was getting no answer, she closed her eyes gently, lost her vigor, and fell back quietly and slowly under the clay. Teig did to her as he had done to the man—he threw the clay back on her, and left the flags down overhead.

He began digging again near the door, but before he had thrown up more than a couple of shovelfuls, he noticed a man's hand laid bare by the spade. "By my soul, I'll go no further, then," said he to himself; "what use is it for me?" And he threw the clay in again on it, and settled the flags as they had been before.

He left the church then, and his heart was heavy enough, but he shut the door and locked it, and left the key where he found it. He sat down on a tombstone that was near the door, and began thinking. He was in great doubt what he should do. He laid his face between his two hands, and cried for grief and fatigue, since he was dead certain at this time that he never would come home alive. He made another attempt to loosen the hands of the corpse that were squeezed round his neck, but they were as tight as if they were clamped; and the more he tried to loosen them, the tighter they squeezed him. He was going to sit down once more, when the cold, horrid lips of the dead man said to him, "Carrick-fhad-vic-Orus," and he remembered the command of the good people to bring the corpse with him to that place if he should be unable to bury it where he had been.

He rose up, and looked about him. "I don't know the way," he said.

As soon as he had uttered the word, the corpse stretched out suddenly its left hand that had been tightened round his neck, and kept it pointing out, showing him the road he ought to follow. Teig went in the direction that the fingers were stretched, and passed out of the churchyard. He found himself on an old rutty, stony road, and he stood still again, not knowing where to turn. The corpse stretched out its bony hand a second time, and pointed out to him another road—not the road by which he had come when approaching the old church. Teig followed that road, and whenever he came to a path or road meeting it, the corpse always stretched out its hand and pointed with its fingers, showing him the way he was to take.

Many was the cross-road he turned down, and many was the crooked *boreen* he walked, until he saw from him an old burying-ground at last, beside the road, but there was neither church nor chapel nor any other building in it. The corpse squeezed him tightly, and he stood. "Bury me, bury me in the burying-ground," said the voice.

Teig drew over towards the old burying-place, and he was not more than about twenty yards from it, when, raising his eyes, he saw hundreds and hundreds of ghosts—men, women, and children—sitting on the top of the wall round about, or standing on the inside of it, or running backwards and forwards, and pointing at him, while he could see their mouths opening and shutting as if they were speaking, though he heard no word, nor any sound amongst them at all.

He was afraid to go forward, so he stood where he was, and the moment he stood, all the ghosts became quiet, and ceased moving. Then Teig understood that it was trying to keep him from going in, that they were. He walked a couple of yards forwards, and immediately the whole crowd rushed together towards the spot to which he was moving, and they stood so thickly together that it seemed to him that he never could break through them, even though he had a mind to try. But he had no mind to try it. He went back broken and dispirited, and when he had gone a couple of hundred yards from the burying-ground, he stood again, for he did not know what way he was to go. He heard the voice of the corpse in his ear, saying "Teampoll-Ronan," and the skinny hand was stretched out again, pointing him out the road.

As tired as he was, he had to walk, and the road was neither short nor even. The night was darker than ever, and it was difficult to make his way. Many was the toss he got, and many a bruise they left on his body. At last he saw Teampoll-Ronan from him in the distance, standing in the middle of the burying-ground. He moved over towards it, and thought he was all right and safe, when he saw no ghosts nor anything else on the wall, and he thought he would never be hindered now from leaving his load off him at last. He moved over to the gate, but as he was passing in, he tripped on the threshold. Before he could recover himself, something that he could not see seized him by the neck, by the hands, and by the feet, and bruised him, and shook him, and choked him, until he was nearly dead; and at last he was lifted up, and carried more than a hundred yards from that place, and then thrown down in an old dyke, with the corpse still clinging to him.

He rose up, bruised and sore, but feared to go near the place again, for he had seen nothing the time he was thrown down and carried away.

"You corpse, up on my back," said he, "shall I go over again to the churchyard?"—but the corpse never answered him. "That's a sign you don't wish me to try it again," said Teig.

He was now in great doubt as to what he ought to do, when the corpse spoke in his ear, and said "Imlogue-Fada."

"Oh, murder!" said Teig, "must I bring you there? If you keep me long walking like this, I tell you I'll fall under you."

He went on, however, in the direction the corpse pointed out to him. He could not have told, himself, how long he had been going, when the dead man behind suddenly squeezed him, and said, "There!"

Teig looked from him, and he saw a little low wall, that was so broken down in places that it was no wall at all. It was in a great wide field, in from the road; and only for three or four great stones at the corners, that were more like rocks than stones, there was nothing to show that there was either graveyard or burying-ground there.

"Is this Imlogue-Fada? Shall I bury you here?" said Teig.

"Yes," said the voice.

"But I see no grave or gravestone, only this pile of stones," said Teig.

The corpse did not answer, but stretched out its long fleshless hand, to show Teig the direction in which he was to go. Teig went on accordingly, but he was greatly terrified, for he remembered what had happened to him at the last place. He went on, "with his heart in his mouth," as he said himself afterwards; but when he came to within fifteen or twenty yards of the little low square wall, there broke out a flash of lightning, bright yellow and red, with blue streaks in it, and went round about the wall in one course, and it swept by as fast as the swallow in the clouds, and the longer Teig remained looking at it the faster it went, till at last it became like a bright ring of flame round the old graveyard, which no one could pass without being burnt by it. Teig never saw, from the time he was born, and never saw afterwards, so wonderful or so splendid a sight as that was. Round went the flame, white and yellow and blue sparks leaping out from it as it went, and although at first it had been no more than a thin, narrow line, it increased slowly until it was at last a great broad band, and it was continually getting broader and higher, and throwing out more brilliant sparks, till there was never a color on the ridge of the earth that was not to be seen in that fire; and lightning never shone and flame never flamed that was so shining and so bright as that.

Teig was amazed; he was half dead with fatigue, and he had no courage left to approach the wall. There fell a mist over his eyes, and there came a *soorawn* in his head, and he was obliged to sit down upon a great stone to recover himself. He could see nothing but the light, and he could hear nothing but the whirr of it as it shot round the paddock faster than a flash of lightning.

As he sat there on the stone, the voice whispered once more in his ear, "Kill-Breedya;" and the dead man squeezed him so tightly that he cried out. He rose again, sick, tired, and trembling, and went forwards as he was directed. The wind was cold, and the road was bad, and the load upon his back was heavy, and the night was dark, and he himself was nearly worn out, and if he had had very much farther to go he must have fallen dead under his burden.

At last the corpse stretched out its hand, and said to him, "Bury me there."

"This is the last burying-place," said Teig in his own mind; "and the little grey man said I'd be allowed to bury him in some of them, so it must be this; it can't be but they'll let him in here."

The first faint streak of the *ring of day* was appearing in the east, and the clouds were beginning to catch fire, but it was darker than ever, for the moon was set, and there were no stars.

"Make haste, make haste!" said the corpse; and Teig hurried forward as well as he could to the graveyard, which was a little place on a bare hill, with only a few graves in it. He walked boldly in through the open gate, and nothing touched him, nor did he either hear or see anything. He came to the middle of the ground, and then stood up and looked round him for a spade or shovel to make a grave. As he was turning round and searching, he suddenly perceived what startled him greatly—a newly-dug grave right before him. He moved over to it, and looked down, and there at the bottom he saw a black coffin. He clambered down into the hole and lifted the lid, and found that (as he thought it would be) the coffin was empty. He had hardly mounted up out of the hole, and was standing on the brink, when the corpse, which had clung to him for more than eight hours, suddenly relaxed its hold of his neck, and loosened its shins from round his hips, and sank down with a *plop* into the open coffin.

Teig fell down on his two knees at the brink of the grave, and gave thanks to God. He made no delay then, but pressed down the coffin lid in its place, and threw in the clay over it with his two hands; and when the grave was filled up, he stamped and leaped on it with his feet, until it was firm and hard, and then he left the place.

The sun was fast rising as he finished his work, and the first thing he did was to return to the road, and look out for a house to rest himself in. He found an inn at last, and lay down upon a bed there, and slept till night. Then he rose up and ate a little, and fell asleep again till morning. When he awoke in the morning he hired a horse and rode home. He was more than twenty-six miles from home where he was, and he had come all that way with the dead body on his back in one night.

All the people at his own home thought that he must have left the country, and they rejoiced greatly when they saw him come back. Everyone began asking him where he had been, but he would not tell anyone except his father.

He was a changed man from that day. He never drank too much; he never lost his money over cards; and especially he would not take the world and be out late by himself of a dark night.

He was not a fortnight at home until he married Mary, the girl he had been in love with; and it's at their wedding the sport was, and it's he was the happy man from that day forward, and it's all I wish that we may be as happy as he was.

SOME OF GULLIVER'S ADVENTURES

BY JONATHAN SWIFT

Justly may I say, that I should have lived happy enough in the country, if my littleness had not exposed me to several ridiculous and troublesome accidents; some of which I shall venture to relate. Glumdalclitch often carried me into the gardens of the court in my smaller box, and would sometimes take me out of it, and hold me in her hand, or set me down to walk. I remember, before the dwarf left the queen, he followed us one day into those gardens, and my nurse having set me down, he and I being close together, near some dwarf apple-trees, I must needs show my wit, by a silly allusion between him and the trees, which happens to hold in their language as it does in ours. Whereupon, the malicious rogue, watching his opportunity, when I was walking under one of them, shook it directly over my head, by which a dozen apples, each of them near as large as a Bristol barrel, came tumbling about my ears; one of them hit me on the back as I chanced to stoop, and knocked me down flat on my face; but I received no other hurt, and the dwarf was pardoned at my desire, because I had given the provocation.

Another day, Glumdalclitch left me on a smooth grass plot to divert myself, while she walked at some distance with her governess. In the meantime, there suddenly fell such a violent shower of hail, that I was immediately, by the force of it, struck to the ground; and when I was down, the hailstones gave me such cruel bangs all over the body, as if I had been pelted with tennis-balls; however, I made a shift to creep on all fours, and shelter myself, by lying flat on my face, on the lee-side of a border of lemon-thyme; but so bruised from head to foot, that I could not go abroad in ten days. Neither is that at all to be wondered at, because nature, in that country, observing the same proportion through all her operations, a hailstone is near eighteen hundred times as large as one in Europe; which I can assert upon experience, having been so curious to weigh and measure them.

But a more dangerous accident happened to me in the same garden, when my little nurse, believing she had put me in a secure place (which I often entreated her to do, that I might enjoy my own thoughts), and having left my box at home, to avoid the trouble of carrying it, went to another part of the garden with her governess and some ladies of her acquaintance. While she was absent and out of hearing, a small white spaniel that belonged to one of the chief gardeners, having got by accident into the garden, happened to range near the place where I lay: the dog, following the scent, came directly up, and taking me in his mouth, ran straight to his master wagging his tail, and set me gently on the ground. By good fortune he had been so well taught, that I was carried between his teeth without the least hurt, or even tearing my clothes. But the poor gardener, who knew me well, and had a great kindness for me, was in a terrible fright; he gently took me up in both his hands, and asked me how I did; but I was so amazed and out of breath, that I could not speak a word. In a few minutes I came to myself, and he carried me safe to my little nurse, who, by this time, had returned to the place where she left me, and was in cruel agonies when I did not appear, nor answer when she called. She severely reprimanded the gardener on account of his dog. But the thing was hushed up, and never known at court, for the girl was afraid of the queen's anger; and truly, as to myself, I thought it would not be for my reputation that such a story should go about.

This accident absolutely determined Glumdalclitch never to trust me abroad for the future out of her sight. I had been long afraid of this resolution, and therefore concealed from her some little unlucky adventures, that happened in those times when I was left by myself. Once a kite, hovering over the garden, made a stoop at me, and if I had not resolutely drawn my hanger, and run under a thick espalier, he would have certainly carried me away in his talons. Another time, walking to the top of a fresh molehill, I fell to my neck in the hole, through which that animal had cast up the earth, and coined some lie, not worth remembering, to excuse myself for spoiling my clothes. I likewise broke my right shin against the shell of a snail, which I happened to stumble over, as I was walking alone and thinking of poor England.

I cannot tell whether I were more pleased or mortified to observe, in those solitary walks, that the smaller birds did not appear to be at all afraid of me, but would hop about within a yard's distance, looking for worms and other food, with as much indifference and security as if no creature at all were near them. I remember, a thrush had the confidence to snatch out of my hand, with his bill, a piece of cake that Glumdalclitch had just given me for my breakfast. When I attempted to catch any of these birds, they would boldly turn against me, endeavoring to peck my fingers, which I durst not venture within their reach; and then they would hop back unconcerned, to hunt for worms or snails, as they did before. But one day, I took a thick cudgel, and threw it with all my strength so luckily, at a linnet, that I knocked him down, and seizing him by the neck with both my hands, ran with him in triumph to my nurse. However, the bird, who had only been stunned, recovering himself, gave me so many boxes with his wings, on both sides of my head and body, though I held him at arm's length, and was out of the reach of his claws, that I was twenty times thinking to let him go. But I was soon relieved by one of our servants, who wrung off the bird's neck, and I had him next day for dinner, by the queen's command. This linnet, as near as I can remember, seemed to be somewhat larger than an English swan.

One day, a young gentleman, who was nephew to my nurse's governess, came and pressed them both to see an execution. It was of a man who had murdered one of that gentleman's intimate acquaintance. Glumdalclitch was prevailed on to be of the company, very much against her inclination, for she was naturally tender-hearted; and as for myself, although I abhorred such kind of spectacles, yet my curiosity tempted me to see something that I thought must be extraordinary. The malefactor was fixed on a chair upon a scaffold erected for that purpose, and his head cut off at one blow, with a sword of about forty feet long. The veins and arteries spouted up such a prodigious quantity of blood, and so high in the air, that the great fountain at Versailles was not equal for the time it lasted; and the head, when it fell on the scaffold floor, gave such a bounce as made me start, although I were at least half an English mile distant.

The queen, who often used to hear me talk of my sea-voyages, and took all occasions to divert me when I was melancholy, asked me whether I understood how to handle a sail or an oar, and whether a little exercise of rowing might not be convenient for my health? I answered that I understood both very well: for although my proper employment had been to be surgeon or doctor to the ship, yet often, upon a pinch, I was forced to work like a common mariner. But I could not see how this could be done in their country, where the smallest wherry was equal to a first-rate man-of-war among us; and such a boat as I could manage would never live in one of their rivers. Her Majesty said, if I would contrive a boat, her own joiner should make it, and she would provide a place for me to sail in. The fellow was an ingenious workman, and by my instructions, in ten days, finished a pleasure-boat, with all its tackling, able conveniently to hold eight Europeans. When it was finished, the queen was so delighted that she ran with it in her lap to the king, who ordered it to be put into a cistern full of water, with me in it, by way of trial; where I could not manage my two sculls, or little oars, for want of room. But the queen had before contrived another project. She ordered the joiner to make a wooden trough of three hundred feet long, fifty broad, and eight deep; which, being well pitched to prevent leaking, was placed on the floor along the wall, in an outer room of the palace. It had a cock near the bottom to let out the water, when it began to grow stale; and two servants could easily fill it in half an hour. Here I often used to row for my own diversion, as well as that of the queen and her ladies, who thought themselves well entertained with my skill and agility. Sometimes I would put up my sail and then my business was only to steer, while the ladies gave me a gale with their fans; and when they were weary, some of their pages would blow my sail forward with their breath, while I showed my art by steering starboard or larboard as I pleased. When I had done, Glumdalclitch always carried back my boat into her closet, and hung it on a nail to dry.

In this exercise I once met an accident, which had like to have cost me my life; for, one of the pages having put my boat into the trough, the governess who attended Glumdalclitch very officiously lifted me up, to place me in the boat; but I happened to slip through her fingers, and should infallibly have fallen down forty feet, upon the floor, if, by the luckiest chance in the world, I had not been stopped by a corking-pin that stuck in the good gentlewoman's stomacher; the head of the pin passed between my shirt and the waistband of my breeches, and thus I was held by the middle in the air, till Glumdalclitch ran to my relief.

Another time, one of the servants, whose office it was to fill my trough every third day with fresh water, was so careless to let a huge frog (not perceiving it) slip out of his pail. The frog lay concealed till I was put into my boat, but then seeing a resting-place, climbed up, and made it to lean so much on one side, that I was forced to balance it with all my weight on the other to prevent overturning. When the frog was got in, it hopped at once half the length of the boat, and then over my head, backward and forward, daubing my face and clothes with its odious slime. The largeness of its features made it appear the most deformed animal that can be conceived. However, I desired Glumdalclitch to let me deal with it alone. I banged it a good while with one of my sculls, and at last forced it to leap out of the boat.

But the greatest danger I underwent in that kingdom was from a monkey, who belonged to one of the clerks of the kitchen. Glumdalclitch had locked me up in her closet, while she went somewhere upon business, or a visit. The weather being very warm, the closet window was left open, as well as the windows and door of my bigger box, in which I usually lived, because of its largeness and conveniency. As I sat quietly meditating at my table, I heard something bounce in at the closet-window, and skip about from one side to the other; whereat, although I was much alarmed, yet I ventured to look out, but not stirring from my seat; and then I saw this frolicsome animal frisking and leaping up and down, till at last he came to my box, which he seemed to view with great pleasure and curiosity, peeping in at the door and every window. I retreated to the further corner of my room, or box; but the monkey, looking in at every side, put me into such a fright, that I wanted presence of mind to conceal myself under the bed, as I might easily have done. After some time spent in peeping, grinning, and chattering, he at last espied me; and reaching one of his paws in at the door, as a cat does when she plays with a mouse, although I often shifted place to avoid him, he at length seized the lappet of my coat (which being made of that country silk, was very thick and strong), and dragged me out. He took me up in his right forefoot, and held me as a nurse does a child; and when I offered to struggle, he squeezed me so hard, that I thought it more prudent to submit. I have good reason to believe that he took me for a young one of his own species, by his often stroking my face very gently with his other paw. In these diversions he was interrupted by a noise at the closet door, as if somebody were opening it; whereupon he suddenly leaped up to the window, at which he had come in, and thence upon the leads and gutters, walking upon three legs, and holding me in the fourth, till he clambered up to a roof that was next to ours. I heard Glumdalclitch give a shriek the moment he was carrying me out. The poor girl was almost distracted; that quarter of the palace was all in an uproar; the servants ran for ladders; the monkey was seen by hundreds in the court, sitting upon the ridge of a building, holding me like a baby in one of his fore-paws, and feeding me with the other, by cramming into my mouth some victuals he had squeezed out of the bag on one side of his chaps, and patting me when I would not eat; whereat many of the rabble below could not forbear laughing; neither do I think they justly ought to be blamed, for, without question, the sight was ridiculous enough to everybody but myself. Some of the people threw up stones, hoping to drive the monkey down; but this was strictly forbidden, or else, very probably, my brains had been dashed out.

The ladders were now applied, and mounted by several men; which the monkey observing, and finding himself almost encompassed, not being able to make speed enough with his three legs, let me drop on a ridge tile, and made his escape. Here I sat for some time, five hundred yards from the ground, expecting every moment to be blown down by the wind, or to fall by my own giddiness, and come tumbling over and over from the ridge to the eaves: but an honest lad, one of my nurse's footmen, climbed up, and putting me into his breeches pocket, brought me down—safe.

I was almost choked with the filthy stuff the monkey had crammed down my throat; but my dear little nurse picked it out of my mouth with a small needle, and then I fell a-vomiting, which gave me great relief. Yet I was so weak and bruised in the sides with the squeezes given me by this odious animal, that I was forced to keep my bed a fortnight. The king, queen, and all the court, sent every day to inquire after my health, and her Majesty made me several visits during my sickness. The monkey was killed, and an order made that no such animal should be kept about the palace.

When I attended the king after my recovery, to return him thanks for his favors, he was pleased to rally me a good deal upon this adventure. He asked me, what my thoughts and speculations were while I lay in the monkey's paw? how I liked the victuals he gave me? his manner of feeding? and whether the fresh air on the roof had sharpened my stomach? He desired to know what I would have done upon such an occasion in my own country? I told his Majesty, that in Europe we had no monkeys except such as were brought for curiosities from other places, and so small that I could deal with a dozen of them together, if they presumed to attack me. And as for that monstrous animal, with whom I was so lately engaged (it was indeed as large as an elephant), if my fears had suffered me to think so far as to make use of my hanger (looking fiercely, and clapping my hand upon the hilt, as I spoke) when he poked his paw into my chamber, perhaps I should have given him such a wound, as would have made him glad to withdraw it, with more haste than he put it in. This I delivered in a firm tone, like a person who was jealous lest his courage should be called in question. However, my speech produced nothing else beside a loud laughter, which all the respect due to his Majesty from those about him could not make them contain. This made me reflect, how vain an attempt it is for a man to endeavor to do himself honor among those who are out of all degree of equality or comparison with him. And yet I have seen the moral of my own behavior very frequently in England since my return; where a little contemptible varlet, without the least title to birth, person, wit, or common-sense, shall presume to look with importance, and put himself upon a foot with the greatest persons of the kingdom.

THE HILL-MAN AND THE HOUSEWIFE

BY JULIANA HORATIA EWING

It is well known that the good people cannot stand mean ways. Now, there once lived a house-wife who had a sharp eye to her own good in this world, and gave alms of what she had no use, for the good of her soul.

One day a man knocked at her door. "Can you lend us a saucepan, good mother?" said he. "There's a wedding on the hill, and all the pots are in use." "Is he to have one?" asked the servant girl who opened the door. "Ay, to be sure," said the house-wife.

But when the maid was taking a saucepan from the self, she pinched her arm and whispered sharply, "Not that, you stupid; get the old one out of the cupboard. It leaks and the hill-men are so neat and such nimble workers that they are sure to mend it before they send it home. So one does a good turn to the good people and saves sixpence from the tinker."

The maid fetched the saucepan, which had been laid by till the tinker's next visit, and gave it to the dwarf, who thanked her and went away.

The saucepan was soon returned neatly mended and ready for use. At supper time the maid filled the pan with milk and set it on the fire for the children's supper, but in a few minutes the milk was so burnt and smoked that no one could touch it, and even the pigs would not drink the wash into which it was thrown.

"Ah, you good-for-nothing slut!" cried the house-wife, as she this time filled the pan herself. "You would ruin the richest, with your careless ways; there's a whole quart of good milk spoilt at once." *"And that's twopence,"* cried a voice from the chimney, a queer whining voice like some old body who was always grumbling over something.

The house-wife had not left the saucepan for two minutes when the milk boiled over, and it was all burnt and smoked as before. "The pan must be dirty," cried the house-wife in a rage; "and there are two full quarts of milk as good as thrown to the dogs." "*And that's fourpence*," said the voice in the chimney.

After a long scrubbing the saucepan was once more filled and set on the fire, but it was not the least use, the milk was burnt and smoked again, and the house-wife burst into tears at the waste, crying out, "Never before did such a thing happen to me since I kept house! Three quarts of milk burnt for one meal!" "*And that's sixpence,*" cried the voice from the chimney. "*You didn't save the tinker after all,*" with which the hill-man himself came tumbling down the chimney, and went off laughing through the door. But from that time the saucepan was as good as any other.

HOW THOMAS CONNOLLY MET THE BANSHEE

BY J. TODHUNTER

Aw, the banshee, sir? Well, sir, as I was striving to tell ye, I was going home from work one day, from Mr. Cassidy's that I tould ye of, in the dusk o' the evening. I had more nor a mile—aye, it was nearer two mile—to thrack to, where I was lodgin' with a dacent widdy woman I knew, Biddy Maguire be name, so as to be near me work.

It was the first week in November, an' a lonesome road I had to travel, an' dark enough, wid threes above it; an' about half-ways there was a bit of a brudge I had to cross, over one o' them little sthrames that runs into the Doddher. I walked on in the middle iv the road, for there was no toe-path at that time, Misther Harry, nor for many a long day afther that; but, as I was sayin', I walked along till I come nigh upon the brudge, where the road was a bit open, an' there, right enough, I seen the hog's back o' the ould-fashioned brudge that used to be there till it was pulled down, an' a white mist steamin' up out o' the wather all around it.

Well, now, Misther Harry, often as I'd passed by the place before, that night it seemed sthrange to me, an' like a place ye might see in a dhrame; an' as I come up to it I began to feel a could wind blowin' through the hollow o' me heart. "Musha Thomas," sez I to meself, "is it yerself that's in it?" sez I; "or, if it is, what's the matter wid ye at all, at all?" sez I; so I put a bould face on it, an' I made a sthruggle to set one leg afore the other, ontil I came to the rise o' the brudge. And there, God be good to us! in a cantle o' the wall I seen an ould woman, as I thought, sittin' on her hunkers, all crouched together, an' her head bowed down, seemin'ly in the greatest affliction.

Well, sir, I pitied the ould craythur, an' thought I wasn't worth a thraneen, for the mortial fright I was in, I up an' sez to her, "That's a cowld lodgin' for ye, ma'am." Well, the sorra ha'porth she sez to that, nor tuk no more notice o' me than if I hadn't let a word out o' me, but kep' rockin' herself to an' fro, as if her heart was breakin'; so I sez to her again, "Eh, ma'am, is there anythin' the matther wid ye?" An' I made for to touch her on the shouldher, on'y somethin' stopt me, for as I looked closer at her I saw she was no more an ould woman nor she was an ould cat. The first thing I tuk notice to, Misther Harry, was her hair, that was sthreelin' down over her showldhers, an' a good yard on the ground on aich side of her. O, be the hoky farmer, but that was the hair! The likes of it I never seen on mortial woman, young or ould, before nor sense. It grew as sthrong out of her as out of e'er a young slip of a girl ye could see; but the colour of it was a misthery to describe. The first squint I got of it I thought it was silvery grey, like an ould crone's; but when I got up beside her I saw, be the glance o' the sky, it was a soart iv an Iscariot colour, an' a shine out of it like floss silk. It ran over her showldhers and the two shapely arms she was lanin' her head on, for all the world like Mary Magdalen's in a picther; and then I persaved that the grey cloak and the green gownd undhernaith it was made of no earthly matarial I ever laid eyes on. Now, I needn't tell ye, sir, that I seen all this in the twinkle of a bed-post—long as I take to make the narration of it. So I made a step back from her, an' "The Lord be betune us an' harm!" sez I, out loud, an' wid that I blessed meself. Well, Misther Harry, the word wasn't out o' me mouth afore she turned her face on me. Aw, Misther Harry, but 'twas that was the awfullest apparation ever I seen, the face of her as she looked up at me! God forgive me for sayin' it, but 'twas more like the face of the "Axy Homo" beyand in Marlboro Sthreet Chapel nor like any face I could mintion—as pale as a corpse, an' a most o' freckles on it, like the freckles on a turkey's egg; an' the two eyes sewn in wid red thread, from the terrible power o' crying the' had to do; an' such a pair iv eyes as the' wor, Misther Harry, as blue as two forget-me-nots, an' as cowld as the moon in a bog-hole of a frosty night, an' a dead-an'-live look in them that sent a cowld shiver through the marra o' me bones. Be the mortial! ye could ha' rung a tay cupful o' cowld paspiration out o' the hair o' me head that minute, so ye could. Well, I thought the life 'ud lave me intirely when she riz up from her hunkers, till, bedad! she looked mostly as tall as Nelson's Pillar; an' wid the two eyes gazin' back at me, an' her two arms stretched out before hor, an' a keine out of her that riz the hair o' me scalp till it was as stiff as the hog's bristles in a new hearth broom, away she glides—glides round the angle o' the brudge, an' down with her into the sthrame that ran undhernaith it. 'Twas then I began to suspect what she was. "Wisha, Thomas!" says I to meself, sez I; an' I made a great struggle to get me two legs into a throt, in spite o' the spavin o' fright the pair o' them wor in; an' how I brought meself home that same night the Lord in heaven only knows, for I never could tell; but I must ha' tumbled agin the door, and shot in head foremost into the middle o' the flure, where I lay in a dead swoon for mostly an hour; and the first I knew was Mrs. Maguire stannin' over me with a jorum o' punch she was pourin' down me throath (throat), to bring back the life into me, an' me head in a pool of cowld wather she dashed over me in her first fright. "Arrah, Mister Connolly," shashee, "what ails ye?" shashee, "to put the scare on a lone woman like that?" shashee. "Am I in this world or the next?" sez I. "Musha! where else would ye be on'y here in my kitchen?" shashee. "O, glory be to God!" sez I, "but I thought I was in Purgathory at the laste, not to mintion an uglier place," sez I, "only it's too cowld I find meself, an' not too hot," sez I. "Faix, an' maybe ye wor more nor half-ways there, on'y for me," shashee; "but what's come to you at all, at all? Is it your fetch ye seen, Mister Connolly?" "Aw, naboclish!" sez I. "Never mind what I seen," sez I. So be degrees I began to come to a little; an' that's the way I met the banshee, Misther Harry!

"But how did you know it really was the banshee after all, Thomas?"

"Begor, sir, I knew the apparition of her well enough; but 'twas confirmed by a sarcumstance that occurred the same time. There was a Misther O'Nales was come on a visit, ye must know, to a place in the neighborhood—one o' the ould O'Nales iv the county Tyrone, a rale ould Irish family—an' the banshee was heard keening round the house that same night, be more then one that was in it; an' sure enough, Misther Harry, he was found dead in his bed the next mornin'. So if it wasn't the banshee I seen that time, I'd like to know what else it could a' been."

THE COMING OF FINN

BY STANDISH JAMES O'GRADY

It was the Eve of Samhain, which we Christians call All Hallows' Eve.

The King of Ireland, Conn, the Hundred-Fighter, sat at supper in his palace at Tara. All his chiefs and mighty men were with him. On his right hand was his only son, Art the Solitary, so called because he had no brothers. The Sons of Morna, who kept the boy Finn out of his rights and were at the time trying to kill him if they could, were here too. Chief amongst them was Gaul mac Morna, a huge and strong warrior, and Captain of all the Fians ever since that battle in which Finn's father had been killed.

And Gaul's men were with him. The great long table was spread for supper. A thousand wax candles shed their light through the chamber, and caused the vessels of gold, silver, and bronze to shine. Yet, though it was a great feast, none of these warriors seemed to care about eating or drinking; every face was sad, and there was little conversation, and no music. It seemed as if they were expecting some calamity. Conn's sceptre, which was a plain staff of silver, lay beside him on the table, and there was a canopy of bright bronze over his head. Gaul mac Morna, Captain of the Fians, sat at the other end of the long table. Every warrior wore a bright banqueting mantle of silk or satin, scarlet or crimson, blue, green, or purple, fastened on the breast either with a great brooch or with a pin of gold or silver. Yet, though their raiment was bright and gay, and though all the usual instruments of festivity were there, and a thousand tall candles shed their light over the scene, no one looked happy.

Then was heard a low sound like thunder, and the earth seemed to tremble, and after that they distinctly heard a footfall like the slow, deliberate tread of a giant. These footfalls sent a chill into every heart, and every face, gloomy before, was now pale.

The King leaned past his son Art the Solitary, and said to a certain Druid who sat beside Art, "Is this the son of Midna come before his time?" "It is not," said the Druid, "but it is the man who is to conquer Midna. One is coming to Tara this night before whose glory all other glory shall wax dim."

Shortly after that they heard the voices of the doorkeepers raised in contention, as if they would repel from the hall someone who wished to enter, then a slight scuffle, and after that a strange figure entered the chamber. He was dressed in the skins of wild beasts, and wore over his shoulders a huge thick cloak of wild boars' skins, fastened on the breast with a white tusk of the same animal. He wore a shield and two spears. Though of huge stature his face was that of a boy, smooth on the cheeks and lips. It was white and ruddy, and very handsome. His hair was like refined gold. A light seemed to go out from him, before which the candles burned dim. It was Finn.

He stood in the doorway, and cried out in a strong and sonorous, but musical, voice:

"Conn the Hundred-Fighter, son of Felimy, the righteous son of Tuthal the legitimate, O King of the Kings of Erin, a wronged and disinherited youth, possessing nowhere one rood of his patrimony, a wanderer and an outlaw, a hunter of the wildernesses and mountains, claims hospitality of thee, illustrious prince, on the eve of the great festival of Samhain."

"Thou art welcome whoever thou art," answered the King, "and doubly welcome because thou art unfortunate. I think, such is thy face and form, that thou art the son of some mighty king on whom disaster has fallen undeserved. The high gods of Erin grant thee speedy restoration and strong vengeance of thy many wrongs. Sit here, O noble youth, between me and my only son, Art, heir to my kingdom."

An attendant took his weapons from the youth and hung them on the wall with the rest, and Finn sat down between the King of Ireland and his only son. Choice food was set before him, which he ate, and old ale, which he drank. From the moment he entered no one thought of anything but of him. When Finn had made an end of eating and drinking, he said to the King:

"O illustrious prince, though it is not right for a guest to even seem to observe aught that may be awry, or not as it should be, in the hall of his entertainer, yet the sorrow of a kindly host is a sorrow, too, to his guest, and sometimes unawares the man of the house finds succor and help in the stranger. There is sorrow in this chamber of festivity. If anyone who is dear to thee and thy people happens to be dead, I can do nothing. But I say it, and it is not a vain boast, that even if a person is at the point of death, I can restore him to life and health, for there are marvelous powers of life-giving in my two hands."

Conn the Hundred-Fighter answered, "Our grief is not such as you suppose; and why should I not tell a cause of shame, which is known far and wide? This, then, is the reason of our being together, and the gloom which is over us. There is a mighty enchanter whose dwelling is in the haunted mountains of Slieve Gullion in the north. His name is Allen, son of Midna, and his enmity to me is as great as his power. Once every year, at this season, it is his pleasure to burn Tara. Descending out of his wizard haunts, he standeth over against the city and shoots balls of fire out of his mouth against it, till it is consumed. Then he goes away mocking and triumphant. This annual building of Tara, only to be annually consumed, is a shame to me, and till this enchanter declared war against me, I have lived without reproach."

"But," said Finn, "how is it that thy young warriors, valiant and swift, do not repel him, or kill him?"

"Alas!" said Conn, "all our valor is in vain against this man. Our hosts encompass Tara on all sides, keeping watch and ward when the fatal night comes. Then the son of Midna plays on his Druidic instrument of music, on his magic pipe and his magic lyre, and as the fairy music falls on our ears, our eyelids grow heavy, and soon all subside upon the grass in deep slumber. So comes this man against the city and shoots his fire-balls against it, and utterly consumes it. Nine years he has burnt Tara in that manner, and this is the tenth. At midnight to-night he will come and do the same. Last year (though it was a shame to me that I, who am the high King over all Ireland, should not be able myself to defend Tara) I summoned Gaul mac Morna and all the Fians to my assistance. They came, but the pipe and lyre of the son of Midna prevailed over them too, so that Tara was burned as at other times. Nor have we any reason to believe that the son of Midna will not burn the city again to-night, as he did last year. All the women and children have been sent out of Tara this day. We are only men of war here, waiting for the time. That, O noble youth, is why we are sad. The 'Pillars of Tara' are broken, and the might of the Fians is as nought before the power of this man."

"What shall be my reward if I kill this man and save Tara?" asked Finn.

"Thy inheritance," answered the King, "be it great or small, and whether it lies in Ireland or beyond Ireland; and for securities I give you my son Art and Gaul mac Morna and the Chief of the Fians."

Gaul and the captains of the Fianna consented to that arrangement, though reluctantly, for their minds misgave them as to who the great youth might be.

After that all arose and armed themselves and ringed Tara round with horse and foot, and thrice Conn the Hundred-Fighter raised his awful regal voice, enjoining vigilance upon his people, and thrice Gaul mac Morna did the same, addressing the Fians, and after that they filled their ears with wax and wool, and kept a stern and fierce watch, and many of them thrust the points of their swords into their flesh.

Now Finn was alone in the banqueting chamber after the rest had gone out, and he washed his face and his hands in pure water, and he took from the bag that was at his girdle the instruments of divination and magic, which had been his father's, and what use he made of them is not known; but ere long a man stood before him, holding a spear in one hand and a blue mantle in the other. There were twenty nails of gold of Arabia in the spear. The nails glittered like stars, and twinkled with live light as stars do in a frosty night, and the blade of it quivered like a tongue of white fire. From haft to blade-point that spear was alive. There were voices in it too, and the war-tunes of the enchanted races of Erin, whom they called the Tuatha De Danan, sounded from it. The mantle, too, was a wonder, for innumerable stars twinkled in the blue, and the likeness of clouds passed through it. The man gave these things to Finn, and when he had instructed him in their use, he was not seen.

Then Finn arose and armed himself, and took the magic spear and mantle and went out. There was a ring of flame round Tara that night, for the Fians and the warriors of Conn had torches in their hands, and all the royal buildings of Tara showed clear in the light, and also the dark serpentine course of the Boyne, which flowed past Tara on the north; and there, standing silent and alert, were the innumerable warriors of all Erin, with spear and shield, keeping watch and ward against the son of Midna, also the Four Pillars of Tara in four dense divisions around the high King, even Conn the Hundred-Fighter.

Finn stood with his back to the palace, which was called the House-of-the-going-round-of-Mead, between the palace and Conn, and he grasped the magic spear strongly with one hand and the mantle with the other.

As midnight drew nigh, he heard far away in the north, out of the mountains of Slieve Gullion, a fairy tune played, soft, low, and slow, as if on a silver flute; and at the same time the roar of Conn the Hundred-Fighter, and the voice of Gaul like thunder, and the responsive shouts of the captains, and the clamor of the host, for the host shouted all together, and clashed their swords against their shields in fierce defiance, when in spite of all obstructions the fairy music of the enchanter began to steal into their souls. That shout was heard all over Ireland, echoing from sea to sea, and the hollow buildings of

Tara reverberated to the uproar. Yet through it all could be heard the low, slow, delicious music that came from Slieve Gullion. Finn put the point of the spear to his forehead. It burned him like fire, yet his stout heart did not fail. Then the roar of the host slowly faded away as in a dream, though the captains were still shouting, and two-thirds of the torches fell to the ground. And now, succeeding the flute music, sounded the music of a stringed instrument exceedingly sweet. Finn pressed the cruel spear-head closer to his forehead, and saw every torch fall, save one which wavered as if held by a drunken man, and beneath it a giant figure that reeled and tottered and strove in vain to keep its feet. It was Conn the Hundred-Fighter. As he fell there was a roar as of many waters; it was the ocean mourning for the high King's fall. Finn passed through the fallen men and stood alone on the dark hill-side. He heard the feet of the enchanter splashing through the Boyne, and saw his huge form ascending the slopes of Tara. When the enchanter saw that all was silent and dark there he laughed and from his mouth blew a red fire-ball at the Teck-Midcuarta, which he was accustomed first to set in flames. Finn caught the fire-ball in the magic mantle. The enchanter blew a second and a third, and Finn caught them both. The man saw that his power over Tara was at an end, and that his magic arts had been defeated. On the third occasion he saw Finn's face, and recognized his conqueror. He turned to flee, and though slow was his coming, swifter than the wind was his going, that he might recover the protection of his enchanted palace before the "fair-faced youth clad in skins" should overtake him. Finn let fall the mantle as he had been instructed, and pursued him, but in vain. Soon he perceived that he could not possibly overtake the swift enchanter. Then he was aware that the magic spear struggled in his hand like a hound in a leash. "Go, then, if thou wilt," he said, and, poising, cast the spear from him. It shot through the dark night hissing and screaming. There was a track of fire behind it. Finn followed, and on the threshold of the enchanted palace he found the body of Midna. He was quite dead, with the blood pouring through a wound in the middle of his back; but the spear was gone. Finn drew his sword and cut off the enchanter's head, and returned with it to Tara. When he came to the spot where he had dropped the mantle it was not seen, but smoke and flame issued there from a hole in the ground. That hole was twenty feet deep in the earth, and at the bottom of it there was a fire always from that night, and it was never extinguished. It was called the fire of the son of Midna. It was in a depression on the north side of the hill of Tara, called the Glen of the Mantle, Glen-a-Brat.

Finn, bearing the head, passed through the sleepers into the palace and spiked the head on his own spear, and drove the spear-end into the ground at

Conn's end of the great hall. Then the sickness and faintness of death came upon Finn, also a great horror and despair overshadowed him, so that he was about to give himself up for utterly lost. Yet he recalled one of his marvelous attributes, and approaching a silver vessel, into which pure water ever flowed and which was always full, he made a cup with his two hands and, lifting it to his mouth, drank, and the blood began to circulate in his veins, and strength returned to his limbs, and the cheerful hue of rosy health to his cheeks.

Having rested himself sufficiently he went forth and shouted to the sleeping host, and called the captains by their names, beginning with Conn. They awoke and rose up, though dazed and stupid, for it was difficult for any man, no matter how he had stopped his ears, to avoid hearing Finn when he sent forth his voice of power. They were astonished to find that Tara was still standing, for though the night was dark, the palaces and temples, all of hewn timber, were brilliantly colored and of many hues, for in those days men delighted in splendid colors.

When the captains came together Finn said, "I have slain Midna." "Where is his head?" they asked, not because they disbelieved him, but because the heads of men slain in battle were always brought away for trophies. "Come and see," answered Finn. Conn and his only son and Gaul mac Morna followed the young hero into the Teck-Midcuarta, where the spear-long waxen candles were still burning, and when they saw the head of Midna impaled there at the end of the hall, the head of the man whom they believed to be immortal and not to be wounded or conquered, they were filled with great joy, and praised their deliverer and paid him many compliments.

"Who art thou, O brave youth?" said Conn. "Surely thou art the son of some great king or champion, for heroic feats like thine are not performed by the sons of inconsiderable and unknown men."

Then Finn flung back his cloak of wild boars' skins, and holding his father's treasure-bag in his hand before them all, cried in a loud voice:

"I am Finn, the son of Cool, the son of Trenmor, the son of Basna; I am he whom the sons of Morna have been seeking to destroy from the time that I was born; and here to-night, O King of the Kings of Erin, I claim the fulfillment of thy promise, and the restoration of my inheritance, which is the Fian leadership of Fail."

Thereupon Gaul mac Morna put his right hand into Finn's, and became his man. Then his brothers and his sons, and the sons of his brothers, did so in succession, and after that all the chief men of the Fians did the same, and that night Finn was solemnly and surely installed in the Fian leadership of Erin, and put in possession of all the woods and forests and waste places, and all the hills and mountains and promontories, and all the streams and rivers of Erin, and the harbors and estuaries and the harbor-dues of the merchants, and all ships and boats and galleys with their mariners, and all that pertained of old time to the Fian leadership of Fail.

AN ESSAY ON THE NOBLE SCIENCE OF SELF-JUSTIFICATION

BY MARIA EDGEWORTH

"For which an eloquence that aims to vex,
With native tropes of anger arms the sex."—*Parnell.*

Endowed as the fair sex indisputably are, with a natural genius for the invaluable art of self-justification, it may not be displeasing to them to see its rising perfection evinced by an attempt to reduce it to a science. Possessed, as are all the fair daughters of Eve, of an hereditary propensity, transmitted to them undiminished through succeeding generations, to be "soon moved with slightest touch of blame;" very little precept and practice will confirm them in the habit, and instruct them in all the maxims of self-justification.

Candid pupil, you will readily accede to my first and fundamental axiom—that a lady can do no wrong.

But simple as this maxim may appear, and suited to the level of the meanest capacity, the talent of applying it on all the important, but more especially on all the most trivial, occurrences of domestic life, so as to secure private peace and public dominion, has hitherto been monopolized by the female adepts in the art of self-justification.

Excuse me for insinuating by this expression, that there may yet be amongst you some novices. To these, if any such, I principally address myself.

And now, lest fired by ambition you lose all by aiming at too much, let me explain and limit my first principle, "That you can do no wrong." You must be aware that real perfection is beyond the reach of mortals, nor would I have you aim at it; indeed it is not in any degree necessary to our purpose. You have heard of the established belief in the infallibility of the sovereign pontiff, which prevailed not many centuries ago:—if man was allowed to be infallible, I see no reason why the same privilege should not be extended to woman;—but times have changed; and since the happy age of credulity is past, leave the opinions of men to their natural perversity—their actions are the best test of their faith. Instead then of a belief in your infallibility, endeavor to enforce implicit submission to your authority. This will give you infinitely less trouble, and will answer your purpose as well.

Right and wrong, if we go to the foundation of things, are, as casuists tell us, really words of very dubious signification, perpetually varying with custom and fashion, and to be adjusted ultimately by no other standards but opinion and force. Obtain power, then, by all means: power is the law of man; make it yours. But to return from a frivolous disquisition about right, let me teach you the art of defending the wrong. After having thus pointed out to you the glorious end of your labors, I must now instruct you in the equally glorious means.

For the advantage of my subject I address myself chiefly to married ladies; but those who have not as yet the good fortune to have that common enemy, a husband, to combat, may in the mean time practice my precepts upon their fathers, brothers, and female friends; with caution, however, lest by discovering their arms too soon, they preclude themselves from the power of using them to the fullest advantage hereafter. I therefore recommend it to them to prefer, with a philosophical moderation, the future to the present.

Timid brides, you have, probably, hitherto been addressed as angels. Prepare for the time when you shall again become mortal. Take the alarm at the first approach of blame; at the first hint of a discovery that you are any thing less than infallible:—contradict, debate, justify, recriminate, rage, weep, swoon, do any thing but yield to conviction.

I take it for granted that you have already acquired sufficient command of voice; you need not study its compass; going beyond its pitch has a peculiarly happy effect upon some occasions. But are you voluble enough to drown all sense in a torrent of words? Can you be loud enough to overpower the voice of all who shall attempt to interrupt or contradict you? Are you mistress of the petulant, the peevish, and the sullen tone? Have you practiced the sharpness which provokes retort, and the continual monotony which by setting your adversary to sleep effectually precludes reply? An event which is always to be considered as decisive of the victory, or at least as reducing it to a drawn battle:—you and Somnus divide the prize.

Thus prepared for an engagement, you will next, if you have not already done it, study the weak part of the character of your enemy—your husband, I mean: if he be a man of high spirit, jealous of command and impatient of control, one who decides for himself, and who is little troubled with the insanity of minding what the world says of him, you must proceed with extreme circumspection; you must not dare to provoke the combined forces of the enemy to a regular engagement, but harass him with perpetual petty skirmishes: in these, though you gain little at a time, you will gradually weary the patience, and break the spirit of your opponent. If he be a man of spirit, he must also be generous; and what man of generosity will contend for trifles with a woman who submits to him in all affairs of consequence, who is in his power, who is weak, and who loves him?

"Can superior with inferior power contend?" No; the spirit of a lion is not to be roused by the teasing of an insect.

But such a man as I have described, besides being as generous as he is brave, will probably be of an active temper: then you have an inestimable advantage; for he will set a high value upon a thing for which you have none—time; he will acknowledge the force of your arguments merely from a dread of their length; he will yield to you in trifles, particularly in trifles which do not militate against his authority; not out of regard for you, but for his time; for what man can prevail upon himself to debate three hours about what could be as well decided in three minutes?

Lest amongst infinite variety the difficulty of immediate selection should at first perplex you, let me point out, that matters of *taste* will afford you, of all others, the most ample and incessant subjects of debate. Here you have no criterion to appeal to. Upon the same principle, next to matters of taste, points of opinion will afford the most constant exercise to your talents. Here you will have an opportunity of citing the opinions of all the living and dead you have ever known, besides the dear privilege of repeating continually:—"Nay, you must allow *that*." Or, "You can't deny this, for it's the universal opinion—every body says so! everybody thinks so! I wonder to hear you express such an opinion! Nobody but yourself is of that way of thinking!" with innumerable other phrases, with which a slight attention to polite conversation will furnish you.

This mode of opposing authority to argument, and assertion to proof, is of such universal utility, that I pray you to practice it.

If the point in dispute be some opinion relative to your character or disposition, allow in general, that "you are sure you have a great many faults;" but to every specific charge reply, "Well, I am sure I don't know, but I did not think *that* was one of my faults! nobody ever accused me of that before! Nay, I was always remarkable for the contrary; at least before I was acquainted with you, sir: in my own family I was always remarkable for the contrary: ask any of my own friends; ask any of them; they must know me best."

But if, instead of attacking the material parts of your character, your husband should merely presume to advert to your manners, to some slight personal habit which might be made more agreeable to him; prove, in the first place, that it is his fault that it is not agreeable to him; ask which is most to blame, "she who ceases to please, or he who ceases to be pleased"—His eyes are changed, or opened. But it may perhaps have been a matter almost of indifference to him, till you undertook its defense: then make it of consequence by rising in eagerness, in proportion to the insignificance of your object; if he can draw consequences, this will be an excellent lesson: if you are so tender of blame in the veriest trifles, how impeachable must you be in matters of importance! As to personal habits, begin by denying that you have any; or in the paradoxical language of Rousseau, declare that the only habit you have is the habit of having none: as all personal habits, if they have been of any long standing, must have become involuntary, the unconscious culprit may assert her innocence without hazarding her veracity.

However, if you happen to be detected in the very fact, and a person cries, "Now, now, you are doing it!" submit, but declare at the same moment—"That it is the very first time in your whole life that you were ever known to be guilty of it; and therefore it can be no habit, and of course nowise reprehensible."

Extend the rage for vindication to all the objects which the most remotely concern you; take even inanimate objects under your protection. Your dress, your furniture, your property, every thing which is or has been yours, defend, and this upon the principles of the soundest philosophy: each of these things all compose a part of your personal merit (Vide Hume); all that connected the most distantly with your idea gives pleasure or pain to others, becomes an object of blame or praise, and consequently claims your support or vindication.

In the course of the management of your house, children, family, and affairs, probably some few errors of omission or commission may strike your husband's pervading eye; but these errors, admitting them to be errors, you will never, if you please, allow to be charged to any deficiency in memory, judgment, or activity, on your part.

There are surely people enough around you to divide and share the blame; send it from one to another, till at last, by universal rejection, it is proved to belong to nobody. You will say, however, that facts remain unalterable; and that in some unlucky instance, in the changes and chances of human affairs, you may be proved to have been to blame. Some stubborn evidence may appear against you; still you may prove an alibi, or balance the evidence. There is nothing equal to balancing evidence; doubt is, you know, the most philosophic state of the human mind, and it will be kind of you to keep your husband perpetually in this skeptical state.

Indeed the short method of denying absolutely all blameable facts, I should recommend to pupils as the best; and if in the beginning of their career they may startle at this mode, let them depend upon it that in their future practice it must become perfectly familiar. The nice distinction of simulation and dissimulation depends but on the trick of a syllable; palliation and extenuation are universally allowable in self-defense; prevarication inevitably follows, and falsehood "is but in the next degree."

Yet I would not destroy this nicety of conscience too soon. It may be of use in your first setting out, because you must establish credit; in proportion to your credit will be the value of your future asseverations.

In the mean time, however, argument and debate are allowed to the most rigid moralist. You can never perjure yourself by swearing to a false opinion.

I come now to the art of reasoning: don't be alarmed at the name of reasoning, fair pupils; I will explain to you my meaning.

If, instead of the fiery-tempered being I formerly described, you should fortunately be connected with a man, who, having formed a justly high opinion of your sex, should propose to treat you as his equal, and who in any little dispute which might arise between you, should desire no other arbiter than reason; triumph in his mistaken candor, regularly appeal to the decision of reason at the beginning of every contest, and deny its jurisdiction at the conclusion. I take it for granted that you will be on the wrong side of every question, and indeed, in general, I advise you to choose the wrong side of an argument to defend; whilst you are young in the science, it will afford the best exercise, and, as you improve, the best display of your talents.

If, then, reasonable pupils, you would succeed in argument, attend to the following instructions.

Begin by preventing, if possible, the specific statement of any position, or if reduced to it, use the most general terms, and take advantage of the ambiguity which all languages and which most philosophers allow. Above all things, shun definitions; they will prove fatal to you; for two persons of sense and candor, who define their terms, cannot argue long without either convincing, or being convinced, or parting in equal good-humor; to prevent which, go over and over the same ground, wander as wide as possible from the point, but always with a view to return at last precisely to the same spot from which you set out. I should remark to you, that the choice of your weapons is a circumstance much to be attended to: choose always those which your adversary cannot use. If your husband is a man of wit, you will of course undervalue a talent which is never connected with judgment: "for your part, you do not presume to contend with him in wit."

But if he be a sober-minded man, who will go link by link along the chain of an argument, follow him at first, till he grows so intent that he does not perceive whether you follow him or not; then slide back to your own station; and when with perverse patience he has at last reached the last link of the chain, with one electric shock of wit make him quit his hold, and strike him to the ground in an instant. Depend upon the sympathy of the spectators, for to one who can understand *reason*, you will find ten who admire *wit*.

But if you should not be blessed with "a ready wit," if demonstration should in the mean time stare you in the face, do not be in the least alarmed—anticipate the blow. Whilst you have it yet in your power, rise with becoming magnanimity, and cry, "I give it up! I give it up! La! let us say no more about it; I do so hate disputing about trifles. I give it up!" Before an explanation on the word trifle can take place, quit the room with flying colors.

If you are a woman of sentiment and eloquence, you have advantages of which I scarcely need apprize you. From the understanding of a man, you have always an appeal to his heart, or, if not, to his affection, to his weakness. If you have the good fortune to be married to a weak man, always choose the moment to argue with him when you have a full audience. Trust to the sublime power of numbers; it will be of use even to excite your own enthusiasm in debate; then as the scene advances, talk of his cruelty, and your sensibility, and sink with "becoming woe" into the pathos of injured innocence.

Besides the heart and the weakness of your opponent, you have still another chance, in ruffling his temper; which, in the course of a long conversation, you will have a fair opportunity of trying; and if—for philosophers will sometimes grow warm in the defense of truth—if he should grow absolutely angry, you will in the same proportion grow calm, and wonder at his rage, though you well know it has been created by your own provocation. The by-standers, seeing anger without any adequate cause, will all be of your side.

Nothing provokes an irascible man, interested in debate, and possessed of an opinion of his own eloquence, so much as to see the attention of his hearers go from him: you will then, when he flatters himself that he has just fixed your eye with his *very best* argument, suddenly grow absent:—your house affairs must call you hence—or you have directions to give to your children—or the room is too hot, or too cold—the window must be opened—or door shut—or the candle wants snuffing. Nay, without these interruptions, the simple motion of your eye may provoke a speaker; a butterfly, or the figure in a carpet may engage your attention in preference to him; or if these objects be absent, the simply averting your eye, looking through the window in quest of outward objects, will show that your mind has not been abstracted, and will display to him at least your wish of not attending. He may, however, possibly have lost the habit of watching your eye for approbation; then you may assault his ear: if all other resources fail, beat with your foot that dead march of the spirits, that incessant tattoo, which so well deserves its name. Marvelous must be the patience of the much-enduring man whom some or other of these devices do not provoke: slight causes often produce great effects; the simple scratching of a pick-axe, properly applied to certain veins in a mine, will cause the most dreadful explosions.

Hitherto we have only professed to teach the defensive; let me now recommend to you the offensive part of the art of justification. As a supplement to reasoning comes recrimination: the pleasure of proving that you are right is surely incomplete till you have proved that your adversary is wrong; this might have been a secondary, let it now become a primary object with you; rest your own defense on it for further security: you are no longer to consider yourself as obliged either to deny, palliate, argue, or declaim, but simply to justify yourself by criminating another; all merit, you know, is judged of by comparison. In the art of recrimination, your memory will be of the highest service to you; for you are to open and keep an account current of all the faults, mistakes, neglects, unkindnesses of those you live with; these you are to state against your own: I need not tell you that the balance will always be in your favor. In stating matters or opinion, produce the words of the very same person which passed days, months, years before, in contradiction to what he is then saying. By displacing, disjointing words and sentences, by misunderstanding the whole, or quoting only a part of what has been said, you may convict any man of inconsistency, particularly if he be a man of genius and feeling; for he speaks generally from the impulse of the moment, and of all others can the least bear to be charged with paradoxes. So far for a husband.

Recriminating is also of sovereign use in the quarrels of friends; no friend is so perfectly equable, so ardent in affection, so nice in punctilio, as never to offend: then "Note his faults, and con them all by rote." Say you can forgive, but you can never forget; and surely it is much more generous to forgive and remember, than to forgive and forget. On every new alarm, call the unburied ghosts from former fields of battle; range them in tremendous array, call them one by one to witness against the conscience of your enemy, and ere the battle is begun take from him all courage to engage.

There is one case I must observe to you in which recrimination has peculiar poignancy. If you have had it in your power to confer obligations on any one, never cease reminding them of it: and let them feel that you have acquired an indefeasible right to reproach them without a possibility of their retorting. It is a maxim with some sentimental people, "To treat their servants as if they were their friends in distress."—I have observed that people of this cast make themselves amends, by treating their friends in distress as if they were their servants.

Apply this maxim—you may do it a thousand ways, especially in company. In general conversation, where every one is supposed to be on a footing, if any of your humble companions should presume to hazard an opinion contrary to yours, and should modestly begin with, "I think;" look as the man did when he said to his servant, "You think, sir—what business have you to think?"

Never fear to lose a friend by the habits which I recommend: reconciliations, as you have often heard it said—reconciliations are the cement of friendship; therefore friends should quarrel to strengthen their attachment, and offend each other for the pleasure of being reconciled.

I beg pardon for digressing: I was, I believe, talking of your husband, not of your friend—I have gone far out of the way.

If in your debates with your husband you should want "eloquence to vex him," the dull prolixity of narration, joined to the complaining monotony of voice which I formerly recommended, will supply its place, and have the desired effect: Somnus will prove propitious; then, ever and anon as the soporific charm begins to work, rouse him with interrogatories, such as, "Did not you say so? Don't you remember? Only answer me that!"

By-the-by, interrogatories artfully put may lead an unsuspicious reasoner, you know, always to your own conclusion.

In addition to the patience, philosophy, and other good things which Socrates learned from his wife, perhaps she taught him this mode of reasoning.

But, after all, the precepts of art, and even the natural susceptibility of your tempers, will avail you little in the sublime of our science, if you cannot command that ready enthusiasm which will make you enter into the part you are acting; that happy imagination which shall make you believe all you fear and all you invent.

Who is there amongst you who cannot or who will not justify when they are accused? Vulgar talent! the sublime of our science is to justify before we are accused. There is no reptile so vile but what will turn when it is trodden on; but of a nicer sense and nobler species are those whom nature has endowed with antennas, which perceive and withdraw at the distant approach of danger. Allow me another allusion: similes cannot be crowded too close for a female taste; and analogy, I have heard, my fair pupils, is your favorite mode of reasoning.

The sensitive plant is too vulgar an allusion; but if the truth of modern naturalists may be depended upon, there is a plant which, instead of receding timidly from the intrusive touch, angrily protrudes its venomous juices upon all who presume to meddle with it:—do not you think this plant would be your fittest emblem?

Let me, however, recommend it to you, nice souls, who, of the mimosa kind, "fear the dark cloud, and feel the coming storm," to take the utmost precaution lest the same susceptibility which you cherish as the dear means to torment others should insensibly become a torment to yourselves.

Distinguish then between sensibility and susceptibility; between the anxious solicitude not to give offence, and the captious eagerness of vanity to prove that it ought not to have been taken; distinguish between the desire of praise and the horror of blame: can any two things be more different than the wish to improve, and the wish to demonstrate that you have never been to blame?

Observe, I only wish you to distinguish these things in your own minds; I would by no means advise you to discontinue the laudable practice of confounding them perpetually in speaking to others.

When you have nearly exhausted human patience in explaining, justifying, vindicating; when, in spite of all the pains you have taken, you have more than half betrayed your own vanity; you have a never-failing resource, in paying tribute to that of your opponent, as thus:—

"I am sure you must be sensible that I should never take so much pains to justify myself if I were indifferent to your opinion.—I know that I ought not to disturb myself with such trifles; but nothing is a trifle to me which concerns you. I confess I am too anxious to please; I know it's a fault, but I cannot cure myself of it now.—Too quick sensibility, I am conscious, is the defect of my disposition; it would be happier for me if I could be more indifferent, I know."

Who could be so brutal as to blame so amiable, so candid a creature? Who would not submit to be tormented with kindness?

When once your captive condescends to be flattered by such arguments as these, your power is fixed; your future triumphs can be bounded only by your own moderation; they are at once secured and justified.

Forbear not, then, happy pupils; but, arrived at the summit of power, give a full scope to your genius, nor trust to genius alone: to exercise in all its extent your privileged dominion, you must acquire, or rather you must pretend to have acquired, infallible skill in the noble art of physiognomy; immediately the thoughts as well as the words of your subjects are exposed to your inquisition.

Words may flatter you, but the countenance never can deceive you; the eyes are the windows of the soul, and through them you are to watch what passes in the inmost recesses of the heart. There, if you discern the slightest ideas of doubt, blame, or displeasure; if you discover the slightest symptoms of revolt, take the alarm instantly. Conquerors must maintain their conquests; and how easily can they do this, who hold a secret correspondence with the minds of the vanquished! Be your own spies then; from the looks, gestures, slightest motions of your enemies, you are to form an alphabet, a language intelligible only to yourselves, yet by which you shall condemn them; always remembering that in sound policy suspicion justifies punishment. In vain, when you accuse your friends of the high treason of blaming you, in vain let them plead their innocence, even of the intention. "They did not say a word which could be tortured into such a meaning." No, "but they looked daggers, though they used none."

And of this you are to be the sole judge, though there were fifty witnesses to the contrary.

How should indifferent spectators pretend to know the countenance of your friend as well as you do—you, that have a nearer, a dearer interest in attending to it? So accurate have been your observations, that no thought of their souls escapes you; nay, you often can tell even what they are going to think of.

The science of divination certainly claims your attention; beyond the past and the present, it shall extend your dominion over the future; from slight words, half-finished sentences, from silence itself, you shall draw your omens and auguries.

"I know what you were going to say;" or, "I know such a thing was a sign you were inclined to be displeased with me."

In the ardor of innocence, the culprit, to clear himself from such imputations, incurs the imputation of a greater offence. Suppose, to prove that you were mistaken, to prove that he could not have meant to blame you, he should declare that at the moment you mention, "You were quite foreign to his thoughts; he was not thinking at all about you."

Then in truth you have a right to be angry. To one of your class of justificators, this is the highest offence. Possessed as you are of the firm opinion that all persons, at all times, on all occasions, are intent upon you alone, is it not less mortifying to discover that you were thought ill of, than that you were not thought of at all? "Indifference, you know, sentimental pupils, is more fatal to love than even hatred."

Thus, my dear pupils, I have endeavored to provide precepts adapted to the display of your several talents; but if there should be any amongst you who have no talents, who can neither argue nor persuade, who have neither sentiment nor enthusiasm, I must indeed—congratulate them;—they are peculiarly qualified for the science of Self-justification: indulgent nature, often even in the weakness, provides for the protection of her creatures; just Providence, as the guard of stupidity, has enveloped it with the impenetrable armor of obstinacy.

Fair idiots! let women of sense, wit, feeling, triumph in their various arts: yours are superior. Their empire, absolute as it sometimes may be, is perpetually subject to sudden revolutions. With them, a man has some chance of equal sway: with a fool he has none. Have they hearts and understandings? Then the one may be touched, or the other in some unlucky moment convinced; even in their very power lies their greatest danger:—not so with you. In vain let the most candid of his sex attempt to reason with you; let him begin with, "Now, my dear, only listen to reason:"—you stop him at once with, "No, my dear, you know I do not pretend to reason; I only say, that's my opinion."

Let him go on to prove that yours is a mistaken opinion:—you are ready to acknowledge it long before he desires it. "You acknowledge it may be a wrong opinion; but still it is your opinion." You do not maintain it in the least, either because you believe it to be wrong or right, but merely because it is yours. Exposed as you might have been to the perpetual humiliation of being convinced, nature seems kindly to have denied you all perception of truth, or at least all sentiment of pleasure from the perception.

With an admirable humility, you are as well contented to be in the wrong as in the right; you answer all that can be said to you with a provoking humility of aspect.

"Yes; I do not doubt but what you say may be very true, but I cannot tell; I do not think myself capable of judging on these subjects; I am sure you must know much better than I do. I do not pretend to say but that your opinion is very just; but I own I am of a contrary way of thinking; I always thought so, and I always shall."

Should a man with persevering temper tell you that he is ready to adopt your sentiments if you will only explain them; should he beg only to have a reason for your opinion—no, you can give no reason. Let him urge you to say something in its defense:—no; like Queen Anne, you will only repeat the same thing over again, or be silent. Silence is the ornament of your sex; and in silence, if there be not wisdom, there is safety. You will, then, if you please, according to your custom, sit listening to all entreaties to explain, and speak—with a fixed immutability of posture, and a pre-determined deafness of eye, which shall put your opponent utterly out of patience; yet still by persevering with the same complacent importance of countenance, you shall half persuade people you could speak if you would; you shall keep them in doubt by that true want of meaning, "which puzzles more than wit;" even because they cannot conceive the excess of your stupidity, they shall actually begin to believe that they themselves are stupid. Ignorance and doubt are the great parents of the sublime.

Your adversary, finding you impenetrable to argument, perhaps would try wit:—but, "On the impassive ice the lightnings play." His eloquence or his kindness will avail less; when in yielding to you after a long harangue, he expects to please you, you will answer undoubtedly with the utmost propriety, "That you should be very sorry he yielded his judgment to you; that he is very good; that you are much obliged to him; but that, as to the point in dispute, it is a matter of perfect indifference to you; for your part, you have no choice at all about it; you beg that he will do just what he pleases; you know that it is the duty of a wife to submit; but you hope, however, you may have an *opinion* of your own."

Remember, all such speeches as these will lose above half their effect, if you cannot accompany them with the vacant stare, the insipid smile, the passive aspect of the humbly perverse.

Whilst I write, new precepts rush upon my recollection; but the subject is inexhaustible. I quit it with regret, though fully sensible of my presumption in having attempted to instruct those who, whilst they read, will smile in the consciousness of superior powers. Adieu! then, my fair readers: long may you prosper in the practice of an art peculiar to your sex! Long may you maintain unrivalled dominion at home and abroad; and long may your husbands rue the hour when first they made you promise *"to obey!"*

SEA-STORIES

BY LADY GREGORY

I was told by:

A Man on the Height near Dun Conor:

It's said there's everything in the sea the same as on the land, and we know there's horses in it. This boy here saw a horse one time out in the sea, a grey one, swimming about. And there were three men from the north island caught a horse in their nets one night when they were fishing for mackerel, but they let it go; it would have broke the boat to bits if they had brought it in, and anyhow they thought it was best to leave it. One year at Kinvara, the people were missing their oats that was eaten in the fields, and they watched one night and it was five or six of the sea-horses they saw eating the oats, but they could not take them, they made off to the sea.

And there was a man on the north island fishing on the rocks one time, and a mermaid came up before him, and was partly like a fish and the rest like a woman. But he called to her in the name of God to be off, and she went and left him.

There was a boy was sent over here one morning early by a friend of mine on the other side of the island, to bring over some cattle that were in a field he had here, and it was before daylight, and he came to the door crying, and said he heard thirty horses or more galloping over the roads there, where you'd think no horse could go.

Surely those things are on the sea as well as on the land. My father was out fishing one night off Tyrone and something came beside the boat that had eyes shining like candles. And then a wave came in, and a storm rose of a moment, and whatever was in the wave, the weight of it had like to sink the boat. And then they saw that it was a woman in the sea that had the shining eyes. So my father went to the priest, and he bid him always to take a drop of holy water and a pinch of salt out in the boat with him, and nothing would harm him.

A Galway Bay Lobster-Seller:

They are on the sea as well as on the land, and their boats are often to be seen on the bay, sailing boats and others. They look like our own, but when you come near them they are gone in an instant.

My mother one time thought she saw our own boat come in to the pier with my father and two other men in it, and she got the supper ready, but when she went down to the pier and called them there was nothing there, and the boat didn't come in till two hours after.

There were three or four men went out one day to fish, and it was a dead calm; but all of a sudden they heard a blast and they looked, and within about three mile of the boat they saw twelve men from the waist, the rest of them was under water. And they had sticks in their hands and were striking one another. And where they were, and the blast, it was rough, but smooth and calm on each side.

There's a sort of a light on the sea sometimes; some call it a "Jack O'Lantern" and some say it is sent by *them* to mislead them.

There's many of them out in the sea, and often they pull the boats down. It's about two years since four fishermen went out from Aran, two fathers and two sons, where they saw a big ship coming in and flying the flag for a pilot, and they thought she wanted to be brought in to Galway. And when they got near the ship, it faded away to nothing and the boat turned over and they were all four drowned.

There were two brothers of my own went to fish for the herrings, and what they brought up was like the print of a cat, and it turned with the inside of the skin outside, and no hair. So they pulled up the nets, and fished no more that day. There was one of *them* lying on the strand here, and some of the men of the village came down of a sudden and surprised him. And when he saw he was taken he began a great crying. But they only lifted him down to the sea and put him back into it. Just like a man they said he was. And a little way out there was another just like him, and when he saw that they treated the one on shore so kindly, he bowed his head as if to thank them.

Whatever's on the land, there's the same in the sea, and between the islands of Aran they can often see the horses galloping about at the bottom.

There was a sort of a big eel used to be in Tully churchyard, used to come and to root up the bodies, but I didn't hear of him of late—he may be done away with now.

There was one Curran told me one night he went down to the strand where he used to be watching for timber thrown up and the like. And on the strand, on the dry sands, he saw a boat, a grand one with sails spread and all, and it up farther than any tide had ever reached. And he saw a great many people round about it, and it was all lighted up with lights. And he got afraid and went away. And four hours after, after sunrise, he went there again to look at it, and there was no sign of it, or of any fire, or of any other thing. The Mara-warra (mermaid) was seen on the shore not long ago, combing out her hair. She had no fish's tail, but was like another woman.

John Corley:

There is no luck if you meet a mermaid and you out at sea, but storms will come, or some ill will happen.

There was a ship on the way to America, and a mermaid was seen following it, and the bad weather began to come. And the captain said, "It must be some man in the ship she's following, and if we knew which one it was, we'd put him out to her and save ourselves." So they drew lots, and the lot fell on one man, and then the captain was sorry for him, and said he'd give him a chance till tomorrow. And the next day she was following them still, and they drew lots again, and the lot fell on the same man. But the captain said he'd give him a third chance, but the third day the lot fell on him again. And when they were going to throw him out he said, "Let me alone for a while." And he went to the end of the ship and he began to sing a song in Irish, and when he sang, the mermaid began to be quiet and to rock like as if she was asleep. So he went on singing till they came to America, and just as they got to the land the ship was thrown up into the air, and came down on the water again. There's a man told me that was surely true.

And there was a boy saw a mermaid down by Spiddal not long ago, but he saw her before she saw him, so she did him no harm. But if she'd seen him first, she'd have brought him away and drowned him.

Sometimes a light will come on the sea before the boats to guide them to the land. And my own brother told me one day he was out and a storm came on of a sudden, and the sail of the boat was let down as quick and as well as if two men were in it. Some neighbor or friend it must have been that did that for him. Those that go down to the sea after the tide going out, to cut the weed, often hear under the sand the sound of the milk being churned. There's some didn't believe that till they heard it themselves.

A Man from Roundstone:

One night I was out on the boat with another man, and we saw a big ship near us with about twenty lights. She was as close to us as that rock (about thirty yards), but we saw no one on board. And she was like some of the French ships that sometimes come to Galway. She went on near us for a while, and then she turned towards the shore and then we knew that she was not a right ship. And she went straight on to the land, and when she touched it, the lights went out and we saw her no more.

There was a comrade of mine was out one night, and a ship came after him, with lights, and she full of people. And as they drew near the land, he heard them shouting at him and he got afraid, and he went down and got a coal of fire and threw it at the ship, and in a minute it was gone.

A Schoolmaster:

A boy told me last night of two men that went with poteen to the Island of Aran. And when they were on the shore they saw a ship coming as if to land, and they said, "We'll have the bottle ready for those that are coming." But when the ship came close to the land, it vanished. And presently they got their boat ready and put out to sea. And a sudden blast came and swept one of them off. And the other saw him come up again, and put out the oar across his breast for him to take hold of it. But he would not take it but said, "I'm all right again now," and sank down again and was never seen no more.

John Nagle:

For one there's on the land there's ten on the sea. When I lived at Ardfry there was never a night but there was a voice heard crying and roaring, by them that were out in the bay. A baker he was from Loughrea, used to give short weight and measure, and so he was put there for a punishment.

I saw a ship that was having a race with another go suddenly down into the sea, and no one could tell why. And afterwards one of the Government divers was sent down to look for her, and he told me he'd never as long as he'd live go down again, for there at the bottom he found her, and the captain and the saloon passengers, and all sitting at the table and eating their dinner, just as they did before.

A Little Girl:

One time a woman followed a boat from Galway twenty miles out, and when they saw that she was some bad thing, wanting some of them, they drowned her.

Mrs. Casey:

I was at home and I got some stories from a man I had suspected of having newses. And he told me that when he was a youngster he was at a height where there used to be a great many of them. And all of a sudden he saw them fly out to where a boat was coming from Duras with seaweed. And they went in two flights, and so fast that they swept the water away from each side the boat, and it was left on the sand, and this they did over and over, just to be humbugging the man in the boat, and he was kept there a long time. When they first rose up, they were like clouds of dust, but with all sorts of colors, and then he saw their faces turned, but they kept changing color every minute. Laughing and humbugging they seemed to be.

My uncle that used to go out fishing for mackerel told me that one night some sort of a monster came under the boat and it wasn't a fish, and it had them near upset.

At an evening gathering in Inishmaan, by a Son of the House:

There was a man on this island was down on the beach one evening with his dog, and some black thing came up out of the sea, and the dog made for it and began to fight it. And the man began to run home and he called the dog, and it followed him, but every now and again it would stop and begin to fight again. And when he got to the house he called the dog in and shut the door, and whatever was outside began hitting against the door but it didn't get in. But the dog went in under the bed in the room, and before morning it was dead.

The Man of the House:

A horse I've seen myself on the sea and on the rocks—a brown one, just like another. And I threw a stone at it, and it was gone in a minute. We often heard there was fighting amongst *these.* And one morning before daybreak I went down to the strand with some others, and the whole of the strand, and it low tide, was covered with blood.

Colman Kane:

I knew a woman on this island and she and her daughter went down to the strand one morning to pick weed, and a wave came and took the daughter away. And a week after that, the mother saw her coming to the house, but she didn't speak to her.

There was a man coming from Galway here and he had no boatman. And on the way he saw a man that was behind him in the boat, that was putting up the sail and taking the management of everything, and he spoke no word. And he was with him all the way, but when the boat came to land, he was gone, and the man isn't sure, but he thinks it was his brother.

You see that sand below on the south side. When the men are out with the mackerel boats at early morning, they often see those sands covered with boys and girls.

There were some men out fishing in the bay one time, and a man came and held on to the boat, and wanted them to make room for him to get in, and after a time he left them. He was one of *those.* And there was another of them came up on the rocks one day, and called out to Martin Flaherty that was going out and asked what was his name.

There's said to be another island out there that's enchanted, and there are some that see it. And it's said that a fisherman landed on it one time, and he saw a little house, and he went in, and a very nice-looking young woman came out and said, "What will you say to me?" and he said, "You are a very nice lady." And a second came and asked him the same thing and a third, and he made the same answer. And after that they said, "You'd best run for your life," and so he did, and his curragh was floating along and he had but just time to get into it, and the island was gone. But if he had said "God bless you," the island would have been saved.

A Fisherman on Kilronan Pier:

I don't give in to these things myself, but they'd make you believe them in the middle island. Mangan, that I lodged with there, told me of seeing a ship when he was out with two other men, that followed them and vanished. And he said one of the men took to his bed from that time and died. And Doran told me about the horse he saw, that was in every way like a horse you'd see on land. And a man on the south island told me how he saw a calf one morning on the strand, and he thought it belonged to a neighbor, and was going to drive it up to his field, when its mother appeared on the sea, and it went off to her.

They are in the sea as well as on the land. That is well known by those that are out fishing by the coast. When the weather is calm, they can look down sometimes and see cattle and pigs and all such things as we have ourselves. And at nights their boats come out and they can be seen fishing, but they never last out after one o'clock.

The cock always crows on the first of March every year at one o'clock. And there was a man brought a cock out with him in his boat to try them. And the first time when it crowed they all vanished. That is how they were detected.

There are more of them in the sea than on the land, and they sometimes try to come over the side of the boat in the form of fishes, for they can take their choice shape.

Pat O'Hagan:

There were two fine young women—red-haired women—died in my village about six months ago. And I believe they're living yet. And there are some have seen them appear. All I ever saw myself was one day I was out fishing with two others, and we saw a canoe coming near us, and we were afraid it would come near enough to take away our fish. And as we looked it turned into a three-masted ship, and people in it. I could see them well, dark-coloured and dressed like sailors. But it went away and did us no harm.

One night I was going down to the curragh, and it was a night in harvest, and the stars shining, and I saw a ship fully rigged going towards the coast of Clare where no ship could go. And when I looked again, she was gone.

And one morning early, I and other men that were with me, and one of them a friend of the man here, saw a ship coming to the island, and he thought she wanted a pilot, and put out in the curragh. But when we got to where she was, there was no sign of her, but where she was the water was covered with black gulls, and I never saw a black gull before, thousands and crowds of them, and not one white bird among them. And one of the boys that was with me took a tar-pin and threw it at one of the gulls and hit it on the head, and when he did, the curragh went down to the rowlocks in the water—up to that—and it's nothing but a miracle she ever came up again, but we got back to land. I never went to a ship again, for the people said it was on account of me helping in the Preventive Service it happened, and that if I'd hit at one of the gulls myself, there would have been a bad chance for us. But those were no right gulls, and the ship was no living ship.

The Old Man in the Kitchen:

It's in the middle island the most of them are, and I'll tell you a thing that I know of myself that happened not long ago. There was a young girl, and one evening she was missing, and they made search for her everywhere and they thought that she was drowned or that she had gone away with some man. And in the evening of the next day there was a boy out in a curragh, and as he passed by a rock that is out in the sea there was the girl on it, and he brought her off. And surely she could not go there by herself. I suppose she wasn't able to give much account of it, and now she's after going to America.

And in Aran there were three boys and their uncle went out to a ship they saw coming, to pilot her into the bay. But when they got to where she was, there was no ship, and a sea broke over the canoe, and they were drowned, all fine strong men. But a man they had with them that was no use or of no account, he came safe to land. And I know a man in this island saw curraghs and curraghs full of people about the island of a Sunday morning early, but I never saw them myself. And one Sunday morning in my time there were scores and scores lying their length by the sea on the sand below, and they saw a woman in the sea, up to her waist, and she racking her hair and settling herself and as clean and as nice as if she was on land. Scores of them saw that.

There's a house up there where the family have to leave a plate of potatoes ready every night, and all's gone in the morning.

They are said to have all things the same as ourselves under the sea, and one day a cow was seen swimming as if for the headland, but before she got to it she turned another way and went down. And one time I got a small muc-warra (porpoise) and I went to cut it up to get what was good of it, for it had about two inches of fat, and when I cut it open the heart and the liver and every bit of it were for all the world like a pig you would cut up on land.

There's a house in the village close by this that's haunted. My sister was sitting near it one day, and it empty and locked, and some other little girls, and they heard a noise in it, and at the same time the flags they were sitting on grew red-hot, that they had to leave them. And another time the woman of the house was sick, and a little girl that was sitting by the fire in the kitchen saw standing in the door the sister of the woman that was sick, and she a good while dead, and she put up her arm, as if to tell her not to notice her. And the poor woman of that house, she had no luck, nothing but miscarriages or dead babies. And one child lived to be nine months old, and there was less flesh on it at the end of the nine months than there was the day it was born. She has a little girl now that's near a year old, but her arm isn't the size of that, and she's crabbed and not like a child as she should be. Many a one that's long married without having a child goes to the fortune-teller in Galway, and those that think anything of themselves go to Roundstone.

A Man near Loughmore:

I know a woman was washed and laid out, and it went so far that two half-penny candles were burned over her. And then she sat up, came back again, and spoke to her husband, and told him how to divide his property, and to manage the children well. And her step-son began to question her, and he might have got a lot out of her but her own son stopped him and said to let her alone. And then she turned over on her side and died. She was not to say an old woman. It's not often the old are taken. What use would there be for them? But a woman to be taken young, you know there's demand for her. It's the people in the middle island know about these things. There were three boys from there lost in a curragh at the point near the lighthouse, and for long after their friends were tormented when they came there fishing, and they would see ships there when the people of this island that were out at the same time couldn't see them. There were three or four out in a curragh near the lighthouse, and a conger-eel came and upset it, and they were all saved but one, but he was brought down and for the whole day they could hear him crying and screeching under the sea. And they were not the only ones, but a fisherman that was there from Galway had to go away and leave it, because of the screeching.

There was a coast-guard's wife there was all but gone, but she was saved after. And there's a boy here now was for a long time that they'd give the world he was gone altogether with the state he was in, and now he's as strong as any boy in the island; and if ever any one was away and came back again, it was him. Children used often to be taken, but there's a great many charms in use in these days that saves them. A big sewing-needle you'll see the woman looking for to put with a baby, and as long as that's with it, it's safe. But anyway they're always put back again into the world before they die in the place of some young person. And even a beast of any consequence if anything happens to it, no one in the island would taste it; there might be something in it, some old woman or the like.

There were a few young men from here were kept in Galway for a day, and they went to a woman there that works the cards. And she told them of deaths that would come in certain families. And it wasn't a fortnight after that five boys were out there, just where you see the curragh now, and they were upset and every one drowned, and they were of the families that she had named on the cards.

My uncle told me that one night they were all up at that house up the road, making a match for his sister, and they stopped till near morning, and when they went out, they all had a drop taken. And he was going along home with two or three others and one of them, Michael Flaherty, said he saw people on the shore. And another of them said that there were not, and my uncle said, "If Flaherty said that and it not true, we have a right to bite the ear off him, and it would be no harm." And then they parted, and my uncle had to pass by the beach, and then he saw whole companies of people coming up from the sea, that he didn't know how he'd get through them, but they opened before him and let him pass.

There were men going to Galway with cattle one morning from the beach down there, and they saw a man up to his middle in the sea—all of them saw it.

There was a man was down early for lobsters on the shore at the middle island, and he saw a horse up to its middle in the sea, and bowing its head down as if to drink. And after he had watched it awhile it disappeared.

There was a woman walking over by the north shore—God have mercy on her—she's dead since—and she looked out and saw an island in the sea, and she was a long time looking at it. It's known to be there, and to be enchanted, but only few can see it.

There was a man had his horse drawing seaweed up there on the rocks, the way you see them drawing it every day, in a basket on the mare's back. And on this day every time he put the load on, the mare would let its leg slip and it would come down again, and he was vexed and he had a stick in his hand and he gave the mare a heavy blow. And that night she had a foal that was dead, not come to its full growth, and it had spots over it, and every spot was of a different color. And there was no sire on the island at that time, so whatever was the sire must have come up from the sea.

A Man Watching the Weed-gatherers:

There's no doubt at all about the sea-horses. There was a man out at the other side of the island, and he saw one standing on the rocks and he threw a stone at it and it went off in the sea. He said it was grand to see it swimming, and the mane and the tail floating on the top of the water.

A Woman from the Connemara Side:

I was told there was a mare that had a foal, and it had never had a horse. And one day the mare and foal were down by the sea, and a horse put up its head and neighed, and away went the foal to it and came back no more.

And there was a man on this island watched his field one night where he thought the neighbours' cattle were eating his grass, and what he saw was horses and foals coming up from the sea. And he caught a foal and kept it, and set it racing, and no horse or no pony could ever come near it, till one day the race was on the strand, and away with it into the sea, and the jockey along with it, and they never were seen again.

Mrs. O'Dea and Mrs. Daly:

There was a cow seen come up out of the sea one day and it walked across the strand, and its udder like as if it had been lately milked. And Tommy Donohue was running up to tell his father to come down and see it, and when he looked back it was gone out to sea again.

There was a man here was going to build a new house, and he brought a wise woman to see would it be in the right place. And she made five heaps of stones in five places, and said, "Whatever heap isn't knocked in the night, build it there." And in the morning all the heaps were knocked but one, and so he built it there.

One time I was out over by that island with another man, and we saw three women standing by the shore, beating clothes with a beetle. And while we looked, they vanished, and then we heard the cry of a child passing over our heads twenty feet in the air.

I know they go out fishing like ourselves, for Father Mahony told me so; and one night I was out myself with my brother, beyond where that ship is, and we heard talk going on, so we knew that a boat was near, and we called out to let them know we heard them, and then we saw the boat and it was just like any other one, and the talk went on, but we couldn't understand what they were saying. And then I turned to light my pipe, and while I lighted it, the boat and all in it were gone.

Mrs. Casey:

I got a story from an old man down by the sea at Tyrone. He says there was a man went down one night to move his boat from the shore where it was to the pier. And when he had put out, he found it was going out to sea, instead of to touch the pier, and he felt it very heavy in the water, and he looked behind him and there on the back of the boat were six men in shiny black clothes like sailors, and there was one like a harvest-man dressed in white flannel with a belt round his waist. And he asked what they were doing, and the man in white said he had brought the others out to make away with them there, and he took and cut their bodies in two and threw them one by one over the boat, and then he threw himself after them into the sea. And the boat went under water too, and the poor man himself lost his wits, but it came up again and he said he had never seen as many people as he did in that minute under the water. And then he got home and left the boat, and in the morning he came down to it, and there was blood in it; and first he washed it and then he painted it, but for all he could do, he couldn't get rid of the blood.

Peter Donohue:

There was a woman, a friend of this man's, living out in the middle island, and one day she came down to where a man of this island was putting out his curragh to come back, and she said, "I just saw a great crowd of them—that's the Sheogue—going over to your island like a cloud." And when he got home he went up to a house there beyond, where the old woman used to be selling poteen on the sly. And while he was there her little boy came running in and cried, "Hide away the poteen, for the police are on the island! Such a man called to me from his curragh to give warning, for he saw the road full of them with the crowd of them and they with their guns and cutlasses and all the rest." But the man was in the house first knew well what it was, after what he heard from the woman on the other island, and that they were no right police, and sure enough no other one ever saw them. And that same day, my mother had put out wool to dry in front of where that house is with the three chimneys, near the Chapel. And I was there talking to some man, one on each side of the yard, and the wall between us. And the day was as fine as this day is and finer, and not a breath of air stirring. And a woman that lived near by had her wool out drying too. And the wool that was in my mother's yard began to rise up, as if something was under it, and I called to the other man to help me to hold it down, but for all we could do it went up in the air, a hundred feet and more, till we could see it no more. And after a couple of hours it began to drop again, like snow, some on the thatch and some on the rocks and some in the gardens. And I think it was a fortnight before my mother had done gathering it. And one day she was spinning it, I don't know what put it in my mind, but I asked her did she lose much of that wool. And what she said was, "If I didn't get more than my own, I didn't get less." That's true and no lie, for I never told a lie in my life—I think. But the wool belonging to the neighboring woman was never stirred at all.

And the woman that had the wool that wasn't stirred, she is the woman I married after, and that's now my wife.

There was a man, one Power, died in this island, and one night that was bright there was a friend of his going out for mackerel, and he saw these sands full of people hurling, and he well knew Power's voice that he heard among them.

There was a cousin of my own built a new house, and when they were first in it and sitting round the fire, the woman of the house that was singing for them saw a great blot of blood come down the chimney on to the floor, and they thought there would be no luck in the house and that it was a wrong place. But they had nothing but good luck ever after.

Peter Dolan:

There was a man that died in the middle island, that had two wives. And one day he was out in the curragh he saw the first wife appear. And after that one time the son of the second wife was sick, and the little girl, the first wife's daughter, was out tending cattle, and a can of water with her and she had a waistcoat of her father's put about her body, where it was cold. And her mother appeared to her in the form of a sheep, and spoke to her, and told her what herbs to find, to cure the step-brother, and sure enough they cured him. And she bid her leave the waistcoat there and the can, and she did. And in the morning the waistcoat was folded there, and the can standing on it. And she appeared to her in her own shape another time, after that. Why she came like a sheep the first time was that she wouldn't be frightened. The girl is in America now, and so is the step-brother that got well.

A Galway Woman:

One time myself, I was up at the well beyond, and looking into it, a very fine day, and no breath of air stirring, and the stooks were ripe standing about me. And all in a minute a noise began in them, and they were like as if knocking at each other and fighting like soldiers all about me.

Mary Moran:

There was a girl here that had been to America and came back, and one day she was coming over from Liscannor in a curragh, and she looked back and there behind the curragh was the "Gan ceann" the headless one. And he followed the boat a great way, but she said nothing. But a gold pin that was in her hair fell out, and into the sea, that she had brought from America, and then it disappeared. And her sister was always asking her where was the pin she brought from America, and she was afraid to say. But at last she told her, and the sister said, "It's well for you it fell out, for what was following you would never have left you, till you threw it a ring or something made of gold." It was the sister herself that told me this.

Up in the village beyond they think a great deal of these things and they won't part with a drop of milk on May Eve, and last Saturday week that was May Eve there was a poor woman dying up there, and she had no milk of her own, and as is the custom, she went out to get a drop from one or other of the neighbors. But not one would give it because it was May Eve. I declare I cried when I heard it, for the poor woman died on the second day after.

And when my sister was going to America she went on the first of May and we had a farewell party the night before, and in the night a little girl that was there saw a woman from that village go out, and she watched her, and saw her walk round a neighbor's house, and pick some straw from the roof.

And she told of it, and it happened a child had died in that house and the father said the woman must have had a hand in it, and there was no good feeling to her for a long while. Her own husband is lying sick now, so I hear.

DEVEREUX'S DREAM

BY JOSEPH SHERIDAN LE FANU

I give you this story only at second-hand; but you have it in substance—and he wasted few words over it—as Paul Devereux told it me.

It was not the only queer story he could have told about himself if he had chosen, by a good many, I should say. Paul's life had been an eminently unconventional one: the man's face certified to that—hard, bronzed, war-worn, seamed and scarred with strange battle-marks—the face of a man who had dared and done most things.

It was not his custom to speak much of what he had done, however. Probably only because he and I were little likely to meet again that he told me this I am free to tell you now.

We had come across one another for the first time for years that afternoon on the Italian Boulevart. Paul had landed a couple of weeks previously at Marseilles from a long yacht-cruise in southern waters, the monotony of which we heard had been agreeably diversified by a little pirate-hunting and slaver-chasing—the evil tongues called it piracy and slave-running; and certainly Devereux was quite equal to either *métier*; and he was about starting on a promising little filibustering expedition across the Atlantic, where the chances were he would be shot, and the certainty was that he would be starved. So perhaps he felt inclined to be a trifle more communicative than usual, as we sat late that night over a blazing pyre of logs and in a cloud of Cavendish. At all events he was, and after this fashion.

I forget now exactly how the subject was led up to. Expression of some philosophic incredulity on my part regarding certain matters, followed by a ten-minutes' silence on his side pregnant with unwonted words to come—that was it, perhaps. At last he said, more to himself, it seemed, than to me:

"'Such stuff as dreams are made of.' Well, who knows? You're a Sadducee, Bertie; you call this sort of thing, politely, indigestion. Perhaps you're right. But yet I had a queer dream once."

"Not unlikely," I assented.

"You're wrong; I never dream, as a rule. But, as I say, I had a queer dream once; and queer because it came literally true three years afterward."

"Queer indeed, Paul."

"Happens to be true. What's queerer still, my dream was the means of my finding a man I owed a long score, and a heavy one, and of my paying him in full."

"Bad for the payee!" I thought.

Paul's face had grown terribly eloquent as he spoke those last words. On a sudden the expression of it changed—another memory was stirring in him. Wonderfully tender the fierce eyes grew; wonderfully tender the faint, sad smile, that was like sunshine on storm-scathed granite. That smile transfigured the man before me.

"Ah, poor child—poor Lucille!" I heard him mutter.

That was it, was it? So I let him be. Presently he lifted his head. If he had let himself get the least thing out of hand for a moment, he had got back his self-mastery the next.

"I'll tell you that queer story, Bertie, if you like," he said.

The proposition was flatteringly unusual, but the voice was quite his own.

"Somehow I'd sooner talk than think about—*her*," he went on after a pause.

I nodded. He might talk about this, you see, but *I* couldn't. He began with a question—an odd one:

"Did you ever hear I'd been married?"

Paul Devereux and a wife had always seemed and been to me a most unheard-of conjunction. So I laconically said:

"No."

"Well, I was once, years ago. She was my wife—that child—for a week. And then———"

I easily filled up the pause; but, as it happened, I filled it up wrongly; for he added:

"And then she was murdered."

I was not unused to our Paul's stony style of talk; but this last sentence was sufficiently startling.

"Eh?"

"Murdered—in her sleep. They never found the man who did it either, though I had Durbec and all the Rue de Jérusalem at work. But I forgave them that, for I found the man myself, and killed him."

He was filling his pipe again as he told me this, and he perhaps rammed the Cavendish in a little tighter, but that was all. The thing was a matter of course; I knew my Paul, well enough to know that. Of course he killed him.

"Mind you," he continued, kindling the black *brûle-gueule* the while—"mind you, I'd never seen this man before, never known of his existence, except in a way that—however, it was this way."

He let his grizzled head drop back on the cushions of his chair, and his eyes seemed to see the queer story he was telling enacted once more before him in the red hollows of the fire.

"As I said, it was years ago. I was waiting here in Paris for some fellows who were to join me in a campaign we'd arranged against the African big game. I never was more fit for anything of that sort than I was then. I only tell you this to show you that the thing can't be accounted for by my nerves having been out of order at all.

"Well: I was dining alone that day, at the Café Anglais. It was late when I sat down to my dinner in the little salon as usual. Only two other men were still lingering over theirs. All the time they stayed they bored me so persistently with some confounded story of a murder they were discussing, that I was once or twice more than half-inclined to tell them so. At last, though, they went away.

"But their talk kept buzzing abominably in my head. When the waiter brought me the evening paper, the first thing that caught my eye was a circumstantial account of the *probable* way the fellow did his murder. I say probable, for they never caught him; and, as you will see directly, they could only suppose how it occurred.

"It seemed that a well-known Paris banker, who was ascertained beyond doubt to have left one station alive and well, and with a couple of hundred thousand francs in a leathern *sac* under his seat, arrived at the next station the train stopped at with his throat cut and *minus* all his money, except a few banknotes to no great amount, which the assassin had been wise enough to leave behind him. The train was a night express on one of the southern lines; the banker travelled quite alone, in a first-class carriage; and the murder must have taken place between midnight and 1 a.m. next morning. The newspapers supposed—rightly enough, I think—that the murderer must have entered the carriage *from without*, stabbed his victim in his sleep—there were no signs of any struggle—opened the *sac*, taken what he wanted, and retreated, loot and all, by the way he came. I fully indorsed my particular writer's opinion that the murderer was an uncommonly cool and clever individual, especially as I fancy he got clear off and was never afterward laid hands on.

"When I had done that I thought I had done with the affair altogether. Not at all. I was regularly ridden with this confounded murder. You see the banker was rather a swell; everybody knew him: and that, of course, made it so shocking. So everybody kept talking about him: they were talking about him at the Opera, and over the *baccarat* and *bouillotte* at La Topaze's later. To escape him I went to bed and smoked myself to sleep. And then a queer thing came to pass: I had a dream—I who never dream; and this is what I dreamed:

"I saw a wide, rich country that I knew. A starless night hung over it like a pall. I saw a narrow track running through it, straight, both ways, for leagues. Something sped along this track with a hurtling rush and roar. This something that at first had looked like a red-eyed devil, with dark sides full of dim fire, resolved itself, as I watched it, presently, into a more conventional night express-train. It flew along, though, as no express-train ever travelled yet; for all that, I was able to keep it quite easily in view. I could count the carriages as they whirled by. One—two—three—four—five—six; but I could only see distinctly into one. Into that one with perfect distinctness. Into that one I seemed forced to look.

"It was the fourth carriage. Two people were in it. They sat in opposite corners; both were sleeping. The one who sat facing forward was a woman—a girl, rather. I could see that; but I couldn't see her face. The blind was drawn across the lamp in the roof, and the light was very dim; moreover, this girl lay back in the shadow. Yet I seemed to know her, and I knew that her face was very fair. She wore a cloak that shrouded her form completely, yet her form was familiar to me.

"The figure opposite to her was a man's. Strangely familiar to me too this figure was. But, as he slept, his head had sunk upon his breast, and the shadow cast upon his face by the low-drawn travelling-cap he wore hid it from me. Yet if I had seemed to know the girl's face, I was certain I knew the man's. But as I could see, so I could remember, neither. And there was an absolute torture in this which I can't explain to you,—in this inability, and in my inability to wake them from their sleep.

"From the first I had been conscious of a desire to do that. This desire grew stronger every second. I tried to call to them, and my tongue wouldn't move. I tried to spring toward them, to thrust out my arms and touch them, and my limbs were paralyzed. And then I tried to shut my eyes to what I *knew* must happen, and my eyes were held open and dragged to look on in spite of me. And I saw this:

"I saw the door of the carriage where these two sleepers, whose sleep was so horribly sound, were sitting—I saw this door open, and out of the thick darkness another face look in.

"The light, as I have said, was very dim, but I could see his face as plainly as I can see yours. A large yellow face it was, like a wax mask. The lips were full, and lustful and cruel. The eyes were little eyes of an evil gray. Thin yellow streaks marked the absence of the eyebrows; thin yellow hair showed itself under a huge fur travelling-cap. The whole face seemed to grow slowly into absolute distinctness as I looked, by the sort of devilish light that it, as it were, radiated. I had chanced upon a good many damnable visages before then; but there was a cold fiendishness about this one such as I had seen on no man's face, alive or dead, till then.

"The next moment the man this face belonged to was standing in the carriage, that seemed to plunge and sway more furiously, as though to waken them that still slept on. He wore a long fur travelling-robe, girt about the waist with a fur girdle. Abnormally tall and broad as he was, he looked in this dress gigantic. Yet there was a marvellous cat-like lightness and agility about all his movements.

"He bent over the girl lying there helpless in her sleep. I don't make rash bargains as a rule, but I felt I would have given years of my life for five minutes of my lost freedom of limb just then. I tell you the torture was infernal.

"The assassin—I knew he was an assassin—bent awhile, gloatingly, over the girl. His great yellow hands were both bare, and on the forefinger of the right hand I could see some great stone blazing like an evil eye. In that right hand there gleamed something else. I saw him draw it slowly from his sleeve, and, as he drew it, turn round and look at the other sleeper with an infernal triumphant malignity and hate the Devil himself might have envied. But the man he looked at slept heavily on. And then—God! I feel the agony I felt in my dream then now!—then I saw the great yellow hand, with the great evil eye upon it, lifted murderously, and the bright steel it held shimmer as the assassin turned again and bent his yellow face down closer to that other face hidden from me in the shadow—the girl's face, that I knew was so fair.

"How can I tell this?... The blade flashed and fell.... There was the sound of a heavy sigh stifled under a heavy hand....

"Then the huge form of the assassin was reared erect, and the bloated yellow face seemed to laugh silently, while the hand that held the steel pointed at the sleeping man in diabolical menace.

"And so the huge form and the bloated yellow face seemed to fade away while I watched.

"The express rushed and roared through the blinding darkness without; the sleeping man slept on still; till suddenly a strong light fell full upon him, and he woke.

"And then I saw why I had been so certain that I knew him. For as he lifted his head, I saw his face in the strong light.

"*And the face was my own face; and the sleeper was myself!*"

Paul Devereux made a pause in his queer story here. Except when he had spoken of the girl, he had spoken in his usual cool, hard way. The pipe he had been smoking all the time was smoked out. He took time to fill another before he went on. I said never a word, for I guessed who the sleeping girl was.

"Well," Paul remarked presently, "that was a devilish queer dream, wasn't it? You'll account for it by telling me I'd been so pestered with the story of the banker's murder that I naturally had nightmare; perhaps, too, that my digestion was out of order. Call it a nightmare, call it dyspepsia, if you like. I *don't*, because——— But you'll see why I don't directly.

"At the same moment that my dream-self awoke in my dream, my actual self woke in reality, and with the same ghastly horror.

"I say the *same* horror, for neither then nor afterward could I separate my one self from my other self. They seemed identical; so that this queer dream made a more lasting impression upon me than you'd think. However, in the life I led that sort of thing couldn't last very long. Before I came back from Africa I had utterly forgotten all about it. Before I left Paris, though, and while it was quite fresh in my memory, I sketched the big murderer just as I had seen him in my dream. The great yellow face, the great broad frame in the fur travelling-robe, the great hand with the great evil eye upon it—everything, carefully and minutely, as though I had been going to paint a portrait that I wanted to make lifelike. I think at the time I had some such intention. If I had, I never fulfilled it. But I made the sketch, as I say, carefully; and then I forgot all about it.

"Time passed—three years nearly. I was wintering in the south of France that year. There it was that I met her—Lucille. Old D'Avray, her father, and I had met before in Algeria. He was dying now. He left the child on his death-bed to me. The end was I married her.

"Poor little thing! I think I might have made her happy—who knows? She used to tell me often she was happy with me. Poor little thing!

"Well, we were to come straight to London. That was Lucille's notion. She wanted to go to my London first—nowhere else. Now I would rather have gone anywhere else; but, naturally, I let the child have her way. She seemed nervously eager about it, I remembered afterward; seemed to have a nervous objection to every other place I proposed. But I saw or suspected nothing to make me question her very closely, or the reasons for her preference for our grimy old Pandemonium. What could I suspect? Not the truth. If I only had! If I had only guessed what it was that made her, as she said, long to be safe there already. Safe? What had she to fear with me? Ah, what indeed!

"So we started on our journey to England. It was a cold, dark night, early in March. We reached Lyons somewhere about seven. I should have stayed there that night but for Lucille. She entreated me so earnestly and with such strange vehemence to go on by the night-mail to Paris, that at last, to satisfy her, I consented; though it struck me unpleasantly at the time that I had let her travel too long already, and that this feverishness was the consequence of over-fatigue. But she became pacified at once when I told her it should be as she wanted; and declared she should sleep perfectly well in the carriage with me beside her. She should feel quite safe then, she said.

"Safe! Where safer? you might ask. Nowhere, I believe. Alone with me—surely nowhere safer. The Paris express was a short train that night; but I managed to secure a compartment for ourselves. I left Lucille in her corner there while I went across to the *buffet* to fill a flask. I was gone barely five minutes; but when I came back the change in the child's face fairly startled me. I had seen it last with the smile it always wore for me on it, looking so childishly happy in the lamp-light. Now it was all gray-pale and distorted; and the great blue eyes told me directly with what.

"Fear—sudden, terrible fear—I thought. But *fear*? Fear of what? I asked her. She clung close to me half-sobbing awhile before she could answer; and then she told me—nothing. There was nothing the matter; only she had felt a pain—a cruel pain—at her heart; and it had frightened her. Yes, that was it; it had frightened her, but it had passed; and she was well, quite well again now.

"All this time her eyes seemed to be telling me another story; but I said nothing; she was obviously too excited already. I did my best to soothe her, and I succeeded. She told me she felt quite well once more before we started. No, she had rather, much rather go on to Paris, as I had promised her she should. She should sleep all the way, if no one came into the carriage to disturb her. No one could come in? Then nothing could be better.

"And so it was that she and I started that night by the Paris mail.

"I made her up a bed of rugs and wraps upon the cushions; but she had rather rest her head upon my shoulder, she said, and feel my arm about her; nothing could hurt her then. Ah, strange how she harped on that.

"She lay there, then, as she loved best—with her head resting on my shoulder, not sleeping much or soundly; uneasily, with sudden waking starts, and with glances round her; till I would speak to her. And then she would look up into my face and smile; and so drop into that uneasy sleep again. And I would think she was over-tired, that was all; and reproach myself with having let her come on. And three or four hours passed like this; and then we had got as far as Dijon.

"But the child was fairly worn out now; and she offered no opposition when I asked her to let me pillow her head on something softer than my shoulder. So I folded, a great thick shawl she was too well cloaked to need, and she made that her pillow.

"We were rushing full swing through the wild, dark night, when she lifted up her face and bade me kiss her and bid her sleep well. And I put my arm round her, and kissed the child's loving lips—for the last time while she lived. Then I flung myself on the seat opposite her; and, watching her till she slept soundly and peacefully, slept at last myself also. I had drawn the blind across the lamp in the roof, and the light in the carriage was very dim.

"How long I slept I don't know; it couldn't have been more than an hour and a half, because the express was slackening speed for its first halt beyond Dijon. I had slept heavily I knew; but I woke with a sudden, sharp sense of danger that made me broad awake, and strung every nerve in a moment. The sort of feeling you have when you wake on a prairie, where you have come across 'Indian sign;' on outpost-duty, when your *feldwebel* plucks gently at your cloak. You know what I mean.

"I was on my feet at once. As I said, the light in the carriage was very dim, and the shadow was deepest where Lucille lay. I looked there instinctively. She must have moved in her sleep, for her face was turned away from me; and the cloak I had put so carefully about her had partly fallen off. But she slept on still. Only soundly, very soundly; she scarcely seemed to breathe. And—*did* she breathe?

"A ghastly fear ran through my blood, and froze it. I understood why I had wakened. In my nostrils was an awful odor that I knew well enough. I bent over her; I touched her. Her face was very cold; her eyes glared glassily at me; my hands were wet with something. My hands were wet with blood—her blood!

"I tore away the blind from the lamp, and then I could see that my wife of a week lay there stabbed straight to the heart—dead—dead beyond doubting; murdered in her sleep."

Devereux's stern, low voice shook ever so little as he spoke those last words; and we both sat very silent after them for a good while. Only when he could trust his utterance again he went on.

"A curious piece of devilry, wasn't it? That child—whom had she ever harmed? Who could hate her like this? I remember I thought that, in a dull, confused sort of way, when I found myself alone in that carriage with her lying dead on the cushions before me. *Alone* with her—you understand? It was confusing.

"I pass over what immediately followed. The express came duly to a halt; and then I called people to me, and—and the Paris express went on without that particular carriage.

"The inquiry began before some local authority next day. Very little came of it. What could come of it, unless they had convicted *me* of the murder of this child I would have given my own life to save?

"They might have done that at home; but they knew better here, and didn't. They couldn't find me the actual assassin, however; though I believe they did their best. All they found was his weapon, which he most purposely have left behind. I asked for this, and got it. It gave their police no clue; and it gave me none. But I had a fancy for it.

"It was a plain, double-edged, admirably-tempered dagger—a very workmanlike article indeed. On the cross hilt of it I swore one day that I would live thenceforth for one thing alone—the discovery of the murderer of old D'Avray's child, whom I had promised him to care for before all. When I had found this man, whoever he was, I also swore that I would kill him. Kill him myself, you understand; without any of the law's delay or uncertainty, without troubling *bourreau* or hangman. Kill him as he had killed her—to do this was what I meant to live for. There was war to the knife between him and me.

"I started, of course, under one heavy disadvantage. He knew me, probably, whereas I didn't know him at all. When he found that his amiable intention of fixing the crime on me had been frustrated, it must, I imagined, have occurred to him that the said crime might eventually be fixed by me on him. And he had proved himself to be a person who didn't stick at trifles. It behooved me, therefore, to go to work cautiously. But I hadn't fought Indians for nothing; and I *was* very cautious. I waited quiet till I got a clue. It was a curious one; and I got it in this way. It struck me one day, suddenly, that I had heard of a murder precisely similar to this already. I could not at first call the thing to mind; but presently I remembered—my dream. And then I asked myself this:

Had not this murder been done before my eyes three years ago?

"I came to the conclusion that the circumstances of the murder in my dream were absolutely identical with the circumstances of the actual crime. Yes; the girl whose face in that dream I had never been able to see was Lucille. Yes; the assassin whose face I had seen so plainly in that dream was the real assassin. In short, I believe that the murder had been *rehearsed* before me three years previous to its actual committal.

"Now this sounds rather wild. Yet I came to this conviction quite coolly and deliberately. It *was* a conviction. Assuming it to be true, the odds against me grew shorter directly; *for I had the portrait of the man I wanted drawn by myself the day after I had seen him in my dream.* And the original of that portrait was a man not to be easily mistaken, supposing him to exist at all. The day I came across that sketch of him in that old forgotten sketch-book of mine, I was as sure he did exist as that I was alive myself. What I had to do was to find this man, and then I never doubted I should find the man I wanted. You see how the odds had shortened. If he knew me I knew him now, and he had no notion that I did know him. It was a good deal fairer fight between us.

"I fought it out alone. My story was hardly one the Rue de Jérusalem would have acted upon; and, besides, I wanted no interference. So, with the portrait before me, I sat down and began to consider who this man was, and why he had murdered that child. The big, burly frame, the heavy yellow face, the sandy-yellow hair, the physiognomy generally, was Teutonic. My man I put down as a North German. Now there were, and are probably, plenty of men who would have no objection whatever to put a knife into me, if they got the chance; but this man, whom I had never met, could have had no such quarrel as theirs with me. His quarrel with me must have been, then, Lucille. Yes, that was it—Lucille. I began to see clearly: a thwarted, devilish passion—a cool, infernal revenge. The child had feared something of this sort; had perhaps seen him that night. This explained her nervous terror, her nervous anxiety to stop nowhere, to travel on. In that carriage of that express-train, alone with me—where could she be safer? This accounted, too, for her anxiety to reach England. He would not dare follow her there, she had thought, or, at least, could not without my noticing him. And then she would have told me. She had not told me before evidently because she had feared for *me* too, in a quarrel with this man. She must, innocent child as she was, have had some instinctive knowledge of what he was capable.... Ay, a cool, infernal revenge, indeed. To kill her; to fix the murder on me. That dagger he had left behind. . . . The apparent impossibility of any one's entering the carriage as he must have entered it at all, to say nothing of the almost absolute impossibility of his doing so without disturbing either of us,—you see it might have gone hard with me if a British jury had had to decide on the case.

"Well, to cut this as short as may be, I made up my mind that the man I wanted was a North German; that he had conceived a hideous passion for Lucille before I knew her; that she had shrunk from it and him so unmistakably, that he knew he had no chance; that my taking her away as my wife, to which he might have been a witness, drove him to as hideous a revenge; that, hearing we were going to England, and seeing that we were likely to stop nowhere on the way, and so give him a chance of doing what he had made up his mind to do, he had decided to do what he had done as he had done it,—counting on finding us asleep as he had found us, or on his strength if it came to a fight between him and me; but coolly reckless enough to brave everything in any case. And the devil aiding, he had in great part and only too well succeeded. He was now either so far satisfied that, if I made no move against him—and how, he might think, could I?—he, feeling himself all safe, would let me be; or, on the other hand, he did not feel safe, and was not satisfied, and was arranging for my being disposed of by and by. I considered the latter frame of mind as his most probable one; I went to work cautiously, as I say. I ascertained that Lucille had made no mention of any obnoxious *prétendant* at any time; I didn't expect to find she had, her terror of the man was too intense. But this man must have met her somewhere—where?

"When old D'Avray came home to die, his daughter was just leaving her Paris *pensionnat*. All through his last illness he had seen no visitor but me, and Lucille had never quitted him. Besides, I had been there all the time. I presumed, then, that this man and she had met in Paris; and I believe they were only likely to have met at one of the half-dozen houses where the child would now and again be asked. I got a list of all these. One name only struck me; it happened to be a German name—Steinmetz. I wondered if Monsieur Steinmetz was my man. In the mean time, who was he? I had no trouble in finding that out: Monsieur Steinmetz was a German banker of good standing and repute, reasonably well off, and recently left a widower. Personally? *Dame*, personally Monsieur Steinmetz was a great man and a fat, with a big face and blond hair, and the appearance of what he really was—a *bon vivant* and a *bon enfant* yet *n'avait jamais fait de mal à personne—allez!*—All, yes; in effect, Madame had died about a year ago, and Monsieur had been inconsolable for a long time. He had changed his residence now, and inhabited a house in one of the new streets off the Champs Elysées.

"From another source I discovered that in the lifetime of Madame Steinmetz Lucille was frequently at the house. She had ceased to come there about the date of the commencement of Madame's sudden illness. I got this information by degrees, while I lay *perdu* in an old haunt of mine in the Pays Latin yonder; for I had always had an idea that I should find the man I wanted in Paris. When I had got it, I thought I should like to see Monsieur Steinmetz, the agreeable banker. One night I strolled up as far as his new residence in the street off the Champs Elysées. Monsieur Steinmetz lived on the first-floor. There was a brilliant light there: Monsieur Steinmetz was entertaining friends, it seemed.

"It was a fine night; I established myself out of sight under the doorway of an unfinished house opposite, and waited. I don't know why; perhaps I fancied that when his friends were gone, the fineness of the night might induce Monsieur Steinmetz to take a stroll, and that then I should be able to gratify my curiosity. You see, I knew that if he were my man, I should know him directly. I waited a good while: shadows crossed the lighted blinds; once a big, broad shadow appeared there, that made me fancy I mightn't have been waiting for nothing after all, somehow. Presently Monsieur Steinmetz's guests departed, and in a little while after there appeared on the little balcony of Monsieur Steinmetz's apartment *the man I wanted.* There was a moon that night, and the cold white light fell on the great yellow face, with the full lustful lips, and the full cruel chin, just as I had seen the light fall on it in my dream. It was the same face, Bertie; the same face, the same man. I couldn't be mistaken. I had no doubt; I *knew* that the assassin of my wife, of that tender, innocent, helpless child, stood there, twenty yards from me, on that balcony.

"I had got myself pretty well in hand; and it was as well. I never moved. The face I knew turned presently toward the spot where I stood hidden,—the face I had seen in my dream, beyond all doubting. The evil gray eyes glanced carelessly into the shadow, and up and down the quiet street; and then Monsieur Steinmetz, humming an air, got inside the window again, and closed it after him. Once more the great burly shadow that had at first told me I should not wait in that dark doorway in vain crossed the blinds; and then it disappeared. I saw my man no more that night; but I had seen enough. I knew who he was now, and where to find him.

"As I walked along home I thought what I would do. I quite meant to kill Monsieur Steinmetz; but I also meant to have no *démêlés* with an Impérial Procureur and the Cour d'Assizes for doing so. I didn't want to murder him, either. I thought I would wait a little for the chance of a suitable opportunity for settling my business satisfactorily. And I did wait. I turned this delay to account, and got together a case of circumstantial evidence against my man that, though perhaps it might have broken down in a law-court, would have been alone amply sufficient for me.

"The reason why Lucille's visits to the banker's house ceased was, it appeared, because Madame Steinmetz had conceived all at once a jealous dislike to her. How far this was owing to Lucille herself I could well understand; but I could understand Madame's jealousy equally well. Madame's illness, strangely sudden, dated from the cessation of Lucille's visits. Was it hard to find a *cause* for that illness—a cause for the wife's subsequent suspected death? I thought not. Then had followed Lucille's departure from Paris. The child's anxiety for her father hid her *other fear* from his eyes and mine; but that fear must have been on her then. With us she forgot it in time; yet it or another reason had always prevented all mention of what had occasioned it. She became my wife. At that very time I easily ascertained that Steinmetz was absent from Paris; less easily, but indubitably, that he had, at all events, been as far south as Lyons. At Lyons it must have been that Lucille first discovered he was dogging us. Hence her alarm, which I had remembered, and her anxiety to proceed on our journey without stopping for the night, as I had previously arranged. The morning after the murder Steinmetz reappeared in Paris. From the hour at which he was seen at the *gare*, it was certain that he had travelled by the night express train in which Lucille and I had started from Lyons; and he wore that morning a travelling-coat of fur in all respects similar to the one I remembered so well.

"If I had ever had any doubt of my man after actually seeing him, I should probably have convinced myself that he was my man by the general tendency of these facts, which I got at slowly and one by one. But I had no need of such evidence; and of course no case, even with such evidence, for a court of law. However, courts of law I had never intended to trouble in the matter.

"The opportunity I was waiting was some time before it offered. Monsieur Steinmetz was a man of regular habits, I found—from his first-floor in the street off the Champs Elysées, every morning at eleven, to the Bourse; thence to his bureau hard by till four; from his bureau to his café, where he read papers and played dominoes till six; and then home slowly by the Boulevarts. He might consider himself tolerably safe from me while he led this sort of life, even supposing he was aware he was incurring any danger. I don't think he troubled much about that; till one night, when, over the count of the beloved domino-points, his eyes met mine fixed right upon him. I had arranged this little surprise to see how it would affect him.

"Perhaps my gaze may have expressed something more than the mere distraction I intended; but I noticed—though a more indifferent observer might easily have failed to notice—how the great yellow face, expanded in childish interest in the childish game, seemed suddenly to grow gray and harden; how the fat smile became a cruel baring of sharp white teeth; how the fat chin squared itself. The man knew me, and scented danger.

"A moment's reflection convinced Monsieur Steinmetz, though, that it could be by no means so certain that I knew him; five minutes' observation of me more than half satisfied him that I did not. Yet what did I want there? What was I doing in Paris? This might concern him nearly, he must have thought.

"I kept my own face in order, and watched his. It wasn't an easy one to read; but you see I had studied it closely, and in a way he couldn't have dreamed of. Monsieur Steinmetz was outwardly his wonted self, but inwardly not quite comfortable when he rose; and I saw the evil eye gleam on his great yellow finger as he took out his purse to pay the *garçon*, just as I had seen it when that finger pointed at *myself* in my dream. I felt curious sensations, Bertie, as I sat there and looked abstractedly at Monsieur Steinmetz. I wondered how long it would be before——But my time hadn't come yet. He went out without another glance at me. I saw his huge form on the other side of the street when I left the café in my turn. This I had expected. Monsieur Steinmetz was naturally curious. It was hardly possible that I could know him; but it was quite certain that he ought to know all about me. So, when I moved on, he moved on; in short, Monsieur Steinmetz dogged me up one street and down another, till he finally dogged me home to my hiding-place in the Pays Latin. He did it very well, too—much better than you would have expected from so apparently unwieldy a *mouchard*. But I *remembered* how lightly he could move.

"Next day I had, of course, disappeared from my old quarters, and gone no one knew where. I suppose Monsieur Steinmetz didn't like this fact when he heard of it. It might have seemed suspicious. Suppose I *had* recognized him? In that case I had evidently a little game of my own, and was as evidently desirous to keep it dark. He was a cool hand; but I fancy my man began to get a little uneasy. He took some trouble to find me again. After a while I permitted him to do that. Once found, he seemed determined that I should not be lost sight of again for want of watching. I permitted that, too; it helped play my game, and I wanted to bring it to an end. To which intent, Monsieur Steinmetz got to hear from sources best known to himself as much of my plans as should bring him to the state I wanted. That was a murderous state. I wanted to get him to think that I was dangerous enough to be worth putting out of the way. I presume he was aware there were, or would be, weak joints in his armor, impenetrable as it seemed; and he preferred not risking the ordeal of legal battle if he could help it. At all events, he elected at last to rid himself of a person who might be dangerous, and was troublesome, by the shortest and the simplest means.

"I say so because when, believing my man was ripe for this, I left Paris about midday for a certain secluded little spot on the sea-coast, I saw one of Monsieur Steinmetz's employees on the platform; and because, two days after my arrival in my secluded spot, I met Monsieur Steinmetz in person, newly arrived also. Now this was exactly what I had intended and anticipated. Monsieur Steinmetz had come down there to put me out of his way, if he could. He passed me, leisurely strolling in the opposite direction, humming his favorite *aria*, bigger and yellower than ever, the evil eye fiery on his finger. His own eyes shot me as evil fire; but he said nothing. . . . I saw he was ripe, though. . . . My time was close at hand.

"It came. Monsieur Steinmetz and I met once more in the very place where I, knowing my ground, had intended we should meet. It was a dip in the cliffs like a hollowed palm, and just there the cliff jutted out a good bit, with a sheer fall on to the rocks below. It was a gray afternoon, at the end of summer. The wind was rising fast; there was a thunder of heavy waves already.

"I think he had been dogging me; but I hadn't chosen to let him get up to me till now. We were quite out of sight when he had reached the level bottom of the dip, where I had halted—quite out of sight, and quite alone. To do him justice, he came on steadily enough. His face was liker the sketch I had made of it, liker the face I had seen in my dream, than it had ever looked before. Evidently he had made up his mind. . . . At last, then!. . . Well, I had been waiting long!. . . He was close beside me.

"'*Ah! bon jour, cher Monsieur Steinmetz.*'

"'So?' he said, his little eyes contracting like a cobra's. 'Ah! Monsieur knows my name?'

"'Among other things about you—yes.'

"'So!' The yellow face was turning grayer and harder every minute—liker and liker to my likeness of it. 'And what other things? Has it never appeared to you that this you do, have been doing—this meddling, may be dangerous, *hein*?'

"He had changed his tone, as he had changed the person in which he addressed me. Yes, he had certainly made up his mind. And his big right hand was hidden inside his waistcoat, so that I could not see the evil eye I knew was on his finger.

"'Dangerous?' he repeated slowly.

"'Possibly.'

"'Ay, surely; I shall crush you!'

"'Try.'

"'In good time; wait. You plot against me. Take care; I am strong; I warn you. There must be an end of this, you understand, or——'

"He nodded his big head significantly.

"'You are right,' I told him; 'there must be an end. It is coming.'

"'So?'

"'Yes; I know you. You know me now.'

"'I know you. What do you want?'

"'To kill you.'

"'So?'

"'Yes; as you killed her.'

"'As I killed her? That is it, then? You know that?'

"'I know that.'

"'Well, it is true. I killed her. Now you can guess what I am going to do to you—to you, curse you!—whom she loved.'

"The very face I had seen in my dream now, Bertie, the very face! There was something besides the evil eye that gleamed in his right hand when he drew it from his breast. Once more he spoke.

"'Yes, I killed her. I meant worse for you. You escaped that; but you will not escape me now. Fool! were you mad to do this? Did not I hate you enough? And I would have let you be. Ah, die, then, if you will have it so!'

"His heavy right arm swung high as he spoke, and I saw the sharp steel gleam as it turned to fall. And I twisted from his grip, and caught the falling arm, and bent it till the dagger dropped to the ground. And then, for a fierce, desperate, devilish minute, I had him in my clutch, dragging him nearer the smooth, slippery edge. He was no match for me at this I knew, and he knew; but he held me with the hold of his despair, and I could not loose myself. Both of us together, he meant; but not I. Yet I only freed myself just as he rolled exhausted, but clutching at the tough, short bushes wildly, toward the brink, and partly over it. . . . Only the hold of his hands between him and his death.

And I knelt above him, with the knife in my hand that was stained with *her* blood.

"The great yellow face, ashen now in its mortal agony, looked silently up at me—for three or four awful seconds; and then—then it disappeared.

"Bah!" Paul concluded, "that was the end of it."

THE YOUNG KING

BY OSCAR WILDE

It was the night before the day fixed for his coronation, and the young King was sitting alone in his beautiful chamber. His courtiers had all taken their leave of him, bowing their heads to the ground, according to the ceremonious usage of the day, and had retired to the Great Hall of the Palace, to receive a few last lessons from the Professor of Etiquette; there being some of them who had still quite natural manners, which in a courtier is, I need hardly say, a very grave offence.

The lad–for he was only a lad, being but sixteen years of age–was not sorry at their departure, and had flung himself back with a deep sigh of relief on the soft cushions of his embroidered couch, lying there, wild-eyed and open-mouthed, like a brown woodland Faun, or some young animal of the forest newly snared by the hunters.

And, indeed, it was the hunters who had found him, coming upon him almost by chance as, bare-limbed and pipe in hand, he was following the flock of the poor goatherd who had brought him up, and whose son he had always fancied himself to be. The child of the old King's only daughter by a secret marriage with one much beneath her in station–a stranger, some said, who, by the wonderful magic of his lute-playing, had made the young Princess love him; while others spoke of an artist from Rimini, to whom the Princess had shown much, perhaps too much honour, and who had suddenly disappeared from the city, leaving his work in the Cathedral unfinished–he had been, when but a week old, stolen away from his mother's side, as she slept, and given into the charge of a common peasant and his wife, who were without children of their own, and lived in a remote part of the forest, more than a day's ride from the town. Grief, or the plague, as the court physician stated, or, as some suggested, a swift Italian poison administered in a cup of spiced wine, slew, within an hour of her wakening, the white girl who had given him birth, and as the trusty messenger who bare the child across his saddle-bow stooped from his weary horse and knocked at the rude door of the goatherd's hut, the body of the Princess was being lowered into an open grave that had been dug in a deserted churchyard, beyond the city gates, a grave where it was said that another body was also lying, that of a young man of marvellous and foreign beauty, whose hands were tied behind him with a knotted cord, and whose breast was stabbed with many red wounds.

Such, at least, was the story that men whispered to each other. Certain it was that the old King, when on his deathbed, whether moved by remorse for his great sin, or merely desiring that the kingdom should not pass away from his line, had had the lad sent for, and, in the presence of the Council, had acknowledged him as his heir.

And it seems that from the very first moment of his recognition he had shown signs of that strange passion for beauty that was destined to have so great an influence over his life. Those who accompanied him to the suite of rooms set apart for his service, often spoke of the cry of pleasure that broke from his lips when he saw the delicate raiment and rich jewels that had been prepared for him, and of the almost fierce joy with which he flung aside his rough leathern tunic and coarse sheepskin cloak. He missed, indeed, at times the fine freedom of his forest life, and was always apt to chafe at the tedious Court ceremonies that occupied so much of each day, but the wonderful palace–*Joyeuse*, as they called it–of which he now found himself lord, seemed to him to be a new world fresh-fashioned for his delight; and as soon as he could escape from the council-board or audience-chamber, he would run down the great staircase, with its lions of gilt bronze and its steps of bright porphyry, and wander from room to room, and from corridor to corridor, like one who was seeking to find in beauty an anodyne from pain, a sort of restoration from sickness.

Upon these journeys of discovery, as he would call them–and, indeed, they were to him real voyages through a marvellous land, he would sometimes be accompanied by the slim, fair-haired Court pages, with their floating mantles, and gay fluttering ribands; but more often he would be alone, feeling through a certain quick instinct, which was almost a divination, that the secrets of art are best learned in secret, and that Beauty, like Wisdom, loves the lonely worshipper.

Many curious stories were related about him at this period. It was said that a stout Burgomaster, who had come to deliver a florid oratorical address on behalf of the citizens of the town, had caught sight of him kneeling in real adoration before a great picture that had just been brought from Venice, and that seemed to herald the worship of some new gods. On another occasion he had been missed for several hours, and after a lengthened search had been discovered in a little chamber in one of the northern turrets of the palace gazing, as one in a trance, at a Greek gem carved with the figure of Adonis. He had been seen, so the tale ran, pressing his warm lips to the marble brow of an antique statue that had been discovered in the bed of the river on the occasion of the building of the stone bridge, and was inscribed with the name of the Bithynian slave of Hadrian. He had passed a whole night in noting the effect of the moonlight on a silver image of Endymion.

All rare and costly materials had certainly a great fascination for him, and in his eagerness to procure them he had sent away many merchants, some to traffic for amber with the rough fisher-folk of the north seas, some to Egypt to look for that curious green turquoise which is found only in the tombs of kings, and is said to possess magical properties, some to Persia for silken carpets and painted pottery, and others to India to buy gauze and stained ivory, moonstones and bracelets of jade, sandal-wood and blue enamel and shawls of fine wool.

But what had occupied him most was the robe he was to wear at his coronation, the robe of tissued gold, and the ruby-studded crown, and the sceptre with its rows and rings of pearls. Indeed, it was of this that he was thinking to-night, as he lay back on his luxurious couch, watching the great pinewood log that was burning itself out on the open hearth. The designs, which were from the hands of the most famous artists of the time, had been submitted to him many months before, and he had given orders that the artificers were to toil night and day to carry them out, and that the whole world was to be searched for jewels that would be worthy of their work. He saw himself in fancy standing at the high altar of the cathedral in the fair raiment of a King, and a smile played and lingered about his boyish lips, and lit up with a bright lustre his dark woodland eyes.

After some time he rose from his seat, and leaning against the carved penthouse of the chimney, looked round at the dimly-lit room. The walls were hung with rich tapestries representing the Triumph of Beauty. A large press, inlaid with agate and lapis-lazuli, filled one corner, and facing the window stood a curiously wrought cabinet with lacquer panels of powdered and mosaiced gold, on which were placed some delicate goblets of Venetian glass, and a cup of dark-veined onyx. Pale poppies were broidered on the silk coverlet of the bed, as though they had fallen from the tired hands of sleep, and tall reeds of fluted ivory bare up the velvet canopy, from which great tufts of ostrich plumes sprang, like white foam, to the pallid silver of the fretted ceiling. A laughing Narcissus in green bronze held a polished mirror above its head. On the table stood a flat bowl of amethyst.

Outside he could see the huge dome of the cathedral, looming like a bubble over the shadowy houses, and the weary sentinels pacing up and down on the misty terrace by the river. Far away, in an orchard, a nightingale was singing. A faint perfume of jasmine came through the open window. He brushed his brown curls back from his forehead, and taking up a lute, let his fingers stray across the cords. His heavy eyelids drooped, and a strange languor came over him. Never before had he felt so keenly, or with such exquisite joy, the magic and the mystery of beautiful things.

When midnight sounded from the clock-tower he touched a bell, and his pages entered and disrobed him with much ceremony, pouring rose-water over his hands, and strewing flowers on his pillow. A few moments after that they had left the room, he fell asleep.

And as he slept he dreamed a dream, and this was his dream.

He thought that he was standing in a long, low attic, amidst the whir and clatter of many looms. The meagre daylight peered in through the grated windows, and showed him the gaunt figures of the weavers bending over their cases. Pale, sickly-looking children were crouched on the huge crossbeams. As the shuttles dashed through the warp they lifted up the heavy battens, and when the shuttles stopped they let the battens fall and pressed the threads together. Their faces were pinched with famine, and their thin hands shook and trembled. Some haggard women were seated at a table sewing. A horrible odour filled the place. The air was foul and heavy, and the walls dripped and streamed with damp.

The young King went over to one of the weavers, and stood by him and watched him.

And the weaver looked at him angrily, and said, 'Why art thou watching me? Art thou a spy set on us by our master?'

'Who is thy master?' asked the young King.

'Our master!' cried the weaver, bitterly. 'He is a man like myself. Indeed, there is but this difference between us–that he wears fine clothes while I go in rags, and that while I am weak from hunger he suffers not a little from overfeeding.'

'The land is free,' said the young King, 'and thou art no man's slave.'

'In war,' answered the weaver, 'the strong make slaves of the weak, and in peace the rich make slaves of the poor. We must work to live, and they give us such mean wages that we die. We toil for them all day long, and they heap up gold in their coffers, and our children fade away before their time, and the faces of those we love become hard and evil. We tread out the grapes, and another drinks the wine. We sow the corn, and our own board is empty. We have chains, though no eye beholds them; and are slaves, though men call us free.'

'Is it so with all?' he asked,

'It is so with all,' answered the weaver, 'with the young as well as with the old, with the women as well as with the men, with the little children as well as with those who are stricken in years. The merchants grind us down, and we must needs do their bidding. The priest rides by and tells his beads, and no man has care of us. Through our sunless lanes creeps Poverty with her hungry eyes, and Sin with his sodden face follows close behind her. Misery wakes us in the morning, and Shame sits with us at night. But what are these things to thee? Thou art not one of us. Thy face is too happy.' And he turned away scowling, and threw the shuttle across the loom, and the young King saw that it was threaded with a thread of gold.

And a great terror seized upon him, and he said to the weaver, 'What robe is this that thou art weaving?'

'It is the robe for the coronation of the young King,' he answered; 'what is that to thee?'

And the young King gave a loud cry and woke, and lo! he was in his own chamber, and through the window he saw the great honey-coloured moon hanging in the dusky air.

And he fell asleep again and dreamed, and this was his dream.

He thought that he was lying on the deck of a huge galley that was being rowed by a hundred slaves. On a carpet by his side the master of the galley was seated. He was black as ebony, and his turban was of crimson silk. Great earrings of silver dragged down the thick lobes of his ears, and in his hands he had a pair of ivory scales.

The slaves were naked, but for a ragged loin-cloth, and each man was chained to his neighbour. The hot sun beat brightly upon them, and the negroes ran up and down the gangway and lashed them with whips of hide. They stretched out their lean arms and pulled the heavy oars through the water. The salt spray flew from the blades.

At last they reached a little bay, and began to take soundings. A light wind blew from the shore, and covered the deck and the great lateen sail with a fine red dust. Three Arabs mounted on wild asses rode out and threw spears at them. The master of the galley took a painted bow in his hand and shot one of them in the throat. He fell heavily into the surf, and his companions galloped away. A woman wrapped in a yellow veil followed slowly on a camel, looking back now and then at the dead body.

As soon as they had cast anchor and hauled down the sail, the negroes went into the hold and brought up a long rope-ladder, heavily weighted with lead. The master of the galley threw it over the side, making the ends fast to two iron stanchions. Then the negroes seized the youngest of the slaves and knocked his gyves off, and filled his nostrils and his ears with wax, and tied a big stone round his waist. He crept wearily down the ladder, and disappeared into the sea. A few bubbles rose where he sank. Some of the other slaves peered curiously over the side. At the prow of the galley sat a shark-charmer, beating monotonously upon a drum.

After some time the diver rose up out of the water, and clung panting to the ladder with a pearl in his right hand. The negroes seized it from him, and thrust him back. The slaves fell asleep over their oars.

Again and again he came up, and each time that he did so he brought with him a beautiful pearl. The master of the galley weighed them, and put them into a little bag of green leather.

The young King tried to speak, but his tongue seemed to cleave to the roof of his mouth, and his lips refused to move. The negroes chattered to each other, and began to quarrel over a string of bright beads. Two cranes flew round and round the vessel.

Then the diver came up for the last time, and the pearl that he brought with him was fairer than all the pearls of Ormuz, for it was shaped like the full moon, and whiter than the morning star. But his face was strangely pale, and as he fell upon the deck the blood gushed from his ears and nostrils. He quivered for a little, and then he was still. The negroes shrugged their shoulders, and threw the body overboard.

And the master of the galley laughed, and, reaching out, he took the pearl, and when he saw it he pressed it to his forehead and bowed. 'It shall be,' he said, 'for the sceptre of the young King,' and he made a sign to the negroes to draw up the anchor.

And when the young King heard this he gave a great cry, and woke, and through the window he saw the long grey fingers of the dawn clutching at the fading stars.

And he fell asleep again, and dreamed, and this was his dream.

He thought that he was wandering through a dim wood, hung with strange fruits and with beautiful poisonous flowers. The adders hissed at him as he went by, and the bright parrots flew screaming from branch to branch. Huge tortoises lay asleep upon the hot mud. The trees were full of apes and peacocks.

On and on he went, till he reached the outskirts of the wood, and there he saw an immense multitude of men toiling in the bed of a dried-up river. They swarmed up the crag like ants. They dug deep pits in the ground and went down into them. Some of them cleft the rocks with great axes; others grabbled in the sand.

They tore up the cactus by its roots, and trampled on the scarlet blossoms. They hurried about, calling to each other, and no man was idle.

From the darkness of a cavern Death and Avarice watched them, and Death said, 'I am weary; give me a third of them and let me go.' But Avarice shook her head. 'They are my servants,' she answered.

And Death said to her, 'What hast thou in thy hand?'

'I have three grains of corn,' she answered; 'what is that to thee?'

'Give me one of them,' cried Death, 'to plant in my garden; only one of them, and I will go away.'

'I will not give thee anything,' said Avarice, and she hid her hand in the fold of her raiment.

And Death laughed, and took a cup, and dipped it into a pool of water, and out of the cup rose Ague. She passed through the great multitude, and a third of them lay dead. A cold mist followed her, and the water-snakes ran by her side.

And when Avarice saw that a third of the multitude was dead she beat her breast and wept. She beat her barren bosom, and cried aloud. 'Thou hast slain a third of my servants,' she cried, 'get thee gone. There is war in the mountains of Tartary, and the kings of each side are calling to thee. The Afghans have slain the black ox, and are marching to battle. They have beaten upon their shields with their spears, and have put on their helmets of iron. What is my valley to thee, that thou shouldst tarry in it? Get thee gone, and come here no more.'

'Nay,' answered Death, 'but till thou hast given me a grain of corn I will not go.'

But Avarice shut her hand, and clenched her teeth. 'I will not give thee anything,' she muttered.

And Death laughed, and took up a black stone, and threw it into the forest, and out of a thicket of wild hemlock came Fever in a robe of flame. She passed through the multitude, and touched them, and each man that she touched died. The grass withered beneath her feet as she walked.

And Avarice shuddered, and put ashes on her head. 'Thou art cruel,' she cried; 'thou art cruel. There is famine in the walled cities of India, and the cisterns of Samarcand have run dry. There is famine in the walled cities of Egypt, and the locusts have come up from the desert. The Nile has not overflowed its banks, and the priests have cursed Isis and Osiris. Get thee gone to those who need thee, and leave me my servants.'

'Nay,' answered Death, 'but till thou hast given me a grain of corn I will not go.'

'I will not give thee anything,' said Avarice.

And Death laughed again, and he whistled through his fingers, and a woman came flying through the air. Plague was written upon her forehead, and a crowd of lean vultures wheeled round her. She covered the valley with her wings, and no man was left alive.

And Avarice fled shrieking through the forest, and Death leaped upon his red horse and galloped away, and his galloping was faster than the wind.

And out of the slime at the bottom of the valley crept dragons and horrible things with scales, and the jackals came trotting along the sand, sniffing up the air with their nostrils.

And the young King wept, and said: 'Who were these men, and for what were they seeking?'

'For rubies for a king's crown,' answered one who stood behind him.

And the young King started, and, turning round, he saw a man habited as a pilgrim and holding in his hand a mirror of silver.

And he grew pale, and said: 'For what king?'

And the pilgrim answered: 'Look in this mirror, and thou shalt see him.'

And he looked in the mirror, and, seeing his own face, he gave a great cry and woke, and the bright sunlight was streaming into the room, and from the trees of the garden and pleasaunce the birds were singing.

And the Chamberlain and the high officers of State came in and made obeisance to him, and the pages brought him the robe of tissued gold, and set the crown and the sceptre before him.

And the young King looked at them, and they were beautiful. More beautiful were they than aught that he had ever seen. But he remembered his dreams, and he said to his lords: 'Take these things away, for I will not wear them.'

And the courtiers were amazed, and some of them laughed, for they thought that he was jesting.

But he spake sternly to them again, and said: 'Take these things away, and hide them from me. Though it be the day of my coronation, I will not wear them. For on the loom of Sorrow, and by the white hands of Pain, has this my robe been woven. There is Blood in the heart of the ruby, and Death in the heart of the pearl.' And he told them his three dreams.

And when the courtiers heard them they looked at each other and whispered, saying: 'Surely he is mad; for what is a dream but a dream, and a vision but a vision? They are not real things that one should heed them. And what have we to do with the lives of those who toil for us? Shall a man not eat bread till he has seen the sower, nor drink wine till he has talked with the vinedresser?'

And the Chamberlain spake to the young King, and said, 'My lord, I pray thee set aside these black thoughts of thine, and put on this fair robe, and set this crown upon thy head. For how shall the people know that thou art a king, if thou hast not a king's raiment?'

And the young King looked at him. 'Is it so, indeed?' he questioned. 'Will they not know me for a king if I have not a king's raiment?'

'They will not know thee, my lord,' cried the Chamberlain.

'I had thought that there had been men who were kinglike,' he answered, 'but it may be as thou sayest. And yet I will not wear this robe, nor will I be crowned with this crown, but even as I came to the palace so will I go forth from it.'

And he bade them all leave him, save one page whom he kept as his companion, a lad a year younger than himself. Him he kept for his service, and when he had bathed himself in clear water, he opened a great painted chest, and from it he took the leathern tunic and rough sheepskin cloak that he had worn when he had watched on the hillside the shaggy goats of the goatherd. These he put on, and in his hand he took his rude shepherd's staff.

And the little page opened his big blue eyes in wonder, and said smiling to him, 'My lord, I see thy robe and thy sceptre, but where is thy crown?'

And the young King plucked a spray of wild briar that was climbing over the balcony, and bent it, and made a circlet of it, and set it on his own head.

'This shall be my crown,' he answered.

And thus attired he passed out of his chamber into the Great Hall, where the nobles were waiting for him.

And the nobles made merry, and some of them cried out to him, 'My lord, the people wait for their king, and thou showest them a beggar,' and others were wroth and said, 'He brings shame upon our state, and is unworthy to be our master.' But he answered them not a word, but passed on, and went down the bright porphyry staircase, and out through the gates of bronze, and mounted upon his horse, and rode towards the cathedral, the little page running beside him.

And the people laughed and said, 'It is the King's fool who is riding by,' and they mocked him.

And he drew rein and said, 'Nay, but I am the King.' And he told them his three dreams.

And a man came out of the crowd and spake bitterly to him, and said, 'Sir, knowest thou not that out of the luxury of the rich cometh the life of the poor? By your pomp we are nurtured, and your vices give us bread. To toil for a hard master is bitter, but to have no master to toil for is more bitter still. Thinkest thou that the ravens will feed us? And what cure hast thou for these things? Wilt thou say to the buyer, "Thou shalt buy for so much," and to the seller, "Thou shalt sell at this price"? I trow not. Therefore go back to thy Palace and put on thy purple and fine linen. What hast thou to do with us, and what we suffer?'

'Are not the rich and the poor brothers?' asked the young King.

'Ay,' answered the man, 'and the name of the rich brother is Cain.'

And the young King's eyes filled with tears, and he rode on through the murmurs of the people, and the little page grew afraid and left him.

And when he reached the great portal of the cathedral, the soldiers thrust their halberts out and said, 'What dost thou seek here? None enters by this door but the King.'

And his face flushed with anger, and he said to them, 'I am the King,' and waved their halberts aside and passed in.

And when the old Bishop saw him coming in his goatherd's dress, he rose up in wonder from his throne, and went to meet him, and said to him, 'My son, is this a king's apparel? And with what crown shall I crown thee, and what sceptre shall I place in thy hand? Surely this should be to thee a day of joy, and not a day of abasement.'

'Shall Joy wear what Grief has fashioned?' said the young King. And he told him his three dreams.

And when the Bishop had heard them he knit his brows, and said, 'My son, I am an old man, and in the winter of my days, and I know that many evil things are done in the wide world. The fierce robbers come down from the mountains, and carry off the little children, and sell them to the Moors. The lions lie in wait for the caravans, and leap upon the camels. The wild boar roots up the corn in the valley, and the foxes gnaw the vines upon the hill. The pirates lay waste the sea-coast and burn the ships of the fishermen, and take their nets from them. In the salt-marshes live the lepers; they have houses of wattled reeds, and none may come nigh them. The beggars wander through the cities, and eat their food with the dogs. Canst thou make these things not to be? Wilt thou take the leper for thy bedfellow, and set the beggar at thy board? Shall the lion do thy bidding, and the wild boar obey thee? Is not He who made misery wiser than thou art? Wherefore I praise thee not for this that thou hast done, but I bid thee ride back to the Palace and make thy face glad, and put on the raiment that beseemeth a king, and with the crown of gold I will crown thee, and the sceptre of pearl will I place in thy hand. And as for thy dreams, think no more of them. The burden of this world is too great for one man to bear, and the world's sorrow too heavy for one heart to suffer.'

'Sayest thou that in this house?' said the young King, and he strode past the Bishop, and climbed up the steps of the altar, and stood before the image of Christ.

He stood before the image of Christ, and on his right hand and on his left were the marvellous vessels of gold, the chalice with the yellow wine, and the vial with the holy oil. He knelt before the image of Christ, and the great candles burned brightly by the jewelled shrine, and the smoke of the incense curled in thin blue wreaths through the dome. He bowed his head in prayer, and the priests in their stiff copes crept away from the altar.

And suddenly a wild tumult came from the street outside, and in entered the nobles with drawn swords and nodding plumes, and shields of polished steel. 'Where is this dreamer of dreams?' they cried. 'Where is this King who is apparelled like a beggar–this boy who brings shame upon our state? Surely we will slay him, for he is unworthy to rule over us.'

And the young King bowed his head again, and prayed, and when he had finished his prayer he rose up, and turning round he looked at them sadly.

And lo! through the painted windows came the sunlight streaming upon him, and the sun-beams wove round him a tissued robe that was fairer than the robe that had been fashioned for his pleasure. The dead staff blossomed, and bare lilies that were whiter than pearls. The dry thorn blossomed, and bare roses that were redder than rubies. Whiter than fine pearls were the lilies, and their stems were of bright silver. Redder than male rubies were the roses, and their leaves were of beaten gold.

He stood there in the raiment of a king, and the gates of the jewelled shrine flew open, and from the crystal of the many-rayed monstrance shone a marvellous and mystical light. He stood there in a king's raiment, and the Glory of God filled the place, and the saints in their carven niches seemed to move. In the fair raiment of a king he stood before them, and the organ pealed out its music, and the trumpeters blew upon their trumpets, and the singing boys sang.

And the people fell upon their knees in awe, and the nobles sheathed their swords and did homage, and the Bishop's face grew pale, and his hands trembled. 'A greater than I hath crowned thee,' he cried, and he knelt before him.

And the young King came down from the high altar, and passed home through the midst of the people. But no man dared look upon his face, for it was like the face of an angel.

RESOLUTIONS WHEN I COME TO BE OLD

BY JONATHAN SWIFT

Not to Marry a young Woman.

Not to keep young company unless they really desire it.

Not to be peevish or morose, or suspicious.

Not to scorn present ways, or wits, or fashions, or men, or war, etc.

Not to be fond of children, or let them come near me hardly.

Not to tell the same story over and over to the same people.

Not to be covetous.

Not to neglect decency, or cleanliness, for fear of falling into nastiness.

Not to be over severe with young people, but give allowances for their youthful follies, and weaknesses.

Not to be influenced by, or give ear to knavish tattling servants, or others.

Not to be too free of advice nor trouble any but those that desire it.

Not to desire some good friends to inform me which of these resolutions I break, or neglect, & wherein; and reform accordingly.

Not to talk much, nor of my self.

Not to boast of my former beauty, or strength, or favor with ladies, etc.

Not to hearken to flatteries, nor conceive I can be beloved by a young woman.

Not to be positive or opinionated.

Not to sett up for observing all these rules, for fear I should observe none.

THE PIPER AND THE PÚCA

BY DOUGLAS HYDE

(Translated literally from the Irish of the *Leabhar Sgeulaigheachta.*)

In the old times, there was a half fool living in Dunmore, in the county Galway, and although he was excessively fond of music, he was unable to learn more than one tune, and that was the "Black Rogue." He used to get a good deal of money from the gentlemen, for they used to get sport out of him. One night the piper was coming home from a house where there had been a dance, and he half drunk. When he came to a little bridge that was up by his mother's house, he squeezed the pipes on, and began playing the "Black Rogue" (an rógaire dubh). The Púca came behind him, and flung him up on his own back. There were long horns on the Púca, and the piper got a good grip of them, and then he said—

"Destruction on you, you nasty beast, let me home. I have a ten-penny piece in my pocket for my mother, and she wants snuff."

"Never mind your mother," said the Púca, "but keep your hold. If you fall, you will break your neck and your pipes." Then the Púca said to him, "Play up for me the 'Shan Van Vocht' (an t-seann-bhean bhocht)."

"I don't know it," said the piper.

"Never mind whether you do or you don't," said the Púca. "Play up, and I'll make you know."

The piper put wind in his bag, and he played such music as made himself wonder.

"Upon my word, you're a fine music-master," says the piper then; "but tell me where you're for bringing me."

"There's a great feast in the house of the Banshee, on the top of Croagh Patric to-night," says the Púca, "and I'm for bringing you there to play music, and, take my word, you'll get the price of your trouble."

"By my word, you'll save me a journey, then," says the piper, "for Father William put a journey to Croagh Patric on me, because I stole the white gander from him last Martinmas."

The Púca rushed him across hills and bogs and rough places, till he brought him to the top of Croagh Patric. Then the Púca struck three blows with his foot, and a great door opened, and they passed in together, into a fine room.

The piper saw a golden table in the middle of the room, and hundreds of old women (cailleacha) sitting round about it. The old women rose up, and said, "A hundred thousand welcomes to you, you Púca of November (na Samhna). Who is this you have with you?"

"The best piper in Ireland," says the Púca.

One of the old women struck a blow on the ground, and a door opened in the side of the wall, and what should the piper see coming out but the white gander which he had stolen from Father William.

"By my conscience, then," says the piper, "myself and my mother ate every taste of that gander, only one wing, and I gave that to Moy-rua (Red Mary), and it's she told the priest I stole his gander."

The gander cleaned the table, and carried it away, and the Púca said, "Play up music for these ladies."

The piper played up, and the old women began dancing, and they were dancing till they were tired. Then the Púca said to pay the piper, and every old woman drew out a gold piece, and gave it to him.

"By the tooth of Patric," said he, "I'm as rich as the son of a lord."

"Come with me," says the Púca, "and I'll bring you home."

They went out then, and just as he was going to ride on the Púca, the gander came up to him, and gave him a new set of pipes. The Púca was not long until he brought him to Dunmore, and he threw the piper off at the little bridge, and then he told him to go home, and says to him, "You have two things now that you never had before—you have sense and music (ciall agus ceól)."

The piper went home, and he knocked at his mother's door, saying, "Let me in, I'm as rich as a lord, and I'm the best piper in Ireland."

"You're drunk," said the mother.

"No, indeed," says the piper, "I haven't drunk a drop."

The mother let him in, and he gave her the gold pieces, and, "Wait now," says he, "till you hear the music I'll play."

He buckled on the pipes, but instead of music, there came a sound as if all the geese and ganders in Ireland were screeching together. He wakened the neighbours, and they were all mocking him, until he put on the old pipes, and then he played melodious music for them; and after that he told them all he had gone through that night.

The next morning, when his mother went to look at the gold pieces, there was nothing there but the leaves of a plant.

The piper went to the priest, and told him his story, but the priest would not believe a word from him, until he put the pipes on him, and then the screeching of the ganders and geese began.

"Leave my sight, you thief," says the priest.

But nothing would do the piper till he would put the old pipes on him to show the priest that his story was true.

He buckled on the old pipes, and he played melodious music, and from that day till the day of his death, there was never a piper in the county Galway was as good as he was.

'IT WAS HIS FIRST CHRISTMAS DINNER'

BY JAMES JOYCE

A great fire, banked high and red, flamed in the grate and under the ivy-twined branches of the chandelier the Christmas table was spread. They had come home a little late and still dinner was not ready: but it would be ready in a jiffy his mother had said. They were waiting for the door to open and for the servants to come in, holding the big dishes covered with their heavy metal covers.

All were waiting: uncle Charles, who sat far away in the shadow of the window, Dante and Mr Casey, who sat in the easy-chairs at either side of the hearth, Stephen, seated on a chair between them, his feet resting on the toasted boss. Mr Dedalus looked at himself in the pierglass above the mantelpiece, waxed out his moustache ends and then, parting his coat-tails, stood with his back to the glowing fire: and still from time to time he withdrew a hand from his coat-tail to wax out one of his moustache ends. Mr Casey leaned his head to one side and, smiling, tapped the gland of his neck with his fingers. And Stephen smiled too for he knew now that it was not true that Mr Casey had a purse of silver in his throat. He smiled to think how the silvery noise which Mr Casey used to make had deceived him. And when he had tried to open Mr Casey's hand to see if the purse of silver was hidden there he had seen that the fingers could not be straightened out: and Mr Casey had told him that he had got those three cramped fingers making a birthday present for Queen Victoria. Mr Casey tapped the gland of his neck and smiled at Stephen with sleepy eyes: and Mr Dedalus said to him:

—Yes. Well now, that's all right. O, we had a good walk, hadn't we, John? Yes... I wonder if there's any likelihood of dinner this evening. Yes... O, well now, we got a good breath of ozone round the Head today. Ay, bedad.

He turned to Dante and said:

—You didn't stir out at all, Mrs Riordan?

Dante frowned and said shortly:

—No.

Mr Dedalus dropped his coat-tails and went over to the sideboard. He brought forth a great stone jar of whisky from the locker and filled the decanter slowly, bending now and then to see how much he had poured in. Then replacing the jar in the locker he poured a little of the whisky into two glasses, added a little water and came back with them to the fireplace.

—A thimbleful, John, he said, just to whet your appetite.

Mr Casey took the glass, drank, and placed it near him on the mantelpiece. Then he said:

—Well, I can't help thinking of our friend Christopher manufacturing...

He broke into a fit of laughter and coughing and added:

—...manufacturing that champagne for those fellows.

Mr Dedalus laughed loudly.

—Is it Christy? he said. There's more cunning in one of those warts on his bald head than in a pack of jack foxes.

He inclined his head, closed his eyes, and, licking his lips profusely, began to speak with the voice of the hotel keeper.

—And he has such a soft mouth when he's speaking to you, don't you know. He's very moist and watery about the dewlaps, God bless him.

Mr Casey was still struggling through his fit of coughing and laughter. Stephen, seeing and hearing the hotel keeper through his father's face and voice, laughed.

Mr Dedalus put up his eyeglass and, staring down at him, said quietly and kindly:

—What are you laughing at, you little puppy, you?

The servants entered and placed the dishes on the table. Mrs Dedalus followed and the places were arranged.

—Sit over, she said.

Mr Dedalus went to the end of the table and said:

—Now, Mrs Riordan, sit over. John, sit you down, my hearty.

He looked round to where uncle Charles sat and said:

—Now then, sir, there's a bird here waiting for you.

When all had taken their seats he laid his hand on the cover and then said quickly, withdrawing it:

—Now, Stephen.

Stephen stood up in his place to say the grace before meals:

Bless us, O Lord, and these Thy gifts which through Thy bounty we are about to receive through Christ our Lord. Amen.

All blessed themselves and Mr Dedalus with a sigh of pleasure lifted from the dish the heavy cover pearled around the edge with glistening drops.

Stephen looked at the plump turkey which had lain, trussed and skewered, on the kitchen table. He knew that his father had paid a guinea for it in Dunn's of D'Olier Street and that the man had prodded it often at the breastbone to show how good it was: and he remembered the man's voice when he had said:

—Take that one, sir. That's the real Ally Daly.

Why did Mr Barrett in Clongowes call his pandybat a turkey? But Clongowes was far away: and the warm heavy smell of turkey and ham and celery rose from the plates and dishes and the great fire was banked high and red in the grate and the green ivy and red holly made you feel so happy and when dinner was ended the big plum pudding would be carried in, studded with peeled almonds and sprigs of holly, with bluish fire running around it and a little green flag flying from the top.

It was his first Christmas dinner and he thought of his little brothers and sisters who were waiting in the nursery, as he had often waited, till the pudding came. The deep low collar and the Eton jacket made him feel queer and oldish: and that morning when his mother had brought him down to the parlour, dressed for mass, his father had cried. That was because he was thinking of his own father. And uncle Charles had said so too.

Mr Dedalus covered the dish and began to eat hungrily. Then he said:

—Poor old Christy, he's nearly lopsided now with roguery.

—Simon, said Mrs Dedalus, you haven't given Mrs Riordan any sauce.

Mr Dedalus seized the sauceboat.

—Haven't I? he cried. Mrs Riordan, pity the poor blind. Dante covered her plate with her hands and said:

—No, thanks.

Mr Dedalus turned to uncle Charles.

—How are you off, sir?

—Right as the mail, Simon.

—You, John?

—I'm all right. Go on yourself.

—Mary? Here, Stephen, here's something to make your hair curl.

He poured sauce freely over Stephen's plate and set the boat again on the table. Then he asked uncle Charles was it tender. Uncle Charles could not speak because his mouth was full; but he nodded that it was.

—That was a good answer our friend made to the canon. What? said Mr Dedalus.

—I didn't think he had that much in him, said Mr Casey.

—*I'll pay your dues, Father, when you cease turning the house of God into a polling-booth.*

—A nice answer, said Dante, for any man calling himself a catholic to give to his priest.

—They have only themselves to blame, said Mr Dedalus suavely. If they took a fool's advice they would confine their attention to religion.

—It is religion, Dante said. They are doing their duty in warning the people.

—We go to the house of God, Mr Casey said, in all humility to pray to our Maker and not to hear election addresses.

—It is religion, Dante said again. They are right. They must direct their flocks.

—And preach politics from the altar, is it? asked Mr Dedalus.

—Certainly, said Dante. It is a question of public morality. A priest would not be a priest if he did not tell his flock what is right and what is wrong.

Mrs Dedalus laid down her knife and fork, saying:

—For pity sake and for pity sake let us have no political discussion on this day of all days in the year.

—Quite right, ma'am, said uncle Charles. Now, Simon, that's quite enough now. Not another word now.

—Yes, yes, said Mr Dedalus quickly.

He uncovered the dish boldly and said:

—Now then, who's for more turkey?

Nobody answered. Dante said:

—Nice language for any catholic to use!

—Mrs Riordan, I appeal to you, said Mrs Dedalus, to let the matter drop now.

Dante turned on her and said:

—And am I to sit here and listen to the pastors of my church being flouted?

—Nobody is saying a word against them, said Mr Dedalus, so long as they don't meddle in politics.

—The bishops and priests of Ireland have spoken, said Dante, and they must be obeyed.

—Let them leave politics alone, said Mr Casey, or the people may leave their church alone.

—You hear? said Dante, turning to Mrs Dedalus.

—Mr Casey! Simon! said Mrs Dedalus, let it end now.

—Too bad! Too bad! said uncle Charles.

—What? cried Mr Dedalus. Were we to desert him at the bidding of the English people?

—He was no longer worthy to lead, said Dante. He was a public sinner.

—We are all sinners and black sinners, said Mr Casey coldly.

—*Woe be to the man by whom the scandal cometh!* said Mrs Riordan. *It would be better for him that a millstone were tied about his neck and that he were cast into the depths of the sea rather than that he should scandalize one of these, my least little ones.* That is the language of the Holy Ghost.

—And very bad language if you ask me, said Mr Dedalus coolly.

—Simon! Simon! said uncle Charles. The boy.

—Yes, yes, said Mr Dedalus. I meant about the... I was thinking about the bad language of the railway porter. Well now, that's all right. Here, Stephen, show me your plate, old chap. Eat away now. Here.

He heaped up the food on Stephen's plate and served uncle Charles and Mr Casey to large pieces of turkey and splashes of sauce. Mrs Dedalus was eating little and Dante sat with her hands in her lap. She was red in the face. Mr Dedalus rooted with the carvers at the end of the dish and said:

—There's a tasty bit here we call the pope's nose. If any lady or gentleman. . .

He held a piece of fowl up on the prong of the carving fork. Nobody spoke. He put it on his own plate, saying:

—Well, you can't say but you were asked. I think I had better eat it myself because I'm not well in my health lately.

He winked at Stephen and, replacing the dish-cover, began to eat again.

There was a silence while he ate. Then he said:

—Well now, the day kept up fine after all. There were plenty of strangers down too.

Nobody spoke. He said again:

—I think there were more strangers down than last Christmas.

He looked round at the others whose faces were bent towards their plates and, receiving no reply, waited for a moment and said bitterly:

—Well, my Christmas dinner has been spoiled anyhow.

—There could be neither luck nor grace, Dante said, in a house where there is no respect for the pastors of the church.

Mr Dedalus threw his knife and fork noisily on his plate.

—Respect! he said. Is it for Billy with the lip or for the tub of guts up in Armagh? Respect!

—Princes of the church, said Mr Casey with slow scorn.

—Lord Leitrim's coachman, yes, said Mr Dedalus.

They are the Lord's anointed, Dante said. They are an honour to their country.

—Tub of guts, said Mr Dedalus coarsely. He has a handsome face, mind you, in repose. You should see that fellow lapping up his bacon and cabbage of a cold winter's day. O Johnny!

He twisted his features into a grimace of heavy bestiality and made a lapping noise with his lips.

—Really, Simon, you should not speak that way before Stephen. It's not right.

—O, he'll remember all this when he grows up, said Dante hotly—the language he heard against God and religion and priests in his own home.

—Let him remember too, cried Mr Casey to her from across the table, the language with which the priests and the priests' pawns broke Parnell's heart and hounded him into his grave. Let him remember that too when he grows up.

—Sons of bitches! cried Mr Dedalus. When he was down they turned on him to betray him and rend him like rats in a sewer. Low-lived dogs! And they look it! By Christ, they look it!

—They behaved rightly, cried Dante. They obeyed their bishops and their priests. Honour to them!

—Well, it is perfectly dreadful to say that not even for one day in the year, said Mrs Dedalus, can we be free from these dreadful disputes!

Uncle Charles raised his hands mildly and said:

—Come now, come now, come now! Can we not have our opinions whatever they are without this bad temper and this bad language? It is too bad surely.

Mrs Dedalus spoke to Dante in a low voice but Dante said loudly:

—I will not say nothing. I will defend my church and my religion when it is insulted and spit on by renegade catholics.

Mr Casey pushed his plate rudely into the middle of the table and, resting his elbows before him, said in a hoarse voice to his host:

—Tell me, did I tell you that story about a very famous spit?

—You did not, John, said Mr Dedalus.

—Why then, said Mr Casey, it is a most instructive story. It happened not long ago in the county Wicklow where we are now.

He broke off and, turning towards Dante, said with quiet indignation:

—And I may tell you, ma'am, that I, if you mean me, am no renegade catholic. I am a catholic as my father was and his father before him and his father before him again, when we gave up our lives rather than sell our faith.

—The more shame to you now, Dante said, to speak as you do.

—The story, John, said Mr Dedalus smiling. Let us have the story anyhow.

—Catholic indeed! repeated Dante ironically. The blackest protestant in the land would not speak the language I have heard this evening.

Mr Dedalus began to sway his head to and fro, crooning like a country singer.

—I am no protestant, I tell you again, said Mr Casey, flushing.

Mr Dedalus, still crooning and swaying his head, began to sing in a grunting nasal tone:

O, come all you Roman catholics That never went to mass.

He took up his knife and fork again in good humour and set to eating, saying to Mr Casey:

—Let us have the story, John. It will help us to digest.

Stephen looked with affection at Mr Casey's face which stared across the table over his joined hands. He liked to sit near him at the fire, looking up at his dark fierce face. But his dark eyes were never fierce and his slow voice was good to listen to. But why was he then against the priests? Because Dante must be right then. But he had heard his father say that she was a spoiled nun and that she had come out of the convent in the Alleghanies when her brother had got the money from the savages for the trinkets and the chainies. Perhaps that made her severe against Parnell. And she did not like him to play with Eileen because Eileen was a protestant and when she was young she knew children that used to play with protestants and the protestants used to make fun of the litany of the Blessed Virgin. *Tower of ivory*, they used to say, *house of gold!* How could a woman be a tower of ivory or a house of gold? Who was right then? And he remembered the evening in the infirmary in Clongowes, the dark waters, the light at the pierhead and the moan of sorrow from the people when they had heard.

Eileen had long white hands. One evening when playing tig she had put her hands over his eyes: long and white and thin and cold and soft. That was ivory: a cold white thing. That was the meaning of *tower of ivory.*

—The story is very short and sweet, Mr Casey said. It was one day down in Arklow, a cold bitter day, not long before the chief died. May God have mercy on him!

He closed his eyes wearily and paused. Mr Dedalus took a bone from his plate and tore some meat from it with his teeth, saying:

—Before he was killed, you mean.

Mr Casey opened his eyes, sighed and went on:

—It was down in Arklow one day. We were down there at a meeting and after the meeting was over we had to make our way to the railway station through the crowd. Such booing and baaing, man, you never heard. They called us all the names in the world. Well there was one old lady, and a drunken old harridan she was surely, that paid all her attention to me. She kept dancing along beside me in the mud bawling and screaming into my face: *Priest-hunter! The Paris funds! Mr Fox! Kitty O'Shea!*

—And what did you do, John? asked Mr Dedalus.

—I let her bawl away, said Mr Casey. It was a cold day and to keep up my heart I had (saving your presence, ma'am) a quid of Tullamore in my mouth and sure I couldn't say a word in any case because my mouth was full of tobacco juice.

—Well, John?

—Well. I let her bawl away, to her heart's content, *Kitty O'Shea* and the rest of it till at last she called that lady a name that I won't sully this Christmas board nor your ears, ma'am, nor my own lips by repeating.

He paused. Mr Dedalus, lifting his head from the bone, asked:

—And what did you do, John?

—Do! said Mr Casey. She stuck her ugly old face up at me when she said it and I had my mouth full of tobacco juice. I bent down to her and *Phth!* says I to her like that.

He turned aside and made the act of spitting.

—*Phth*! says I to her like that, right into her eye.

He clapped his hand to his eye and gave a hoarse scream of pain.

—*O Jesus, Mary and Joseph!* says she. *I'm blinded! I'm blinded and drownded!*

He stopped in a fit of coughing and laughter, repeating:

—*I'm blinded entirely.*

Mr Dedalus laughed loudly and lay back in his chair while uncle Charles swayed his head to and fro.

Dante looked terribly angry and repeated while they laughed:

—Very nice! Ha! Very nice!

It was not nice about the spit in the woman's eye.

But what was the name the woman had called Kitty O'Shea that Mr Casey would not repeat? He thought of Mr Casey walking through the crowds of people and making speeches from a wagonette. That was what he had been in prison for and he remembered that one night Sergeant O'Neill had come to the house and had stood in the hall, talking in a low voice with his father and chewing nervously at the chinstrap of his cap. And that night Mr Casey had not gone to Dublin by train but a car had come to the door and he had heard his father say something about the Cabinteely road.

He was for Ireland and Parnell and so was his father: and so was Dante too for one night at the band on the esplanade she had hit a gentleman on the head with her umbrella because he had taken off his hat when the band played *God Save the Queen* at the end.

Mr Dedalus gave a snort of contempt.

—Ah, John, he said. It is true for them. We are an unfortunate priest-ridden race and always were and always will be till the end of the chapter.

Uncle Charles shook his head, saying:

—A bad business! A bad business!

Mr Dedalus repeated:

—A priest-ridden Godforsaken race!

He pointed to the portrait of his grandfather on the wall to his right.

—Do you see that old chap up there, John? he said. He was a good Irishman when there was no money in the job. He was condemned to death as a whiteboy. But he had a saying about our clerical friends, that he would never let one of them put his two feet under his mahogany.

Dante broke in angrily:

—If we are a priest-ridden race we ought to be proud of it! They are the apple of God's eye. *Touch them not,* says Christ, *for they are the apple of My eye.*

—And can we not love our country then? asked Mr Casey. Are we not to follow the man that was born to lead us?

—A traitor to his country! replied Dante. A traitor, an adulterer! The priests were right to abandon him. The priests were always the true friends of Ireland.

—Were they, faith? said Mr Casey.

He threw his fist on the table and, frowning angrily, protruded one finger after another.

—Didn't the bishops of Ireland betray us in the time of the union when Bishop Lanigan presented an address of loyalty to the Marquess Cornwallis?

Didn't the bishops and priests sell the aspirations of their country in 1829 in return for catholic emancipation? Didn't they denounce the fenian movement from the pulpit and in the confession box? And didn't they dishonour the ashes of Terence Bellew MacManus?

His face was glowing with anger and Stephen felt the glow rise to his own cheek as the spoken words thrilled him. Mr Dedalus uttered a guffaw of coarse scorn.

—O, by God, he cried, I forgot little old Paul Cullen! Another apple of God's eye!

Dante bent across the table and cried to Mr Casey:

—Right! Right! They were always right! God and morality and religion come first.

Mrs Dedalus, seeing her excitement, said to her:

—Mrs Riordan, don't excite yourself answering them.

—God and religion before everything! Dante cried. God and religion before the world.

Mr Casey raised his clenched fist and brought it down on the table with a crash.

—Very well then, he shouted hoarsely, if it comes to that, no God for Ireland!

—John! John! cried Mr Dedalus, seizing his guest by the coat sleeve.

Dante stared across the table, her cheeks shaking. Mr Casey struggled up from his chair and bent across the table towards her, scraping the air from before his eyes with one hand as though he were tearing aside a cobweb.

—No God for Ireland! he cried. We have had too much God In Ireland. Away with God!

—Blasphemer! Devil! screamed Dante, starting to her feet and almost spitting in his face.

Uncle Charles and Mr Dedalus pulled Mr Casey back into his chair again, talking to him from both sides reasonably. He stared before him out of his dark flaming eyes, repeating:

—Away with God, I say!

Dante shoved her chair violently aside and left the table, upsetting her napkin-ring which rolled slowly along the carpet and came to rest against the foot of an easy-chair. Mrs Dedalus rose quickly and followed her towards the door. At the door Dante turned round violently and shouted down the room, her cheeks flushed and quivering with rage:

—Devil out of hell! We won! We crushed him to death! Fiend!

The door slammed behind her.

Mr Casey, freeing his arms from his holders, suddenly bowed his head on his hands with a sob of pain.

—Poor Parnell! he cried loudly. My dead king!

He sobbed loudly and bitterly.

Stephen, raising his terror-stricken face, saw that his father's eyes were full of tears.

THE TINKER'S DOG

BY EDITH SOMERVILLE AND MARTIN ROSS

"Can't you head 'em off, Patsey? Run, you fool! *run*, can't you?"

Sounds followed that suggested the intemperate use of Mr. Freddy Alexander's pocket-handkerchief, but that were, in effect, produced by his struggle with a brand new hunting-horn. To this demonstration about as much attention was paid by the nine couple of buccaneers whom he was now exercising for the first time as might have been expected, and it was brought to abrupt conclusion by the sudden charge of two of them from the rear. Being coupled, they mowed his legs from under him as irresistibly as chain shot and being puppies, and of an imbecile friendliness they remained to lick his face and generally make merry over him as he struggled to his feet.

By this time the leaders of the pack were well away up a ploughed field, over a fence and into a furze brake, from which their rejoicing yelps streamed back on the damp breeze. The Master of the Craffroe Hounds picked himself up, and sprinted up the hill after the Whip and Kennel Huntsman—a composite official recently promoted from the stable yard—in a way that showed that his failure in horn-blowing was not the fault of his lungs. His feet were held by the heavy soil, he tripped in the muddy ridges; none the less he and Patsey plunged together over the stony rampart of the field in time to see Negress and Lily springing through the furze in kangaroo leaps, while they uttered long squeals of ecstasy. The rest of the pack, with a confidence gained in many a successful riot, got to them as promptly as if six Whips were behind them, and the whole faction plunged into a little wood on the top of what was evidently a burning scent.

"Was it a fox, Patsey?" said the Master excitedly.

"I dunno, Master Freddy: it might be 'twas a hare," returned Patsey, taking in a hurried reef in the strap that was responsible for the support of his trousers.

Freddy was small and light, and four short years before had been a renowned hare in his school paper-chases: he went through the wood at a pace that gave Patsey and the puppies all they could do to keep with him, and dropped into a road just in time to see the pack streaming up a narrow lane near the end of the wood. At this point they were reinforced by a yellow dachshund who, with wildly flapping ears, and at that caricature of a gallop peculiar to his kind, joined himself to the hunters.

"Glory be to Mercy!" exclaimed Patsey, "the misthress's dog!"

Almost simultaneously the pack precipitated themselves into a ruined cabin at the end of the lane; instantly from within arose an uproar of sounds—crashes of an ironmongery sort, yells of dogs, raucous human curses; then the ruin exuded hounds, hens and turkeys at every one of the gaps in its walls, and there issued from what had been the doorway a tall man with a red beard, armed with a large frying-pan, with which he rained blows on the fleeing Craffroe Pack. It must be admitted that the speed with which these abandoned their prey, whatever it was, suggested a very intimate acquaintance with the wrath of cooks and the perils of resistance.

Before their lawful custodians had recovered from this spectacle, a tall lady in black was suddenly merged in the *mêlée*, alternately calling loudly and incongruously for "Bismarck," and blowing shrill blasts on a whistle.

"If the tinker laves a sthroke of the pan on the misthress's dog, the Lord help him!" said Patsey, starting in pursuit of Lily, who, with tail tucked in and a wounded hind leg buckled up, was removing herself swiftly from the scene of action.

Mrs. Alexander shoved her way into the cabin, through a filthy group of gabbling male and female tinkers, and found herself involved in a wreck of branches and ragged tarpaulin that had once formed a kind of tent, but was now strewn on the floor by the incursion and excursion of the chase. Earthquake throes were convulsing the tarpaulin; a tinker woman, full of zeal, dashed at it and flung it back, revealing, amongst other *débris*, an old wooden bedstead heaped with rags. On either side of one of its legs protruded the passion-fraught faces of the coupled hound-puppies, who, still linked together, had passed through the period of unavailing struggle into a state of paralyzed insanity of terror. Muffled squeals and tinny crashes told that conflict was still raging beneath the bed; the tinker women screamed abuse and complaint; and suddenly the dachshund's long yellow nose, streaming with blood, worked its way out of the folds. His mistress snatched at his collar and dragged him forth, and at his heels followed an infuriated tom cat, which, with its tail as thick as a muff, went like a streak through the confusion, and was lost in the dark ruin of the chimney.

Mrs. Alexander stayed for no explanations: she extricated herself from the tinker party, and, filled with a righteous wrath, went forth to look for her son. From a plantation three fields away came the asphyxiated bleats of the horn and the desolate bawls of Patsey Crimmeen. Mrs. Alexander decided that it was better for the present to leave the *personnel* of the Craffroe Hunt to their own devices.

It was but three days before these occurrences that Mr. Freddy Alexander had stood on the platform of the Craffroe Station, with a throbbing heart, and a very dirty paper in his hand containing a list of eighteen names, that ranged alphabetically from "Batchellor" to "Warior." At his elbow stood a small man with a large moustache, and the thinnest legs that were ever buttoned into gaiters, who was assuring him that to no other man in Ireland would he have sold those hounds at such a price; a statement that was probably unimpeachable.

"The only reason I'm parting them is I'm giving up me drag, and selling me stock, and going into partnership with a veterinary surgeon in Rugby. You've some of the best blood in Ireland in those hounds."

"Is it blood?" chimed in an old man who was standing, slightly drunk, at Mr. Alexander's other elbow. "The most of them hounds is by the Kerry Rapparee, and he was the last of the old Moynalty Baygles. Black dogs they were, with red eyes! Every one o' them as big as a yearling calf, and they'd hunt anything that'd roar before them!" He steadied himself on the new Master's arm. "I have them gethered in the ladies' waiting-room, sir, the way ye'll have no throuble. 'Twould be as good for ye to lave the muzzles on them till ye'll be through the town."

Freddy Alexander cannot to this hour decide what was the worst incident of that homeward journey; on the whole, perhaps, the most serious was the escape of Governess, who subsequently ravaged the country for two days, and was at length captured in the act of killing Mrs. Alexander's white Leghorn cock. For a young gentleman whose experience of hounds consisted in having learned at Cambridge to some slight and painful extent that if he rode too near them he got sworn at, the purchaser of the Kerry Rapparee's descendants had undertaken no mean task.

On the morning following on the first run of the Craffroe Hounds, Mrs. Alexander was sitting at her escritoire, making up her weekly accounts and entering in her poultry-book the untimely demise of the Leghorn cock. She was a lady of secret enthusiasms which sheltered themselves behind habits of the most business-like severity. Her books were models of order, and as she neatly inscribed the Leghorn cock's epitaph, "Killed by hounds," she could not repress the compensating thought that she had never seen Freddy's dark eyes and olive complexion look so well as when he had tried on his new pink coat.

At this point she heard a step on the gravel outside; Bismarck uttered a bloodhound bay and got under the sofa. It was a sunny morning in late October, and the French window was open; outside it, ragged as a Russian poodle and nearly as black, stood the tinker who had the day before wielded the frying-pan with such effect.

"Me lady," began the tinker, "I ax yer ladyship's pardon, but me little dog is dead."

"Well?" said Mrs. Alexander, fixing a gaze of clear grey rectitude upon him.

"Me lady," continued the tinker, reverentially but firmly, "'twas afther he was run by thim dogs yestherday, and 'twas your ladyship's dog that finished him. He tore the throat out of him under the bed!" He pointed an accusing forefinger at Bismarck, whose lambent eyes of terror glowed from beneath the valance of the sofa.

"Nonsense! I saw your dog; he was twice my dog's size," said Bismarck's mistress decidedly, not, however, without a remembrance of the blood on Bismarck's nose. She adored courage, and had always cherished a belief that Bismarck's sharklike jaws implied the possession of latent ferocity.

"Ah, but he was very wake, ma'am, afther he bein' hunted," urged the tinker. "I never slep' a wink the whole night, but keepin' sups o' milk to him and all sorts. Ah, ma'am, ye wouldn't like to be lookin' at him!"

The tinker was a very good-looking young man, almost apostolic in type, with a golden red aureole of hair and beard and candid blue eyes. These latter filled with tears as their owner continued:—

"He was like a brother for me; sure he follied me from home. 'Twas he was dam wise! Sure at home all me mother'd say to him was, "Where's the ducks, Captain?" an' he wouldn't lave wather nor bog-hole round the counthry but he'd have them walked and the ducks gethered. The pigs could be in their choice place, wherever they'd be he'd go around them. If ye'd tell him to put back the childhren from the fire, he'd ketch them by the sleeve and dhrag them."

The requiem ceased, and the tinker looked grievingly into his hat.

"What is your name?" asked Mrs. Alexander sternly. "How long is it since you left home?"

Had the tinker been as well acquainted with her as he was afterwards destined to become, he would have been aware that when she was most judicial she was frequently least certain of what her verdict was going to be.

"Me name's Willy Fennessy, me lady," replied the tinker, "an' I'm goin' the roads no more than three months. Indeed, me lady, I think the time too long that I'm with these blagyard thravellers. All the friends I have was poor Captain, and he's gone from me."

"Go round to the kitchen," said Mrs. Alexander.

The results of Willy Fennessy's going round to the kitchen were far-reaching. Its most immediate consequences were that (1) he mended the ventilator of the kitchen range; (2) he skinned a brace of rabbits for Miss Barnet, the cook; (3) he arranged to come next day and repair the clandestine devastations of the maids among the china.

He was pronounced to be a very agreeable young man.

Before luncheon (of which meal he partook in the kitchen) he had been consulted by Patsey Crimmeen about the chimney of the kennel boiler, had single-handed reduced it to submission, and had, in addition, boiled the meal for the hounds with a knowledge of proportion and an untiring devotion to the use of the potstick which produced "stirabout" of a smoothness and excellence that Miss Barnet herself might have been proud of.

"You know, mother," said Freddy that evening, "you do want another chap in the garden badly."

"Well it's not so much the garden," said Mrs. Alexander with alacrity, "but I think he might be very useful to you, dear, and it's such a great matter his being a teetotaler, and he seems so fond of animals. I really feel we ought to try and make up to him somehow for the loss of his dog; though, indeed, a more deplorable object than that poor mangy dog I never saw!"

"All right: we'll put him in the back lodge, and we'll give him Bizzy as a watch dog. Won't we, Bizzy?" replied Freddy, dragging the somnolent Bismarck from out of the heart of the hearthrug, and accepting without repugnance the comprehensive lick that enveloped his chin.

From which it may be gathered that Mrs. Alexander and her son had fallen, like their household, under the fatal spell of the fascinating tinker.

At about the time that this conversation was taking place, Mr. Fennessy, having spent an evening of valedictory carouse with his tribe in the ruined cottage, was walking, somewhat unsteadily, towards the wood, dragging after him by a rope a large dog. He did not notice that he was being followed by a barefooted woman, but the dog did, and, being an intelligent dog, was in some degree reassured. In the wood the tinker spent some time in selecting a tree with a projecting branch suitable to his purpose, and having found one he proceeded to hang the dog. Even in his cups Mr. Fennessy made sentiment subservient to common sense.

It is hardly too much to say that in a week the tinker had taken up a position in the Craffroe household only comparable to that of Ygdrasil, who in Norse mythology forms the ultimate support of all things. Save for the incessant demands upon his skill in the matter of solder and stitches, his recent tinkerhood was politely ignored, or treated as an escapade excusable in a youth of spirit. Had not his father owned a farm and seven cows in the county Limerick, and had not he himself three times returned the price of his ticket to America to a circle of adoring and wealthy relatives in Boston? His position in the kitchen and yard became speedily assured. Under his *régime* the hounds were valeted as they had never been before. Lily herself (newly washed, with "blue" in the water) was scarcely more white than the concrete floor of the kennel yard, and the puppies, Ruby and Remus, who had unaccountably developed a virulent form of mange, were immediately taken in hand by the all-accomplished tinker, and anointed with a mixture whose very noisomeness was to Patsey Crimmeen a sufficient guarantee of its efficacy, and was impressive even to the Master, fresh from much anxious study of veterinary lore.

"He's the best man we've got!" said Freddy proudly to a dubious uncle, "there isn't a mortal thing he can't put his hand to."

"Or lay his hands on," suggested the dubious uncle. "May I ask if his colleagues are still within a mile of the place?"

"Oh, he hates the very sight of 'em!" said Freddy hastily, "cuts 'em dead whenever he sees 'em."

"It's no use your crabbing him, George," broke in Mrs. Alexander, "we won't give him up to you! Wait till you see how he has mended the lock of the hall door!"

"I should recommend you to buy a new one at once," said Sir George Ker, in a way that was singularly exasperating to the paragon's proprietors.

Mrs. Alexander was, or so her friends said, somewhat given to vaunting herself of her paragons, under which heading, it may be admitted, practically all her household were included. She was, indeed, one of those persons who may or may not be heroes to their valets, but whose valets are almost invariably heroes to them. It was, therefore, excessively discomposing to her that, during the following week, in the very height of apparently cloudless domestic tranquility, the housemaid and the parlor-maid should in one black hour successively demand an audience, and successively, in the floods of tears proper to such occasions, give warning. Inquiry as to their reasons was fruitless. They were unhappy: one said she wouldn't get her appetite, and that her mother was sick; the other said she wouldn't get her sleep in it, and there was things—sob—going on—sob.

Mrs. Alexander concluded the interview abruptly, and descended to the kitchen to interview her queen paragon, Barnet, on the crisis.

Miss Barnet was a stout and comely English lady, of that liberal forty that frankly admits itself in advertisements to be twenty-eight. It was understood that she had only accepted office in Ireland because, in the first place, the butler to whom she had long been affianced had married another, and because, in the second place, she had a brother buried in Belfast. She was, perhaps, the one person in the world whose opinion about poultry Mrs. Alexander ranked higher than her own. She now allowed a restrained acidity to mingle with her dignity of manner, scarcely more than the calculated lemon essence in her faultless castle puddings, but enough to indicate that she, too, had grievances. *She* didn't know why they were leaving. She had heard some talk about a fairy or something, but she didn't hold with such nonsense.

"Gerrls is very frightful!" broke in an unexpected voice; "owld standards like meself maybe wouldn't feel it!"

A large basket of linen had suddenly blocked the scullery door, and from beneath it a little woman, like an Australian aborigine, delivered herself of this dark saying.

"What are you talking about, Mrs. Griffen?" demanded Mrs. Alexander, turning in vexed bewilderment to her laundress, "what does all this mean?"

"The Lord save us, ma'am, there's some says it means a death in the house!" replied Mrs. Griffen with unabated cheerfulness, "an' indeed 'twas no blame for the little gerrls to be frightened an' they meetin' it in the passages—"

"Meeting *what*?" interrupted her mistress. Mrs. Griffen was an old and privileged retainer, but there were limits even for Mrs. Griffen.

"Sure, ma'am, there's no one knows what was in it," returned Mrs. Griffen, "but whatever it was they heard it goin' on before them always in the panthry passage, an' it walkin' as sthrong as a man. It whipped away up the stairs, and they seen the big snout snorting out at them through the banisters, and a bare back on it the same as a pig; and the two cheeks on it as white as yer own, and away with it! And with that Mary Anne got a wakeness, and only for

Willy Fennessy bein' in the kitchen an' ketching a hold of her, she'd have cracked her head on the range, the crayture!"

Here Barnet smiled with ineffable contempt.

"What I'm tellin' them is," continued Mrs. Griffen, warming with her subject, "maybe that thing was a pairson that's dead, an' might be owin' a pound to another one, or has something that way on his soul, an' it's in the want o' some one that'll ax it what's throublin' it. The like o' thim couldn't spake till ye'll spake to thim first. But, sure, gerrls has no courage—"

Barnet's smile was again one of wintry superiority.

"Willy Fennessy and Patsey Crimmeen was afther seein' it too last night," went on Mrs. Griffen, "an' poor Willy was as much frightened! He said surely 'twas a ghost. On the back avenue it was, an' one minute 'twas as big as an ass, an' another minute it'd be no bigger than a bonnive—"

"Oh, the Lord save us!" wailed the kitchen-maid irrepressibly from the scullery.

"I shall speak to Fennessy myself about this," said Mrs. Alexander, making for the door with concentrated purpose, "and in the meantime I wish to hear no more of this rubbish."

"I'm sure Fennessy wishes to hear no more of it," said Barnet acridly to Mrs. Griffen, when Mrs. Alexander had passed swiftly out of hearing, "after the way those girls have been worryin' on at him about it all the morning. Such a set out!"

Mrs. Griffen groaned in a polite and general way, and behind Barnet's back put her tongue out of the corner of her mouth and winked at the kitchen-maid.

Mrs. Alexander found her conversation with Willy Fennessy less satisfactory than usual. He could not give any definite account of what he and Patsey had seen: maybe they'd seen nothing at all; maybe—as an obvious impromptu—it was the calf of the Kerry cow; whatever was in it, it was little he'd mind it, and, in easy dismissal of the subject, would the misthress be against his building a bit of a coal-shed at the back of the lodge while she was away?

That evening a new terror was added to the situation. Jimmy the boot-boy, on his return from taking the letters to the evening post, fled in panic into the kitchen, and having complied with the etiquette invariable in such cases by having "a wakeness," he described to a deeply sympathetic audience how he had seen something that was like a woman in the avenue, and he had called to it and it returned him no answer, and how he had then asked it three times in the name o' God what was it, and it soaked away into the trees from him, and then there came something rushing in on him and grunting at him to bite him, and he was full sure it was the Fairy Pig from Lough Clure.

Day by day the legend grew, thickened by tales of lights that had been seen moving mysteriously in the woods of Craffroe. Even the hounds were subpœnaed as witnesses; Patsey Crimmeen's mother stating that for three nights after Patsey had seen that Thing they were singing and screeching to each other all night.

Had Mrs. Crimmeen used the verb scratch instead of screech she would have been nearer the mark. The puppies, Ruby and Remus, had, after the manner of the young, human and canine, not failed to distribute their malady among their elders, and the pack, straitly coupled, went for dismal constitutionals, and the kennels reeked to heaven of remedies, and Freddy's new hunter, Mayboy, from shortness of work, smashed the partition of the loose box and kicked his neighbor, Mrs. Alexander's cob, in the knee.

"The worst of it is," said Freddy confidentially to his ally and adviser, the junior subaltern of the detachment at Enniscar, who had come over to see the hounds, "that I'm afraid Patsey Crimmeen—the boy whom I'm training to whip to me, you know"—(as a matter of fact, the Whip was a year older than the Master)—"is beginning to drink a bit. When I came down here before breakfast this mornin"'—when Freddy was feeling more acutely than usual his position as an M.F.H., he cut his g's and talked slightly through his nose, even, on occasion, going so far as to omit the aspirate in talking of his hounds—"there wasn't a sign of him—kennel door not open or anything. I let the poor brutes out into the run. I tell you, what with the paraffin and the carbolic and everything the kennel was pretty high—"

"It's pretty thick now," said his friend, lighting a cigarette.

"Well, I went into the boiler-house," continued Freddy impressively, "and there he was, asleep on the floor, with his beastly head on my kennel coat, and one leg in the feeding trough!"

Mr. Taylour made a suitable ejaculation.

"I jolly soon kicked him on to his legs," went on Freddy, "not that they were much use to him—he must have been on the booze all night. After that I went on to the stable yard, and if you'll believe me, the two chaps there had never turned up at all—at half-past eight, mind you!—and there was Fennessy doing up the horses. He said he believed that there'd been a wake down at Enniscar last night. I thought it was rather decent of him doing their work for them."

"You'll sack 'em, I suppose?" remarked Mr. Taylour, with martial severity.

"Oh well, I don't know," said Mr. Alexander evasively, "I'll see. Anyhow, don't say anything to my mother about it; a drunken man is like a red rag to a bull to her."

Taking this peculiarity of Mrs. Alexander into consideration, it was perhaps as well that she left Craffroe a few days afterwards to stay with her brother. The evening before she left both the Fairy Pig and the Ghost Woman were seen again on the avenue, this time by the coachman, who came into the kitchen considerably the worse for liquor and announced the fact, and that night the household duties were performed by the maids in pairs, and even, when possible, in trios.

As Mrs. Alexander said at dinner to Sir George, on the evening of her arrival, she was thankful to have abandoned the office of Ghostly Comforter to her domestics. Only for Barnet she couldn't have left poor Freddy to the mercy of that pack of fools; in fact, even with Barnet to look after them, it was impossible to tell what imbecility they were not capable of.

"Well, if you like," said Sir George, "I might run you over there on the motor car some day to see how they're all getting on. If Freddy is going to hunt on Friday, we might go on to Craffroe after seeing the fun."

The topic of Barnet was here shelved in favor of automobiles. Mrs. Alexander's brother was also a person of enthusiasms.

But what were these enthusiasms compared to the deep-seated ecstasy of Freddy Alexander as in his new pink coat he rode down the main street of Enniscar, Patsey in equal splendor bringing up the rear, unspeakably conscious of the jibes of his relatives and friends. There was a select field, consisting of Mr. Taylour, four farmers, some young ladies on bicycles, and about two dozen young men and boys on foot, who, in order to be prepared for all contingencies, had provided themselves with five dogs, two horns, and a ferret. It is, after all, impossible to please everybody, and from the cyclists' and foot people's point of view the weather left nothing to be desired. The sun shone like a glistering shield in the light blue November sky, the roads were like iron, the wind, what there was of it, like steel. There was a line of white on the northerly side of the fences, that yielded grudgingly and inch by inch before the march of the pale sunshine: the new pack could hardly have had a more unfavorable day for their *début*.

The new Master was, however, wholly undaunted by such crumples in the rose-leaf. He was riding Mayboy, a big trustworthy horse, whose love of jumping had survived a month of incessant and arbitrary schooling, and he left the road as soon as was decently possible, and made a line across country for the covert that involved as much jumping as could reasonably be hoped for in half a mile. At the second fence Patsey Crimmeen's black mare put her nose in the air and swung round; Patsey's hands seemed to be at their worst this morning, and what their worst felt like the black mare alone knew. Mr. Taylour, as Deputy Whip, waltzed erratically round the nine couple on a very flippant polo pony; and the four farmers, who had wisely adhered to the road, reached the covert sufficiently in advance of the hunt to frustrate Lily's project of running sheep in a neighboring field.

The covert was a large, circular enclosure, crammed to the very top of its girdling bank with furze-bushes, bracken, low hazel, and stunted Scotch firs. Its primary idea was woodcock, its second rabbits; beaters were in the habit of getting through it somehow, but a ride feasible for fox hunters had never so much as occurred to it. Into this, with practical assistance from the country boys, the deeply reluctant hounds were pitched and flogged; Freddy very nervously uplifted his voice in falsetto encouragement, feeling much as if he were starting the solo of an anthem; and Mr. Taylour and Patsey, the latter having made it up with the black mare, galloped away with professional ardor to watch different sides of the covert. This, during the next hour, they had ample opportunities for doing. After the first outburst of joy from the hounds on discovering that there were rabbits in the covert, and after the retirement of the rabbits to their burrows on the companion discovery that there were hounds in it, a silence, broken only by the far-away prattle of the lady bicyclists on the road, fell round Freddy Alexander. He bore it as long as he could, cheering with faltering whoops the invisible and unresponsive pack, and wondering what on earth huntsmen were expected to do on such occasions; then, filled with that horrid conviction which assails the lonely watcher, that the hounds have slipped away at the far side, he put spurs to Mayboy, and cantered down the long flank of the covert to find some one or something. Nothing had happened on the north side, at all events, for there was the faithful Taylour, pirouetting on his hill-top in the eye of the wind. Two fields more (in one of which he caught his first sight of any of the hounds, in the shape of Ruby, carefully rolling on a dead crow), and then, under the lee of a high bank, he came upon Patsey Crimmeen, the farmers, and the country boys, absorbed in the contemplation of a fight between Tiger, the butcher's brindled cur, and Watty, the kennel terrier.

The manner in which Mr. Alexander dispersed this entertainment showed that he was already equipped with one important qualification of a Master of Hounds—a temper laid on like gas, ready to blaze at a moment's notice. He pitched himself off his horse and scrambled over the bank into the covert in search of his hounds. He pushed his way through briars and furze-bushes, and suddenly, near the middle of the wood, he caught sight of them. They were in a small group, they were very quiet and very busy. As a matter of fact they were engaged in eating a dead sheep.

After this episode, there ensued a long and disconsolate period of wandering from one bleak hillside to another, at the bidding of various informants, in search of apocryphal foxes, slaughterers of flocks of equally apocryphal geese and turkeys—such a day as is discreetly ignored in all hunting annals, and, like the easterly wind that is its parent, is neither good for man nor beast.

By half-past three hope had died, even in the sanguine bosoms of the Master and Mr. Taylour. Two of the farmers had disappeared, and the lady bicyclists, with faces lavender blue from waiting at various windy cross roads, had long since fled away to lunch. Two of the hounds were limping; all, judging by their expressions, were on the verge of tears. Patsey's black mare had lost two shoes; Mr. Taylour's pony had ceased to pull, and was too dispirited even to try to kick the hounds, and the country boys had dwindled to four. There had come a time when Mr. Taylour had sunk so low as to suggest that a drag should be run with the assistance of the ferret's bag, a scheme only frustrated by the regrettable fact that the ferret and its owner had gone home.

"Well we had a nice bit of schooling, anyhow, and, it's been a real educational day for the hounds," said Freddy, turning in his saddle to look at the fires of the frosty sunset. "I'm glad they had it. I think we're in for a go of hard weather. I don't know what I should have done only for you, old chap. Patsey's gone all to pieces: it's my belief he's been on the drink this whole week, and where he gets it—"

"Hullo! Hold hard!" interrupted Mr. Taylour. "What's Governor after?"

They were riding along a grass-grown farm road outside the Craffroe demesne; the grey wall made a sharp bend to the right, and just at the corner Governor had begun to gallop, with his nose to the ground and his stern up. The rest of the pack joined him in an instant, and all swung round the corner and were lost to sight.

"It's a fox!" exclaimed Freddy, snatching up his reins; "they always cross into the demesne just here!"

By the time he and Mr. Taylour were round the corner the hounds had checked fifty yards ahead, and were eagerly hunting to and fro for the lost scent, and a little further down the old road they saw a woman running away from them.

"Hi, ma'am!" bellowed Freddy, "did you see the fox?"

The woman made no answer.

"Did you see the fox?" reiterated Freddy in still more stentorian tones. "Can't you answer me?"

The woman continued to run without even looking behind her.

The laughter of Mr. Taylour added fuel to the fire of Freddy's wrath: he put the spurs into Mayboy, dashed after the woman, pulled his horse across the road in front of her, and shouted his question point-blank at her, coupled with a warm inquiry as to whether she had a tongue in her head.

The woman jumped backwards as if she were shot, staring in horror at Freddy's furious little face, then touched her mouth and ears and began to jabber inarticulately and talk on her fingers.

The laughter of Mr. Taylour was again plainly audible.

"Sure that's a dummy woman, sir," explained the butcher's nephew, hurrying up. "I think she's one of them tinkers that's outside the town." Then with a long screech, "Look! Look over! Tiger, have it! Hulla, hulla, hulla!"

Tiger was already over the wall and into the demesne, neck and neck with Fly, the smith's half-bred greyhound; and in the wake of these champions clambered the Craffroe Pack, with strangled yelps of ardor, striving and squealing and fighting horribly in the endeavor to scramble up the tall smooth face of the wall.

"The gate! The gate further on!" yelled Freddy, thundering down the turfy road, with the earth flying up in lumps from his horse's hoofs.

Mr. Taylour's pony gave two most uncomfortable bucks and ran away; even Patsey Crimmeen and the black mare shared an unequal thrill of enthusiasm, as the latter, wholly out of hand, bucketed after the pony.

* * * * *

The afternoon was very cold, a fact thoroughly realized by Mrs. Alexander, on the front seat of Sir George's motor-car, in spite of enveloping furs, and of Bismarck, curled like a fried whiting, in her lap. The grey road rushed smoothly backwards under the broad tyres; golden and green plover whistled in the quiet fields, starlings and huge missel thrushes burst from the wayside trees as the "Bollée," uttering that hungry whine that indicates the desire of such creatures to devour space, tore past. Mrs. Alexander wondered if birds' beaks felt as cold as her nose after they had been cleaving the air for an afternoon; at all events, she reflected, they had not the consolation of tea to look forward to. Barnet was sure to have some of her best hot cakes ready for Freddy when he came home from hunting. Mrs. Alexander and Sir George had been scouring the roads since a very early lunch in search of the hounds, and her mind reposed on the thought of the hot cakes.

The front lodge gates stood wide open, the motor-car curved its flight and skimmed through. Half-way up the avenue they whizzed past three policemen, one of whom was carrying on his back a strange and wormlike thing.

"Janet," called out Sir George, "you've been caught making potheen! They've got the worm of a still there."

"They're only making a short cut through the place from the bog; I'm delighted they've found it!" screamed back Mrs. Alexander.

The "Bollée" was at the hall door in another minute, and the mistress of the house pulled the bell with numbed fingers. There was no response.

"Better go round to the kitchen," suggested her brother. "You'll find they're talking too hard to hear the bell."

His sister took the advice, and a few minutes afterwards she opened the hall door with an extremely perturbed countenance.

"I can't find a creature anywhere," she said, "either upstairs or down—I can't understand Barnet leaving the house empty—"

"Listen!" interrupted Sir George, "isn't that the hounds?"

They listened.

"They're hunting down by the back avenue! come on, Janet!"

The motor-car took to flight again; it sped, soft-footed, through the twilight gloom of the back avenue, while a disjointed, travelling clamor of hounds came nearer and nearer through the woods. The motor-car was within a hundred yards of the back lodge, when out of the rhododendron-bush burst a spectral black-and-white dog, with floating fringes of ragged wool and hideous bald patches on its back.

"Fennessy's dog!" ejaculated Mrs. Alexander, falling back in her seat.

Probably Bismarck never enjoyed anything in his life as much as the all too brief moment in which, leaning from his mistress's lap in the prow of the flying "Bollée," he barked hysterically in the wake of the piebald dog, who, in all its dolorous career had never before had the awful experience of being chased by a motor-car. It darted in at the open door of the lodge; the pursuers pulled up outside. There were paraffin lamps in the windows, the open door was garlanded with evergreens; from it proceeded loud and hilarious voices and the jerky strains of a concertina. Mrs. Alexander, with all, her most cherished convictions toppling on their pedestals, stood in the open doorway and stared, unable to believe the testimony of her own eyes. Was that the immaculate Barnet seated at the head of a crowded table, in her—Mrs. Alexander's—very best bonnet and velvet cape, with a glass of steaming potheen punch in her hand, and Willy Fennessy's arm round her waist?

The glass sank from the paragon's lips, the arm of Mr. Fennessy fell from her waist; the circle of servants, tinkers, and country people vainly tried to efface themselves behind each other.

"Barnet!" said Mrs. Alexander in an awful voice, and even in that moment she appreciated with an added pang the feathery beauty of a slice of Barnet's sponge-cake in the grimy fist of a tinker.

"Mrs. Fennessy, m'm, if you please," replied Barnet, with a dignity that, considering the bonnet and cape, was highly creditable to her strength of character.

At this point a hand dragged Mrs. Alexander backwards from the doorway, a barefooted woman hustled past her into the house, slammed the door in her face, and Mrs. Alexander found herself in the middle of the hounds.

"We'd give you the brush, Mrs. Alexander," said Mr. Taylour, as he flogged solidly all round him in the dusk, "but as the other lady seems to have gone to ground with the fox I suppose she'll take it!"

* * * * *

Mrs. Fennessy paid out of her own ample savings the fines inflicted upon her husband for potheen-making and selling drink in the Craffroe gate lodge without a license, and she shortly afterwards took him to America.

Mrs. Alexander's friends professed themselves as being not in the least surprised to hear that she had installed the afflicted Miss Fennessy (sister to the late occupant) and her scarcely less afflicted companion, the Fairy Pig, in her back lodge. Miss Fennessy, being deaf and dumb, is not perhaps a paragon lodge-keeper, but having, like her brother, been brought up in a work-house kitchen, she has taught Patsey Crimmeen how to boil stirabout *à merveille*.

BRENNAN ON THE MOOR

Traditional

Tis of a brave young highwayman this story I will tell.
His name was Willie Brennan and in Ireland he did dwell.

It was on the Kilworth mountains he commenced his wild career,
Where many of a wealthy gentleman before him shook with fear.

And it's Brennan on the Moor, Brennan on the Moor
Bold, brave and undaunted was young Brennan on the Moor.

A brace of loaded pistols, he carried night and day.
He never robbed a poor man upon the King's highway.
But what he'd taken from the rich, like Turpin and Black Bess,
He always did divide it with the widow in distress.

And it's Brennan on the Moor, Brennan on the Moor
Bold, brave and undaunted was young Brennan on the Moor.

One night he robbed a packman, by name of Pedlar Bawn.
They traveled on together til the day began to dawn.
The pedlar saw his money gone, likewise his watch and chain,
He at once encountered Brennan and he robbed him back again.

And it's Brennan on the Moor, Brennan on the Moor
Bold, brave and undaunted was young Brennan on the Moor.

One day upon the highway, as Willie he went down,

He met the Mayor of Cashel, a mile outside the town.
The mayor he knew his features and he said "Young man" said he,
"Your name is Willie Brennan, you must come along with me."

And it's Brennan on the Moor, Brennan on the Moor
Bold, brave and undaunted was young Brennan on the Moor.

Now Brennan's wife had come to town, provisions for to buy,
And when she saw her Willie there, she commenced to weep and cry.
He said, "Give to me that ten-penny." As soon as Willie spoke,
She handed him a blunderbuss from underneath her cloak.

And it's Brennan on the Moor, Brennan on the Moor
Bold, brave and undaunted was young Brennan on the Moor.

Now with this loaded blunderbuss, the truth I will unfold,
He made the Mayor to tremble, and he robbed him of his gold.
One hundred pounds was offered for his apprehension there,
So he with horse and saddle to the mountains did repair.

And it's Brennan on the Moor, Brennan on the Moor
Bold, brave and undaunted was young Brennan on the Moor.

Then Brennan being an outlaw, upon the mountains high,
When cavalry and infantry to take they did try,
He laughed at them with scorn, until at last 'tis said,
By a false-hearted young man he basely was betrayed.

And it's Brennan on the Moor, Brennan on the Moor
Bold, brave and undaunted was young Brennan on the Moor.

In the county of Tipperary, in a place they call Clonmore,
Willie Brennan and his comrade, that day did suffer sore.
They lay amongst the fern, which was thick upon the field,
And nine deep wounds did he receive, before that he did yield.

And it's Brennan on the Moor, Brennan on the Moor
Bold, brave and undaunted was young Brennan on the Moor.

So they were taken prisoner, in irons they were bound,
And both conveyed to Clonmel jail, strong walls did them surround.
They were tried and there found guilty, the Judge made this reply:
"For robbing on the King's highway, you're both condemned to die."

And it's Brennan on the Moor, Brennan on the Moor
Bold, brave and undaunted was young Brennan on the Moor.

Farewell unto my dear wife, and to my children three.
And to my aged father, he may shed tears for me.
And to my loving mother, who tore her locks and cried,
Saying, "I wish my Willie Brennan in your cradle you had died!"

And it's Brennan on the Moor, Brennan on the Moor
Bold, brave and undaunted was young Brennan on the Moor.

MURTOUGH AND THE WITCH WOMAN

BY ELEANOR HULL

In the days when Murtough Mac Erca was in the High Kingship of Ireland, the country was divided between the old beliefs of paganism and the new doctrines of the Christian teaching. Part held with the old creed and part with the new, and the thought of the people was troubled between them, for they knew not which way to follow and which to forsake. The faith of their forefathers clung close around them, holding them by many fine and tender threads of memory and custom and tradition; yet still the new faith was making its way, and every day it spread wider and wider through the land.

The family of Murtough had joined itself to the Christian faith, and his three brothers were bishops and abbotts of the Church, but Murtough himself remained a pagan, for he was a wild and lawless prince, and the peaceful teachings of the Christian doctrine, with its forgiveness of enemies, pleased him not at all. Fierce and cruel was his life, filled with dark deeds and bloody wars, and savage and tragic was his death, as we shall hear.

Now Murtough was in the sunny summer palace of Cletty, which Cormac, son of Art, had built for a pleasure house on the brink of the slow-flowing Boyne, near the Fairy Brugh of Angus the Ever Young, the God of Youth and Beauty. A day of summer was that day, and the King came forth to hunt on the borders of the Brugh, with all his boon companions around him. But when the high-noon came the sun grew hot, and the King sat down to rest upon the fairy mound, and the hunt passed on beyond him, and he was left alone.

There was a witch woman in that country whose name was "Sigh, Sough, Storm, Rough Wind, Winter Night, Cry, Wail, and Groan." Star-bright and beautiful was she in face and form, but inwardly she was cruel as her names. And she hated Murtough because he had scattered and destroyed the Ancient Peoples of the Fairy Tribes of Erin, her country and her fatherland, and because in the battle which he fought at Cerb on the Boyne her father and her mother and her sister had been slain. For in those days women went to battle side by side with men.

She knew, too, that with the coming of the new faith trouble would come upon the fairy folk, and their power and their great majesty would depart from them, and men would call them demons, and would drive them out with psalm-singing and with the saying of prayers, and with the sound of little tinkling bells. So trouble and anger wrought in the witch woman, and she waited the day to be revenged on Murtough, for he being yet a pagan, was still within her power to harm.

So when Sheen (for Sheen or "Storm" was the name men gave to her) saw the King seated on the fairy mound and all his comrades parted from him, she arose softly, and combed her hair with her comb of silver adorned with little ribs of gold, and she washed her hands in a silver basin wherein were four golden birds sitting on the rim of the bowl, and little bright gems of carbuncle set round about the rim. And she donned her fairy mantle of flowing green, and her cloak, wide and hooded, with silvery fringes, and a brooch of fairest gold. On her head were tresses yellow like to gold, plaited in four locks, with a golden drop at the end of each long tress. The hue of her hair was like the flower of the iris in summer or like red gold after the burnishing thereof. And she wore on her breasts and at her shoulders marvelous clasps of gold, finely worked with the tracery of the skilled craftsman, and a golden twisted torque around her throat. And when she was decked she went softly and sat down beside Murtough on the turfy hunting mound. And after a space Murtough perceived her sitting there, and the sun shining upon her, so that the glittering of the gold and of her golden hair and the bright shining of the green silk of her garments, was like the yellow iris-beds upon the lake on a sunny summer's day. Wonder and terror seized on Murtough at her beauty, and he knew not if he loved her or if he hated her the most; for at one moment all his nature was filled with longing and with love of her, so that it seemed to him that he would give the whole of Ireland for the loan of one hour's space of dalliance with her; but after that he felt a dread of her, because he knew his fate was in her hands, and that she had come to work him ill. But he welcomed her as if she were known to him and he asked her wherefore she was come. "I am come," she said, "because I am beloved of Murtough, son of Erc, King of Erin, and I come to seek him here." Then Murtough was glad, and he said, "Dost thou not know me, maiden?" "I do," she answered, "for all secret and mysterious things are known to me and thou and all the men of Erin are well known."

After he had conversed with her awhile, she appeared to him so fair that the King was ready to promise her anything in life she wished, so long as she would go with him to Cletty of the Boyne. "My wish," she said, "is that you take me to your house, and that you put out from it your wife and your children because they are of the new faith, and all the clerics that are in your house, and that neither your wife nor any cleric be permitted to enter the house while I am there."

"I will give you," said the King, "a hundred head of every herd of cattle that is within my kingdom, and a hundred drinking horns, and a hundred cups, and a hundred rings of gold, and a feast every other night in the summer palace of Cletty. But I pledge thee my word, oh, maiden, it were easier for me to give thee half of Ireland than to do this thing that thou hast asked." For Murtough feared that when those that were of the Christian faith were put out of his house, she would work her spells upon him, and no power would be left with him to resist those spells.

"I will not take thy gifts," said the damsel, "but only those things that I have asked; moreover, it is thus, that my name must never be uttered by thee, nor must any man or woman learn it."

"What is thy name," said Murtough, "that it may not come upon my lips to utter it?"

And she said, "Sigh, Sough, Storm, Rough Wind, Winter Night, Cry, Wail, Groan, this is my name, but men call me Sheen, for 'Storm' or Sheen is my chief name, and storms are with me where I come."

Nevertheless, Murtough was so fascinated by her that he brought her to his home, and drove out the clerics that were there, with his wife and children along with them, and drove out also the nobles of his own clan, the children of Niall, two great and gallant battalions. And Duivsech, his wife, went crying along the road with her children around her to seek Bishop Cairnech, the half-brother of her husband, and her own soul-friend, that she might obtain help and shelter from him.

But Sheen went gladly and light-heartedly into the House of Cletty, and when she saw the lovely lightsome house and the goodly nobles of the clan of Niall, and the feasting and banqueting and the playing of the minstrels and all the joyous noise of that kingly dwelling, her heart was lifted within her, and "Fair as a fairy palace is this house of Cletty," said she.

"Fair, indeed, it is," replied the King; "for neither the Kings of Leinster nor the Kings of mighty Ulster, nor the lords of the clans of Owen or of Niall, have such a house as this; nay, in Tara of the Kings itself, no house to equal this house of mine is found." And that night the King robed himself in all the splendor of his royal dignity, and on his right hand he seated Sheen, and a great banquet was made before them, and men said that never on earth was to be seen a woman more goodly of appearance than she. And the King was astonished at her, and he began to ask her questions, for it seemed to him that the power of a great goddess of the ancient time was in her; and he asked her whence she came, and what manner was the power that he saw in her. He asked her, too, did she believe in the God of the clerics, or was she herself some goddess of the older world? For he feared her, feeling that his fate was in her hands.

She laughed a careless and a cruel laugh, for she knew that the King was in their power, now that she was there alone with him, and the clerics and the Christian teachers gone. "Fear me not, O Murtough," she cried; "I am, like thee, a daughter of the race of men of the ancient family of Adam and of Eve; fit and meet my comradeship with thee; therefore, fear not nor regret. And as to that true God of thine, worker of miracles and helper of His people, no miracle in all the world is there that I, by mine own unaided power, cannot work the like. I can create a sun and moon; the heavens I can sprinkle with radiant stars of night. I can call up to life men fiercely fighting in conflict, slaughtering one another. Wine I could make of the cold water of the Boyne, and sheep of lifeless stones, and swine of ferns. In the presence of the hosts I can make gold and silver, plenty and to spare; and hosts of famous fighting men I can produce from naught. Now, tell me, can thy God work the like?"

"Work for us," says the King, "some of these great wonders." Then Sheen went forth out of the house, and she set herself to work spells on Murtough, so that he knew not whether he was in his right mind or no. She took of the water of the Boyne and made a magic wine thereout, and she took ferns and spiked thistles and light puff-balls of the woods, and out of them she fashioned magic swine and sheep and goats, and with these she fed Murtough and the hosts. And when they had eaten, all their strength went from them, and the magic wine sent them into an uneasy sleep and restless slumbers. And out of stones and sods of earth she fashioned three battalions, and one of the battalions she placed at one side of the house, and the other at the further side beyond it, and one encircling the rest southward along the hollow windings of the glen. And thus were these battalions, one of them all made of men stark-naked and their color blue, and the second with heads of goats with shaggy beards and horned; but the third, more terrible than they, for these were headless men, fighting like human beings, yet finished at the neck; and the sound of heavy shouting as of hosts and multitudes came from the first and the second battalion, but from the third no sound save only that they waved their arms and struck their weapons together, and smote the ground with their feet impatiently. And though terrible was the shout of the blue men and the bleating of the goats with human limbs, more horrible yet was the stamping and the rage of those headless men, finished at the neck.

And Murtough, in his sleep and in his dreams, heard the battle-shout, and he rose impetuously from off his bed, but the wine overcame him, and his strength departed from him, and he fell helplessly upon the floor. Then he heard the challenge a second time, and the stamping of the feet without, and he rose again, and madly, fiercely, he set on them, charging the hosts and scattering them before him, as he thought, as far as the fairy palace of the Brugh. But all his strength was lost in fighting phantoms, for they were but stones and sods and withered leaves of the forest that he took for fighting men.

Now Duivsech, Murtough's wife, knew what was going on. She called upon Cairnech to arise and to gather together the clans of the children of his people, the men of Owen and of Niall, and together they went to the fort; but Sheen guarded it well, so that they could by no means find an entrance. Then Cairnech was angry, and he cursed the place, and he dug a grave before the door, and he stood up upon the mound of the grave, and rang his bells and cursed the King and his house, and prophesied his downfall. But he blessed the clans of Owen and of Niall, and they returned to their own country.

Then Cairnech sent messengers to seek Murtough and to draw him away from the witch woman who sought his destruction, but because she was so lovely the King would believe no evil of her; and whenever he made any sign to go to Cairnech, she threw her spell upon the King, so that he could not break away. When he was so weak and faint that he had no power left, she cast a sleep upon him, and she went round the house, putting everything in readiness. She called upon her magic host of warriors, and set them round the fortress, with their spears and javelins pointed inwards towards the house, so that the King would not dare to go out amongst them. And that night was a night of Samhain-tide, the eve of Wednesday after All Souls' Day.

Then she went everywhere throughout the house, and took lighted brands and burning torches, and scattered them in every part of the dwelling. And she returned into the room wherein Murtough slept, and lay down by his side. And she caused a great wind to spring up, and it came soughing through the house from the north-west; and the King said, "This is the sigh of the winter night." And Sheen smiled, because, unwittingly, the King had spoken her name, for she knew by that that the hour of her revenge had come. "'Tis I myself that am Sigh and Winter Night," she said, "and I am Rough Wind and Storm, a daughter of fair nobles; and I am Cry and Wail, the maid of elfin birth, who brings ill-luck to men."

After that she caused a great snowstorm to come round the house; and like the noise of troops and the rage of battle was the storm, beating and pouring in on every side, so that drifts of deep snow were piled against the walls, blocking the doors and chilling the folk that were feasting within the house. But the King was lying in a heavy, unresting sleep, and Sheen was at his side. Suddenly he screamed out of his sleep and stirred himself, for he heard the crash of falling timbers and the noise of the magic hosts, and he smelled the strong smell of fire in the palace.

He sprang up. "It seems to me," he cried, "that hosts of demons are around the house, and that they are slaughtering my people, and that the house of Cletty is on fire." "It was but a dream," the witch maiden said. Then he slept again, and he saw a vision, to wit, that he was tossing in a ship at sea, and the ship floundered, and above his head a griffin, with sharp beak and talons, sailed, her wings outspread and covering all the sun, so that it was dark as middle-night; and lo! as she rose on high, her plumes quivered for a moment in the air; then down she swooped and picked him from the waves, carrying him to her eyrie on the dismal cliff outhanging o'er the ocean; and the griffin began to pierce him and to prod him with her talons, and to pick out pieces of his flesh with her beak; and this went on awhile, and then a flame, that came he knew not whence, rose from the nest, and he and the griffin were enveloped in the flame. Then in her beak the griffin picked him up, and together they fell downward over the cliff's edge into the seething ocean; so that, half by fire and half by water, he died a miserable death.

When the King saw that vision, he rose screaming from his sleep, and donned his arms; and he made one plunge forward seeking for the magic hosts, but he found no man to answer him. The damsel went forth from the house, and Murtough made to follow her, but as he turned the flames leaped out, and all between him and the door was one vast sheet of flame. He saw no way of escape, save the vat of wine that stood in the banqueting hall, and into that he got; but the burning timbers of the roof fell upon his head and the hails of fiery sparks rained on him, so that half of him was burned and half was drowned, as he had seen in his dream.

The next day, amid the embers, the clerics found his corpse, and they took it up and washed it in the Boyne, and carried it to Tuilen to bury it. And they said, "Alas! that Mac Erca, High King of Erin, of the noble race of Conn and of the descendants of Ugaine the Great, should die fighting with sods and stones! Alas! that the Cross of Christ was not signed upon his face that he might have known the witchdoms of the maiden what they were."

As they went thus, bewailing the death of Murtough and bearing him to his grave, Duivsech, wife of Murtough, met them, and when she found her husband dead, she struck her hands together and she made a great and mournful lamentation; and because weakness came upon her she leaned her back against the ancient tree that is in Aenech Reil; and a burst of blood broke from her heart, and there she died, grieving for her husband. And the grave of Murtough was made wide and deep, and there they laid the Queen beside him, two in the one grave, near the north side of the little church that is in Tuilen.

Now, when the burial was finished, and the clerics were reciting over his grave the deeds of the King, and were making prayers for Murtough's soul that it might be brought out of hell, for Cairnech showed great care for this, they saw coming towards them across the sward a lonely woman, star-bright and beautiful, and a kirtle of priceless silk upon her, and a green mantle with its fringes of silver thread flowing to the ground. She reached the place where the clerics were, and saluted them, and they saluted her.

And they marveled at her beauty, but they perceived on her an appearance of sadness and of heavy grief. They asked of her, "Who art thou, maiden, and wherefore art thou come to the house of mourning? For a king lies buried here." "A king lies buried here, indeed," said she, "and I it was who slew him, Murtough of the many deeds, of the race of Conn and Niall, High King of Ireland and of the West. And though it was I who wrought his death, I myself will die for grief of him."

And they said, "Tell us, maiden, why you brought him to his death, if so be that he was dear to thee?" And she said, "Murtough was dear to me, indeed, dearest of the men of the whole world; for I am Sheen, the daughter of Sige, the son of Dian, from whom Ath Sigi or the 'Ford of Sige' is called to-day. But Murtough slew my father, and my mother and sister were slain along with him, in the battle of Cerb upon the Boyne, and there was none of my house to avenge their death, save myself alone. Moreover, in his time the Ancient Peoples of the Fairy Tribes of Erin were scattered and destroyed, the folk of the underworld and of my fatherland; and to avenge the wrong and loss he wrought on them I slew the man I loved. I made poison for him; alas! I made for him magic drink and food which took his strength away, and out of the sods of earth and puff-balls that float down the wind, I wrought men and armies of headless, hideous folk, till all his senses were distraught. And, now, take me to thee, O Cairnech, in fervent and true repentance, and sign the Cross of Christ upon my brow, for the time of my death is come."

Then she made penitence for the sin that she had sinned, and she died there upon the grave of grief and of sorrow after the King. And they digged a grave lengthways across the foot of the wide grave of Murtough and his spouse, and there they laid the maiden who had wrought them woe. And the clerics wondered at those things, and they wrote them and revised them in a book.

THE THIEF

BY PATRICK PEARSE

One day when the boys of Gortmore were let out from school, after the Glencaha boys and the Derrybanniv boys had gone east, the Turlagh boys and the Inver boys stayed to have a while's chat before separating at the Rossnageeragh road. The master's house is exactly at the head of the road, its back to the hill and its face to Loch Ellery.

'I heard that the master's bees were swarming,' says Michileen Bartly Enda.

'In with you into the garden till we look at them,' says Daragh Barbara of the Bridge.

'I'm afraid,' says Michileen.

'What are you afraid of?'says Daragh.

'By my word, the master and the mistress will be out presently.'

'Who'll stay to give us word when the master will be coming?' says Daragh.

'I will,' says little Anthony Manning.

'That'll do,' says Daragh. 'Let a whistle when you see him leaving the school.'

In over the fence with him. In over the fence with the other boys after him.

'Have a care that none of you will get a sting,' says Anthony.

'Little fear,' says Daragh. And off forever with them.

Anthony sat on the fence, and his back to the road. He could see the master over his right shoulder if he'd leave the schoolhouse. What a nice garden the master had, thought Anthony. He had rose-trees and gooseberry-trees and apple-trees. He had little white stones round the path. He had big white stones in a pretty rockery, and moss and maiden-hair fern and common fern growing between them. He had . . .

Anthony saw a wonder greater than any wonder the master had in the garden. He saw a little, beautiful wee house under the shade of one of the rose-trees; it made of wood; two stories in it; white color on the lower story and red color on the upper story; a little green door on it; three windows of glass on it, one downstairs and two upstairs; house furniture in it, between tables and chairs and beds and delf, and the rest; and, says Anthony to himself, look at the lady of the house sitting in the door!

Anthony never saw a doll's house before, and it was a wonder to him, its neatness and order, for a toy. He knew that it belonged to the master's little girl, little Nance. A pity that his own little sister hadn't one like it— Eibhlin, the creature, that was stretched on her bed for a long three months, and she weak and sick! A pity she hadn't the doll itself! Anthony put the covetousness of his heart in that doll for Eibhlin. He looked over his right shoulder—neither master nor mistress was to be seen. He looked over his left shoulder—the other boys were out of sight. He didn't think the second thought. He gave his best leap from the fence; he seized the doll; he stuck it under his jacket; he clambered out over the ditch again, and away with him home.

'I have a present for you,' says he to Eibhlin, when he reached the house. 'Look!' and with that he showed her the doll.

There came a blush on the wasted cheeks of the little sick girl, and a light into her eyes.

'*Ora*, Anthony, love, where did you get it?' says she.

'The master's little Nance, that sent it to you for a present,' says Anthony.

Their mother came in.

'Oh, mameen, treasure,' says Eibhlin, 'look at the present that the master's little Nance sent me!'

'In earnest?' says the mother.

'Surely,' says Eibhlin. 'Anthony, it was, that brought it in to me now.'

Anthony looked down at his feet, and began counting the toes that were on them.

'My own pet,' says the mother, 'isn't it she that was good to you! *Muise*, Nance! I'll go bail that that present will put great improvement on my little girl.'

And there came tears in the mother's eyes out of gratitude to little Nance because she remembered the sick child. Though he wasn't able to look his mother between the eyes, or at Eibhlin, with the dint of fear, Anthony was glad that he committed the theft.

He was afraid to say his prayers that night, and he lay down on his bed without as much as an 'Our Father.' He couldn't say the Act of Contrition, for it wasn't truthfully he'd be able to say to God that he was sorry for that sin. It's often he started in the night, imagining that little Nance was coming seeking the doll from Eibhlin, that the master was taxing him with the robbery before the school, that there was a miraculous swarm of bees rising against him, and Daragh Barbara of the Bridge and the other boys exciting them with shouts and with the music of drums. But the next morning he said to himself: 'I don't care. The doll will make Eibhlin better.'

When he went to school the boys asked him why he went off unawares the evening before that, and he after promising them he'd keep watch.

'My mother sent for me,' says Anthony. 'She'd a task for me.'

When little Nance came into the school, Anthony looked at her under his brows. He fancied that she was after being crying; he thought that he saw the track of the tears on her cheeks. The first time the master called him by his name he jumped, because he thought that he was going to tax him with the fault or to cross-question him about the doll. He never put in as miserable a day as that day at school. But when he went home and saw the great improvement on Eibhlin, and she sitting up in the bed for the first time for a month, and the doll clasped in her arms, says he to himself: 'I don't care. The doll is making Eibhlin better.'

In his bed in the night-time he had bad dreams again. He thought that the master was after telling the police that he stole the doll, and that they were on his track; he imagined one time that there was a policeman hiding under the bed and that there was another hunkering behind the window-curtain. He screamed out in his sleep.

'What's on you?' says his father to him.

'The peeler that's going to take me,' says Anthony.

'You're only rambling, boy,' says his father to him. 'There's no peeler in it. Go to sleep.'

There was the misery of the world on the poor fellow from that out. He used think they would be pointing fingers at him, and he going the road. He used think they would be shaking their heads and saying to each other, 'There's a thief,' or, 'Did you hear what Anthony Pharaig Manning did? Her doll he stole from the master's little Nance. Now what do you say?' But he didn't suffer rightly till he went to Mass on Sunday and till Father Ronan started preaching a sermon on the Seventh Commandment: 'Thou shalt not steal; and if you commit a theft it will not be forgiven you until you make restitution.' Anthony was full sure that it was a mortal sin. He knew that he ought to go to confession and tell the sin to the priest. But he couldn't go to confession, for he knew that the priest would say to him that he must give the doll back. And he wouldn't give the doll back. He hardened his heart and he said that he'd never give the doll back, for that the doll was making Eibhlin better every day.

One evening he was sitting by the bed-foot in serious talk with Eibhlin when his mother ran in a hurry, and says she—

'Here's the mistress and little Nance coming up the bohereen!'

Anthony wished the earth would open and swallow him. His face was red up to his two ears. He was in a sweat. He wasn't able to say a word or to think a thought! But these words were running through his head: 'They'll take the doll from Eibhlin.' It was all the same to him what they'd say or what they'd do to himself. The only answer he'd have would be, 'The doll's making Eibhlin better.'

The mistress and little Nance came into the room. Anthony got up. He couldn't look them in the face. He began at his old clatter, counting the toes of his feet. Five on each foot; four toes and a big toe; or three toes, a big toe, and a little toe; that's five; twice five are ten; ten in all. He couldn't add to their number or take from them. His mother was talking, the mistress was talking, but Anthony paid no heed to them. He was waiting till something would be said about the doll. There was nothing for him to do till that but count his toes. One, two, three. . .

What was that? Eibhlin was referring to the doll. Anthony listened now.

'Wasn't it good of you to send me the doll?' she was saying to Nance. 'From the day Anthony brought it in to me a change began coming on me.'

'It did that,' says her mother. 'We'll be forever grateful to you for that same doll you sent to her. May God increase your store, and may He requite you for it a thousand times.

Neither Nance nor the mistress spoke. Anthony looked at Nance shyly. His two eyes were stuck in the doll, for the doll was lying cosy in the bed beside Eibhlin. It had its mouth half open, and the wonder of the world on it at the sayings of Eibhlin and her mother.

'It's with trouble I believed Anthony when he brought it into me,' says Eibhlin, 'and when he told me you sent it to me as a present.'

Nance looked over at Anthony. Anthony lifted his head slowly, and their eyes met. It will never be known what Nance read in Anthony's eyes. What Anthony read in Nance's eyes was mercy, love and sweetness. Nance spoke to Eibhlin.

'Do you like it?' says she.

'Over anything,' says Eibhlin. 'I'd rather it than anything I have in the world.'

'I have the little house it lives in,' says Nance. 'I must send it to you. Anthony will bring it to you to-morrow.'

'Ora!' says Eibhlin, and she clapping her two little thin palms together.

'You'll miss it, love,' says Eibhlin's mother to Nance.

'No,' said Nance. 'It will put more improvement on Eibhlin. I have lots of things.'

'Let her do it, Cait,' said the mistress to the mother.

'Ye are too good,' says the poor woman.

Anthony thought that it's dreaming he was. Or he thought that it's not a person of this world little Nance was at all, but an angel come down out of heaven. He wanted to go on his knees to her.

When the mistress and little Nance went off, Anthony ran out the back door and tore across the garden, so that he'd be before them at the boher-een-foot, and they going out on the road.

'Nance,' says he, 'I s-stole it,—the d-doll.'

'Never mind, Anthony,' says Nance, 'you did good to Eibhlin.'

Anthony stood like a stake in the road, he couldn't speak another word.

Isn't it he was proud bringing the doll's house home to Eibhlin after school the next day! And isn't it they had the fun that evening settling the house and polishing the furniture and putting the doll to sleep on its little bed!

The Saturday following Anthony went to confession, and told his sin to the priest. The penance the priest put on him was to clean the doll's house once in the week for Eibhlin, till she would be strong enough to clean it herself. Eibhlin was strong enough for it by the end of a month. By the end of another month she was at school again. There wasn't a Saturday evening from that out that they wouldn't hear a little, light tapping at the master's door. On the mis-tress going out Anthony would be standing at the door.

'Here's a little present for Nance,' he'd say, stretching towards her half-a-dozen duck's eggs, or a bunch of heather, or, at the least, the full of his fist of duileasg, and then he'd rush off with him without giving the mistress time to say 'thank you.'

THE DEVIL, THE DEMON CAT

BY LADY WILDE

There was a woman in Connemara, the wife of a fisherman; as he had always good luck, she had plenty of fish at all times stored away in the house ready for market. But, to her great annoyance, she found that a great cat used to come in at night and devour all the best and finest fish. So she kept a big stick by her, and determined to watch.

One day, as she and a woman were spinning together, the house suddenly became quite dark; and the door was burst open as if by the blast of the tempest, when in walked a huge black cat, who went straight up to the fire, then turned round and growled at them.

"Why, surely this is the devil," said a young girl, who was by, sorting fish.

"I'll teach you how to call me names," said the cat; and, jumping at her, he scratched her arm till the blood came. "There, now," he said, "you will be more civil another time when a gentleman comes to see you." And with that he walked over to the door and shut it close, to prevent any of them going out, for the poor young girl, while crying loudly from fright and pain, had made a desperate rush to get away.

Just then a man was going by, and hearing the cries, he pushed open the door and tried to get in; but the cat stood on the threshold, and would let no one pass. On this the man attacked him with his stick, and gave him a sound blow; the cat, however, was more than a match in the fight, for it flew at him and tore his face and hands so badly that the man at last took to his heels and ran away as fast as he could.

"Now, it's time for my dinner," said the cat, going up to examine the fish that was laid out on the tables. "I hope the fish is good to-day. Now, don't disturb me, nor make a fuss; I can help myself." With that he jumped up, and began to devour all the best fish, while he growled at the woman.

"Away, out of this, you wicked beast," she cried, giving it a blow with the tongs that would have broken its back, only it was a devil; "out of this; no fish shall you have to-day."

But the cat only grinned at her, and went on tearing and spoiling and devouring the fish, evidently not a bit the worse for the blow. On this, both the women attacked it with sticks, and struck hard blows enough to kill it, on which the cat glared at them, and spit fire; then, making a leap, it tore their heads and arms till the blood came, and the frightened women rushed shrieking from the house.

But presently the mistress returned, carrying with her a bottle of holy water; and, looking in, she saw the cat still devouring the fish, and not minding. So she crept over quietly and threw holy water on it without a word. No sooner was this done than a dense black smoke filled the place, through which nothing was seen but the two red eyes of the cat, burning like coals of fire. Then the smoke gradually cleared away, and she saw the body of the creature burning slowly till it became shriveled and black like a cinder, and finally disappeared. And from that time the fish remained untouched and safe from harm, for the power of the evil one was broken, and the demon cat was seen no more.

THE ENCHANTED CAVE OF CESH CORRAN

BY JAMES STEPHENS

*

Fionn mac Uail was the most prudent chief of an army in the world, but he was not always prudent on his own account. Discipline sometimes irked him, and he would then take any opportunity that presented for an adventure; for he was not only a soldier, he was a poet also, that is, a man of science, and whatever was strange or unusual had an irresistible attraction for him. Such a soldier was he that, single-handed, he could take the Fianna out of any hole they got into, but such an inveterate poet was he that all the Fianna together could scarcely retrieve him from the abysses into which he tumbled. It took him to keep the Fianna safe, but it took all the Fianna to keep their captain out of danger. They did not complain of this, for they loved every hair of Fionn's head more than they loved their wives and children, and that was reasonable for there was never in the world a person more worthy of love than Fionn was.

Goll mac Morna did not admit so much in words, but he admitted it in all his actions, for although he never lost an opportunity of killing a member of Fionn's family (there was deadly feud between clann-Baiscne and clann-Morna), yet a call from Fionn brought Goll raging to his assistance like a lion that rages tenderly by his mate. Not even a call was necessary, for Goll felt in his heart when Fionn was threatened, and he would leave Fionn's own brother only half-killed to fly where his arm was wanted. He was never thanked, of course, for although Fionn loved Goll he did not like him, and that was how Goll felt towards Fionn.

Fionn, with Conán the Swearer and the dogs Bran and Sceólan, was sitting on the hunting-mound at the top of Cesh Corran. Below and around on every side the Fianna were beating the coverts in Legney and Brefny, ranging the fastnesses of Glen Dallan, creeping in the nut and beech forests of Carbury, spying among the woods of Kyle Conor, and ranging the wide plain of Moy Conal.

The great captain was happy: his eyes were resting on the sights he liked best—the sunlight of a clear day, the waving trees, the pure sky, and the lovely movement of the earth; and his ears were filled with delectable sounds—the baying of eager dogs, the clear calling of young men, the shrill whistling that came from every side, and each sound of which told a definite thing about the hunt. There was also the plunge and scurry of the deer, the yapping of badgers, and the whirr of birds driven into reluctant flight.

* *

Now the king of the Shí of Cesh Corran, Conaran, son of Imidel, was also watching the hunt, but Fionn did not see him, for we cannot see the people of Faery until we enter their realm, and Fionn was not thinking of Faery at that moment. Conaran did not like Fionn, and, seeing that the great champion was alone, save for Conán and the two hounds Bran and Sceólan, he thought the time had come to get Fionn into his power. We do not know what Fionn had done to Conaran, but it must have been bad enough, for the king of the Shí of Cesh Cotran was filled with joy at the sight of Fionn thus close to him, thus unprotected, thus unsuspicious.

This Conaran had four daughters. He was fond of them and proud of them, but if one were to search the Shí's of Ireland or the land of Ireland, the equal of these four would not be found for ugliness and bad humor and twisted temperaments.

Their hair was black as ink and tough as wire: it stuck up and poked out and hung down about their heads in bushes and spikes and tangles. Their eyes were bleary and red. Their mouths were black and twisted, and in each of these mouths there was a hedge of curved yellow fangs. They had long scraggy necks that could turn all the way round like the neck of a hen. Their arms were long and skinny and muscular, and at the end of each finger they had a spiked nail that was as hard as horn and as sharp as a briar. Their bodies were covered with a bristle of hair and fur and fluff, so that they looked like dogs in some parts and like cats in others, and in other parts again they looked like chickens. They had moustaches poking under their noses and woolly wads growing out of their ears, so that when you looked at them the first time you never wanted to look at them again, and if you had to look at them a second time you were likely to die of the sight.

They were called Caevóg, Cuillen, and Iaran. The fourth daughter, Iarnach, was not present at that moment, so nothing need be said of her yet.

Conaran called these three to him.

"Fionn is alone," said he. "Fionn is alone, my treasures."

"Ah!" said Caevóg, and her jaw crunched upwards and stuck outwards, as was usual with her when she was satisfied.

"When the chance comes take it," Conaran continued, and he smiled a black, beetle-browed, unbenevolent smile.

"It's a good word," quoth Cuillen, and she swung her jaw loose and made it waggle up and down, for that was the way she smiled.

"And here is the chance," her father added.

"The chance is here," Iaran echoed, with a smile that was very like her sister's, only that it was worse, and the wen that grew on her nose joggled to and fro and did not get its balance again for a long time.

Then they smiled a smile that was agreeable to their own eyes, but which would have been a deadly thing for anybody else to see.

"But Fionn cannot see us," Caevóg objected, and her brow set downwards and her chin set upwards and her mouth squeezed sidewards, so that her face looked like a badly disappointed nut.

"And we are worth seeing," Cuillen continued, and the disappointment that was set in her sister's face got carved and twisted into hers, but it was worse in her case.

"That is the truth," said Iaran in a voice of lamentation, and her face took on a gnarl and a writhe and a solidity of ugly woe that beat the other two and made even her father marvel.

"He cannot see us now," Conaran replied, "but he will see us in a minute."

"Won't Fionn be glad when he sees us!" said the three sisters.

And then they joined hands and danced joyfully around their father, and they sang a song, the first line of which is:

"Fionn thinks he is safe. But who knows when the sky will fall?"

Lots of the people in the Shí learned that song by heart, and they applied it to every kind of circumstance.

* * *

By his arts Conaran changed the sight of Fionn's eyes, and he did the same for Conán.

In a few minutes Fionn stood up from his place on the mound. Everything was about him as before, and he did not know that he had gone into Faery. He walked for a minute up and down the hillock. Then, as by chance, he stepped down the sloping end of the mound and stood with his mouth open, staring. He cried out:

"Come down here, Conán, my darling."

Conán stepped down to him.

"Am I dreaming?" Fionn demanded, and he stretched out his finger before him.

"If you are dreaming," said Conán, "I'm dreaming too. They weren't here a minute ago," he stammered.

Fionn looked up at the sky and found that it was still there. He stared to one side and saw the trees of Kyle Conor waving in the distance. He bent his ear to the wind and heard the shouting of hunters, the yapping of dogs, and the clear whistles, which told how the hunt was going.

"Well!" said Fionn to himself.

"By my hand!" quoth Conán to his own soul.

And the two men stared into the hillside as though what they were looking at was too wonderful to be looked away from.

"Who are they?" said Fionn.

"What are they?" Conán gasped. And they stared again.

For there was a great hole like a doorway in the side of the mound, and in that doorway the daughters of Conaran sat spinning. They had three crooked sticks of holly set up before the cave, and they were reeling yarn off these. But it was enchantment they were weaving.

"One could not call them handsome," said Conán.

"One could," Fionn replied, "but it would not be true."

"I cannot see them properly," Fionn complained. "They are hiding behind the holly."

"I would be contented if I could not see them at all," his companion grumbled.

But the Chief insisted.

"I want to make sure that it is whiskers they are wearing."

"Let them wear whiskers or not wear them," Conán counseled. "But let us have nothing to do with them."

"One must not be frightened of anything," Fionn stated.

"I am not frightened," Conán explained. "I only want to keep my good opinion of women, and if the three yonder are women, then I feel sure I shall begin to dislike females from this minute out."

"Come on, my love," said Fionn, "for I must find out if these whiskers are true."

He strode resolutely into the cave. He pushed the branches of holly aside and marched up to Conaran's daughters, with Conán behind him.

* * * * *

The instant they passed the holly a strange weakness came over the heroes. Their fists seemed to grow heavy as lead, and went dingle-dangle at the ends of their arms; their legs became as light as straws and began to bend in and out; their necks became too delicate to hold anything up, so that their heads wibbled and wobbled from side to side.

"What's wrong at all?" said Conán, as he tumbled to the ground.

"Everything is," Fionn replied, and he tumbled beside him.

The three sisters then tied the heroes with every kind of loop and twist and knot that could be thought of.

"Those are whiskers!" said Fionn.

"Alas!" said Conán.

"What a place you must hunt whiskers in?" he mumbled savagely. "Who wants whiskers?" he groaned.

But Fionn was thinking of other things.

"If there was any way of warning the Fianna not to come here," Fionn murmured.

"There is no way, my darling," said Caevóg, and she smiled a smile that would have killed Fionn, only that he shut his eyes in time.

After a moment he murmured again:

"Conán, my dear love, give the warning whistle so that the Fianna will keep out of this place."

A little whoof, like the sound that would be made by a baby and it asleep, came from Conán.

"Fionn," said he, "there isn't a whistle in me. We are done for," said he.

"You are done for, indeed," said Cuillen, and she smiled a hairy and twisty and fangy smile that almost finished Conán.

By that time some of the Fianna had returned to the mound to see why Bran and Sceólan were barking so outrageously. They saw the cave and went into it, but no sooner had they passed the holly branches than their strength went from them, and they were seized and bound by the vicious hags. Little by little all the members of the Fianna returned to the hill, and each of them was drawn into the cave, and each was bound by the sisters.

Oisín and Oscar and mac Lugac came, with the nobles of clann-Baiscne, and with those of clann-Corcoran and clann-Smól; they all came, and they were all bound.

It was a wonderful sight and a great deed this binding of the Fianna, and the three sisters laughed with a joy that was terrible to hear and was almost death to see. As the men were captured they were carried by the hags into dark mysterious holes and black perplexing labyrinths.

"Here is another one," cried Caevóg as she bundled a trussed champion along.

"This one is fat," said Cuillen, and she rolled a bulky Fenian along like a wheel.

"Here," said Iaran, "is a love of a man. One could eat this kind of man," she murmured, and she licked a lip that had whiskers growing inside as well as out.

And the corded champion whimpered in her arms, for he did not know but eating might indeed be his fate, and he would have preferred to be coffined anywhere in the world rather than to be coffined inside of that face. So far for them.

* * * * *

Within the cave there was silence except for the voices of the hags and the scarcely audible moaning of the Fianna-Finn, but without there was a dreadful uproar, for as each man returned from the chase his dogs came with him, and although the men went into the cave the dogs did not.

They were too wise.

They stood outside, filled with savagery and terror, for they could scent their masters and their masters' danger, and perhaps they could get from the cave smells till then unknown and full of alarm.

From the troop of dogs there arose a baying and barking, a snarling and howling and growling, a yelping and squealing and bawling for which no words can be found. Now and again a dog nosed among a thousand smells and scented his master; the ruff of his neck stood up like a hog's bristles and a netty ridge prickled along his spine. Then with red eyes, with bared fangs, with a hoarse, deep snort and growl he rushed at the cave, and then he halted and sneaked back again with all his ruffles smoothed, his tail between his legs, his eyes screwed sideways in miserable apology and alarm, and a long thin whine of woe dribbling out of his nose.

The three sisters took their wide-channeled, hard-tempered swords in their hands, and prepared to slay the Fianna, but before doing so they gave one more look from the door of the cave to see if there might be a straggler of the Fianna who was escaping death by straggling, and they saw one coming towards them with Bran and Sceólan leaping beside him, while all the other dogs began to burst their throats with barks and split their noses with snorts and wag their tails off at sight of the tall, valiant, white-toothed champion, Goll mor mac Morna. "We will kill that one first," said Caevóg.

"There is only one of him," said Cuillen.

"And each of us three is the match for an hundred," said Iaran.

The uncanny, misbehaved, and outrageous harridans advanced then to meet the son of Morna, and when he saw these three Goll whipped the sword from his thigh, swung his buckler round, and got to them in ten great leaps.

Silence fell on the world during that conflict. The wind went down; the clouds stood still; the old hill itself held its breath; the warriors within ceased to be men and became each an ear; and the dogs sat in a vast circle round the combatants, with their heads all to one side, their noses poked forward, their mouths half open, and their tails forgotten. Now and again a dog whined in a whisper and snapped a little snap on the air, but except for that there was neither sound nor movement.

It was a long fight. It was a hard and a tricky fight, and Goll won it by bravery and strategy and great good luck; for with one shrewd slice of his blade he carved two of these mighty termagants into equal halves, so that there were noses and whiskers to his right hand and knees and toes to his left: and that stroke was known afterwards as one of the three great sword-strokes of Ireland. The third hag, however, had managed to get behind Goll, and she leaped on to his back with the bound of a panther, and hung here with the skilful, many-legged, tight-twisted clutching of a spider. But the great champion gave a twist of his hips and a swing of his shoulders that whirled her around him like a sack. He got her on the ground and tied her hands with the straps of a shield, and he was going to give her the last blow when she appealed to his honor and bravery.

"I put my life under your protection," said she. "And if you let me go free I will lift the enchantment from the Fianna-Finn and will give them all back to you again."

"I agree to that," said Goll, and he untied her straps. The harridan did as she had promised, and in a short time Fionn and Oisín and Oscar and Conán were released, and after that all the Fianna were released.

* * * * *

As each man came out of the cave he gave a jump and a shout; the courage of the world went into him and he felt that he could fight twenty. But while they were talking over the adventure and explaining how it had happened, a vast figure strode over the side of the hill and descended among them. It was Conaran's fourth daughter.

If the other three had been terrible to look on, this one was more terrible than the three together. She was clad in iron plate, and she had a wicked sword by her side and a knobby club in her hand. She halted by the bodies of her sisters, and bitter tears streamed down into her beard.

"Alas, my sweet ones," said she, "I am too late."

And then she stared fiercely at Fionn.

"I demand a combat," she roared.

"It is your right," said Fionn. He turned to his son.

"Oisín, my heart, kill me this honourable hag." But for the only time in his life Oisín shrank from a combat.

"I cannot do it," he said, "I feel too weak."

Fionn was astounded. "Oscar," he said, "will you kill me this great hag?"

Oscar stammered miserably. "I would not be able to," he said.

Conán also refused, and so did Caelte mac Ronán and mac Lugac, for there was no man there but was terrified by the sight of that mighty and valiant harridan.

Fionn rose to his feet. "I will take this combat myself," he said sternly.

And he swung his buckler forward and stretched his right hand to the sword. But at that terrible sight Goll mac Morna blushed deeply and leaped from the ground.

"No, no," he cried; "no, my soul, Fionn, this would not be a proper combat for you. I take this fight."

"You have done your share, Goll," said the captain.

"I should finish the fight I began," Goll continued, "for it was I who killed the two sisters of this valiant hag, and it is against me the feud lies."

"That will do for me," said the horrible daughter of Conaran. "I will kill Goll mor mac Morna first, and after that I will kill Fionn, and after that I will kill every Fenian of the Fianna-Finn."

"You may begin, Goll," said Fionn, "and I give you my blessing."

Goll then strode forward to the fight, and the hag moved against him with equal alacrity. In a moment the heavens rang to the clash of swords on bucklers.

It was hard to withstand the terrific blows of that mighty female, for her sword played with the quickness of lightning and smote like the heavy crashing of a storm. But into that din and encirclement Goll pressed and ventured, steady as a rock in water, agile as a creature of the sea, and when one of the combatants retreated it was the hag that gave backwards. As her foot moved a great shout of joy rose from the Fianna. A snarl went over the huge face of the monster and she leaped forward again, but she met Goll's point in the road; it went through her, and in another moment Goll took her head from its shoulders and swung it on high before Fionn.

As the Fianna turned homewards Fionn spoke to his great champion and enemy.

"Goll," he said, "I have a daughter."

"A lovely girl, a blossom of the dawn," said Goll.

"Would she please you as a wife?" the chief demanded.

"She would please me," said Goll.

"She is your wife," said Fionn.

But that did not prevent Goll from killing Fionn's brother Cairell later on, nor did it prevent Fionn from killing Goll later on again, and the last did not prevent Goll from rescuing Fionn out of hell when the Fianna-Finn were sent there under the new God. Nor is there any reason to complain or to be astonished at these things, for it is a mutual world we live in, a give-and-take world, and there is no great harm in it.

THE STAR-CHILD

BY OSCAR WILDE

Once upon a time two poor Woodcutters were making their way home through a great pine-forest. It was winter, and a night of bitter cold. The snow lay thick upon the ground, and upon the branches of the trees: the frost kept snapping the little twigs on either side of them, as they passed: and when they came to the Mountain-Torrent she was hanging motionless in air, for the Ice-King had kissed her.

So cold was it that even the animals and the birds did not know what to make of it.

'Ugh!' snarled the Wolf, as he limped through the brushwood with his tail between his legs, 'this is perfectly monstrous weather. Why doesn't the Government look to it?'

'Weet! weet! weet!' twittered the green Linnets, 'the old Earth is dead and they have laid her out in her white shroud.'

'The Earth is going to be married, and this is her bridal dress,' whispered the Turtle-doves to each other. Their little pink feet were quite frost-bitten, but they felt that it was their duty to take a romantic view of the situation.

'Nonsense!' growled the Wolf. 'I tell you that it is all the fault of the Government, and if you don't believe me I shall eat you.' The Wolf had a thoroughly practical mind, and was never at a loss for a good argument.

'Well, for my own part,' said the Woodpecker, who was a born philosopher, 'I don't care an atomic theory for explanations. If a thing is so, it is so, and at present it is terribly cold.'

Terribly cold it certainly was. The little Squirrels, who lived inside the tall fir-tree, kept rubbing each other's noses to keep themselves warm, and the

Rabbits curled themselves up in their holes, and did not venture even to look out of doors. The only people who seemed to enjoy it were the great horned Owls. Their feathers were quite stiff with rime, but they did not mind, and they rolled their large yellow eyes, and called out to each other across the forest, 'Tu-whit! Tu-whoo! Tu-whit! Tu-whoo! what delightful weather we are having!'

On and on went the two Woodcutters, blowing lustily upon their fingers, and stamping with their huge iron-shod boots upon the caked snow. Once they sank into a deep drift, and came out as white as millers are, when the stones are grinding; and once they slipped on the hard smooth ice where the marsh-water was frozen, and their faggots fell out of their bundles, and they had to pick them up and bind them together again; and once they thought that they had lost their way, and a great terror seized on them, for they knew that the Snow is cruel to those who sleep in her arms. But they put their trust in the good Saint Martin, who watches over all travellers, and retraced their steps, and went warily, and at last they reached the outskirts of the forest, and saw, far down in the valley beneath them, the lights of the village in which they dwelt.

So overjoyed were they at their deliverance that they laughed aloud, and the Earth seemed to them like a flower of silver, and the Moon like a flower of gold.

Yet, after that they had laughed they became sad, for they remembered their poverty, and one of them said to the other, 'Why did we make merry, seeing that life is for the rich, and not for such as we are? Better that we had died of cold in the forest, or that some wild beast had fallen upon us and slain us.'

'Truly,' answered his companion, 'much is given to some, and little is given to others. Injustice has parcelled out the world, nor is there equal division of aught save of sorrow.'

But as they were bewailing their misery to each other this strange thing happened. There fell from heaven a very bright and beautiful star. It slipped down the side of the sky, passing by the other stars in its course, and, as they watched it wondering, it seemed to them to sink behind a clump of willow-trees that stood hard by a little sheepfold no more than a stone's-throw away.

'Why! there is a crook of gold for whoever finds it,' they cried, and they set to and ran, so eager were they for the gold.

And one of them ran faster than his mate, and outstripped him, and forced his way through the willows, and came out on the other side, and lo! there was indeed a thing of gold lying on the white snow. So he hastened towards it, and stooping down placed his hands upon it, and it was a cloak of golden tissue, curiously wrought with stars, and wrapped in many folds. And he cried out to his comrade that he had found the treasure that had fallen from the sky, and when his comrade had come up, they sat them down in the snow, and loosened the folds of the cloak that they might divide the pieces of gold. But, alas! no gold was in it, nor silver, nor, indeed, treasure of any kind, but only a little child who was asleep.

And one of them said to the other: 'This is a bitter ending to our hope, nor have we any good fortune, for what doth a child profit to a man? Let us leave it here, and go our way, seeing that we are poor men, and have children of our own whose bread we may not give to another.'

But his companion answered him: 'Nay, but it were an evil thing to leave the child to perish here in the snow, and though I am as poor as thou art, and have many mouths to feed, and but little in the pot, yet will I bring it home with me, and my wife shall have care of it.'

So very tenderly he took up the child, and wrapped the cloak around it to shield it from the harsh cold, and made his way down the hill to the village, his comrade marvelling much at his foolishness and softness of heart.

And when they came to the village, his comrade said to him, 'Thou hast the child, therefore give me the cloak, for it is meet that we should share.'

But he answered him: 'Nay, for the cloak is neither mine nor thine, but the child's only,' and he bade him Godspeed, and went to his own house and knocked.

And when his wife opened the door and saw that her husband had returned safe to her, she put her arms round his neck and kissed him, and took from his back the bundle of faggots, and brushed the snow off his boots, and bade him come in.

But he said to her, 'I have found something in the forest, and I have brought it to thee to have care of it,' and he stirred not from the threshold.

'What is it?' she cried. 'Show it to me, for the house is bare, and we have need of many things.' And he drew the cloak back, and showed her the sleeping child.

'Alack, goodman!' she murmured, 'have we not children of our own, that thou must needs bring a changeling to sit by the hearth? And who knows if it will not bring us bad fortune? And how shall we tend it?' And she was wroth against him.

'Nay, but it is a Star-Child,' he answered; and he told her the strange manner of the finding of it.

But she would not be appeased, but mocked at him, and spoke angrily, and cried: 'Our children lack bread, and shall we feed the child of another? Who is there who careth for us? And who giveth us food?'

'Nay, but God careth for the sparrows even, and feedeth them,' he answered.

'Do not the sparrows die of hunger in the winter?' she asked. 'And is it not winter now?'

And the man answered nothing, but stirred not from the threshold.

And a bitter wind from the forest came in through the open door, and made her tremble, and she shivered, and said to him: 'Wilt thou not close the door? There cometh a bitter wind into the house, and I am cold.'

'Into a house where a heart is hard cometh there not always a bitter wind?' he asked. And the woman answered him nothing, but crept closer to the fire.

And after a time she turned round and looked at him, and her eyes were full of tears. And he came in swiftly, and placed the child in her arms, and she kissed it, and laid it in a little bed where the youngest of their own children was lying. And on the morrow the Woodcutter took the curious cloak of gold and placed it in a great chest, and a chain of amber that was round the child's neck his wife took and set it in the chest also.

So the Star-Child was brought up with the children of the Woodcutter, and sat at the same board with them, and was their playmate. And every year he became more beautiful to look at, so that all those who dwelt in the village were filled with wonder, for, while they were swarthy and black-haired, he was white and delicate as sawn ivory, and his curls were like the rings of the daffodil. His lips, also, were like the petals of a red flower, and his eyes were like violets by a river of pure water, and his body like the narcissus of a field where the mower comes not.

Yet did his beauty work him evil. For he grew proud, and cruel, and selfish. The children of the Woodcutter, and the other children of the village, he despised, saying that they were of mean parentage, while he was noble, being sprang from a Star, and he made himself master over them, and called them his servants. No pity had he for the poor, or for those who were blind or maimed or in any way afflicted, but would cast stones at them and drive them forth on to the highway, and bid them beg their bread elsewhere, so that none save the outlaws came twice to that village to ask for alms. Indeed, he was as one enamoured of beauty, and would mock at the weakly and ill-favoured, and make jest of them; and himself he loved, and in summer, when the winds were still, he would lie by the well in the priest's orchard and look down at the marvel of his own face, and laugh for the pleasure he had in his fairness.

Often did the Woodcutter and his wife chide him, and say: 'We did not deal with thee as thou dealest with those who are left desolate, and have none to succour them. Wherefore art thou so cruel to all who need pity?'

Often did the old priest send for him, and seek to teach him the love of living things, saying to him: 'The fly is thy brother. Do it no harm. The wild birds that roam through the forest have their freedom. Snare them not for thy pleasure. God made the blind-worm and the mole, and each has its place. Who art thou to bring pain into God's world? Even the cattle of the field praise Him.'

But the Star-Child heeded not their words, but would frown and flout, and go back to his companions, and lead them. And his companions followed him, for he was fair, and fleet of foot, and could dance, and pipe, and make music. And wherever the Star-Child led them they followed, and whatever the Star-Child bade them do, that did they. And when he pierced with a sharp reed the dim eyes of the mole, they laughed, and when he cast stones at the leper they laughed also. And in all things he ruled them, and they became hard of heart even as he was.

Now there passed one day through the village a poor beggar-woman. Her garments were torn and ragged, and her feet were bleeding from the rough road on which she had travelled, and she was in very evil plight. And being weary she sat her down under a chestnut-tree to rest.

But when the Star-Child saw her, he said to his companions, 'See! There sitteth a foul beggar-woman under that fair and green-leaved tree. Come, let us drive her hence, for she is ugly and ill-favoured.'

So he came near and threw stones at her, and mocked her, and she looked at him with terror in her eyes, nor did she move her gaze from him. And when the Woodcutter, who was cleaving logs in a haggard hard by, saw what the Star-Child was doing, he ran up and rebuked him, and said to him: 'Surely thou art hard of heart and knowest not mercy, for what evil has this poor woman done to thee that thou shouldst treat her in this wise?'

And the Star-Child grew red with anger, and stamped his foot upon the ground, and said, 'Who art thou to question me what I do? I am no son of thine to do thy bidding.'

'Thou speakest truly,' answered the Woodcutter, 'yet did I show thee pity when I found thee in the forest.'

And when the woman heard these words she gave a loud cry, and fell into a swoon. And the Woodcutter carried her to his own house, and his wife had care of her, and when she rose up from the swoon into which she had fallen, they set meat and drink before her, and bade her have comfort.

But she would neither eat nor drink, but said to the Woodcutter, 'Didst thou not say that the child was found in the forest? And was it not ten years from this day?'

And the Woodcutter answered, 'Yea, it was in the forest that I found him, and it is ten years from this day.'

'And what signs didst thou find with him?' she cried. 'Bare he not upon his neck a chain of amber? Was not round him a cloak of gold tissue broidered with stars?'

'Truly,' answered the Woodcutter, 'it was even as thou sayest.' And he took the cloak and the amber chain from the chest where they lay, and showed them to her.

And when she saw them she wept for joy, and said, 'He is my little son whom I lost in the forest. I pray thee send for him quickly, for in search of him have I wandered over the whole world.'

So the Woodcutter and his wife went out and called to the Star-Child, and said to him, 'Go into the house, and there shalt thou find thy mother, who is waiting for thee.'

So he ran in, filled with wonder and great gladness. But when he saw her who was waiting there, he laughed scornfully and said, 'Why, where is my mother? For I see none here but this vile beggar-woman.'

And the woman answered him, 'I am thy mother.'

'Thou art mad to say so,' cried the Star-Child angrily. 'I am no son of thine, for thou art a beggar, and ugly, and in rags. Therefore get thee hence, and let me see thy foul face no more.'

'Nay, but thou art indeed my little son, whom I bare in the forest,' she cried, and she fell on her knees, and held out her arms to him. 'The robbers stole thee from me, and left thee to die,' she murmured, 'but I recognised thee when I saw thee, and the signs also have I recognised, the cloak of golden tissue and the amber chain. Therefore I pray thee come with me, for over the whole world have I wandered in search of thee. Come with me, my son, for I have need of thy love.'

But the Star-Child stirred not from his place, but shut the doors of his heart against her, nor was there any sound heard save the sound of the woman weeping for pain.

And at last he spoke to her, and his voice was hard and bitter. 'If in very truth thou art my mother,' he said, 'it had been better hadst thou stayed away, and not come here to bring me to shame, seeing that I thought I was the child of some Star, and not a beggar's child, as thou tellest me that I am. Therefore get thee hence, and let me see thee no more.'

'Alas! my son,' she cried, 'wilt thou not kiss me before I go? For I have suffered much to find thee.'

'Nay,' said the Star-Child, 'but thou art too foul to look at, and rather would I kiss the adder or the toad than thee.'

So the woman rose up, and went away into the forest weeping bitterly, and when the Star-Child saw that she had gone, he was glad, and ran back to his playmates that he might play with them.

But when they beheld him coming, they mocked him and said, 'Why, thou art as foul as the toad, and as loathsome as the adder. Get thee hence, for we will not suffer thee to play with us,' and they drave him out of the garden.

And the Star-Child frowned and said to himself, 'What is this that they say to me? I will go to the well of water and look into it, and it shall tell me of my beauty.'

So he went to the well of water and looked into it, and lo! his face was as the face of a toad, and his body was sealed like an adder. And he flung himself down on the grass and wept, and said to himself, 'Surely this has come upon me by reason of my sin. For I have denied my mother, and driven her away, and been proud, and cruel to her. Wherefore I will go and seek her through the whole world, nor will I rest till I have found her.'

And there came to him the little daughter of the Woodcutter, and she put her hand upon his shoulder and said, 'What doth it matter if thou hast lost thy comeliness? Stay with us, and I will not mock at thee.'

And he said to her, 'Nay, but I have been cruel to my mother, and as a punishment has this evil been sent to me. Wherefore I must go hence, and wander through the world till I find her, and she give me her forgiveness.'

So he ran away into the forest and called out to his mother to come to him, but there was no answer. All day long he called to her, and, when the sun set he lay down to sleep on a bed of leaves, and the birds and the animals fled from him, for they remembered his cruelty, and he was alone save for the toad that watched him, and the slow adder that crawled past.

And in the morning he rose up, and plucked some bitter berries from the trees and ate them, and took his way through the great wood, weeping sorely. And of everything that he met he made inquiry if perchance they had seen his mother.

He said to the Mole, 'Thou canst go beneath the earth. Tell me, is my mother there?'

And the Mole answered, 'Thou hast blinded mine eyes. How should I know?'

He said to the Linnet, 'Thou canst fly over the tops of the tall trees, and canst see the whole world. Tell me, canst thou see my mother?'

And the Linnet answered, 'Thou hast clipt my wings for thy pleasure. How should I fly?'

And to the little Squirrel who lived in the fir-tree, and was lonely, he said, 'Where is my mother?'

And the Squirrel answered, 'Thou hast slain mine. Dost thou seek to slay thine also?'

And the Star-Child wept and bowed his head, and prayed forgiveness of God's things, and went on through the forest, seeking for the beggar-woman. And on the third day he came to the other side of the forest and went down into the plain.

And when he passed through the villages the children mocked him, and threw stones at him, and the carlots would not suffer him even to sleep in the byres lest he might bring mildew on the stored corn, so foul was he to look at, and their hired men drave him away, and there was none who had pity on him. Nor could he hear anywhere of the beggar-woman who was his mother, though for the space of three years he wandered over the world, and often seemed to see her on the road in front of him, and would call to her, and run after her till the sharp flints made his feet to bleed. But overtake her he could not, and those who dwelt by the way did ever deny that they had seen her, or any like to her, and they made sport of his sorrow.

For the space of three years he wandered over the world, and in the world there was neither love nor loving-kindness nor charity for him, but it was even such a world as he had made for himself in the days of his great pride.

And one evening he came to the gate of a strong-walled city that stood by a river, and, weary and footsore though he was, he made to enter in. But the soldiers who stood on guard dropped their halberts across the entrance, and said roughly to him, 'What is thy business in the city?'

'I am seeking for my mother,' he answered, 'and I pray ye to suffer me to pass, for it may be that she is in this city.'

But they mocked at him, and one of them wagged a black beard, and set down his shield and cried, 'Of a truth, thy mother will not be merry when she sees thee, for thou art more ill-favoured than the toad of the marsh, or the adder that crawls in the fen. Get thee gone. Get thee gone. Thy mother dwells not in this city.'

And another, who held a yellow banner in his hand, said to him, 'Who is thy mother, and wherefore art thou seeking for her?'

And he answered, 'My mother is a beggar even as I am, and I have treated her evilly, and I pray ye to suffer me to pass that she may give me her forgiveness, if it be that she tarrieth in this city.' But they would not, and pricked him with their spears.

And, as he turned away weeping, one whose armour was inlaid with gilt flowers, and on whose helmet couched a lion that had wings, came up and made inquiry of the soldiers who it was who had sought entrance. And they said to him, 'It is a beggar and the child of a beggar, and we have driven him away.'

'Nay,' he cried, laughing, 'but we will sell the foul thing for a slave, and his price shall be the price of a bowl of sweet wine.'

And an old and evil-visaged man who was passing by called out, and said, 'I will buy him for that price,' and, when he had paid the price, he took the Star-Child by the hand and led him into the city.

And after that they had gone through many streets they came to a little door that was set in a wall that was covered with a pomegranate tree. And the old man touched the door with a ring of graved jasper and it opened, and they went down five steps of brass into a garden filled with black poppies and green jars of burnt clay. And the old man took then from his turban a scarf of figured silk, and bound with it the eyes of the Star-Child, and drave him in front of him. And when the scarf was taken off his eyes, the Star-Child found himself in a dungeon, that was lit by a lantern of horn.

And the old man set before him some mouldy bread on a trencher and said, 'Eat,' and some brackish water in a cup and said, 'Drink,' and when he had eaten and drunk, the old man went out, locking the door behind him and fastening it with an iron chain.

And on the morrow the old man, who was indeed the subtlest of the magicians of Libya and had learned his art from one who dwelt in the tombs of the Nile, came in to him and frowned at him, and said, 'In a wood that is nigh to the gate of this city of Giaours there are three pieces of gold. One is of white gold, and another is of yellow gold, and the gold of the third one is red. To-day thou shalt bring me the piece of white gold, and if thou bringest it not back, I will beat thee with a hundred stripes. Get thee away quickly, and at sunset I will be waiting for thee at the door of the garden. See that thou bringest the white gold, or it shall go ill with thee, for thou art my slave, and I have bought thee for the price of a bowl of sweet wine.' And he bound the eyes of the Star-Child with the scarf of figured silk, and led him through the house, and through the garden of poppies, and up the five steps of brass. And having opened the little door with his ring he set him in the street.

And the Star-Child went out of the gate of the city, and came to the wood of which the Magician had spoken to him.

Now this wood was very fair to look at from without, and seemed full of singing birds and of sweet-scented flowers, and the Star-Child entered it gladly. Yet did its beauty profit him little, for wherever he went harsh briars and thorns shot up from the ground and encompassed him, and evil nettles stung him, and the thistle pierced him with her daggers, so that he was in sore distress. Nor could he anywhere find the piece of white gold of which the Magician had spoken, though he sought for it from morn to noon, and from noon to sunset. And at sunset he set his face towards home, weeping bitterly, for he knew what fate was in store for him.

But when he had reached the outskirts of the wood, he heard from a thicket a cry as of some one in pain. And forgetting his own sorrow he ran back to the place, and saw there a little Hare caught in a trap that some hunter had set for it.

And the Star-Child had pity on it, and released it, and said to it, 'I am myself but a slave, yet may I give thee thy freedom.'

And the Hare answered him, and said: 'Surely thou hast given me freedom, and what shall I give thee in return?'

And the Star-Child said to it, 'I am seeking for a piece of white gold, nor can I anywhere find it, and if I bring it not to my master he will beat me.'

'Come thou with me,' said the Hare, 'and I will lead thee to it, for I know where it is hidden, and for what purpose.'

So the Star-Child went with the Hare, and lo! in the cleft of a great oak-tree he saw the piece of white gold that he was seeking. And he was filled with joy, and seized it, and said to the Hare, 'The service that I did to thee thou hast rendered back again many times over, and the kindness that I showed thee thou hast repaid a hundred-fold.'

'Nay,' answered the Hare, 'but as thou dealt with me, so I did deal with thee,' and it ran away swiftly, and the Star-Child went towards the city.

Now at the gate of the city there was seated one who was a leper. Over his face hung a cowl of grey linen, and through the eyelets his eyes gleamed like red coals. And when he saw the Star-Child coming, he struck upon a wooden bowl, and clattered his bell, and called out to him, and said, 'Give me a piece of money, or I must die of hunger. For they have thrust me out of the city, and there is no one who has pity on me.'

'Alas!' cried the Star-Child, 'I have but one piece of money in my wallet, and if I bring it not to my master he will beat me, for I am his slave.'

But the leper entreated him, and prayed of him, till the Star-Child had pity, and gave him the piece of white gold.

And when he came to the Magician's house, the Magician opened to him, and brought him in, and said to him, 'Hast thou the piece of white gold?' And the Star-Child answered, 'I have it not.' So the Magician fell upon him, and beat him, and set before him an empty trencher, and said, 'Eat,' and an empty cup, and said, 'Drink,' and flung him again into the dungeon.

And on the morrow the Magician came to him, and said, 'If to-day thou bringest me not the piece of yellow gold, I will surely keep thee as my slave, and give thee three hundred stripes.'

So the Star-Child went to the wood, and all day long he searched for the piece of yellow gold, but nowhere could he find it. And at sunset he sat him down and began to weep, and as he was weeping there came to him the little Hare that he had rescued from the trap,

And the Hare said to him, 'Why art thou weeping? And what dost thou seek in the wood?'

And the Star-Child answered, 'I am seeking for a piece of yellow gold that is hidden here, and if I find it not my master will beat me, and keep me as a slave.'

'Follow me,' cried the Hare, and it ran through the wood till it came to a pool of water. And at the bottom of the pool the piece of yellow gold was lying.

'How shall I thank thee?' said the Star-Child, 'for lo! this is the second time that you have succoured me.'

'Nay, but thou hadst pity on me first,' said the Hare, and it ran away swiftly.

And the Star-Child took the piece of yellow gold, and put it in his wallet, and hurried to the city. But the leper saw him coming, and ran to meet him, and knelt down and cried, 'Give me a piece of money or I shall die of hunger.'

And the Star-Child said to him, 'I have in my wallet but one piece of yellow gold, and if I bring it not to my master he will beat me and keep me as his slave.'

But the leper entreated him sore, so that the Star-Child had pity on him, and gave him the piece of yellow gold.

And when he came to the Magician's house, the Magician opened to him, and brought him in, and said to him, 'Hast thou the piece of yellow gold?' And the Star-Child said to him, 'I have it not.' So the Magician fell upon him, and beat him, and loaded him with chains, and cast him again into the dungeon.

And on the morrow the Magician came to him, and said, 'If to-day thou bringest me the piece of red gold I will set thee free, but if thou bringest it not I will surely slay thee.'

So the Star-Child went to the wood, and all day long he searched for the piece of red gold, but nowhere could he find it. And at evening he sat him down and wept, and as he was weeping there came to him the little Hare.

And the Hare said to him, 'The piece of red gold that thou seekest is in the cavern that is behind thee. Therefore weep no more but be glad.'

'How shall I reward thee?' cried the Star-Child, 'for lo! this is the third time thou hast succoured me.'

'Nay, but thou hadst pity on me first,' said the Hare, and it ran away swiftly.

And the Star-Child entered the cavern, and in its farthest corner he found the piece of red gold. So he put it in his wallet, and hurried to the city. And the leper seeing him coming, stood in the centre of the road, and cried out, and said to him, 'Give me the piece of red money, or I must die,' and the Star-Child had pity on him again, and gave him the piece of red gold, saying, 'Thy need is greater than mine.' Yet was his heart heavy, for he knew what evil fate awaited him.

But lo! as he passed through the gate of the city, the guards bowed down and made obeisance to him, saying, 'How beautiful is our lord!' and a crowd of citizens followed him, and cried out, 'Surely there is none so beautiful in the whole world!' so that the Star-Child wept, and said to himself, 'They are mocking me, and making light of my misery.' And so large was the concourse of the people, that he lost the threads of his way, and found himself at last in a great square, in which there was a palace of a King.

And the gate of the palace opened, and the priests and the high officers of the city ran forth to meet him, and they abased themselves before him, and said, 'Thou art our lord for whom we have been waiting, and the son of our King.'

And the Star-Child answered them and said, 'I am no king's son, but the child of a poor beggar-woman. And how say ye that I am beautiful, for I know that I am evil to look at?'

Then he, whose armour was inlaid with gilt flowers, and on whose helmet crouched a lion that had wings, held up a shield, and cried, 'How saith my lord that he is not beautiful?'

And the Star-Child looked, and lo! his face was even as it had been, and his comeliness had come back to him, and he saw that in his eyes which he had not seen there before.

And the priests and the high officers knelt down and said to him, 'It was prophesied of old that on this day should come he who was to rule over us. Therefore, let our lord take this crown and this sceptre, and be in his justice and mercy our King over us.'

But he said to them, 'I am not worthy, for I have denied the mother who bare me, nor may I rest till I have found her, and known her forgiveness. Therefore, let me go, for I must wander again over the world, and may not tarry here, though ye bring me the crown and the sceptre.' And as he spake he turned his face from them towards the street that led to the gate of the city, and lo! amongst the crowd that pressed round the soldiers, he saw the beggar-woman who was his mother, and at her side stood the leper, who had sat by the road.

And a cry of joy broke from his lips, and he ran over, and kneeling down he kissed the wounds on his mother's feet, and wet them with his tears. He bowed his head in the dust, and sobbing, as one whose heart might break, he said to her: 'Mother, I denied thee in the hour of my pride. Accept me in the hour of my humility. Mother, I gave thee hatred. Do thou give me love. Mother, I rejected thee. Receive thy child now.' But the beggar-woman answered him not a word.

And he reached out his hands, and clasped the white feet of the leper, and said to him: 'Thrice did I give thee of my mercy. Bid my mother speak to me once.' But the leper answered him not a word.

And he sobbed again and said: 'Mother, my suffering is greater than I can bear. Give me thy forgiveness, and let me go back to the forest.' And the beggar-woman put her hand on his head, and said to him, 'Rise,' and the leper put his hand on his head, and said to him, 'Rise,' also.

And he rose up from his feet, and looked at them, and lo! they were a King and a Queen.

And the Queen said to him, 'This is thy father whom thou hast succoured.'

And the King said, 'This is thy mother whose feet thou hast washed with thy tears.' And they fell on his neck and kissed him, and brought him into the palace and clothed him in fair raiment, and set the crown upon his head, and the sceptre in his hand, and over the city that stood by the river he ruled, and was its lord. Much justice and mercy did he show to all, and the evil Magician he banished, and to the Woodcutter and his wife he sent many rich gifts, and to their children he gave high honour. Nor would he suffer any to be cruel to bird or beast, but taught love and loving-kindness and charity, and to the poor he gave bread, and to the naked he gave raiment, and there was peace and plenty in the land.

Yet ruled he not long, so great had been his suffering, and so bitter the fire of his testing, for after the space of three years he died. And he who came after him ruled evilly.

AN ENCOUNTER

BY JAMES JOYCE

It was Joe Dillon who introduced the Wild West to us. He had a little library made up of old numbers of The Union Jack, Pluck and The Halfpenny Marvel. Every evening after school we met in his back garden and arranged Indian battles. He and his fat young brother Leo, the idler, held the loft of the stable while we tried to carry it by storm; or we fought a pitched battle on the grass. But, however well we fought, we never won siege or battle and all our bouts ended with Joe Dillon's war dance of victory. His parents went to eight-o'clock mass every morning in Gardiner Street and the peaceful odour of Mrs. Dillon was prevalent in the hall of the house. But he played too fiercely for us who were younger and more timid. He looked like some kind of an Indian when he capered round the garden, an old tea-cosy on his head, beating a tin with his fist and yelling:

"Ya! yaka, yaka, yaka!"

Everyone was incredulous when it was reported that he had a vocation for the priesthood. Nevertheless it was true.

A spirit of unruliness diffused itself among us and, under its influence, differences of culture and constitution were waived. We banded ourselves together, some boldly, some in jest and some almost in fear: and of the number of these latter, the reluctant Indians who were afraid to seem studious or lacking in robustness, I was one. The adventures related in the literature of the Wild West were remote from my nature but, at least, they opened doors of escape. I liked better some American detective stories which were traversed from time to time by unkempt fierce and beautiful girls. Though there was nothing wrong in these stories and though their intention was sometimes literary they were circulated secretly at school. One day when Father Butler was hearing the four pages of Roman History clumsy Leo Dillon was discovered with a copy of The Halfpenny Marvel.

"This page or this page? This page Now, Dillon, up! 'Hardly had the day'... Go on! What day? 'Hardly had the day dawned'... Have you studied it? What have you there in your pocket?"

Everyone's heart palpitated as Leo Dillon handed up the paper and everyone assumed an innocent face. Father Butler turned over the pages, frowning.

"What is this rubbish?" he said. "The Apache Chief! Is this what you read instead of studying your Roman History? Let me not find any more of this wretched stuff in this college. The man who wrote it, I suppose, was some wretched fellow who writes these things for a drink. I'm surprised at boys like you, educated, reading such stuff. I could understand it if you were... National School boys. Now, Dillon, I advise you strongly, get at your work or..."

This rebuke during the sober hours of school paled much of the glory of the Wild West for me and the confused puffy face of Leo Dillon awakened one of my consciences. But when the restraining influence of the school was at a distance I began to hunger again for wild sensations, for the escape which those chronicles of disorder alone seemed to offer me. The mimic warfare of the evening became at last as wearisome to me as the routine of school in the morning because I wanted real adventures to happen to myself. But real adventures, I reflected, do not happen to people who remain at home: they must be sought abroad.

The summer holidays were near at hand when I made up my mind to break out of the weariness of school-life for one day at least. With Leo Dillon and a boy named Mahony I planned a day's miching. Each of us saved up sixpence. We were to meet at ten in the morning on the Canal Bridge. Mahony's big sister was to write an excuse for him and Leo Dillon was to tell his brother to say he was sick. We arranged to go along the Wharf Road until we came to the ships, then to cross in the ferryboat and walk out to see the Pigeon House. Leo Dillon was afraid we might meet Father Butler or someone out of the college; but Mahony asked, very sensibly, what would Father Butler be doing out at the Pigeon House. We were reassured: and I brought the first stage of the plot to an end by collecting sixpence from the other two, at the same time showing them my own sixpence. When we were making the last arrangements on the eve we were all vaguely excited. We shook hands, laughing, and Mahony said:

"Till tomorrow, mates!"

That night I slept badly. In the morning I was first-comer to the bridge as I lived nearest. I hid my books in the long grass near the ashpit at the end of the garden where nobody ever came and hurried along the canal bank. It was a mild sunny morning in the first week of June. I sat up on the coping of the bridge admiring my frail canvas shoes which I had diligently pipeclayed overnight and watching the docile horses pulling a tramload of business people up the hill. All the branches of the tall trees which lined the mall were gay with little light green leaves and the sunlight slanted through them on to the water. The granite stone of the bridge was beginning to be warm and I began to pat it with my hands in time to an air in my head. I was very happy.

When I had been sitting there for five or ten minutes I saw Mahony's grey suit approaching. He came up the hill, smiling, and clambered up beside me on the bridge. While we were waiting he brought out the catapult which bulged from his inner pocket and explained some improvements which he had made in it. I asked him why he had brought it and he told me he had brought it to have some gas with the birds. Mahony used slang freely, and spoke of Father Butler as Old Bunser. We waited on for a quarter of an hour more but still there was no sign of Leo Dillon. Mahony, at last, jumped down and said:

"Come along. I knew Fatty'd funk it."

"And his sixpence...?" I said.

"That's forfeit," said Mahony. "And so much the better for us—a bob and a tanner instead of a bob."

We walked along the North Strand Road till we came to the Vitriol Works and then turned to the right along the Wharf Road. Mahony began to play the Indian as soon as we were out of public sight. He chased a crowd of ragged girls, brandishing his unloaded catapult and, when two ragged boys began, out of chivalry, to fling stones at us, he proposed that we should charge them. I objected that the boys were too small and so we walked on, the ragged troop screaming after us: "Swaddlers! Swaddlers!" thinking that we were Protestants because Mahony, who was dark-complexioned, wore the silver badge of a cricket club in his cap. When we came to the Smoothing Iron we arranged a siege; but it was a failure because you must have at least three. We revenged ourselves on Leo Dillon by saying what a funk he was and guessing how many he would get at three o'clock from Mr. Ryan.

We came then near the river. We spent a long time walking about the noisy streets flanked by high stone walls, watching the working of cranes and engines and often being shouted at for our immobility by the drivers of groaning carts. It was noon when we reached the quays and, as all the labourers seemed to be eating their lunches, we bought two big currant buns and sat down to eat them on some metal piping beside the river. We pleased ourselves with the spectacle of Dublin's commerce—the barges signalled from far away by their curls of woolly smoke, the brown fishing fleet beyond Ringsend, the big white sailing-vessel which was being discharged on the opposite quay. Mahony said it would be right skit to run away to sea on one of those big ships and even I, looking at the high masts, saw, or imagined, the geography which had been scantily dosed to me at school gradually taking substance under my eyes. School and home seemed to recede from us and their influences upon us seemed to wane.

We crossed the Liffey in the ferryboat, paying our toll to be transported in the company of two labourers and a little Jew with a bag. We were serious to the point of solemnity, but once during the short voyage our eyes met and we laughed. When we landed we watched the discharging of the graceful three-master which we had observed from the other quay. Some bystander said that she was a Norwegian vessel. I went to the stern and tried to decipher the legend upon it but, failing to do so, I came back and examined the foreign sailors to see had any of them green eyes for I had some confused notion.... The sailors' eyes were blue and grey and even black. The only sailor whose eyes could have been called green was a tall man who amused the crowd on the quay by calling out cheerfully every time the planks fell:

"All right! All right!"

When we were tired of this sight we wandered slowly into Ringsend. The day had grown sultry, and in the windows of the grocers' shops musty biscuits lay bleaching. We bought some biscuits and chocolate which we ate sedulously as we wandered through the squalid streets where the families of the fishermen live. We could find no dairy and so we went into a huckster's shop and bought a bottle of raspberry lemonade each. Refreshed by this, Mahony chased a cat down a lane, but the cat escaped into a wide field. We both felt rather tired and when we reached the field we made at once for a sloping bank over the ridge of which we could see the Dodder.

It was too late and we were too tired to carry out our project of visiting the Pigeon House. We had to be home before four o'clock lest our adventure should be discovered. Mahony looked regretfully at his catapult and I had to suggest going home by train before he regained any cheerfulness. The sun went in behind some clouds and left us to our jaded thoughts and the crumbs of our provisions.

There was nobody but ourselves in the field. When we had lain on the bank for some time without speaking I saw a man approaching from the far end of the field. I watched him lazily as I chewed one of those green stems on which girls tell fortunes. He came along by the bank slowly. He walked with one hand upon his hip and in the other hand he held a stick with which he tapped the turf lightly. He was shabbily dressed in a suit of greenish-black and wore what we used to call a jerry hat with a high crown. He seemed to be fairly old for his moustache was ashen-grey. When he passed at our feet he glanced up at us quickly and then continued his way. We followed him with our eyes and saw that when he had gone on for perhaps fifty paces he turned about and began to retrace his steps. He walked towards us very slowly, always tapping the ground with his stick, so slowly that I thought he was looking for something in the grass.

He stopped when he came level with us and bade us good-day. We answered him and he sat down beside us on the slope slowly and with great care. He began to talk of the weather, saying that it would be a very hot summer and adding that the seasons had changed greatly since he was a boy—a long time ago. He said that the happiest time of one's life was undoubtedly one's school-boy days and that he would give anything to be young again. While he expressed these sentiments which bored us a little we kept silent. Then he began to talk of school and of books. He asked us whether we had read the poetry of Thomas Moore or the works of Sir Walter Scott and Lord Lytton. I pretended that I had read every book he mentioned so that in the end he said:

"Ah, I can see you are a bookworm like myself. Now," he added, pointing to Mahony who was regarding us with open eyes, "he is different; he goes in for games."

He said he had all Sir Walter Scott's works and all Lord Lytton's works at home and never tired of reading them. "Of course," he said, "there were some of Lord Lytton's works which boys couldn't read." Mahony asked why couldn't boys read them—a question which agitated and pained me because I was afraid the man would think I was as stupid as Mahony. The man, however, only smiled. I saw that he had great gaps in his mouth between his yellow teeth. Then he asked us which of us had the most sweethearts. Mahony mentioned lightly that he had three totties. The man asked me how many had I. I answered that I had none. He did not believe me and said he was sure I must have one. I was silent.

"Tell us," said Mahony pertly to the man, "how many have you yourself?"

The man smiled as before and said that when he was our age he had lots of sweethearts.

"Every boy," he said, "has a little sweetheart."

His attitude on this point struck me as strangely liberal in a man of his age. In my heart I thought that what he said about boys and sweethearts was reasonable. But I disliked the words in his mouth and I wondered why he shivered once or twice as if he feared something or felt a sudden chill. As he proceeded I noticed that his accent was good. He began to speak to us about girls, saying what nice soft hair they had and how soft their hands were and how all girls were not so good as they seemed to be if one only knew. There was nothing he liked, he said, so much as looking at a nice young girl, at her nice white hands and her beautiful soft hair. He gave me the impression that he was repeating something which he had learned by heart or that, magnetised by some words of his own speech, his mind was slowly circling round and round in the same orbit. At times he spoke as if he were simply alluding to some fact that everybody knew, and at times he lowered his voice and spoke mysteriously as if he were telling us something secret which he did not wish others to overhear. He repeated his phrases over and over again, varying them and surrounding them with his monotonous voice. I continued to gaze towards the foot of the slope, listening to him.

After a long while his monologue paused. He stood up slowly, saying that he had to leave us for a minute or so, a few minutes, and, without changing the direction of my gaze, I saw him walking slowly away from us towards the near end of the field. We remained silent when he had gone. After a silence of a few minutes I heard Mahony exclaim:

"I say! Look what he's doing!"

As I neither answered nor raised my eyes Mahony exclaimed again:

"I say... He's a queer old josser!"

"In case he asks us for our names," I said, "let you be Murphy and I'll be Smith."

We said nothing further to each other. I was still considering whether I would go away or not when the man came back and sat down beside us again. Hardly had he sat down when Mahony, catching sight of the cat which had escaped him, sprang up and pursued her across the field. The man and I watched the chase. The cat escaped once more and Mahony began to throw stones at the wall she had escaladed. Desisting from this, he began to wander about the far end of the field, aimlessly.

After an interval the man spoke to me. He said that my friend was a very rough boy and asked did he get whipped often at school. I was going to reply indignantly that we were not National School boys to be whipped, as he called it; but I remained silent. He began to speak on the subject of chastising boys. His mind, as if magnetised again by his speech, seemed to circle slowly round and round its new centre. He said that when boys were that kind they ought to be whipped and well whipped. When a boy was rough and unruly there was nothing would do him any good but a good sound whipping. A slap on the hand or a box on the ear was no good: what he wanted was to get a nice warm whipping. I was surprised at this sentiment and involuntarily glanced up at his face. As I did so I met the gaze of a pair of bottle-green eyes peering at me from under a twitching forehead. I turned my eyes away again.

The man continued his monologue. He seemed to have forgotten his recent liberalism. He said that if ever he found a boy talking to girls or having a girl for a sweetheart he would whip him and whip him; and that would teach him not to be talking to girls. And if a boy had a girl for a sweetheart and told lies about it then he would give him such a whipping as no boy ever got in this world. He said that there was nothing in this world he would like so well as that. He described to me how he would whip such a boy as if he were unfolding some elaborate mystery. He would love that, he said, better than anything in this world; and his voice, as he led me monotonously through the mystery, grew almost affectionate and seemed to plead with me that I should understand him.

I waited till his monologue paused again. Then I stood up abruptly. Lest I should betray my agitation I delayed a few moments pretending to fix my shoe properly and then, saying that I was obliged to go, I bade him good-day. I went up the slope calmly but my heart was beating quickly with fear that he would seize me by the ankles. When I reached the top of the slope I turned round and, without looking at him, called loudly across the field:

"Murphy!"

My voice had an accent of forced bravery in it and I was ashamed of my paltry stratagem. I had to call the name again before Mahony saw me and hallooed in answer. How my heart beat as he came running across the field to me! He ran as if to bring me aid. And I was penitent; for in my heart I had always despised him a little.

DIRECTIONS TO SERVANTS

BY JONATHAN SWIFT

When your Master or Lady call a Servant by Name, if that Servant be not in the Way, none of you are to answer, for then there will be no End of your Drudgery: And Masters themselves allow, that if a Servant comes when he is called, it is sufficient.

When you have done a Fault, be always pert and insolent, and behave your self as if you were the injured Person; this will immediately put your Master or Lady off their Mettle.

If you see your Master wronged by any of your Fellow-servants, be sure to conceal it, for fear of being called a Tell-tale: However, there is one Exception, in case of a favourite Servant, who is justly hated by the whole Family; you are therefore bound in Prudence to lay all the Faults you can upon the Favourite.

The Cook, the Butler, the Groom, the Market-man, and every other Servant who is concerned in the Expenses of the Family, should act as if his Master's whole Estate ought to be applied to that Servant's particular Business. For Instance, if the Cook computes his Master's Estate to be a thousand Pounds a Year, he reasonably concludes that a thousand Pounds a Year will afford Meat enough, and therefore, he need not be sparing; the Butler makes the same Judgment, so may the Groom and the Coachman, and thus every Branch of Expense will be filled to your Master's Honour.

When you are chid before Company, (which with Submission to our Masters and Ladies is an unmannerly Practice) it often happens that some Stranger will have the Good-nature to drop a Word in your Excuse; in such a Case, you will have a good Title to justify yourself, and may rightly conclude, that whenever he chides you afterwards on other Occasions, he may be in the wrong; in which Opinion you will be the more confirmed by stating the Case to your Fellow-servants in your own Way, who will certainly decide in your Favour: Therefore, as I have said before, whenever you are chidden, complain as if you were injured.

It often happens that Servants sent on Messages, are apt to stay out somewhat longer than the Message requires, perhaps, two, four, six, or eight Hours, or some such Trifle, for the Temptation to be sure was great, and Flesh and Blood cannot always resist: When you return, the Master storms, the Lady scolds; stripping, cudgelling, and turning off, is the Word: But here you ought to be provided with a Set of Excuses, enough to serve on all Occasions: For Instance, your Uncle came fourscore Miles to Town this Morning, on purpose to see you, and goes back by Break of Day To-morrow: A Brother-Servant that borrowed Money of you when he was out of Place, was running away to *Ireland*: You were taking Leave of an old Fellow-Servant, who was shipping for *Barbados*: Your Father sent a Cow to you to sell, and you could not find a Chapman till Nine at Night: You were taking Leave of a dear Cousin who is to be hanged next *Saturday*: You wrenched your Foot against a Stone, and were forced to stay three Hours in a Shop, before you could stir a Step: Some Nastiness was thrown on you out of a Garret Window, and you were ashamed to come Home before you were cleaned, and the Smell went off: You were pressed for the Sea-service, and carried before a Justice of Peace, who kept you three Hours before he examined you, and you got off with much a-do: A Bailiff by mistake seized you for a Debtor, and kept you the whole Evening in a Spunging-house: You were told your Master had gone to a Tavern, and came to some Mischance, and your grief was so great that you inquired for his Honour in a hundred Taverns between *Pall-mall* and *Temple-bar*.

Take all Tradesmen's Parts against your Master, and when you are sent to buy any Thing, never offer to cheapen it, but generously pay the full Demand. This is highly to your Master's Honour; and may be some Shillings in your Pocket; and you are to consider, if your Master hath paid too much, he can better afford the Loss than a poor Tradesman.

Never submit to stir a Finger in any Business but that for which you were particularly hired. For Example, if the Groom be drunk or absent, and the Butler be ordered to shut the Stable Door, the Answer is ready, An please your Honour, I don't understand Horses: If a Corner of the Hanging wants a single Nail to fasten it, and the Footman be directed to tack it up, he may say, he doth not understand that Sort of Work, but his Honour may send for the Upholsterer.

Masters and Ladies are usually quarrelling with the Servants for not shutting the Doors after them: But neither Masters nor Ladies consider that those Doors must be open before they can be shut, and that the Labour is double to open and shut the Doors; therefore the best and shortest, and easiest Way is to do neither. But if you are so often teased to shut the Door, that you cannot easily forget it, then give the Door such a Clap as you go out, as will shake the whole Room, and make every Thing rattle in it, to put your Master and Lady in Mind that you observe their Directions.

If you find yourself to grow into Favour with your Master or Lady, take some Opportunity, in a very mild Way, to give them Warning, and when they ask the Reason, and seem loth to part with you, answer that you would rather live with them, than any Body else, but a poor Servant is not to be blamed if he strives to better himself; that Service is no Inheritance, that your Work is great, and your Wages very small: Upon which, if your Master hath any Generosity, he will add five or ten Shillings a Quarter rather than let you go: But, if you are baulked, and have no Mind to go off, get some Fellow-servant to tell your Master, that he had prevailed upon you to stay.

Whatever good Bits you can pilfer in the Day, save them to junket with your Fellow-servants at Night, and take in the Butler, provided he will give you Drink.

Write your own Name and your Sweet-heart's with the Smoke of a Candle on the Roof of the Kitchen, or the Servants Hall, to show your Learning.

If you are a young sightly Fellow, whenever you whisper your Mistress at the Table, run your Nose full in her Cheek, or if your Breath be good, breathe full in her Face; this I have known to have had very good Consequences in some Families.

Never come till you have been called three or four Times; for none but Dogs will come at the first Whistle: And when the Master calls (*Who's there?*) no Servant is bound to come; for (*Who's there*) is no Body's Name.

When you have broken all your earthen Drinking Vessels below Stairs (which is usually done in a Week) the Copper Pot will do as well; it can boil Milk, heat Porridge, hold Small-Beer, or in Case of Necessity serve for a Jordan; therefore apply it indifferently to all these Uses; but never wash or scour it, for Fear of taking off the Tin.

Although you are allowed Knives for the Servants Hall, at Meals, yet you ought to spare them, and make Use only of your Master's.

Let it be a constant Rule, that no Chair, Stool or Table in the Servants Hall, or the Kitchen, shall have above three Legs, which hath been the ancient, and constant Practice in all the Families I ever knew, and is said to be founded upon two Reasons; first to show that Servants are ever in a tottering Condition; secondly, it was thought a Point of Humility, that the Servants Chairs and Tables should have at least one Leg fewer than those of their Masters. I grant there hath been an Exception to this Rule, with regard to the Cook, who by old Custom was allowed an easy Chair to sleep in after Dinner; and yet I have seldom seen them with above three Legs. Now this epidemical Lameness of Servants Chairs is by Philosophers imputed to two Causes, which are observed to make the greatest Revolutions in States and Empires; I mean Love and War. A Stool, a Chair or a Table is the first Weapon taken up in a general Romping or Skirmish; and after a Peace, the Chairs if they be not very strong, are apt to suffer in the Conduct of an Amour, the Cook being usually fat and heavy, and the Butler a little in Drink.

I could never endure to see Maid-Servants so ungenteel as to walk the Streets with their Petticoats pinned up; it is a foolish Excuse to allege, their Petticoats will be dirty, when they have so easy a Remedy as to walk three or four times down a clean Pair of Stairs after they come home.

When you stop to tattle with some crony Servant in the same Street, leave your own Street-Door open, that you may get in without knocking, when you come back; otherwise your Mistress may know you are gone out, and you must be chidden.

I do most earnestly exhort you all to Unanimity and Concord. But mistake me not: You may quarrel with each other as much as you please, only bear in Mind that you have a common Enemy, which is your Master and Lady, and you have a common Cause to defend. Believe an old Practitioner; whoever out of Malice to a Fellow-Servant, carries a Tale to his Master, should be ruined by a general Confederacy against him.

The general Place of Rendezvous for all the Servants, both in Winter and Summer, is the Kitchen; there the grand Affairs of the Family ought to be consulted; whether they concern the Stable, the Dairy, the Pantry, the Laundry, the Cellar, the Nursery, the Dining-room, or my Lady's Chamber: There, as in your own proper Element, you can laugh, and squall, and romp, in full Security.

When any Servant comes home drunk, and cannot appear, you must all join in telling your Master, that he is gone to Bed very sick; upon which your Lady will be so good-natured, as to order some comfortable Thing for the poor Man, or Maid.

When your Master and Lady go abroad together, to Dinner, or to Visit for the Evening, you need leave only one Servant in the House, unless you have a Black-guard-boy to answer at the Door, and attend the Children, if there be any. Who is to stay at home is to be determined by short and long Cuts, and the Stayer at home may be comforted by a Visit from a Sweet-heart, without Danger of being caught together. These Opportunities must never be missed, because they come but sometimes; and you are always safe enough while there is a Servant in the House.

When your Master or Lady comes home, and wants a Servant, who happens to be abroad, your Answer must be, that he but just that Minute stepped out, being sent for by a Cousin who was dying.

If your Master calls you by Name, and you happen to answer at the fourth Call, you need not hurry yourself; and if you be chidden for staying, you may lawfully say, you came no sooner, because you did not know what you were called for.

When you are chidden for a Fault, as you go out of the Room, and down Stairs, mutter loud enough to be plainly heard; this will make him believe you are innocent.

Whoever comes to visit your Master or Lady when they are abroad, never burthen your Memory with the Person's Name, for indeed you have too many other Things to remember. Besides it is a Porter's Business, and your Master's Fault he doth not keep one, and who can remember Names; and you will certainly mistake them, and you can neither write nor read.

If it be possible, never tell a Lie to your Master or Lady, unless you have some Hopes that they cannot find it out in less than half an Hour. When a Servant is turned off, all his Faults must be told, although most of them were never known by his Master or Lady; and all Mischiefs done by others, charge to him. (Instance them.) And when they ask any of you, why you never acquainted them before? The Answer is, Sir, or Madam, really I was afraid it would make you angry; and besides perhaps you might think it was Malice in me. Where there are little Masters and Misses in a House, they are usually great Impediments to the Diversions of the Servants; the only Remedy is to bribe them with Goody Goodyes, that they may not tell Tales to Papa and Mamma.

I advise you of the Servants, whose Master lives in the Country, and who expect Vales, always to stand Rank and File when a Stranger is taking his Leave; so that he must of Necessity pass between you; and he must have more Confidence, or less Money than usual, if any of you let him escape, and according as he behaves himself, remember to treat him the next Time he comes.

If you are sent with ready Money to buy any Thing at a Shop, and happen at that Time to be out of Pocket, sink the Money and take up the Goods on your Master's Account. This is for the Honor of your Master and yourself; for he becomes a Man of Credit at your Recommendation.

When your Lady sends for you up to her Chamber, to give you any Orders, be sure to stand at the Door, and keep it open fiddling with the Lock all the while she is talking to you, and keep the Button in your Hand for fear you should forget to shut the Door after you.

If your Master or Lady happen once in their Lives to accuse you wrongfully, you are a happy Servant, for you have nothing more to do, than for every Fault you commit while you are in their Service, to put them in Mind of that false Accusation, and protest yourself equally innocent in the present Case.

When you have a Mind to leave your Master, and are too bashful to break the Matter for fear of offending him, the best way is to grow rude and saucy of a sudden, and beyond your usual Behavior, till he finds it necessary to turn you off, and when you are gone, to revenge yourself, give him and his Lady such a Character to all your Brother-servants, who are out of Place, that none will venture to offer their Service.

Some nice Ladies who are afraid of catching Cold, having observed that the Maids and Fellows below Stairs, often forget to shut the Door after them as they come in or go out into the back Yards, have contrived that a Pulley and a Rope with a large Piece of Lead at the End, should be so fixed as to make the Door shut of itself, and require a strong Hand to open it, which is an immense Toil to Servants, whose Business may force them to go in and out fifty Times in a Morning: But Ingenuity can do much, for prudent Servants have found out an effectual Remedy against this insupportable Grievance, by tying up the Pully in such a Manner, that the Weight of the Lead shall have no Effect; however, as to my own Part, I would rather choose to keep the Door always open, by laying a heavy Stone at the Bottom of it.

The Servants Candlesticks are generally broken, for nothing can last for ever. But you may find out many Expedients: You may conveniently stick your Candle in a Bottle, or with a Lump of Butter against the Wainscot, in a Powder-horn, or in an old Shoe, or in a cleft Stick, or in the Barrel of a Pistol, or upon its own Grease on a Table, in a Coffee Cup or a Drinking Glass, a Horn Can, a Tea Pot, a Twisted Napkin, a Mustard Pot, an Inkhorn, a Marrowbone, a Piece of Dough, or you may cut a Hole in the Loaf, and stick it there.

When you invite the neighboring Servants to junket with you at home in an Evening, teach them a peculiar way of tapping or scraping at the Kitchen Window, which you may hear, but not your Master or Lady, whom you must take Care not to disturb or frighten at such unseasonable Hours.

Lay all Faults upon a Lap-Dog or favorite Cat, a Monkey, a Parrot, a Child, or on the Servant who was last turned off: By this Rule you will excuse yourself, do no Hurt to any Body else, and save your Master or Lady from the Trouble and Vexation of chiding.

When you want proper Instruments for any Work you are about, use all Expedients you can invent, rather than leave your Work undone. For Instance, if the Poker be out of the Way or broken, stir up the Fire with the Tongs; if the Tongs be not at Hand, use the Muzzle of the Bellows, the wrong End of the Fire Shovel, the Handle of the Fire Brush, the End of a Mop, or your Master's Cane. If you want Paper to singe a Fowl, tear the first Book you see about the House. Wipe your Shoes, for want of a Clout, with the Bottom of a Curtain, or a Damask Napkin. Strip your Livery Lace for Garters. If the Butler wants a Jordan, he may use the great Silver Cup.

There are several Ways of putting out Candles, and you ought to be instructed in them all: you may run the Candle End against the Wainscot, which puts the Snuff out immediately: You may lay it on the Floor, and tread the Snuff out with your Foot: You may hold it upside down until it is choked with its own Grease; or cram it into the Socket of the Candlestick: You may whirl it round in your Hand till it goes out: When you go to Bed, after you have made Water, you may dip the Candle End into the Chamber Pot: You may spit on your Finger and Thumb, and pinch the Snuff until it goes out: The Cook may run the Candle's Nose into the Meal Tub or the Groom into a Vessel of Oats, or a Lock of Hay, or a Heap of Litter: The House-maid may put out her Candle by running it against a Looking-glass, which nothing cleans so well as Candle Snuff: But the quickest and best of all Methods, is to blow it out with your Breath, which leaves the Candle clear and readier to be lighted.

There is nothing so pernicious in a Family as a Tell-Tale, against whom it must be the principal Business of you all to unite: Whatever Office he serves in, take all Opportunities to spoil the Business he is about, and to cross him in every Thing. For Instance, if the Butler be the Tell-Tale, break his Glasses whenever he leaves the Pantry Door open: or lock the Cat or the Mastiff in it, who will do as well: Mislay a Fork or a Spoon so as he may never find it. If it be the Cook, whenever she turns her Back, throw a Lump of Soot, or a Handful of Salt in the Pot, or smoking Coals into the Dripping-Pan, or daub the roast Meat with the Back of the Chimney, or hide the Key of the Jack. If a Footman be suspected, let the Cook daub the Back of his new Livery; or when he is going up with a Dish of Soup, let her follow him softly with a Ladle-full, and dribble it all the Way up Stairs to the Dining-room, and then let the House-maid make such a Noise, that her Lady may hear it: The Waitingmaid is very likely to be guilty of this Fault, in hopes to ingratiate herself. In this Case, the Laundress must be sure to tear her Smocks in the washing, and yet wash them but half; and, when she complains, tell all the House that she sweats so much, that her Flesh is so nasty, that she fouls a Smock more in one Hour than the Kitchen-maid doth in a Week.

THE BALLAD OF FATHER GILLIGAN

BY WILLIAM BUTLER YEATS

The old priest Peter Gilligan
Was weary night and day;
For half his flock were in their beds,
Or under green sods lay.

Once, while he nodded on a chair,
At the moth-hour of eve,
Another poor man sent for him,
And he began to grieve.

"I have no rest, nor joy, nor peace,"
For people die and die";
And after cried he, "God forgive!
My body spake, not I!"

He knelt, and leaning on the chair
He prayed and fell asleep;
And the moth-hour went from the fields,
And stars began to peep.

They slowly into millions grew,

And leaves shook in the wind;
And God covered the world with shade,
And whispered to mankind.

Upon the time of sparrow chirp
When the moths came once more,
The old priest Peter Gilligan
Stood upright on the floor.

"Mavrone, mavrone! the man has died,
While I slept on the chair";
He roused his horse out of its sleep,
And rode with little care.

He rode now as he never rode,
By rocky lane and fen;
The sick man's wife opened the door:
"Father! you come again!"

"And is the poor man dead?" he cried,
"He died an hour ago."
The old priest Peter Gilligan
In grief swayed to and fro.

"When you were gone, he turned and died
As merry as a bird."
The old priest Peter Gilligan
He knelt him at that word.

"He who hath made the night of stars
For souls, who tire and bleed,
Sent one of His great angels down
To help me in my need.

"He who is wrapped in purple robes,
With planets in His care,
Had pity on the least of things
Asleep upon a chair."

A HISTORICAL ANECDOTE

BY THOMAS FRANCIS BRENNAN

In about 1850, Elizabeth McMahon and her brother John left the port of Cork in Ireland aboard a ship of the type known as "coffin ships," bound for America. She was 16 years of Age. Her brother was 15. Neither could read or write.

After a long, uncomfortable voyage, they landed in New York City. They knew no one in New York, but they had the name of a relative or a friend of a relative in Rochester, NY. They had just enough money to purchase rail tickets to Rochester.

They arrived at the station on Central Avenue and began to walk south on St. Paul Street. As they progressed, they presumably discussed what they would do now that they had arrived. At the corner of St. Paul Street and Andrews Street they noticed an elaborate stone house set back on a terrace. (There are presently high-rise apartments in this site.)

Elizabeth remarked that the house looked prosperous enough to perhaps have a need for domestic help. She went into the stone house, leaving her brother to wait for her. She must have made an impression on the residents because she was hired as a domestic servant on the spot.

She then went to the door of the house and signaled to her brother that she had found employment. John waved at her and then began on his way along St. Paul Street. Elizabeth never saw or heard from her brother again.

(My source for this story is my father. Elizabeth McMahon was his maternal grandmother.)